FALLING FOR THE ROCKSTAR'S
DAUGHTER BOOK 2

WE & BREATHE

by

WILLA DREW

Moving Words Publishing

PRAISE FOR WILLA DREW

Willa Drew's writing style blew me away.

Highly recommend this author and book without a doubt!

My first book by Willa and it won't be my last!

I look forward to reading other books by this author in the future. Because I went into this one with hope and promise, and it absolutely delivered! Now it's your turn!

This is a great story written by two clearly talented authors. The characters have been put front and centre of this book, with their story and development being what it is all about.

This is the first time I have a read a book by these authors and I enjoyed the collaboration. The book flowed well, seamlessly moving through the story.

I am glad I stumbled on this book and these authors, and I will definitely be adding them to my list of authors to keep my eye out for.

The authors did a wonderful job of writing the characters in a way that I felt connected to them right away.

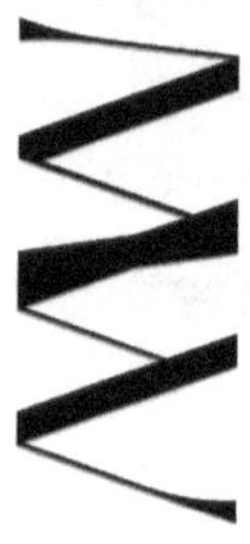

Published by: Moving Words Publishing

www.movingwordspublishing.com

Copyright © 2023 by Willa Drew

Cover: Books and Moods (@booksnmoods on Instagram)

Artwork: María Peña (@me.me.pe on Instagram)

ISBN: 978-1-957897-14-1

First Edition: October 2023

Characters you met in WE Blend:

El Vella aka Melodie Vella Rockerby — wannabe singer-songwriter. Daughter of opera stars Sylvia Vella Rockerby and Mathew Vella (died in a boat accident with El present when she was 10 y.o.). Only child. Her mother is pregnant with her half-brother. She's dyslexic, has perfect pitch, plays the piano and the guitar, is an avid runner, and loves butter tarts. El has blue eyes, is 5'6". She is 18 year old, a redhead and has shoulder-length hair with a streak of colorless hair that appeared after the father's death.

Wil Peters aka Wilhelm Peters, named for his grandfather — is studying sound engineering in Germany, plays the guitar, sings, DJs to support himself (as well as his family), was on a rowing team, constantly writes words and impressions of the world around him in a small black notebook he carries around. Wil is 6'3", has amber eyes and jet-black floppy hair. He turns 20 during WE Blend.

Bill Rockerby, aka Rocker—El's stepdad (Rocker married Sylvia when El was 12 y.o.) and Wil's estranged biological father. Rocker sides with his wife when she instructs El to stay away from a career in music. He is a music producer and has his own company Rocker Inc. where El works during WE Blend. Rocker is 42 years old, 6'3", has amber eyes and jet-black hair. He's expecting what he believes is his first baby in December with his wife and El's mother, Sylvia Vella Rockerby.

Sylvia Vella Rockerby—El's mother. She is a famous opera singer, a widow, and wife of Rocker, expecting her second child. She's from Norway and married Mathew Vella, who's from Malta, after they met in college in Italy studying classical singing. She is 44 years old, has blond hair and blue eyes. Her negative experience with paparazzi after her first husband's death and fame guides her decision to make sure El never has to go through the same.

Hanna Peters—Wil's mother. She had Wil when she was 21. She's an assistant at a doctor's office. She suffers from a severe case of Rheumatoid Arthritis and was accepted to a clinical trial program that requires out-of-pocket payments she cannot afford. Never married. Lives in Bremen, Germany, with her father, Wilhelm Peters aka Opa aka Mr. Peters. Hanna never told Wil who his father is.

Wilhelm Peters, aka Opa, aka Mr. Peters—Wil's grandfather. A retired construction worker. A widower, he helped Hanna raise Wil and became his father-figure. Mr. Peters is not good with technology. He is the one who told Wil who his real father is and concocted the plan of Wil going to America to meet Rocker to get the money for Hanna's treatment.

Zoe Yilmaz—El's cousin. She turns 20 during the book. Zoe is a fashion designer and is a fan of social media. Zoe lives with her parents, Patty and Bob Yilmaz, and is El's best friend.

Mateo Gallardo—Wil's friend from the Starlight Film Foundation competition who Wil lives with during the competition and when he goes to UCLA in the fall. Mateo is from Mexico. He is studying to be a graphic designer at UCLA, is into art, but is also a connector and is the one who gets Wil his ID, so Wil can go to The Devil's Martini bar where he ends up playing the guitar for El's open mic competition.

Sven Andres—Rocker's bodyguard who becomes El's bodyguard after Rocker brings her back from England. Sven completed 8 years with the marines before joining Rocker's team. He loves Superman comics, attends ComiCon dressed up as his hero and has a major sweet tooth. He is an excellent driver, works out a lot, including running with El and has a younger half-brother Travis who often gets in trouble.

Marta Nowak—Rocker's housekeeper. She's Polish, a great cook and turns 55 during WE Blend.

Leonard Astor–famous music video director El hired to film her music video in England.

Melodie Rockerby, 18, is in London, England to film a music video with a famous director to jump-start her career as a singer-songwriter, out of the spotlight of her famous mother/opera star Sylvia and step-father/rockstar Bill Rockerby (aka Rocker). Before she gets the chance, Rocker discovers her deception and arrives to drag her back to their home in Malibu, California. Her mother, Sylvia, is livid that Melodie fled the US without telling her and takes away her credit cards and allowance, forcing her to work with her step-father for the summer. Angry at her parents, Melodie accidentally closes the door on her hand and breaks her fingers.

Wil Peters, 19, leaves his hometown of Bremen Germany and arrives in LA to take part in a film competition as a sound engineer. He rooms in a UCLA dorm with another student, Mateo. However Wil has an ulterior motive to be in the US. Wil's grandfather, Opa, has just revealed that Wil's biological father is Rocker. Wil plans to ask for eighteen years of child support to pay for his sick mother Hanna's clinical trial.

Determined to make enough to reschedule her music video, Melodie sneaks out of the house with the help of her bodyguard, Sven, to enter an open-mic competition at The Devil's Martini. She hides her signature red hair with its distinctive white streak under a blonde wig and uses the stage name El Vella. When she arrives, the guitarist she's hired to play for her since she can't because of her broken fingers is drunk. Drinking with him is Wil. He recognizes El but agrees to step in and play guitar for her. He sees this as an opportunity to use El to get to his father. Although El freezes when she first sets foot on stage, Wil helps her and together they win the coveted weekly paid gig at The Devil's Martini. They now must perform together every Saturday for the next three months.

Wil works on the movie Indigo with his teammates at the Starlight Foundation competition and scores a job on campus working at a coffee shop Blend. El starts her job at Rocker's music production company Rocker Inc. During rehearsals (that her bodyguard, Sven, delivers her to every week) El opens up about her songwriting and Wil helps her with the lyrics.

Wil suggests they busk at the local Farmers' Market to both practice more and earn extra cash. El is afraid she'll get recognized but agrees. Nick, Indigo's movie director, sees Wil and El perform and asks them to write and perform the theme song for the movie. The process of writing the song together brings Wil and El even closer and both start having more-than-friends feelings for each other. During the preview of Indigo, El's cast is finally off and Wil gets to hold her hand.

On Labor Day, El goes running and is accosted by a paparazzi who just found out Sylvia is pregnant. They want to know more about El's brother. Wil sees the recording and panics, thinking the paparazzi found out that he is Rocker's son and El's stepbrother. Wil is relieved this was about the baby, although he's still worried about El's mental state after the encounter, because he knows how difficult her relationship with the press is.

He texts her to check-in and she invites him over to work on her song. She discovers it's his birthday and bakes him blueberry muffins like his mom usually does. At the Rockerby mansion, Wil gets to see what his life would've been like if he lived with Rocker. He wants to tell El the truth about who his father is but doesn't want to break the special bond he and El are forming. Wil is attracted to El but doesn't act on his feelings and sleeps in the guest bedroom. He asks El to attend the Starlight Foundation Gala where their song has been nominated for an award.

The day of the gala, Sven catches Wil and EL busking. Angry that they didn't tell him, Sven pulls her away from Wil before she can retrieve her phone from his bag.

Rocker drags El to a last-minute birthday party for Marta, their housekeeper, and El can't sneak out or contact Wil, who is waiting for her at the gala. When El doesn't show up or reply to his messages, Wil gets drunk and the next day he wakes up hungover. Feeling guilty, El barges into his room at his frat house with apology muffins and assumes he slept with a girl she sees leaving his room. They fight. At their performance at The Devil's Marini they fight/sing, but talk after and reconcile.

El, who is no longer allowed to busk with Wil, asks Wil to DJ at her cousin Zoe's birthday party, so he can earn extra cash but also so she can see him. At the event, she is pushed into the pool and Wil dives in to save her. As Wil consoles her, under the grand piano in the music room at Zoe's house, El shares the story of her father's death during a boating accident when she was ten. She explains why she is afraid of water.

Mateo is throwing a Halloween Party at his and Wil's frat house and Wil persuades Sven to let El attend it in costume. Wil and El perform at the party and dance until Travis, Sven's brother, shows up and needs El's help to bail Sven out of prison. Wil and El borrow money from Mateo and rescue Sven. El pays Mateo back with the money she saved busking and singing at The Devil's Martini. She no longer has the funds to film the music video.

Wil asks his friends from the film competition to help him create a music video for El. During their final performance at The Devil's Martini El forgets her wig. She sings on the stage as herself, without Wil and is no longer afraid. Wil, El, and the rest of the team spend the evening filming at several locations. During filming the ending for the video El needs to kiss someone for the final scene. When Nick volunteers, Wil offers himself instead. Wil and El's first kiss on camera is awkward, but their second kiss is so good they forget there are cameras.

Someone at The Devil's Martini recognizes El and Rocker interrupts the video shoot moments ahead of the paparazzi. Rocker takes El away, angry that she is defying her mother and that she's out without protection. Wil finally sees Rocker in person and could tell him that he's his son, but he is more worried about how Rocker and Sylvia are treating El.

Unable to contact El, Wil sneaks into Rocker Inc. to give El the final recording of her music video. In the elevator, he bumps into Rocker who accuses Wil of brining drugs to the premises when Wil refuses to part with the bag that holds the recording. Wil confronts Rocker and his treatment of El and the fact that he is Rocker's son slips out. El overhears the fact and is hurt by Wil's lie. She trusted him and told him everything, but she now believes he was only using her.

With Sven's help, Wil sneaks into Rocker's mansion to apologize to El. Wil confesses his secret to her and explains the situation with his mom's treatment. El stops him with a kiss because she forgives him. She decides to escape her parents' home and run away with Wil. In Bremen, when Wil arrives at his mother's doorstep with El, he introduces her as his girlfriend. No one knows where they are and they're enjoying the time together in Bremen, away from the press.

CONTENTS

For our families,
no matter how we found you

ONE

I'VE ALWAYS BEEN FAMOUS. Just for the wrong reasons.

My eyes lock on the young girls holding their phones, probably recording me. Me. The music I make, stretching far and wide across the world, is the only reason fame, being scrutinized by people, cameras, being the center of attention, all of it, would be worth the price.

Wil slides into a strum on his guitar as I hit the A-flat in the bridge of the cover of *Love Is Not a Sin*, Blatantly Subtle's biggest hit, and I let the air rush out, pushing the note as far across the small crowd gathered around us as I can manage without a mic. A man in a baseball cap watches me like I'm a contestant on a talent show he's judging. A couple wearing matching scarves and mittens sway to the music. They seem to like what they hear, and to want more. Sure, Carlee Waters owns this song, but I could give her a run for her money.

A little circle has formed around the stationary store we're busking in front of, and as the note ends, the people break into applause. I bow and point to my partner. Wil tips his head. The clapping accelerates.

We don't have any of the equipment we did when we busked at the Farmers' Market back in LA, no amplifier or microphone. Just Wil and his guitar, me and my voice.

I love it.

"One more song?" He shifts the guitar case at our feet, making the euro we've been collecting clink, and glances at me.

Every time Wil's eyes shine at me, a warmth I'm now familiar with, almost comfortable with, blooms inside my chest. "Sure."

My boyfriend grins. "Let's try my favorite one."

I nod, and the blue-and-gray wool beanie slides over my eyes. I push it up, grateful Wil insisted he buy the hat with the word BREMEN plastered across the front on my second day in his hometown. His mom's parka—a size too big, which might qualify for vintage, even if the black material has faded to a muted gray—helps with the chill I can't seem to keep out. But the coat is the warmest thing Hanna had to spare, and right now warmth counts more than couture. I jump, attempting to move the ice crystals forming in my blood. At least I packed jeans and sneakers when I fled Mom and Dad's, otherwise I'd be standing in the town square frozen like a popsicle.

"Next up is our original song," Wil announces.

He strums the opening chords to *Our Lines*. Last week, Wil and I recorded an acoustic rendition in his living room with the Christmas tree behind us and posted the video to my YouTube channel, in addition to other covers I've added since landing in Germany. The song racked up thirty thousand views already. We cowrote *Our Lines* for Wil's movie *Indigo* and won Best Song at the Starlight Young Filmmakers Foundation in September. That was three months ago, but feels like a lifetime.

Wil whisper-sings the opening. "My lines."

"Your lines," I sing-whisper back.

We join our voices on the first verse and crescendo into the chorus.

Go far away,

Forget the past,

Create your life,

That will make you . . .

I sing on, "Happy."

Our gazes meet.

"Laughing . . ." Wil's line lingers in the frozen air.

We smile at each other. His guitar sings under his fingers, giving me a break. The cold air smells of Christmas, pine melding with the aroma of roasted chestnuts. December in Germany is like living inside a Christmas card. Huge bows decorate every lamppost. Mirrored globes hang on the Tannenbaum that dominates the square. Twinkling lights lend cheer to gray skies. The only thing missing is gently falling snow.

To me, it's not really Christmas unless there's snow. Growing up, Mom and I spent as much of December with my aunts and grandparents in Norway as we could. When Dad joined the family, the trips got shorter, but Christmas was always at Mormor's chalet just outside of Sandes.

Mom must be missing the snow. The doctor didn't approve her flying in the last weeks of pregnancy and we planned to spend this Christmas in LA for the first time in years. My heart aches. Now I'm hiding here. My emails assuring them I'm safe, staying with a friend, didn't stop them trying to find out where, with whom, and when I'll be coming home. I'm not letting them drag me back this time. Heat threatens behind my eyes. I raise my chin and watch the enchanted faces of the listeners. This year there might not be snow, or Mom and me sharing the same mug of cocoa on Christmas morning, but it doesn't mean I don't have a reason to celebrate.

I take a deep breath, and the stab of pain in my chest lessens. This Christmas I have something new. I have Wil. and I have freedom.

His voice makes my heart flutter. Singing a love song while in a relationship, after you've admitted feelings for someone, is a million times better than being a hopeless romantic. The man standing beside me once swore he'd never do the girlfriend thing but look at him now. Writing love songs with his girlfriend. Performing before a crowd with his girlfriend.

Our melodies blend as we start the bridge of the song:

"Even if I can't hear it,
As long as you believe it."

I sing the line he wrote about finding the mythical world behind his words directly at my musical partner.

"Transforming the mundane.
And when I close my eyes
I hear it.
I see the castles and the beasts,
the starry galaxies and pirates' bounty amid the elves and feasts,
I hear you."

I hold the last note as long as my diaphragm lets me.

Not recognizing the song, unlike the other covers we played over the last hour, part of the crowd dissipates. The guy in the baseball cap records us now as well. Seems like a fan even though he never smiles or sings. The two girls put their phones away, but they linger, listening. Maybe checking out Wil.

Look all you want girls, he's mine.

My voice cracks on the upper-C, and I'm unable to sustain the note. The cold air is getting to me.

Wil ends the song and addresses the listeners in German. Most people slip away while the few remaining fans clap. He turns to me, his thick eyebrows drawn together. "Are you okay?" The pads of Wil's fingers stroke my chin.

"Fine." I lean into his palm. "My throat's a little dry." His tender touch sends a warm trickle to my frozen toes.

His icy thumb caresses my cheek. "Maybe this wasn't a good idea."

"Singing with you is always a good idea." I put my hand on his, mostly just to feel more of him, but also to heat him up. How can he play with icicles for fingers? "I could do this all day."

Amber eyes search mine, and he must like what he sees because he stoops down and brushes a featherlight kiss on my lips. "Me too." His breath mingles with mine as our foreheads touch. "I love singing with you."

Our mouths meld in a proper kiss, slow and sweet. The unsung song I hear in my mind when it's just Wil and I begins to play. My heart races to the beat. The trickle in my chest turns into a stream. My hand slips up his jacket, over his neck, and into the jet-black hair I love to play with.

Wil's guitar slips from his grasp and hits the ground. The off-key F-note it creates screeches across my nerves like the needle on a record on my vintage powder-blue Victrola. Cold air blasts my cheeks as Wil's lips retreat.

"Entschuldigung," a voice interrupts. I look over Wil's shoulder at the two girls from earlier, arm in arm. The taller blonde speaks. "Kann ich ein Foto von dir machen?"

In a month of living here, I've only picked up a few basic German words and phrases. Danke for thanks, Bitte for please. Thank goodness Kaffee is easy to remember. I turn to Wil for the translation. His eyes sparkle. "They want a picture."

A lump of lead forms in my stomach. Of course they do. I've been here before. Groupies antsy for a photo of Dad—Rocker to the rest of the world. I've taken so many of these, I know to look for the right lighting and to raise the camera up high to fit my rockstar stepfather's tall frame. Wil's tall too, like his dad. I'll have to stand back a few feet to fit him in.

"Sure." I hold out my hand for their phone. The girls squeal and shove their phone at Wil's chest as they bound past him to stand beside me.

Me?

A thrill shoots up my spine as Wil winks. The girls bracket me, and a gloved hand lands on my elbow. I can feel their bodies practically vibrating with excitement. Normally I dread having my picture taken, but this time my smile comes easily.

"Say cheese." He adjusts the phone after each click, then gives us a thumbs-up.

A hand squeezes my arm and a string of syllables rush from the mouth of the girl on my left. I catch two words: "El Vella." My pulse skyrockets. They recognize me. These girls don't want a photo with the unknown busker they stumbled upon on an afternoon at the Christmas Market. They want a photo with El Vella.

My *Don't Give Me Comfort* video still gets hundreds of hits a day since going viral. I check it first thing every morning, but I didn't realize the song crossed to non-English speaking fans. To prove my point, the girls sing a few bars. I try not to cringe at their off-key rendition.

"They love your song." Wil hands back the phone. "They'd like your autograph."

No one has ever asked me for my signature. "My autograph?"

"Apparently you're famous." His words make my heart flutter. Famous because of the song Wil and I created. I can get on board with that.

The other girl rummages in her bag and produces a grocery receipt. We look around for a pen. As usual, Wil comes to the rescue, pulling one out of his satchel. A memory of it tapping against his cheek last night as we worked on the chorus of a new song filters through my mind. My fingers start to write the capital letter M for Melodie, but I catch myself and switch to an E for El. El Vella. My first time signing anything with my stage name. I like seeing Papa's name on the page. He'd be proud of me.

Brighter than the Christmas lights, the girls' smiles beam at me.

"Wait." I stop them from leaving and turn to Wil. "Can you ask them to take a picture of us?"

His cheeks tint the faintest pink as he speaks to the girls in a low tone. They giggle and must agree because he's putting his arm around me.

"Cheese." With the heavy accent, the ee gets the focus.

I snuggle into Wil and smile at the camera, marking the moment forever. My first autograph. I check the photo. I'm smiling like a kid on Christmas morning, but the picture only has Wil's profile. His head is angled down, almost touching mine. The corner of his lip is curled up and he looks . . . like I've never seen him before. Vulnerable? Serene? Happy? I poke Wil's chest. "You're not looking at the camera."

He snatches the phone from my hand. "I'm deleting this."

"No," I yelp. My gaze meets his, and my heart sputters. "Please don't. I love it."

The lines around his eyes iron out. "Fine. But it goes in our private account on the cloud. I better not see this picture on Hollywood Happenings."

A shiver slices through me. Daniel Davison's trashy online gossip fest is a thorn in my side. That man has it out for me and never misses a chance to laugh at Melodie Rockerby's failures and missteps. I don't miss that part of LA life at all.

As if called forth by the mere mention of paparazzi, a phone is shoved into my face. I jerk back and glare at the source of the intrusion. A wiry man with a green-and-gray striped scarf snaking around his neck babbles at me. Wil pushes his hand away from us and snaps, his words short and sharp.

More syllables pour from the man, and again I only recognize two words: "Melodie" and "Rocker." My already cold blood reaches subzero temperatures. No, no, no. They can't find me here. Bremen is a city with over half a million people. No one knows me here. I was supposed to be safe, hidden, like in my grandparents' village in Malta.

The paparazzi aren't supposed to be here.

But they are.

Years of training for this situation kicks in and my feet prepare to run, but I don't know where to go. I'm not even sure which direction Wil's mother's house is. For the first time in over a month, I truly miss Sven. He'd know what to do, where to go, how to get me out.

The man is shouting at me now. Wil moves to step between us. The world goes white, not from snow, but from the flash of a camera.

I can't see.

I can't breathe.

Wil's cool fingers slide into mine.

TWO

EL IS TREMBLING, NOT from the cold. The flashes around us are not many, but they break the bubble we've been in for the last four weeks. I've never seen paparazzi in Bremen. Berlin, yes, but not around here.

"Let's go," El pleads.

Saying yes to her is easy, but I also don't want to give up prime busking time. Letting these guys force us to change our plans—that's not how I roll. I don't want to hide or let them affect our lives. I'm proud of the music we're making, and even more proud to be by El's side while doing it. "We don't have to," I say, but she's already closing the guitar case on our meager earnings. "Let's talk. There's no—"

"Not here." El slings her backpack on her shoulders.

The small crowd that was around us is gone. What I thought was one or two photographers turns into five guys with cameras, who, like some bloody pack animals, are tightening their semi-circle around us.

I grab my Goodboy messenger bag. "This way." My guitar in one hand and El's fingers in the other, I barge into the stationary store.

"We can buy notebooks later." El tries to pull me to the street that will take us to the tram station.

I cradle her and whisper, "Trust me."

We enter the mostly empty store and I maneuver us around stacks of notebooks, desk calendars, high-end ink pen displays, and more paperweights than I remember. By the time we are at the counter where the owner greets me with a smile, the chime on the door goes off and I see the first of the paparazzi enter.

"Can I use the back exit?"

The owner follows my gaze and clocks the second paparazzi, camera in hand, entering the store. "You know the way." He puts on a face that works better than having a bouncer around and moves in front of door while I lift one side of the counter and veer left through the curtains that lead into the storage room.

El's hand is slick with sweat and my jaw tightens at the thought that she is this upset. We squeeze between the shelves with neat boxes, and I push on the back door that leads to an alley with garbage cans and no tourists or paparazzi. "We're good." I press El into me. Even through the layers of clothes I feel her heart beating overtime.

She pushes me away. "No time. We can't let them know where you live."

Most of today's busking proceeds go toward the taxi fare as we instruct the driver to head in the opposite direction of where we are staying. Once we're sure no one's following us, we give him directions to Mum's house. The panic that sent my blood pressure soaring calms when we lock the door and settle on the couch. El is already on her phone and scrolling through her socials looking for a mention of her being in Bremen. When she finds none, she calls Zoe.

"Daniel Davison is a dick." Zoe uses her phone's camera as a mirror and covers her already pink lips in another layer of glittery gloss. "His interview with Langdon Beau was good though. I might be crushing on him now."

El slides her arms through the crook of my elbow and moves as close to me as possible. I don't mind, but instead of the desire to push her against the wall and spend hours kissing every inch of her body, all I can think of is how powerless I am to protect her. What if she's right and the paparazzi show up in front of our duplex? We can't escape out the back door like at the stationary store. Our yard is fenced. Not something I've ever had to worry about.

"Why does it feel like it's personal? Why is he so focused on always making me look the worst way possible?" The anger and weariness in El's voice remind me how grateful I am that I didn't have to go through this as a kid. No Rocker meant no money, but no money means not having to worry about every move and who will be waiting to take unflattering photos of you.

"It's not. He's after the money, and you're hot gossip at a slow time of year. No one has seen you since they caught you shooting your video at Griffith Observatory, which makes finding you busking in Bremen even juicier. Posting flattering photos of you is not profitable." Zoe's eyebrows arch. "You in that ridiculous Bremen hat and a parka that's too long with a mysterious man by your side—that's the money-maker."

"D'you think they'll figure out who Wil is?" says El.

She shouldn't worry about me. My thumb circles the soft skin on her wrist as if I can erase the anxiety that has crept into her words.

Her cousin's lips twitch. "A German boyfriend is juicy and a good excuse to be in Europe, but he's not a celebrity, so I doubt they'll care enough to bother."

El shoots me a glance. We've talked about who should and should not know about my relationship to Rocker. Her reasoning that Zoe is one of the people who'll never tell the paparazzi and will only help us was hard to poke holes in. "Go ahead, tell her," I say.

"Tell me what?" The tiny wand in Zoe's hand freezes in midair.

"You can't tell this to anyone," says El. "I mean it. Not to your mom or anyone."

"When have I ever betrayed you?"

Zoe and El have a silent conversation like some kind of mental pinky swear. El stares at me again. "Wil is sort of . . ."

I give her a look, and she gives me one back, urging me to take over. I sigh and face the screen, where Zoe has inched even closer. "I'm Rocker's son."

"Rocker's . . ." Zoe blinks rapidly. "What? How?"

This is going well. The first person we tell, and she doesn't believe me. "Do I need to explain you how sex works?"

"Yes, I mean, no. It's just . . . how is that possible?"

I asked the same question of Mum and finally heard the story I'd been waiting for my whole life. Zoe gets the highlights. "My mum and Rocker met at some resort in the Alps where she worked one winter. They got snowed in, got to know each other, and it clearly involved enough sex for her to get pregnant. I didn't ask for details."

Zoe's fingers fly up and she starts counting. "How old are you again?"

"Twenty."

"Wow." Zoe widens her eyes. "You are dating your sister."

"No," we both shout in unison.

"She's not my sister," I say.

"Well, technically if you are Rocker's son and she is Rocker's daughter, you are siblings. Brother and sister. Family."

I thread my fingers through El's hand, creating an unbreakable barrier to Zoe's ridiculous words. "Why would you even go there? You know we only met six months ago. We are not biologically related in the least. We didn't grow up together. The man who donated his sperm has only met me once and made it pretty clear he wants nothing to do with me." El's grip tightens on mine. "El's real father is not related to me. We have different mothers. We've never lived under the same roof until we came to my mum's weeks ago. We are not a family. The only thing linking us are some legal papers. There is nothing inappropriate about us dating."

Zoe tilts her head. "How long did it take you to defend yourself and explain that to me? The headline on Daniel Davison's blog certainly won't describe the finer details of your relationship. Once the paparazzi find out about it, they'll have a field day." She pauses. "Wait. Did Rocker know? About Wil? All this time?"

El inches away from me and I hate it. "No. He might not even know now." I have no idea what Sven did with the DNA test. It doesn't matter. Rocker is a continent away, and I don't need him. Even though I didn't get the money for Mum's treatment I went to LA for, between Opa and me, we've got half of the payment for the first installment. I have a few jobs lined up and a DJ gig on New Year's Eve that should cover the rest.

"I think he might. Aunt Sylvia told Mom Rocker changed his will," Zoe says.

"To include Wil?" El's eyes brim with hope.

The hairs on the back of my neck stand on end. "Doubt that." I concentrate on the faded rug under our feet. "Why would Rocker want to do anything with me?"

"Because you're his son," says El. "Family is the thing he cares about most."

The fact that he spent a night with my mother does not make him my family. "After I almost extorted money from him?"

"Extorted Rocker? You've got balls, I give you that." Zoe whistles. "Not just a pretty face and an awesome DJ then."

"Zoe." El gets between me and the phone screen with her cousin's playful grin.

"Fine, fine. I'll play nice with Rocker's new son. He may yet come in handy."

"Oh, he's handy all right." El wraps her arms around my neck and gives me a peck on my cheek. I'd take a million jabs from Zoe to get El back to my side.

"Stop the PDA." Zoe puckers her lips. "I got it. You don't have to rub your girlfriend-boyfriend bliss in." Her face falls. "Does this mean you're staying in Germany and living your romance dreams instead of coming home to help me with my first-ever Fashion Show Extravaganza?" Zoe's talent as a fashion designer shines through every item she makes, but this will be her first real runway show, with celebrities and influencers and whatever else her brilliant mind comes up with.

I can tell El doesn't want to hurt her cousin's feelings, but she can't lie either. "I don't know what I'm doing."

"You can't stay in Bremen forever. What about your music video? Your career?"

"It's only been a month."

"A month? That's like twenty years in social-media time. Right now, you have people's attention, but that will fade if you don't follow it up. Soon." The camera bounces as she sets her phone against something. "Have you written anything new?"

"Wil and I worked on a song yesterday. And I've posted a few covers Wil shot on YouTube."

"Yeah, I saw those." Zoe scrunches her nose. "Good start, but you need to diversify. Get on the new platforms."

A notification covers the top portion of the screen and El jolts forward, my arm forgotten. In the speech bubble is the name CarleeWaters and the words, "Saw your cover of my song."

"What the—" comes out of my mouth while El's jaw almost hits her knees.

"What's going on?" Zoe's voice is as demanding as ever. "What is so scandalous about diversifying?"

El's vibrating beside me. "I'm hallucinating, right?"

"Tell me what's happening," says Zoe.

El stares at her cousin. "Carlee Waters just DMed me."

"Get out," Zoe squeals. "What does she say?"

"She says she watched my cover of her *Love Is Not a Sin*—"

"What?"

"—and she liked it." El's gaze meets mine.

THREE

"What's taking so long?" asks El.

She pulls out her phone and scrolls to the last email from Blatantly Subtle about the final version of the contract we've been going back and forth on. Carlee Waters, the lead singer of the controversial glam-rock band that most just call Subtle, was discovered at The Devil's Martini's open mic competition, and the reason El was determined to win the same event the night we met.

The last email from Carlee's manager clarified the band's tour schedule as well the rehearsal period to learn the songs and basic choreography. El now has a list of events she'll attend and a set of protocols for interactions with the press. She signed an NDA that prevents her from discussing pretty much anything about the group's members, music, or plans. That document was almost as long as the contract for El to be their backup singer.

If she accepts.

"It's supposed to be here by nine." El shakes her foot. "They need the answer by end of day, so . . ."

The laptop on my knees dings with the sound of an incoming email. The account El set up to open her YouTube channel got a fair amount of spam since her *Don't Give Me Comfort* video blew up. The exchange with Blatantly Subtle is probably the only valid email string. The new message stands out in bold.

This victory is El's. I'm proud her talent is recognized, although I think she's far too bright of a star to be someone's backup. But I'll support her if this is the next step she wants to take in her career.

"Open it." El sets her cheek on my shoulder and puts her hands between her thighs, failing at keeping herself still.

"Ready?" I ask.

"Am I ready to prove I can support myself with music?" Even though she messaged Sylvia and Rocker once we reached Bremen telling them she is safe and sound, she declined to reveal her location. Or that she's with me. The reasons she left their house, the bitterness over the way her parents doubt her abilities as a musician, seep through most sentences containing their names. She switches her gaze to the screen in front of us. "As ready as I'll ever be."

The contract lists Melodie Rockerby as the VOCALIST. One of the biggest concessions El had to agree to was to use her legal name instead of her stage one. They didn't outright state that being the stepdaughter of a famous rockstar was one of the reasons for the offer, but even for a group as popular as Subtle, El's relationship to Rocker is beneficial. Any publicity is good publicity, it seems.

I read the contract out loud to help El understand the details. I like being part of the process. "They agreed on the advance upon signing and will reimburse you for any travel-related expenses you submit after you arrive."

El breathes out. Finding the money to get her to Atlanta without dipping into the pot Opa and I set aside for Mum's first treatment was one part of the puzzle we couldn't solve on our own. Opa's suggestion to ask for the cash upfront paid off.

Her gaze meets mine. "This contract is real money. An opportunity that might not come again. Busking in Bremen isn't the most lucrative trade, and I want to sing. Plus, I'll be on the road with Carlee. Six weeks of performing night after night. If I ever write a memoir about my life, this will be the most popular chapter."

Carlee will be the one writing about meeting El in her memoir, because El is going to be a star. *The* star. She's determined to say yes to this contract, and who am I to urge her to say no?

My fear of losing the only girl I've ever loved is selfish. I'm so sure she'll be famous. I can already see El Vella written on billboards and on the side of her personal tour bus, not one she'll share with eleven other crew members in Carlee's band.

"Don't think about the money. We can figure the money out. I've always managed to survive." I bury my nose in her hair and lower my voice to a whisper. "What is it that you want?"

"I want to live and breathe music." She closes her eyes as if in prayer. "To make my way as a working musician. To hear my parents tell me they were wrong and that I can do this."

My lips find their way to her cheek. "You can do this." They create a path to her upper lip. "You can do anything you want," I whisper. El lifts her face, drinking in my words. "I want you to have everything you want, because you are the princess. And music is your kingdom." She's my princess. She shifts the laptop off my knees and straddles me, turning my reassuring kisses into the hungry ones I can never get enough of.

I sink back into the couch and gratefully accept the weight of her body. She's no longer a stranger in a blond wig I found attractive, not a cute girl I had to collaborate with to get money from my birth father. She is the woman I'd do anything for. She is the person I want to be with rain or shine, money or not, busking on the streets of Bremen or singing with on the largest stages in the world. I don't care about where or the name she chooses, because I've seen who El is, and her kindness, loyalty, and creativity are what made me fall for her.

"Son." Opa's voice cuts through the meters that separate the hallway and the couch we're sitting on in the living room. I stifle a groan. Bloody hell, I don't know what's gotten into my grandfather. Yesterday El and I were alone in my bedroom, which is currently her bedroom, for maybe five minutes before he barged in to complain the internet was out. The cause? The router had mysteriously become unplugged. "Hanna'll be home soon. Let's turn on the kettle."

"I'll do it." El stands. I'd much rather make her stay, hold her in place, and not let her go.

When did I get so clingy? I'm making up for months of not being able to touch her, but it's more than that. "No, you stay here and finish reading the contract. I'll make us a cuppa." I settle her back on the couch into the spot that has become hers and head for the kitchen.

"What do you think, Mr. Peters?" El asks. "Should I take the offer?" I love hearing her ask Opa for advice, and he loves giving it.

"It pays, right?" That's Opa. Practical.

I add water and start the kettle. Through the condensation that rings the bottom half of the kitchen window I watch Mum climb up the front steps. The snow that started as a fairy-tale flurry this morning has turned into a proper storm. We should've kept Opa's car. The Passat was an old clunker, but it meant Mum didn't walk to and from work on these cold days.

"I'm home." Mum bustles in, hands laden with shopping bags.

Opa and I rush into the hallway and take the groceries from her as she removes her hat and shakes off the snowflakes clinging to her short blond hair. With the clinical trial starting in January, she can't get overtired or sick. We can't mess that up. "Go sit with El. I'll put the food away," I say.

"Thanks, luv." Mum takes a seat near El and wraps her in a hug. El puts the laptop aside and settles into my mother's embrace. My girlfriend who doesn't like people touching her lets Mum hug her all the time. First thing in the morning, last thing at night, when she comes home from work, when El does something sweet for her. "Did you get it?" Mum asks.

The electricity in El's eyes charges the air in my lungs. "I did. Got almost everything I requested." She turns the screen for Mum to see. "They have a few other conditions, mostly about brand and image, but nothing major."

Over her shoulder, Mum gives me a look like she understands what this means. El will be leaving. Leaving me. "Does that mean you're ready to sign?"

"I think so."

"Are you sure you don't want to send it to your parents, have their lawyers look it over?" Mum asks.

El needs to talk to her parents. I'm just afraid of what's going to happen when she does. How do we get them on board? The moment she steps on stage, Rocker will descend.

"I'm doing this on my own." El's gaze falls to the floor, and she grips the laptop.

I step closer to El's end of the couch. "Mateo got one of his frat brothers to show it to their parents who are contract lawyers. They said it's a standard contract. No red flags."

"I still think her parents would know more." Mum addresses me over El's head. "They're in the business." She rubs El's back and looks at her.

"Maybe as a Christmas present, you give them a call?" Opa jumps in. "Let them hear your voice." His eyes find mine, imploring me to join the argument.

I can't. I saw their overprotectiveness firsthand. I'm on El's side. Always.

El stands and heads to the kitchen. "Hanna, did you get the dried fruit for the stollen?"

Mum promised to make the sweet traditional Christmas cake with El. My search for butter tarts was a failure—no one had a clue what we were talking about. Mum offered to make some but El insisted she preferred to eat like a local while she had authentic German pastry to explore.

A small smile lights Mum's face. "I did. And the secret ingredient." I didn't know our family recipe had a secret ingredient, but Mum's stollen is the best. If she's sharing this secret with El, I'm not jealous. Really, I'm not.

Outside the night and the snowfall wrap our house in a wall of charcoal. Specks of white gather on the window ledge. If this cold front remains, it'll be a rare white Christmas.

Perfect.

I want everything to be perfect for El.

Opa rubs his hands together. "Anyone want a schnapps?"

El looks at me, and her expression of terror is priceless. I suppress a grin. Opa didn't scare her until he brought out the schnapps. The clear liquid is at least 40 percent alcohol, a far cry from the 6 percent in the pilsner that knocked El out when I introduced her to my rowing crew. She was barely able to walk home the night we met Jan and the boys, and I had to carry her halfway. The next morning my girl put on a brave face and accepted my homemade hangover mixture of herring, gherkins, and onion without a word of complaint.

"Not tonight, Opa. Let's save it for Christmas Eve tomorrow." I wink at El, and her hands loosen on her tea mug.

The doorbell rings.

"I'll get it," I say.

"Careful, son. It might be Nikolaus." Opa glances at El. "That's the German version of Santa Claus."

I open the door, and more than the cold air stuns me. I come eye-to-eye with the one person I never wanted to see again.

"Where's my daughter?" says Rocker.

FOUR

THE CUP OF TEA falls out of my hands, hits the wooden surface of the table, and splatters the thankfully lukewarm liquid on the cream tablecloth Wil's grandmother embroidered by hand. My confused limbs aren't quick enough to catch the thick stoneware mug, and it lands with a crack on the tiled kitchen floor.

"You okay?" Hanna bends stiffly and picks up the shards of brown pottery. "Don't move until I run the vacuum." She turns and freezes as she sees the reason I dropped the cup. Dominating the doorway, his thick black hair and leather jacket covered in snow, stands my stepfather, his arm pushing Wil aside.

There's a second crack of porcelain on tile as the pieces Hanna was holding shatter into smaller chunks. A low "oh my" escapes her lips as I reach to steady her in case she falls.

Rocker shoulders Wil out of the way and walks into the kitchen. His Doc Martens leave huge slushy marks in the entryway Wil's grandfather mopped yesterday. I find my voice. "It's my—"

"Melodie." His low baritone sends goosebumps up my neck. Hanna steps in front of me and Dad jolts to a halt. He does a fish-out-of-water impersonation, his mouth gaping as his eyes narrow. Uncertainty gathers his brows. "HP?"

Is Dad having a stroke? What does the brown sauce everyone here slathers on french fries instead of ketchup have to do with Wil's mother?

"Rocker?" Hanna says the nickname millions of people know, but her interpretation sounds nothing like the shouts Dad's fans throw his way on the daily. There's intimacy there. There's history.

He blinks and his gaze ping-pongs between Hanna and me.

"Why are you here?" We all speak at the same time.

"It's my house," says Hanna, as if Dad had directed the question to her.

I say, "I'm staying with Wil."

"She's with me." Wil comes to my side.

I take strength from his hand in mine. Unlike in London last year, Dad can't make me go home with him. I have Wil, a roof over my head, and a small amount of money from busking.

Being free and poor here is better than rich and trapped in the golden cage of my parents' expectations.

Wil moves through the gap between Hanna and me and steps directly in front of my stepfather. "What do you want?"

Dad's head whips to Wil and confusion swirls in the golden eyes that have cried over Mom's miscarriages and sizzled with joy at the sight of the steady heartbeat of the baby boy Mom's carrying. His eyebrows climb, and he angles back like Wil's thrown a phantom punch.

Wil's body stiffens, his fingers like steel rods gripping mine, shoulders pushed back the way they did when I walked in on them at Rocker Inc. when I thought Wil was there for me. My boyfriend radiates defiance. But I can feel the hurt coursing through his veins, can almost hear the pounding of his heart.

The confusion on Dad's face melts into something like understanding. "It's you." His hand runs through his hair and his gaze swivels between Wil and Hanna, landing on her. "I get it now."

"What do you get?" Wil steps up to Dad, and I get it too.

I saw them together in the recording studio, but I didn't really let it sink in. Standing side by side, amber eyes glaring at each other, black hair flopping over their foreheads, you'd have to be blind not to see the resemblance. Daniel Davison would. Wil has a couple of inches on Dad but the way they are standing, the narrow hips and wide shoulders, their eyebrows . . . there's no doubt. Even if I didn't already know, seeing them so close, the truth is clear: Bill Rockerby is Wil's biological dad.

Dad seems torn, like he doesn't know whom to address, Wil or Hanna.

"I get whose son he is," says Dad.

Wil flinches. I squeeze his hand, reassuring him I'm here. No matter what happens.

Dad takes a long breath in and an even longer breath out. He settles his gaze on my boyfriend. "Mine."

"And mine." Hanna grasps Wil's other hand with both of hers, the joints on her fingers swollen from her disease.

Shoulders set, Dad takes a step toward Hanna and crunches what's left of my cup under the thick soles of his boots. "Why didn't you tell me?"

"How dare you?" Mr. Peters's voice rises over the noise of chair legs scraping against the floor. Wil's grandpa flanks his daughter, putting a hand on her elbow, another link in the chain of protection this family offers. The defense line even Dad won't be able to breach. "She contacted you. Many times. You chose to pretend she couldn't be pregnant by you."

"No." Dad shakes his head. More shards crunch as he gets close enough to Hanna to put his hands on her arm. "I'd never do that. What are you talking about?"

She remains silent, her eyes searching Dad's face, as if she can't believe he's here.

I can't believe he's here either. I thought I had more time before he'd figure out where I was. Wil told me busking was a risk, he was filmed by tourists when he did it, but I couldn't not sing. Plus, even living rent-free, the money I brought from home was disappearing.

Mr. Peters grunts. He's not the easiest man to like, but right now he's scaring me. "I'm talking about her emailing and calling and sending you letters twenty years ago, and your replies insisting she stop harassing you." He pokes Dad in the chest, the tip of his finger turning white. "So while you were touring the world, getting laid, and throwing money on more cars and houses than one human can possibly need, she had to raise your son on her own without your help."

"I—" Dad swallows. "I didn't get any of your messages." His gaze stays on Hanna like he's trying to hypnotize her, make her see that he's not lying. "I swear." He puts a hand on Hanna's shoulder and the edges of her lips twitch. Wil burns holes in the side of Dad's face. Dad pitches forward. "I would never." A shiver starts between my shoulder blades and rolls down to my toes. Dad's not lying. Family is everything to him. His eyes glisten with a plea for Hanna to trust him. "I swear to you."

Wil huffs.

Hanna falls out of her trance, shrugs Dad's hands off her shoulder, nudges her father out of the way, and backs into the kitchen. She removes a dustpan and a broom from the under the sink. The four of us watch her calm motions, like we can glean her thoughts through them.

"Take off your boots. There are spare slippers by the door," she tells Dad. He stares at the top of her head, opens his mouth to say something, then closes it and complies.

"Could you start the kettle again?" she asks Mr. Peters. He walks around me, careful not to step on the shards, and takes the kettle to the sink.

Dad comes over wearing the green guest slippers set aside for visitors. They are a bit short, and the heels of his feet touch the floor of the kitchen. "Melodie. Wil." He rolls up the sleeves of his shirt. The gesture is so familiar. Not just because I've seen Dad do it a million times, but because I've seen Wil do it a million times too. How have I not noticed before? "Wil, I didn't know." Dad's gaze jumps my way. "Melodie, Sylvia misses you."

"Why don't you and El take the living room while we get sorted here?" Hanna's words come out like a suggestion, but she's nudging me toward Dad.

"I'll come with." Wil moves in my direction.

Hanna holds Wil's forearm. "Could you go upstairs and bring down one more chair for me?"

Wil's gaze moves between Hanna and me.

"It's okay." I attempt a reassuring smile. "Dad and I should talk." So should he and Dad, but that's a conversation twenty years in the making.

Wil's shoulders slump and he disappears.

With Dad here, the room looks different. Smaller. Maybe drabber. He's the odd man out. Is this how I feel to Hanna or Wil's grandfather? Yet Rocker settles into the worn couch like he's done this before. His elbow on the armrest, one foot bounces on his knee. "Is this your plan?"

"Sorry?"

"Hide in Germany for a few weeks until we . . . what?"

"I'm not." But I *am* hiding. From Mom, and him, and the world I no longer want. He may think I'm the little girl in distress he took care of when he met my mother, but I'm not. This time I'm not just saying it. "I have a plan." I raise my chin. "I'm going on the road with Blatantly Subtle to sing on the next leg of their tour." I steel myself for Dad's fury.

Instead, I see the businessman I've witnessed at board meetings. Calm. Cool. Collected. "As the opening act?"

My stomach tightens. "No. Backup. One of the girls is pregnant and can't continue."

Dad shifts his gaze to the Christmas tree that's a quarter the size of the one we decorate in the media room in Malibu. He hums. "Interesting."

Interesting? That's what I get? I expected "No." "Not happening." "You can't." "Your mother needs you." I should be relieved but the knot in my stomach doesn't release. "The contract's for six weeks with an option to continue. The tour is in the States, mostly West Coast with a week in Las Vegas." His foot bounce speeds up. The motion so like Wil. Or is Wil like him? "They start rehearsals after Christmas."

Wil's footsteps pound down the stairs, and Dad tips his chin in that direction. "Is he coming with you?"

Nausea hits. That is the question I ignored and avoided under the convenient cover of the excitement of Carlee Waters reaching out to me and contract negotiations. Wil and I haven't really talked about what will happen between us. "Maybe."

"So you're more than friends?"

I consider denying our relationship. Telling Zoe was one thing. Admitting Wil and I are together to Dad is another. If he knows, Mom knows. Then Aunt Sylvia. Then . . . I don't want to think about the gossip chain. My feelings for Wil won't just be a secret between a few trusted people. "He's my boyfriend."

"That serious, huh?" Dad presses his lips together and nods to himself. His knee stops bouncing, and he plants his feet on the floor. "Explains a lot. You both can come home for Christmas then?"

"You're not mad?"

"Oh, I'm plenty mad." Dad stands and rubs his face, scrubbing the tired under-eye circles and day-old stubble Mom would've complained about if she were here. "I'm mad for what you did to us. To your mother. Sylvia can't sleep, won't stop crying, sits in the media room watching home movies of you. I don't understand how you of all people could do this to her." He won't look at me. That's worse than the words coming out of his mouth.

"Is everything okay?" I promised Mom I'd be with her during the difficult part of her pregnancy, but she was past that. With less than two months left when I flew to Germany, she and the baby were healthy. They didn't need me anymore.

She has Rocker. She has Aunt Patti and Zoe. She has Marta. She has Sven. A nanny on hold that'll be helping them. A doula. The best OBGYN in LA money can buy. There's nothing that would change if I were there. I'm not messing this birth up for her. She can focus on the new baby.

"She calmed down when she saw the video the private investigator we hired captured, the one of you singing outside that store." Dad crosses his arms. "Still. Couldn't you have waited until your brother was born? Found the right time to declare your independence?"

"There would never be a right time. You'd find another reason to lock her up." Wil is in the doorway, fists clenched at his side.

Dad pivots. "Is that what you think we did? Hold her against her will?"

"I don't think. I saw."

"I assure you, all we care about is Melodie's well-being."

A storm brews in Wil's eyes. Wil's attempt at rescuing me is one of the reasons I'm here. In a good way. The best of ways, but I can't rely on him to be there for me every time I need to defend myself. That'll only undermine what I'm trying to do: set boundaries with Dad. Show him I'm my own person, that I'm taking care of my life without his or Mom's help.

I catch Wil's eye. *I can do this.* I use our connection to tell him without opening my mouth. He props his shoulder against the doorframe in a failed attempt to look relaxed.

To cut the tension, I ask the question I'm sure I don't want the answer to. "Did Mom like my song?"

"Sylvia played it several times." Dad's gaze drops to his Doc Martens.

A non-answer Dad's publicist could have given him an award for.

"Did she like it?" Or did Mom hear the song but still doesn't think I'm good enough?

"She sent the link to your father's parents. They were thrilled. Said you take after their son." Dad sidesteps the issue, trying to distract me from the real answer.

"Papa followed his dreams, and I'm following his example. Singing is not a hobby or a passing fancy, like Mom keeps insisting. This is the real deal, and I'm going to prove to her and to you how serious I am. Carlee's tour is the first step."

Wil leaves his post, his eyes shining with pride. His fingers thread through mine, and I know I can do this. Even if it's just him and me.

Dad's gaze rests on my face. The pain I see in his eyes hits me like a lightning bolt. "Melodie, I understand more than you know, and won't stand in your way." He won't go against Mom's wishes, I know that, so not actively interfering with my choices is a big step. I pull on my hair. Dad drums his nails on the side of his leg. "But can't you compromise? Come home for a couple of days? Spend Christmas with us. It's not that much to ask."

For a split second, I consider giving in, staying with my family for Christmas. The morning hot cocoa with Mom, opening presents by the twelve-foot tree in the family mansion, sleeping under the stars of my bedroom, filling up on Marta's cooking before the tour. The possibility of tasting the sweet and tangy sauce Marta uses on her stuffed peppers makes my mouth water.

I swallow the illusion and ground myself in reality. The warmth of Wil's hand reminds me I can't go back. Because if I do, I might not be able to leave. Mom doesn't want me to sing. She wants her little girl back, and I'm done with Melodie Rockerby, the rockstar's daughter.

I want to be the star, and I can't do that trapped in my mother's smothering embrace.

FIVE

Wil

"Are there any cookies?" Rocker sits at our kitchen table like he owns the place.

Mum smiles at the arse. "Would you like the Leibniz?"

Rage boils under my skin. It's not bad enough that he barges in here unannounced, and now he's eating the cookies we saved up to buy? I concentrate on the steam rising from my tea. He's ruining everything. He ruined Mum's life. If it weren't for Rocker getting her pregnant, she'd have a college degree, a better-paying job, and the ability to cover her medical bills.

Rocker opens his mouth. "I—"

"Why did you keep me?" bursts from my lips. How different would her life be if I hadn't been around to screw it up?

The face that has been my comfort, my cheerleader, my home fills with horror. I want to take the question back. I don't want to know. I want out of this kitchen.

Mum reaches across the table and places her hand on mine. "I wanted a child. Children. Not going to lie, I freaked out when I found out I was pregnant. How was I going to support myself and you? What to do with my plans to go back to school, especially when your father did not respond? But never ever did I question not having you." Her fingers curl around mine as if to prove her words. Her rheumatoid nodules become more visible, but she holds on.

Somehow knowing she wanted me makes me feel better. A puzzle piece that never quite fit rearranges itself in my chest and finally finds its spot. One half of the picture complete. I'm not a burden, a mistake to make up for. She wanted children.

Opa's hand lands on my shoulder. "I couldn't have asked for a better grandson."

My throat thickens with pride.

"I'm sorry I wasn't here." Rocker's platitude screeches into my world like feedback from a microphone. I glare at him, but he is watching Mum. He should be across an ocean in his mansion in Malibu with his perfect wife and the baby on the way. The one he actually wants. His gaze flicks to me, and I look away. He can take his apology and shove it.

"Little late," I say. I expect Rocker to shoot back at me, want him to so I can yell.

Rocker studies his fingers on the handle of his teacup. "If I'd known I would've—"

"Yeah, sure."

Rocker's head snaps up, jaw tight. "I protect my family. You can't blame me for that."

He's not the only one who protects his family. I match his growl. "Glad I'm not part of that. You'd stifle me to death like you did with El."

El squirms in her seat beside me, her features in that mask she wears when she's trying not to upset anyone, not show her emotions. Guilt mixed with rage invades my veins. I got so caught up in my stuff, I forgot to consider her. Not once since running away has she said anything mean about Rocker, even though she has more right than I do. He ignored me, but he stopped her from fulfilling her dreams, held her back. Of course, if he hadn't, she wouldn't have needed me.

"You have to be a parent to understand." Rocker's voice goes from contrite to menacing. I must've hit a nerve. His face hardens like it did that day in the studio at Rocker Inc.

"Stop it you two." El's hand flies to her colorless strand. My heart lurches at the movement, knowing the meaning behind the white streak in her hair. This whole situation bloody sucks, and it's not fair to her.

"I believe Dad. If he says he didn't know—he didn't know."

"So, you don't believe my daughter?" Opa thuds his mug down on the table.

She takes a breath. "I do. I believe Hanna." She offers Mum a smile before turning her gaze back to Opa. "But I know what it's like. People mail him nail and hair clippings. Fans send him underwear and photoshop his image into their pictures to make it look like they're together, sometimes out of obsession, but other times to blackmail him for money. Dad doesn't open his letters or public emails unless they've gone through his PA, or publicist, or bodyguard."

Rocker puts his hand on El's knee. The way he looks at her—the anger flashing in his eyes before replaced with a softness rarely seen in his publicity photos—he cares about El. Everyone in this room can see that.

"What Melodie says is true. In those days there were lots of women who claimed I was the father of their children." His eyes dart to Hanna. "I'll talk to my manager. He was the one who handled my inbound communication then."

Mum straightens. "But you had my number. Why didn't you reach out—"

"I did." Rocker leans in, and it's like they're in their own world. Opa, El, and I don't exist. "I called the number you put into my phone over and over, but something was wrong. I tried so many combinations, spent sleepless nights on the road calling strangers trying to find you."

"Oh, Bill, I"—Mum raises her hand to her mouth—"I didn't know."

El breaks her biscuit in half, and Mum blinks, like she's fighting tears.

"I regret not being there with you. Not seeing my son grow up. Him not having a father figure to look up to." Rocker puts his elbows on the table and buries his face in his hands.

"Well, I think it's time we start dinner." Mum wipes at her eyes. "We're having bratwurst, that okay with you?" she asks Rocker.

Isn't it enough she let him have tea? Now he's eating dinner here? I roll my eyes. That's it. I push my chair back and stand. Skipping dinner sounds like a better option.

"Wil"—Mum thwarts me—"can you bring the potatoes up from the basement?"

I grunt "yes" through my teeth. El calls my name as I stomp down the stairs. Everything's wrong. Mum should be angry with Rocker, instead she's inviting him to stay. Opa should have thrown him out but he's tolerating him. Back for five minutes in El's life and she's defending him again. How am I in the wrong? If she's angry with me, she probably should be. I was dumb to think it was going to take months for Rocker to find her. We should've gone somewhere else. Found a place no one knows us. Instead, I wanted to stay home with my family, in a place I feel comfortable and safe.

I flick on the light, slam the lid of the washer, and barge into the cold cellar.

"Wait," shouts El.

I turn around and she crashes into me. Her arms come around my waist, her head finds the crook of my neck, and she presses her body against mine. My arms do what they do best—hold my girlfriend. The bands of pain wrapped around my heart lessen with the familiar weight of her.

We stay like that for a moment, ignoring the unintelligible hum of voices from above. I kiss her temple. She moves and kisses my cheek, the corner of my mouth, and her soft lips land on mine. The slow sweet kiss doesn't stay that way for long, her giving into my request for more and more. I lose myself in her, the one true thing I know. This thing between us is real. The world shrinks to El and me, just the way I like it.

I find the trim of her sweater and edge underneath to brush her bare skin. I want to touch her everywhere. El opens her mouth, her tongue tasting mine. There's the faint hint of chocolate, but the rest is El. My pulse quickens. I want her.

El's hands are in my hair pulling, tugging, twisting, driving me crazy, my body responding to her desire. She wants me.

This is what I need. Not my stupid father upstairs pretending he wanted to be in my life. Whatever happened or didn't happen with Rocker is in the past. El is my here and now.

My fingers move up, exploring more of the parts I haven't been able to get close to for the last month. The last six months. I've never waited so long, craved someone so much. I drag my thumb down her spine and feel her shiver. I caress her waist, her stomach, unable to stop myself.

Her lips retreat. El presses her for forehead against mine. "We can't," she pants.

"We can." This could be my last chance; she's signing the contract. She's leaving.

"Your mom and Rocker are just upstairs."

Her words are more efficient than a bucket of cold water. "Let them wait. I need more time." I release El. "A month with you is not enough." I didn't mean to sound desperate, but I lose control around El and tell her things I wouldn't admit to anyone.

She takes my face in her hands and forces me to meet her eyes. "This is just the beginning." Her thumbs rub against my temples.

I shouldn't want the words to matter so much, but they do. She better mean them. I'm serious here. Too serious.

"Promise?" I tuck a piece of her flaming red hair behind her ear because I don't trust myself to touch her anywhere else.

Her face glows with determination in the low light of the basement. "I promise."

I believe her. El never lies.

I find the bag of potatoes and haul them up the stairs, El's hand never leaving mine.

On the top step, Rocker's voice rumbles. "That was the pilot. We're grounded because of the snow. Can you recommend a hotel?"

Six

Wil

THE REFRIGERATOR HUMS. THE familiar sound covers the whining wind so strong it feels like it's breathing cold right at me. The heavy velvet curtains don't move but they should—the weather outside has no intention of calming down.

Neither do I.

I can't believe my so-called father, not that I ever plan to call him that, weaseled his way into staying overnight. I roll to my side and remember why I was facing away. The blue flare of Rocker's phone charger is the main source of light in the room. The only source of light. How that tiny thing can be so bright, I have no idea, but it burns through my closed eyelids. I didn't turn the garland on the Christmas tree off only to have his inconsiderate arse not let me sleep because he needs to charge his phone.

Resigned, I lie on my back, the metal bar of the pullout couch hard against my shoulders, and stare at the light fixture in the middle of the ceiling—perfectly visible in the blue glow of the devilish device. Another howl shakes the window. The blue light disappears. Finally.

The room is quiet. Too quiet. I listen and try to understand what's wrong.

"Did the electricity just go out?" Rocker's voice comes from the floor. That's right, I didn't offer the foldout couch I've been sleeping on. Nope, the rockstar doesn't want to find a comfy bed someplace else, he gets what he gets. An old air mattress Opa and I squeezed between my couch and the kitchen wall.

"It'll be back." Hopefully after I fall asleep without his charger setting the room aglow again.

"Should we check if it's the breaker fuse?"

"Probably the whole street. Wait."

"Don't want the house to get too cold."

"The heater is running from the oil tank in the basement. We'll be fine."

I make a show of turning away from Rocker. Damn, he can't see me. I ensure the couch makes as much noise as possible as I move.

"Where's the breaker box? I'll go check." He addresses my back.

"No need. Go to sleep." Rocker's conversation about breaker boxes is hilarious. Like he knows anything about electricity. After years of helping Opa on construction sites, I know electrical work is harder than it looks.

The wind keeps pounding. Sleep doesn't come. I bunch the blanket around me to shield my shoulders from the drift of cold trickling down. I turn back to the other side. The Rocker side.

"Still awake?" He's whispering but he's so close, even his whisper is too loud in this dark room. I wish I was asleep because that means when I wake up, he'll leave, and I can get back to my normal life. "It's been half an hour. Maybe we should go check?"

How does he know how long it's been?

I open my eyes to find Rocker's profile bathed in the blue of his cell phone. Great. More bright light. I tug the blanket over my head and refuse to talk to him.

"Wil, is the breaker box in the basement?"

Rolling my eyes under the blanket doesn't help. I throw the cover off and stuff my feet into my slippers. "I'll fix it."

Since we're practically bedmates, I almost trip on the corner of the air mattress as I try to get to the basement steps. Something pops and a loud hiss fills the room.

"Think we have another problem." Rocker stretches and the hiss gets louder. "The mattress is losing air."

Great.

"Wait. Wil, wait." The glass bell on the Christmas tree sings from impact. Bet Mum wouldn't be so bloody happy if Rocker toppled over our tree, breaking our family heirloom decorations. Might be a fitting end to this disaster of a day. I look back and see him shining the phone's flashlight on the lanky branches in an attempt to still the many moving balls and toys.

"Ouch." Rocker shines the light at his bare feel covered in tiny green needles. Between the needles and how freezing cold the floor is in our house, he'll regret walking barefoot.

The light switch for the basement stairs is on the left and I flick it up. Rocker runs into my back.

"Oh." His breath tickles my neck.

El running into me earlier was a dream come true. Rocker breathing down the collar of my T-shirt is my worst nightmare. He's shining his phone's flashlight in front of him, which now is right into my eyes. I scowl. "Give me your phone."

I reach the bottom of the stairs and see the metal door of the panel. Thankfully Rocker's attempts at blinding me were unsuccessful. I walk over, swing it open, and peer at the switches.

"See here." Rocker stretches his hand over my shoulder. "The fuse blew." He elbows me aside. "Does your grandfather have any spares?"

"Over here."

"Electrical work is the only thing my father spent time with me on. He used to be a lighting engineer." Rocker replaces the fuse and the electricity whirls back up.

"Can we sleep now?"

I go up the steps first and shine the light from his phone so he can see. Injuring a famous rockstar is not a good look for anyone, never mind his newly discovered illegitimate son, even though it'd bring me some much-needed satisfaction. I don't know why I want him to hurt. I didn't care about him being my father. It's not like it matters to me at all.

"Quite the sleepover you and I are having."

Sleepover. We are not in primary school. "This has nothing to do with you. I didn't want Mum to worry."

"I like how protective of your mom you are."

"Someone has to be."

Back in the room, Mum's extra pillow and blanket lie in a sad pile on the floor over the carcass of the deflated mattress. I grind my teeth. Mum would be disappointed if I left it that way. I throw my hands in an "I give up" gesture, get the pump, attach it to the mattress, and start pumping my foot up and down. My efforts are useless. The plug must've failed. There's no rescuing this thing.

"It's okay." Rocker's breathing down my neck again, and I hop away. "I can sleep on the floor."

I sit down on the couch and take off my slippers. Damn, the floor is freezing. No way he can sleep on it and not get sick. I move my pillow to the edge. "You sleep by the window."

Rocker tosses and turns behind me. "Wil."

What now? I pull my cover higher.

"Come back to the States with me."

Not happening.

"You could work with me at Rocker Inc.?"

With him? He means for him. That's what El had to do, intern for months before he let her approach a microphone.

"You'd get hands-on experience."

Working with El, recording her song, taking her voice to new heights was exhilarating. But he's trying to do the same thing he did to El: shape me into a mini version of himself, shove his tastes and desires onto me. "Not interested."

"Okay." Rocker rolls and the couch squeaks. "What about school? You're studying sound engineering, right?"

I grunt.

"We could get you into the new quarter. I'll pay for it."

The program I was in at UCLA was pretty awesome, but the one in Berlin is fine. "I have a life here. Free school. Real family. Not leaving to play house with you."

"I know you think I've been overprotective with Melodie, and maybe I have." He doesn't take the bait. Again. I've been trying to get under his skin, and it's not working. "But you don't know everything."

Oh, but I do. El told me why the paparazzi chase her. They want the story of her father's death. I'd protect El from their prying eyes as well. Even now, just thinking about El as a child, watching her father drown, makes me want to run upstairs and hold her, Opa be damned. No one should relive that, least of all in public for the world to see.

"If you're in the States it'd be easier to see her when she's on tour."

Maybe I should go back to the States with him, create some trouble. That might be fun. What's wrong with me? How can I consider leaving . . . Opa? With El on tour and Mum at the clinic, there's no one who needs me. Back to Berlin, uni, rowing, DJing on the weekends for money. Wait for El to come back to me. There's my plan.

Damn him. "We'll be fine."

"What about when I announce that you're my son? The press will descend on you."

"What? Why would you do that?"

"Well, because you are my son, and it's important. I want the world to know."

Am I supposed to be grateful? He doesn't know me. I punch my pillow with my elbow. "You'll have a new son soon. You don't need me."

"But I want you."

Like I would ever believe him.

"Guten Morgen." Opa stumbles into the kitchen rubbing his hands together. "Still snowing." Opa gets his "Happy Retirement!" mug and fills it to the brim.

"I'll go shovel if it ever stops." It's been my task since before I hit puberty. But last year with me at uni and Mum's physical condition at its worst, Opa took over snow-clearing duties.

"I'll help." Rocker drains his cup.

"We only have one shovel," I say. Maybe I should let him. I could take photos of Rocker shoveling snow. Send them to Mateo who'd sell them to the press. That's one way to find the funds Mum needs. I wish I could do something like that.

Opa sits down at the table next to Rocker. Next. Not opposite. Not the furthest distance away possible. Out of the available four chairs he chooses the one to Rocker's left. "If you're eager to help, there's something better you can do."

"Sure. Anything." Rocker sets his slippered foot on his knee. "What can I do for you?"

"Not for me. For Hanna."

No. Opa's not doing what I think he is.

"Anything for Hanna." Rocker sits up straight, like the coffee's kicked in, and Opa has his attention. I want to puke.

"You know she's sick."

Rocker's hand pauses midair. "Hanna? Sick?"

"Hasn't Wil told you why he went to California in the first place?" Opa glances at me, and I choose to stare at the floor.

"No. There . . . wasn't time." Geez, Rocker thinks he has to cover for me. Wanker.

"The plan wasn't to steal your stepdaughter." Opa slurps his coffee. "He went for his mother. Hanna has an autoimmune disease and it's bad. The last flare-up was the worst yet. She couldn't work. She couldn't walk."

Rocker is drumming his fingers on the table as Opa sighs. "I watched my wife die in my arms. Seeing my daughter in pain and not being able to help her was the next hardest thing. That's when I told Wil the identity of his father."

Rocker's fingers stop moving. "Wait. Wil didn't know?"

"Not until his nineteenth birthday. Hanna couldn't bake him his birthday blueberry muffins. She always bakes them. Every year. It's a tradition. Might be a little thing for you, but that broke me." The coffee pot hisses and clicks off. "I told Wil to find a way to you. To ask you, threaten you, blackmail you—whatever it takes—to get the money Hanna needs for the experimental treatment. The money I could not provide. Selling my car was not enough."

"I thought German medicine is free," says Rocker.

"Everyone contributes from their salaries, so we get good coverage. But not . . . Wil how do you say . . ."

I take a chair. One far away from Rocker. "There's a clinical trial, starting in January, not approved by the health authorities, so they won't pay."

"It's the only option she has. She put on a brave face for you yesterday, but she's constantly in pain."

"So, you need money?" Rocker's brows pull together.

Opa's mouth presses into a line. On any other day a torrent of swear words would spill from his mouth. Instead, his voice is calm, measured. "*We* do not. I have my pension. Wil works. Hanna needs money."

"We have enough for most of the first round," I say.

"We're a thousand euro short." Opa makes a face like when he threw his back out last year.

"How much to cover the whole thing?"

Opa glances at Rocker then stares at his mug. "Twenty thousand euro, give or take."

"That's ridiculous," says Rocker.

"You don't have to cover the second treatment." Opa's voice rises. "Just help us cover the first—"

"Not what I mean. I can cover ten of those. A hundred. It's trivial. It's yours. I'll get my manager to transfer the money—" Rocker pats his shirt. The one Opa lent him. "I need my phone."

While Rocker's rummaging around the living room looking for his phone, I stare at Opa. "I can't believe you just asked him like that."

Opa glares back at me. "I had no choice."

I point to the living room. "We don't need his money."

"We do."

Rocker is talking as he enters the kitchen. "Give me your bank information, and my assistant will transfer the money when the banks open the day after Christmas. What else can I do?"

"That's enough," I grumble.

Rocker stares at me, his phone in his hand. "Why didn't you take the money when I offered it to you in the studio?"

This whole conversation is pissing me off. Opa begging Rocker for money, Rocker calling his bank manager like twenty thousand is nothing to him. "I wasn't going to sell out El. I can take care of Mum." I stand to look him in the eye. "I have a big gig for New Year's that'll cover the rest of the money for the first treatment. I'm back working for Opa's old company.

We'll figure something out. If I must drop out of school for a while—I'll do that."

"No need." Rocker moves like he's going to give me one of those pats on the shoulder he keeps giving El. I step out of his reach. "It's done, Wil. There's nothing to worry about. Not anymore."

Opa shuffles to the coffeemaker and pours another cup. "You don't understand. Hanna will not take it. If Wil would've gotten money from you before, we were going to say it was part of winning the competition, but that's no longer an option. She is a very proud woman. Even learning to accept money from Wil and me took her years. It has always been the three of us against the world."

My hip rests against the counter as Rocker takes this information in. The corners of his mouth curve, and I know that look. It's my look when I'm about to convince someone to do something. "I have an idea, but Wil won't like it."

"If it helps Mum, I'll like it." That'll piss him off. Try me.

"You come work for me. Shadow me, learn the business. A member of my A&R team is leaving, we could use the help. You live with me: no living expenses, free food, and if you decide to go back to UCLA, I'll pay for that too."

"I told you. I'm not going back to the States."

Rocker holds up his hands. "Think about it. As far as Hanna knows, the money you send home will be from your salary. We'll make sure it's plenty to cover Hanna's medical bills"—Rocker looks at Opa and then back at me—"and anything else she needs. Anything."

He can't be serious. I shake my head. "Mum wouldn't want me to go. She wants me to stay."

Rocker crosses his arms. "She's your mother. She loves you. If you tell her that's what you want, explain it'll provide you with opportunities you can't get here—she won't say no. If I know Hanna, she'd never deny anyone a chance at their dreams."

I think of the time Mum got me my first guitar. I begged for the instrument for weeks. I didn't know until later, but she sold her mother's diamond earrings to buy it for my birthday.

"How long do I have to stay?"

Rocker sits at the table. "When does El finish the tour?"

"March?"

"Three months? Stay for three months. You can finish a quarter at UCLA. Is three months of your life with me worth your mother's chance at a long and healthy life?"

It is. And Rocker knows it. He found my weakness. The thought of being in California with him sours the coffee I've been drinking. At least I'll be closer to El. I clench my jaw and push my head down.

He stretches out his hand. "Then we have a deal."

SEVEN

"You did what?" I can't believe my ears. I shake my head like I can unhear him.

"I made a deal with Rocker," Wil whispers.

I came upstairs to clean up after making the stollen, and Wil followed me into the bathroom. Maybe a kiss or getting his sweater off was what I expected, not a betrayal. I turn on the tap and pump the soap dispenser, creating distance from the comfort of him. "Well, at least you're telling me in person."

"What?"

"The last guy who chose Dad over me broke up with me with a text."

Wil grabs my soapy fingers. "I'm *not* breaking up with you. Ever." He squeezes my hands. "I'm doing this for Mum and for you. For us."

"That's a new one." I tug my slippery hands, but he refuses to let go.

"I'm serious."

I raise my eyes and meet his. The usual amber glow is gone. His pinched face seems panicked. My heart lurches at the sight. How could I doubt him? He's sacrificed so much for me already. I relax my fingers and weave them with his. "I don't need you to fight my battles." Even though I like that he cares enough to try.

Wil's features smooth and he lets go. "I know you don't." He bends forward and rinses the soap off, the smell of orange and cinnamon filling the small space. "But I saw an opportunity and I took it."

I shake my head as my hands join his under the water. "So like you. Explain."

He grabs a towel and fills me in on his conversation with Dad and Mr. Peters. "You understand, I had to do it."

I lean in and kiss his cheek. "I do."

The towel tossed on the countertop, Wil locks me in his embrace. As the orange soap scent dissipates, the essence of Wil fills my lungs. I breathe deeply while tucking my head into the crook of his neck. I love being this close to him. Don't think I'll ever get enough. The steady beating of his heart against my chest is like the kick drum line in U2's *Beautiful Day*, my own personal rendition.

Wil pecks my lips once, twice, three times, and I no longer care about what we were discussing or anything outside this room, with its chipped tiles and tiny tub. A year ago, I dreamed of a perfect boyfriend, and tried to fit Dillon into the image I created. Now I have the perfect boyfriend who is anything but the image I had, and I love that. The real Wil is a thousand times better than anything my imagination could come up with.

"See. Now you can't leave me." I feel Wil's smile against my skin. "We'll be in the US together. I'll save my money to fly out and hold a giant sign in the audience with 'I'm her boyfriend' in bold block letters."

I catch my reflection in the mirror and cringe at the fear evident on my face. A knot forms below my rib cage, cinching around my heart. Zoe's taunts about Daniel Davison swirl in my mind. "About that. We should . . ." I don't know how to say this without hurting his feelings. "I think it would be best if we don't tell anyone else about us."

Wil digs his fingers into my waist. "You don't want to be my girlfriend?"

"No," I say quickly. His jaw stiffens, and I trace the hard edge. "I mean yes, of course I want to be your girlfriend." I bounce on my tiptoes and gently brush my lips against his. The muscles of his jaw ease. "I just don't want to stir up trouble."

"There won't be any—"

"There will be." I press my thumb into his chin. "As soon as I'm back in the States and step foot on that stage, the paparazzi will be watching my every move. If my boyfriend"—I caress his face—"is waiting for me offstage, they are going to ask questions to find out who you are."

"Let 'em. They'll find out eventually." Wil's eyes search mine, belying the casual denial in his voice.

I long to be carefree like him, but even more I long to protect his ability to be carefree for as long as possible. My life has been lived in the headlines. I want more for him. "And when they find out you're my stepbrother?"

Wil groans at the ceiling. "Not this again."

I rattle his arms. "The press won't be kind. Especially since I've been absent for over a month. They'll make a big deal if we go public right now." His shoulders slump. I rest my cheek against his chest. "We must be smart about this."

"It's not fair."

"It never is with them. Believe me."

He pulls me closer, his fingers massaging the small of my back. "Okay."

The ties around my heart slacken and I can breathe again knowing Wil is safe from the jabs of the paparazzi for at least a little while longer. He needs time with Dad, time to learn to trust him out of the spotlight.

I snuggle closer. "Promise to text or call me every day."

"Done."

"And I'm taking you up on your promise to fly to see me. I can't not see you for three months." I grip the wool of his sweater. "We'll find a way. In secret if we have to. I'll sneak you in." I wrap my arms around his waist and meet his heated gaze. "Teach you my tricks."

He pushes hair away from my face. "All your tricks?"

Two sharp raps on the door stop Wil's progress to my lips. Mr. Peters clears his throat. "Wilhelm. Your mother needs help downstairs."

"Bloody hell." His voice goes from sultry to gruff. "How does he always know when we're alone?"

"Are you in there, son?"

"Coming, Opa." With a quick kiss on my temple, Wil unlocks the door and heads downstairs.

Without Wil's presence, there's a void in the small room as if the sunlight is gone. This is what signing with the group means. I'll be singing without Wil. I've done it before, but this time I'll know what I'm missing. I stomp on the tendrils of fear that are trying to poison my resolve and face myself in the mirror. "Everything is going to be fine."

Even though I can't stop thinking about Mom celebrating Christmas with only Marta, I choose to appreciate my first holiday without her by my side for what it is: a marker of my independence. Wishing them Merry Christmas on Facetime feels more sad than happy, but Dad coming here so close to Christmas was Mom's idea. No lavish presents were exchanged despite Dad's efforts to venture into the snow-covered streets of Bremen on Christmas eve to pick up some last-minute gifts. I had to squeeze Wil's thigh too many times to count to stop him from rolling his eyes through Dad's impromptu present: a mini concert of Hanna's favorite Rocker songs.

"What else do you need to pack?" Wil digs his fingers into my waist, like he can keep me longer this way.

I let him. I never want to leave this couch. Never leave his hands. Never leave him. "Hopefully nothing. Thank you for lending me the extra T-shirts. Are you sure you don't need them?"

"I won't miss two T-shirts." A flash of green from the Christmas tree twinkles in Wil's eyes. The presents are opened, and the room feels hollower. "Thinking of you wearing them will hold me over until I get to see you."

Dad's pilot confirmed everything will be clear to fly tomorrow morning. Dad, Wil, and I, bound for the States. Tomorrow, I get off the plane in Atlanta and walk away from Wil. My arms encircle him, cementing myself to Wil. The tour is over at the beginning of March. My chest compresses as Wil tightens his hold on me. "One month. I won't see you for a whole month."

"Might as well be an eternity." His fingers massage the nape of my neck, teasing my craving for contact with his skin. "When do you get to Las Vegas?"

"We arrive on the twenty-third and stay till the end of the month." My Christmas present, the bracelet Wil created out of leather strips from his old guitar strap, twists on my wrist. Something to remind me of him.

"Perfect. Vegas is only a six-hour drive from LA, and I don't want you to spend your birthday alone."

My fingers trace the ridges of his stomach. "What happened to flying?"

His muscles contract under my touch. "Too expensive."

"You can borrow Rocker's jet? He won't mind."

"No. I want to use as little of Rocker's stuff as possible. We have a deal, but it doesn't mean I have to trust him."

Hanna's laughter filters in from the kitchen. "I always hoped there was some reference to me in *Candlelight Nights*," she says.

Wil's jaw tightens. I graze his chin with the tip of my finger. "He's a good guy, you know."

"Sure." Wil's gaze could cut steel.

I massage the base of his neck to release the tension gripping his shoulders. "I know you think he made the bargain to force your hand, and he did, but he only wants to get to know his son."

"He has his precious new baby boy that'll be here in a few weeks." Wil squirms like his clothes itch. "I'm just a biological responsibility. Too old to play catch in the park with or have the birds and bees conversation with before prom."

I tilt my head up and force Wil to look me in the eyes. "I felt the same way when he started seeing my mom. Why would he like me? I was someone else's child. I came with issues."

Wil pulls me closer. "Don't say that. You don't have issues. After what you went through with your dad, anyone would be scared of water."

"Plus my dyslexia."

"One part of your brain works differently than the other, so you hear the world around you in a way like no one I've ever known." His finger traces my earlobe. "*I* certainly don't hear the world that way." I shiver. Will knows how to spin anything so even a negative looks positive.

"Didn't make it less stressful on my parents. When Rocker married Mom, he got a moody almost-teenager who sulked around his house for months and balked at his attempts to spend time with me and bond. But he never forced me to call him dad. He assured me he knew he could never replace my papa. Over time"—I loop my fingers through the belt on Wil's jeans—"he earned the right to be called dad." I twist the rough fabric. "I wanted to hate him for making me share Mom, but I couldn't. He's completely lovable." I find Wil's gaze again. "Just like his son."

"But . . ."

"But what?" I whisper the words against his lips.

He matches my tone. "What if he doesn't like me?"

My chest reverberates with laughter. "Not possible."

"You don't know that." Wil's head jerks away. "I'm . . ."

"Arrogant, a know-it-all, too smart for your own good?"

"Hey." His face relaxes.

"Stubborn," I say. He kisses my nose. "Thinks T-shirts count as formal wear, impulsive," I continue. He peppers my cheeks and forehead with more kisses. "Cocky." I hold my palm to block the kiss he aims at my lips.

He takes my hand in both of his and captures it under his chin. "Okay, okay, I get the point."

"No, Wil, you don't." The longing I've been pushing away because I miss Mom and couldn't spend Christmas with her for the first time in my life mixes with the memory of my first one without Papa. Wil doesn't understand that he still has a chance to be with his father. One I will never have again. With a tug on his hair, Wil looks at me. I cherish his face, glowing in the dim light of the fire. "The point is you don't know until you try. Won't you please try?" My nerves surge at the vulnerability and fear I see in him. "For me? And for you?"

He shakes his head, his gaze not leaving mine. "I don't know if I can do this."

"If I can go on stage without you, you can give Dad a chance." The corners of my mouth twitch, trying to smile, but it doesn't materialize. Instead, my bottom lip trembles. "What if I freeze? What if I can't sing on stage without you?"

"You're past that. Plus—" He finds my wrist and tugs on my bracelet. "I'll be there." He presses his lips against my cheek. "Always."

I take a sharp breath to protest, but Wil stops me with a kiss. It wipes away my fears and fills me with the confidence he has in me. The power of us. Even when we are not in the same room, he's by my side.

A melody, high and sweet, light and pure like Wil, ripples through my mind. I squeeze my eyes, as if I can trap this moment in my head, the joy and sadness, hope and hurt playing a cacophony of sounds in my ears. Flutes versus tubas.

"You were born to do this." Wil's voice calms the noise. I relax into him, passing the strength back to Wil.

How am I supposed to live without this?

My fingers slip under the collar of Wil's shirt, and the song inside me roars, desperate for more, desperate to make him mine.

"More schnapps?" Mr. Peters bellows from the kitchen.

A warning bell chimes somewhere in the recesses of my mind. I rushed my first time with Dillon. I don't want to rush my first time with Wil. Not now. We deserve better. With more effort than I would ever admit to him, I crowbar myself away from my boyfriend.

"I have something for you." I retrieve a brown paper bag from the coffee table. "A going-away present."

The evenings fire crackles in the fireplace, bathing the crammed living room in a cozy orange glow. It shimmers in Wil's hair. "A going-away present? I didn't get you one."

"You didn't need to. It's silly." I shove the bag back. He'll think I'm a sentimental fool.

Wil grabs my hand, pulling it and the bag into his lap. He peers inside and removes the water bottle he brought from

Germany to LA. The first thing that was truly ours beside the music we made together. He pushes the water bottle he told me to keep toward me. "No. I'm not taking it back."

"Turn it over."

He does as I ask. I watch delight bloom on his face as he reads the W&E I wrote in thick black marker on the metal bottom. "I need you to take care of it for me. I don't want to lose it."

I know this is an excuse. He knows it's an excuse. He runs his finger over the ampersand that connects our initials. "I can do that. But the moment the tour is over, it goes back to you."

"Maybe then we share it." I hope he hears a promise in my voice. Three months, for a lifetime together.

His eyes sparkle and my pulse double-times. "Deal."

EIGHT

THE TAXI DRIVER SWERVES into the left lane with a jolt and I grip my mostly empty coffee cup. He's no Sven. Nor is this tiny electric car the Rolls. Taking a rideshare from the Atlanta airport to Carlee's house in Tuxedo Park wasn't an option since they need a credit card. El Vella doesn't have one, and I'm not using the American Express tucked into the back of my wallet. Melodie Vella Rockerby may have signed the contract with Blatantly Subtle, but El Vella is making it on her own dime.

I bring the screen with Carlee's lively face closer and tune back into last year's Grammys. Carlee sings the first line of *Love Is Not a Sin* onstage during the ceremony. She's always on pitch. No autotune needed. What isn't she good at? Dancing, singing, writing songs, winning competitions. Her love for harmonies was one of the first things that made Subtle stand out from other glam-rock groups. The addition of backup singers isn't an industry standard, and no one could've predicted it would contribute to their worldwide success.

On the plane, I sat holding Wil's hand and obsessing over every single interview of hers, with and without Blatantly Subtle. With no famous parents or a recognizable last name, Carlee made it from the suburbs of Atlanta to her stratospheric level of fame all on her own.

My stomach lurches. A cup of airport coffee as my breakfast wasn't a good idea. Luckily living expenses are taken care of for the next few months, but with less than a hundred dollars of the advance left to my name and two weeks until I get paid, coffee is the multitasker I'm after: energy, fills my stomach, and minimum budget. I drain the last drops of the weak brown liquid that tastes more like eau d'coffee. Not sure there's enough caffeine in here to wake an ant.

It's only a thirty-minute ride to the gated community of Carlee's house. The woman at the gate booth asks for my name and my driver's license, and scans the code on my phone that confirms I'm allowed on the estate. A bodyguard and a fancy car used to act like VIP passes without me having to lift a finger. Not anymore.

Welcome to my new life.

A stunning panorama of the hills greets us. We pass streets with low-end McMansions and fully customized buildings that will never rival Rocker's Malibu property. The empty cup in my hand shakes. My throat is less dry but my heart pinches, missing Wil's metal bottle already. I ignore the discomfort and point to the woman standing in the driveway up ahead. "That's it."

Once out of the cramped taxi, I grip the handle of my one piece of luggage, bright and yellow, matching the Georgia sun. I wait for the lightness of freedom to inhabit my lungs. Instead, a snake of anticipation coils in my stomach.

From coffee or uncertainty? The hollowness inside feels closer to loneliness than freedom. I'll miss introducing Marta to Wil and showing him the ropes at Rocker Inc. I'll even miss Zoe's exuberant welcome home hug, but sacrifices must be made. One viral YouTube video does not a star make.

"I'm Josie." A preppy woman in a black sundress who's closer to Mom's age than mine pays the driver before I have a chance. "You're the last to arrive."

"Oh." I check my phone. I can't be late. "The email said to arrive at 10 a.m."

She pushes open the front door, and we exchange the blinding sun for a dark hallway. "Guess the other girls wanted a head start."

As usual, the words aren't available when I need them. They go through the shredder of my anxiety as soon as they form, and I don't have time to piece them back together. My knees shake as Josie leads me down a corridor lined with gold and platinum records, ending in a living room large enough to host a Rocker-scale party.

Three dark-brown leather couches occupy the center of the space. The light from the tall windows bracketing the large fireplace reflects on the surface of a square glass coffee table. In the corner sits a grand piano with a crystal chandelier hanging over it, like something out of a black-and-white movie. Two girls sit at a long marble table on the opposite end of the room. Carlee, Beau, and Kamo—the three members of Blatantly Subtle—face them.

"Everyone, this is Melodie," says Josie.

A look of recognition filters across the face of the girl with shoulder-length flat-ironed hair that shines like a blade. I adjust my shirt. The jitters that started on my way here are now a full-blown revolt. I'm both sweating and hiding my ice-cold fingers in my pockets. The hurricane in my chest is so much like stage fright, and I'm nowhere near a stage yet. The first time I ran away, the second time Wil was there to get me though it. What do I do today?

I offer a small wave, pull on my press conference façade, and slide into the empty spot at the head of the table opposite the group. The legs of the chair squeak an off-key C as I drag it forward. I wince at the dissonance between the sour note and the sweet hope for my future music career.

This is the first day for everyone, not just me. I take a long breath. Even though these other girls look older than my almost-nineteen, we're equals, here because each of us has something the group wants. I twist my new bracelet. Wil's advice comes into my head: *Picture them naked.*

"Are we ready to rock?" Carlee glances at the clock showing five to ten in the kitchen that's littered with what looks like brunch at the Ritz. I'm either hallucinating from my coffee high or I smell bacon, and my stomach reminds me of the lack of food. "I handpicked everyone here to be part of this inner circle." Her gaze meets each of us, one at a time, me last.

Without her bold makeup, the pink strand in her shoulder-length blonde hair is the sole trace of color. Her clothes echo her signature head-to-toe black but lack the studs and sequins. She's more fragile, a shadow of the fearless self I've seen in footage of her on stage.

"Hold on." Beau crosses his arm over a black collared shirt open so far, I can see the tattoo of a heart across his sternum. "I helped a little."

Kamo punches him in the shoulder, her black tank top showing off her toned arms. The girls next to me are head-to-toe black as well. I slide my gaze to my pink shirt with a giant white bass clef, a leftover from Zoe's batch of music-inspired outfits she ended up scrapping last year. Why didn't I wear something more Rocker-like? I stand out like a giant pink thumb.

"We all helped," says Carlee.

Kamo dips her chin, her long braids swishing with the movement. "Damn right."

Carlee places a hand on Beau's elbow. "We're a team."

His arms drop and I feel like a tension balloon just popped.

"You've met Josie, who has been the backup singer for us since Langdon and I," Carlee tilts her head in Beau's direction, "or Beau as the world knows him, formed Blatantly Subtle six years ago. She'll be your day-to-day contact. Her job is to bring you up to speed on the songs, chorography, stuff like that, before you join us for rehearsals next week." Carlee reaches for the coffee cup in front of her. "She'll give you details later. But first, we'll be spending a lot of time together on the road, so let's get to know each other."

The girl with the perfect hair straightens. "I'm Annalyn." Her accent is British, but I'm not acquainted with the different parts of the UK enough to place where she's from. "I've been singing since I was born. Mom says the whole of Makati could hear me until we moved to the UK when I was three." Her gaze pauses on each of our faces for a second. "I started my YouTube channel at fifteen and have almost six hundred thousand subscribers. My two latest covers hit over three million views."

Don't Give Me Comfort's video still gets hits every day, but it hasn't hit two million yet.

The girl with a nose ring and a perfectly outlined pout tucks her thumbs behind the waistband of her black jeans and smiles. Her whole face changes from hardness to bright sunshine. "I'm Yolanda, but my friends call me Yoli. I'm from LA." She sounds like a valley girl. "Like Annalyn, I've been singing as long as I remember, but I got my start busking on the beach. Some tourists filmed me, and I became social-media famous. I post recordings my boyfriend makes of me. Some covers. Some original stuff. I play the guitar, banjo, and am learning piano. I guess I just like music. If I could be a one-woman band, I probably would."

Josie faces me. "And of course, everyone knows Melodie Rockerby."

If they didn't, they do now.

"Hi." I wiggle in my seat. "I prefer El. Born in Malta but lived in LA the last six years. Like Annalyn, I've been singing all my life. Mostly play the piano, but my dad has been teaching me guitar and he's amazing at it." There's a collection of half-laughs. Of course they know Rocker is amazing. "I have one song that I made a video for, an original, and that sorta blew up last month. Like Yoli, I also busked for a bit. Oh, and I worked at a recording studio, so I've been on the inside and outside of the recording process."

"Your dad's studio?" Annalyn says.

"Yeah." I try to meet her eye and fail.

"*Don't Give Me Comfort* spoke to me." Beau's lean body edges forward. "Did you write it?"

A flush of confidence surges through my veins. This I can talk about nonstop. "I did. Collaborated with my"—my tongue stumbles on the word boyfriend—"my friend. We're working on two more songs."

Carlee's cup clanks on its saucer. "My advice is to pause that. Tour life is brutal and you're here to sing."

"Correct." Josie taps on her phone. "We're in Atlanta for three weeks of rehearsals, then the six-week West Coast tour begins. I'm emailing you the stops, bus days, and hotel days."

When I get mine, I scroll and stifle a groan. The text jumps around. I push down the returning anxiety, reminding myself I can study the details later.

Carlee rises. "Things might change as we adapt but expect long days. Today however, we celebrate you joining Blatantly Subtle." Carlee steers our attention to the food in the kitchen. "Welcome to our family."

"Come on." Josie invites us to follow her.

My phone explodes with "Come talk to me, come talk to me, come talk to me." I should change Zoe's ringtone to something less . . . Zoe. I fumble for the mute button and type.

Me: Busy right now.

The tray closest to me is piled with mini muffins and I stuff a chocolate one into my mouth. Memories of baking them for Wil's birthday and him staying in the guest bedroom he'll probably live in now overlays the image of the chattering people I'll spend the next three months with. The sweetness of chocolate brings tears to my eyes. I kissed Wil on the plane and walked away only a few hours ago, yet I miss him already. The thought of not seeing him for a month lodges the poorly chewed muffin in my throat. I cough and tears escape my eyes, but at least I have a good cover for why I'm crying.

"Take this." Carlee extends a glass of water my way, her other hand resting between my shoulder blades.

"Thanks," I croak.

She gives me a mischievous look that reminds me of Zoe. Now I miss Zoe as well.

"Come with me." She heads to the piano. A collection of photos in silver frames decorate the lid. "I was you seven years ago." She points to a picture of a young Carlee without the pink hair, pointing to the neon sign of The Devil's Martini above her. "I promise you; we'll be your new family."

My heart squeezes, wishing Mom and Rocker would accept my career choice like this, but maybe a new family is what I need. My gaze finds a familiar face in the collection of photos. Rocker has his arm across Carlee's shoulder, both smiling at the camera. A cold knife of suspicion that it was Dad who arranged this deal slices into my back. The fear I wasn't selected based on my skills but my connection, that my self-proclaimed independence is his doing, burns in my chest. "You know Dad?"

"Know? Not really. We sat at the same table at the Grammys two years ago. He clearly adores your mother. They were holding hands the entire time. Not something I expected based on his stage persona. But then I'm not my stage persona either." She grins at me. Her lips are curving up but her eyes well with sadness. I don't know what to do. "We have our roles to play." Her voice lowers. "My advice is: listen to Josie. She's good people. She'll help you navigate the spotlight and the press. Remember you signed the NDA. Be careful what you share, and with whom."

Beau appears beside Carlee and whispers something in her ear. She raises her eyebrows and her eyes narrow. "I guess it's time." Carlee threads her arm through Beau's. "We're glad you decided to join us, El."

"Me too."

She gestures to the kitchen. "Go eat. We'll talk again soon."

The part of the muffin that reaches my stomach does nothing to make me less hungry. I load a plate with scrambled eggs, bacon, toast, grapes, and strawberries, and pour a glass of orange juice to avoid another choking incident.

"Sucking up to Carlee already?" Yoli hands Annalyn a glass of champagne.

I play with the fruit on my plate to hide my unease. "She showed me a picture of the bar where she got her start. I sang there too."

"Daddy get you that gig too?" Annalyn sneers.

So much for making friends.

NINE

Wil

Sven's hulking body and stony eyes are the first thing I see as we walk down the plane's stairs into the heat of the LA December afternoon.

"Welcome back, Mr. Rockerby." Sven strides alongside as we leave.

This is no LAX. The smaller Hollywood Burbank Airport doesn't have the crowds I saw Rocker and El parade through on my very first day in LA. Yet there are still people staring and recognizing the rockstar, lifting their phones to record our exit. I tug my beanie down. The sensation that I'm on display decreases only when I climb into the back seat of the familiar electric Rolls Royce and Sven closes the doors.

Rocker's phone rings and he smiles as he puts it to his ear. "Just another hour or so till we're ho—"

His features change from a sunny day into the moment right before a thunderstorm, when the air is tense and heavy with rain.

"Three minutes apart? Why didn't you tell me?" His eyebrows furrow. "Yes, I couldn't have made the plane go any faster, but I would've liked to kno—" I'm not sure if there's a way to furrow his eyebrows any further without them popping off his face. "I'll tell Sven to gun it. We'll meet you at the hospital." The tight line of his mouth quirks in a tiny smile. "Love you."

"Mount Sinai?" Sven asks.

"As fast as you can." Rocker slants forward, like he can make the car go faster with his body's motion. "Speeding tickets are a small price to pay for seeing my son's birth."

Sven swerves and runs a light that turns red way before we get to the middle of the intersection. I grab the seat with the hand not holding my phone texting El the baby is on the way. Speeding tickets might be nothing for Rocker, but I do value my life.

"Sven knows what he's doing. He won't put us in danger, even if might feel like a race. It's very controlled." Rocker's hand lands beside my white knuckles on the leather separating us. "I trust Sven with not only my life but my kids' lives. He's never betrayed me."

I find Sven's eyes in the rearview mirror. Rocker might think Sven and my silent exchange is about the speed with which the car is moving, but we know what happened in El's room the day she left LA, and who got me there. Maybe Rocker should trust Sven a little less.

"By the way, I'm assigning Sven as your driver for the duration of your stay."

I rip my eyes from the rearview mirror and meet Rocker's for the first time in hours. "I don't need a chauffeur."

"Wil Peters didn't need one. Wil Rockerby definitely does."

"Not happening." I glare at him, hating how it's like looking in a time-warped mirror of myself. "Neither the chauffeur nor me taking your name."

"We'll discuss it with my publicist and see what's the best way to spin this is. As soon as we announce you're my son, your world will be a paparazzi circus. And not a ha-ha fun kind of circus either. It's imperative we are ahead of the story every step of the way. You will be a target of more than cameras."

El's words land in my head. The bubble wrap she mentioned seemed like a rich-people problem. I text El about Sven.

El: Don't think about him as something to deal with. Think about him as a friend. Another Nick or Mateo but with muscles and a scary stare.

Sven as a friend. Hell will freeze over before that happens.

"We're going through the staff entrance." Sven glides the car into a parking spot.

Rocker set his shades on his nose, and the two of them exit the car as if we're on a mission to save the world, one baby at a time. I trail behind, not really sure what the hell I'm supposed to do with myself.

With Sven at the head of our procession people part like he has the power of opposing magnets. The moment the staff realizes who we are, doors open, personnel update us on Sylvia's status, and we exit the elevator fully up to speed. I don't know what normal hospital suites look like in the US, but the room we enter is not it. It's like a high-end hotel, plus medical equipment. There are three women standing by the window. One is Zoe, one is a lighter-haired version of Zoe, and the last one is a heart-wrenching mix of El and a paler version of the polished face that mistook me for Rocker at Zoe's birthday party.

Sylvia Vella Rockerby's big blue eyes are full of fear that changes to relief the moment she sees Rocker. The feeling of not belonging hits me like a slap to the face. I should've stayed in the car or got a rideshare to the mansion.

"You made it." She kisses him like there aren't five other people in the room.

"I would've made it even if I had to stop LA traffic." He strokes her hair and nuzzles her nose. I'd say get a room, but that's what got us here in the first place.

"Mom and I will leave you alone." Zoe and the other woman hug El's mom and pass by me on their way out.

Sylvia's gaze follows, then narrows as it lands on me, roams over my face, my body, and stops at my fingers that are rapping a nervous song on my jeans. I clench my fist.

"This is Wil." Rocker juts his chin at me. "And this is the love of my life." The way he looks at El's mother shouts who she is to him without any need to voice it aloud.

"We've met," Sylvia says before I have a chance to open my mouth. "I should've trusted my gut then." She doubles over and a nurse runs to steady her on one side, Rocker on the other, and they lead her to the bed.

"Coffee." Sven sets his palm on my back and not-so-gently-directs me out of the room, greeting the two similarly dressed large men on either side of the door as we pass.

After the espresso that might have been made of the tears of an angel on Rocker's plane, the steaming cup of a coffee-adjacent brew from the machine on a lower floor gets my head out of the clouds and grounds me in reality. I'm in LA. I'm about to have a baby brother, and an insta-family I never wanted. I pull my phone out and text Mum and Opa that I arrived safely. I spare them the details and switch to chat with El.

Me: The nurse is helping your mum. Rocker's there as well. Sven and I are drinking possibly the worst coffee I've ever tasted. I miss you.

El: How's she doing? Miss you too.

Me: In pain? Unhappy to see me? Almost mauled Rocker when he got there?

El: Their PDA is a lot. You'll get used to it. I always thought they were the teenagers in the house and not me.

Me: Not planning on spending enough time at the mansion to find out. I'll sleep there but I don't live there.

El: It's not all bad. There's the studio downstairs. And my room. You can pretend I'm there.

Me: I can't wait for these three months to be over and us not needing to pretend about anything.

Sven taps my shoe. "Baby Pickle is here."

"Baby Pickle?" I process the phrase. "They named the baby Pickle?"

"Nickname." Sven tosses his coffee cup. "Let's go." He sails through the mostly empty atrium toward the elevators without looking over his shoulder to see if I'm following.

Maybe he's used to El doing what he says, but I'm not El. I cross my ankle over my knee and sip the hot liquid despite the horrid taste.

"This is the first and the last time I'll tell you this." Sven's voice is low and booming at the same time. "I'm in charge of you now. Even though you don't think you need me, you need me. No matter what you think about Mr. and Mrs. Rockerby, you're not getting the chance to make one of the best days of their lives worse by being an ass and not being there when the kid they've been waiting for arrives into this world. If I have to cuff you, paint a smile on your face, and drag you up to their suite, I will do it. But if you want my help any time in the future, you'll get up, and no matter what you actually feel, be the most pleasant version of yourself."

I shake my foot. "It's not my job to make them happy."

"Maybe not, but it's my job to protect them. Even if it's from ungrateful people like you." Sven crosses his arms and I fear for the seams of his suit jacket. "I thought you valued family."

His accusation sticks in my ribs. "They are not my family. I didn't live with them. They didn't get me to school on time, they didn't cheer at my rowing events. They are strangers to me."

Sven stomps forward and glares down at me. "Rocker would've wiped your snotty nose had he known about you. None of us can take back the past. Let him be a father now. What is there to lose?"

Myself? What if he changes me? I can't let him. This is about the money for Mum.

Sven inches forward. "What will it be? Me dragging you, or are you able to walk?"

I get up and throw the mostly full cup in the bin.

"Smile." Sven instructs me outside Sylvia's door.

I pull my lips into the best imitation of happiness I can muster and enter the room. Instead of just Sylvia and Rocker, there are three other people in the room. One of them is doing something with the baby in a transparent plastic container under bright lights. His tiny mewls are cute. His eyes are more closed than open, but when he turns his head my way, something happens to my chest. It both expands and contracts. The little human sends invisible tendrils my way, and my fake as hell smile falls. My real smile tugs at the corners of my lips. "He's sorta cute in a squished kind of way," I hear myself say.

"Hi, baby Pickle." I step toward the baby and the nurse or doctor who is attending to him beckons me over. "Can I?"

"As long as it's okay with Mom."

I look over at Sylvia, who's holding Rocker's hand. "Greet your brother," she says. The glow in her eyes is full force.

"Wash your hands first," the nurse instructs.

I lather and rinse while singing Happy Birthday to myself twice, then walk over to the baby. He stops his noises. I brush his tiny fist with my finger that looks giant in comparison. His baby hand grabs onto me, his grip stronger than I anticipated. He's so small and fragile. "Hi" is the only thing I can think of saying.

"My two sons together. We just need El here and our family will be complete."

Sylvia sniffles. I catch her wipe her eyes. She wants El here.

I want El here too.

TEN

THAT ALERT FLASHES AT the top of my screen and I hold my breath. What does Daniel Davison have to say about me this time? The link leads to an article on his blog. I scan for my name, my finger tracing under the lines, trying to keep the letters from jumping.

"Are you on dating apps too?" Annalyn stares at me from the other side of the couch, the episode of *Love Island* reflecting in her wide eyes. "Don't tell me you plan on sneaking out on dates in the middle of the night like Yoli."

"No. I have a—" I shut up before I mention that I have a boyfriend. "I'm not." I drop my phone in my lap. "Just playing a game."

"Want anything from the kitchen?" She stands and stretches like we've been huddled here for hours instead of twenty minutes. "I need tea before we start rehearsals."

"A cappuccino?" I already made myself a cup in the morning. Carlee's machine is almost identical to the one at home, the one I used to make Wil coffee for his birthday. I've made coffee a million times, but that's the memory that constantly resurfaces. "One pump of caramel?"

"Reminds me of my parents pub. Although the coffee machine they have isn't as fancy as Carlee's." Annalyn leaves the den attached to the three bedrooms in this wing of Carlee's mansion. The architecture and layout are different from the Malibu house I've spent the last six years in, but the feel of luxury is the same. After the month with Wil in Bremen, I notice things I took for granted before. Like the coffee machine.

I resume reading the article. There's a grainy picture of Mom and Dad shuffling an infant car seat into an SUV outside the hospital and speculation on his name and hair color. Why does anyone care what color a baby's hair is? From the onslaught of photos Mom, Dad, Aunt Patti, Wil, Zoe, and even Sven have sent me, Pickle has less hair than my balding grandfather in Malta, just tufts that cover the middle of his head exactly where grandpa lost his. Pickle sort of suits: tiny and bold with his puff of hair where the stem would be.

Three paragraphs later I find my name.

He is also the half brother of Melodie Rockerby, Rocker's adopted daughter.

That's it? I press my hand against my sternum to dampen the burning in my chest. I recline on the couch and take a calming breath, pushing the agitation away. I should be happy I'm only a footnote in this article. I shift on the couch. Is this concern for my new brother? Doubt it. He's got Dad and Mom to look after him. Not to mention a compound full of bodyguards. Sven wouldn't let anything happen, not on his watch. I shove my hair behind my ear and reread the article to make sure I didn't miss anything.

Wil isn't mentioned at all. Relief fills my head. His secret is safe. For now. If the press is in such a frenzy over a newborn, I don't want to imagine the field day they'll have over Rocker's long-lost son. I tuck my nose into the sleeve of Wil's T-shirt that still smells like Hanna's detergent and send Wil a text.

Me: Miss you.

My shoulders slump at the lack of dots indicating he's writing back. I tuck my phone in the pocket of my jeans. It's been a little over a week and while we've found a routine of early morning calls that seems to work, I miss knowing where he is, what he's doing, and, most of all, when I'll see him again.

The only solid plan we agreed on is him visiting me in Vegas for my nineteenth birthday in a month. Being in his arms will be a great present. My body sings the familiar tune that could be Wil's leitmotif if we were a movie. Spending a night alone in a hotel room—that might be the best present I've ever received in my life. My cheeks blaze at the scenarios of what I could do to him, and with him. I press my lips together to hide my smile.

Keeping myself from thinking about Wil before we left for Germany was hard. Staying away from him now, when I know the taste of him, the comfort of his arms, the feel of his palms exploring my skin—this is what torture feels like. I squeeze my thighs, close my eyes, and sink deeper into the fantasies of Wil's breath over my ear, his fingers tangled in my hair. I hum as a pool of pleasure melts my core.

"El." Carlee's voice cuts across my imagination. "Do you have a minute?"

I sit straight and run my hand over my burning face, erasing any trace of my dreams of Wil. "Sure. What's up?"

Carlee strolls over and perches on the coffee table. She snags the remote and pauses *Love Island*. "Sorry, can't think with that thing on."

The screen freezes with an image of one of the couples deep in a kiss. The flush creeps back up my neck.

"I wasn't really watching it."

We glance at the still, and I'm glad she might think my pink cheeks are because of the show, not the thoughts in my head. She turns off the TV.

"I'm not into reality shows." I stretch my lips into an apologetic smile. Why am I making excuses? Am I trying to impress Carlee? I've been living in her house for over a week and besides that first day, we haven't really spoken.

My mornings start with Josie running us through rounds of the harmonies we need to learn for each song, followed by choreography in the afternoon. Carlee and Beau attended a few sessions and gave notes to Josie on what to improve.

"I've been rewatching your cover of *Love Is Not a Sin* on your YouTube channel." Carlee lays her hands in her lap. "You have quite a collection of covers of other artists, but I didn't realize you have several originals. Did you write those?"

Even if I would've wanted to lie and say yes, I can't. Without Wil, I wouldn't have done those songs justice. "I wrote the songs with a coauthor."

"Did you?" The interest on her face piques. "So you're comfortable working with others on new songs?"

"Absolutely." Not sure how this matters for me as a backup singer. Harmonizing, memorizing, and retaining the choreography appear to be the three major skills Josie required of Annalyn, Yoli, and me over the last week.

"Do you write the music or the words? Or both?" Carlee's fascination with Wil and my writing process is not what I expected, but as a songwriter, she's probably interested in other people's processes, just like I would die to know how she and Beau write their songs.

"Melodies come first usually, but I've been getting better at words. Once we have the core of the song, we both go over the music and the lyrics, moving things around, testing what feels right and what doesn't. There's a lot of give and take. I have my pet peeves, he has his."

"He?"

"Yeah." Wil's name is on the tip of my tongue. If she digs deeper, she'll be able to find his name, and potentially his connection to Rocker. I don't want that, so I grind my teeth to keep from telling her who he is. This is not lying.

"You like that part?" Carlee doesn't push, and a knot under my breastbone loosens. "The songwriting?"

Like? That's such a weak word. Even my mind that struggles with finding the right ones scoffs at "like" where songwriting is concerned. "I live for it."

Carlee scoots to the edge of the table. "Are you working on something now?"

"Only always."

"What is it about?"

How do I explain the song we started in Bremen? "Love?" My answer sounds more like a question.

"Love." Carlee smiles and worries her lip. "A universal topic. Can't wait till you post that one." She rises. "Or, if you ever want me to look over what you've got, I can—"

"Really?" Her offer has to be an empty gesture. Carlee Waters cannot possibly be interested in what Wil and I are fumbling with. "We're struggling with this chorus."

"Oh?" She sits back down. "What's not working?"

"We're trying for words sung by two people, but not a conversation. More like two separate monologues, yet they play over each other. We have the melodies down, but the words are not falling into place."

"Can I hear it?"

Carlee Walters wants to hear my song. A buzz of worry fills my ears. "Now?"

"Why not?"

The rehearsal starts in half an hour, but I don't have to go yet. I take my phone out of my pocket, locate the latest version of the song, and hit play. The world diminishes as the two loves of my life fill the room: music and Wil. Fizzy excitement shoots across my forearms at the low baritone of Wil's voice, his words not whispered in my ear like in Bremen but still as potent. My voice joins him and we fade in and out, the lyrics struggling to convey the parallel conversations. The track ends, and silence stretches, morphing into discomfort.

I can't make myself look at Carlee. Does she hate it? Have I screwed up? Will she laugh like Wil did when he heard my first version of *Don't Give Me Comfort*?

Carlee's hand brushes my knee. "Such a cool concept, but I see what you mean. The impact is lost."

"I didn't know if you wanted any sugar in yours." Annalyn stops in the doorway with two cups in her hands.

Carlee retracts her hand and raises her eyebrows at Annalyn.

"Carlee?" She approaches us. "Are you joining us at the rehearsals today?"

I take the cup of coffee out of Annalyn's hands. The note design she created in milk foam shows she's done latte art for a while to get to this level of skill. "Thank you."

"No, I'm heading out for the day, but Josie said you both are doing an amazing job. She's proud of your progress." Carlee stands again and addresses me. "Send that file to me. I'll give it another listen. I might just have a thought on how to go about fixing it."

ELEVEN

SAME COUNTRY. SAME-ISH CITY. Very different life. Rocker's Malibu mansion is less than forty miles from the UCLA campus where I spent my first week in LA six months ago. That first week was about getting used to rooming with Mateo, sharing a shower with a whole floor of guys who had worse hygiene standards than me as a tween, and trying to stay alive with dry ramen as a major food group.

Last night the cook/housekeeper/stand-in-grandmother Marta made enough food to feed my entire rowing team. This morning she's mixing something by hand, totally ignoring the machine in the corner my mum would give her back teeth to use. I scan the drying rack I left our water bottle on last night. It's empty. A fissure of panic licks the back of my neck. No.

They won't throw it away. It might be banged up and the paint chipped all over, but who discards water bottles?

"Wil." Marta wipes her hands on her apron. "You're up early."

"Couldn't sleep." I take a guess as to which of the line of ceiling-height cupboards might contain water bottles and pull on a knob. Nope. Looks like a collection of egg cups shaped like people dressed in Nordic outfits.

Marta's right beside me. "Can I help?"

"My water bottle?"

"Here." She points to the cupboard over a chrome-clad contraption sunk into the backsplash. I open the door and our water bottle stands—or more like stands out—next to a dozen pristine bottles in various sizes. Like me next to Rocker and his entourage. "Mr. Rockerby doesn't use plastic. Try not to use the black ones. They're his favorites."

Relief washes over me as I tip our bottle and make sure El's writing is still on the bottom. I start toward the sink to turn on the tap like a regular person, but Marta reaches out. "May I?" I pass her the bottle. She unscrews the lid, places the bottle in the alcove of the machine, and presses a button. The machine whirs to life.

"Thanks." I stand there with nothing to do as the bottle fills.

"The brioche won't be ready for another hour or so. Do you want me to make you something else for breakfast?" Her smile erases my intention to forgo breakfast here and eat something on campus. I can't offend her.

"Thought I might try out the gym first," I say. Rocker pointed out the separate building during the grand tour, along with the tennis court, five-car garage, and guest house that is home to the three bodyguards on staff.

The sun isn't up yet as I cross the lawn the sprinklers just finished watering. It feels weird to be wearing only my sweats and Energie Berlin T-shirt. According to Mum the freak snowstorm in Bremen didn't last long but a cold snap had settled in. She promised to pack every sweater for her stay at the clinic and the wool socks El and I gave her as a Christmas present. Avoiding colds and viruses doing her RA trial is essential.

I enter the gym. "Bloody hell."

My voice bounces off the walls of the unoccupied space. If Rocker ever needed additional income, he could rent this out for personal trainers, because calling this a workout room is woefully underselling things. Free weights, treadmills, elliptical, rowing machine, machines I've never seen before, and other stuff my trainer at the club would drool over form neat rows.

After stretching, I move to the bench and start with a lighter set of weights. It's been over a month since my last real workout. Eight presses in, the door into the studio opens and I freeze mid-push. My mind tells me there is no threat. No intruder can get through the fences, gates, and security, but my body is on high alert.

At the flash of white-blond hair my muscles relax. Sven's broad shoulders look as tense as mine. Our gazes lock. Whether he's on my side or not varies day by day. One thing hasn't changed—he never smiles. The expression on his face right now is closer to disgust.

He glances at the clock on the wall, then back at me. "It's five fifteen."

"Good morning." I push the bar up, rest it on the metal stands, and sit.

"Come back at six fifteen." Sven sets down a water bottle similar to the clones in the cupboard above the filtration machine, but it's hard to tell the color because it's covered in blue and red Superman stickers. One says Comic-Con and I stifle a laugh. By the way his arms are crossed, this is not the time to mock his superhero obsession.

Guess someone's not a morning person.

"What about first come, first served?" I try my grin on him. Hasn't worked yet, but I don't have anything else in my arsenal.

"Doesn't work that way." He spits the words like each one is a monumental effort.

"I'll be done after two more sets." I lie back on the bench. "Then it's all yours."

A muscle in his jaw ticks. "I need the space."

I look around. The eight hundred square feet, at least, can accommodate a dozen people, maybe two. "There's more than enough room. I promise I won't fart."

"This is my time."

I don't know if it's because I have no place of my own in this mansion or if Sven is pissing me off, but I'm not leaving. "I won't be in your way."

"Not a negotiation." He spreads his legs and glares. I glare back. "Come back after six fifteen. We don't leave until seven thirty."

My fingers grip the side of the bench. "El's calling at 6:30." The hard line of Sven's mouth softens like butter left in the sun. I take the opening. "It's the only time we can talk. Can I stay? I promise to remain six feet away at all times."

Sven grunts.

Was that a yes?

He walks past me to the stretching machine. "Remind her she has my number."

"So we're good?" I wipe the sweat pouring off my forehead.

"No talking." He glances at the weights on my bar and one corner of his mouth goes up.

If he thinks that's the most I can lift, I'm going to show him this was just a warm-up. I remove the lighter plates off the bar and add the weight I pressed last spring before moving here.

The first five are . . . not exactly easy, but I manage. I press six, and my arms shake on the seventh. I should probably stop. I find Sven's gaze on me. This is not the time to be a wimp. I go for the eighth lift and my chest muscles disagree with my decision. I'm pushing up but the bar is only getting closer to my neck.

"Stupid." Sven's fingers curl around the bar in the middle just as it touches my Adam's apple. "El would kill me if you hurt yourself."

My heart is in my ears. I rest my fingers on my neck and make sure I can still swallow.

"Who trained you?" The bar clanks as Sven returns it to its rightful place. "You never, ever do critical weights without someone standing by."

"I know." My voice sounds normal. I think I'll live.

"Knowing and doing are not the same." He lifts the bar and hands it to me. "Six reps this time. Got it?"

"Okay." I restart the set. Sven remains above my head. He's not moving back to the stretching station. On my sixth rep, he takes the bar and places it on the stands. "If we're spotting each other we start at four fifty."

"Okay." Does this mean I'm invited back?

He stares down at me. "Don't mention this to anyone."

"I can keep a secret." I vacate the bench and move to where he stood, ready to spot him.

Sven grunts as he loads more plates. "No secrets." He glares at me and whatever invisible ground I might have won slips away. "Just don't brag."

I point at my chest and feign being offended. "Me? Brag?"

Sven shakes his head as he prepares for his lifts.

By six fifteen, you could mop the floor with my T-shirt. Unlike the material straining to cover Sven's chest, which has but a hint of sweat stains. My first proof he is not a superhuman.

"Tomorrow's leg day." Sven holds open the door. "Be at the garage at seven thirty. We'll take the Rolls."

The sky outside is now streaked with pink clouds. "We?"

Sven wipes his brow with a towel as we start on the path to the main house. "Where you go, I go."

"I don't think so." I shake my head. "Who do you think you are? My bodyguard?"

A hint of a smile pulls at the corner of his mouth, and I know I'm not going to like what he says. "Actually yes. You didn't want a driver, so I got upgraded to your bodyguard."

"No bloody way." The cold sweat on my back heats again. "I don't need a babysitter. And I'm not El. No one knows who I am. I'm safe."

"For now." His arms are crossed again, and the camaraderie from inside the gym evaporates. Sven the man is gone. Sven the bodyguard is on.

"What if I want to go somewhere I don't want you to know about." Not that I have anywhere but school and my new job at Rocker Inc. I cancelled my new Year's gig in Bremen and even bailed on the New Year's party Mateo invited me to, not interested if El can't be with me.

"You won't."

"I get no privacy?"

"Correct."

I swear there's a hint of delight in Sven's cold blue stare before he turns and walks away.

"I didn't sign up for that."

He raises his hand in the air. "Talk to your father."

"He's not . . ." He is my father in name only. Not even in name.

Marta insists I have a slice of the brioche she just took out of the oven as I cut through the kitchen. No sign of Rocker,

Sylvia, or the baby. Pickle must not be awake yet. Bloody hell, I'm calling him Pickle now too. How hard is it to come up with a name for a baby? Even though they ended up putting William on his birth certificate as they originally planned, I guess with three Williams in the house, things might get confusing. But the kid needs a real name at some point.

I beeline for my temporary room. When Rocker dropped my bag in here, I had to hide my grin and pretend I hadn't seen this place or slept in that massive bed the night El asked me to stay over after the incident with the paparazzi. Move over Asher Menken, there's a new Oscar-worthy actor living in the neighborhood.

El's ringtone, her singing Queen's *Somebody to Love*, chimes as I close the door. Her face fills the screen of the new phone Rocker insisted he buy for me and my heart leaps.

I don't fight the smile. "Hi."

Her eyes light up. "There you are." The lips I have not had enough chances to kiss grin back at me. She is so beautiful. A crinkle forms between her brows. "Are you wet?"

I look down at my damp shirt. "Worked out with Sven. He says hi, by the way."

Her eyelashes flutter with a few rapid blinks. "Tell him I miss him."

"What about me?" The words are out before I can stop them.

Her mouth hitches to the side. "I miss you the most."

The compliment shouldn't make me feel better, but it does. Talking over video the last two weeks has been odd, like there is a chasm between us. Part of me wants to steal Rocker's jet and fly to Atlanta just to hold her in my arms, reassure myself she is real and the month we had in Germany wasn't a dream.

"How's it going with Rocker?"

The mention of her stepfather acts like a bucket of cold water on my heated thoughts. "Apparently I need a bodyguard now."

The bubble of laughter that bursts out of her should not make me so happy.

"It's not funny."

She's clutching her middle, and I push my lips together to maintain my grumpy expression.

"Right." Her hand covers her mouth. "Not funny at all."

"Can we not talk about it?" Her red hair stands out against the soft gray walls of the room she's in. "Tell me about yesterday." I was still in class when she passed out after rehearsals. I hate being three hours behind her. At least when she's on tour in a few days we'll be in the same time zone. "How did the rehearsal go?"

The giggles stop, and I immediately want them back. My chest aches at the doubt in her eyes. "I did okay. Most of the songs are classic Blatantly Subtle. There are only two off the new album in the first set so not much to memorize."

"That's good." I wish I had better words of encouragement, a way to support her. My empty hand itches to hold hers. I should've found a way to stay in Atlanta, stay with her for at least for the rehearsals.

"I'm getting the harmonies, but it's hard not to sing lead." I hate that she's not the star. I know this is her choice and how she wants to prove herself, but she deserves more. "Carlee is amazing, but I like how we altered the bridge on *Pages of You*. The key change—" She sings our version of the bridge as she folds her hand over her heart. I nod in agreement. El made a great song amazing with her arrangement. "I have to stop myself from singing that version in rehearsals."

She rolls her lips inward and puffs out air. "And apparently I have two left feet."

I scoot to the edge of my seat. "What?"

"Annalyn is like a professional dancer and picked up the choreography on the spot. I stepped on Yoli's foot and she had to sit out the last run-through."

"Hey, now you know why I learned guitar. Hard to dance holding one." That wins me a small chuckle and the noose around my heart loosens.

"Beau said something similar." I ignore the stitch in my chest at the mention of the lead guitarist. "I think you'd like him. You have a lot in common." I bite the inside of my cheek to avoid insisting I'm nothing like the musician with a reputation of sleeping with a different girl every night of the week. She wrinkles her nose. "He writes a lot of the lyrics."

"Good for him." I don't want to talk about Beau. She's spending too much time with him. I scratch my stubble, searching for a better topic. "How's your roommate, Yoli?"

"Argh." El's exasperation rolls off the screen. "She snuck out last night and went to a club. Came home completely drunk and tried to crawl into bed with me. I miss having a room to myself."

My eyebrows rise. "Can you switch roommates?"

"Don't think Annalyn likes me much either." She looks away, and the chill in her voice makes my stomach contract. Something's bothering her, and I'm about to ask what when her phone alarm beeps.

Twelve

THERE'S NEVER ENOUGH TIME with Wil.

"I have to go," I say. "Same time tomorrow?"

Wil's smile makes my heart accelerate and my fingertips prickle, wishing they could brush the rogue jet-black hair out of his eyes. I miss the silky strands I got to play with for our short time in Germany, the luxury of his hugs, the sweetness of his kisses.

"You can count on it."

I want to say something else, express how much he means to me, how much I'd rather be there with him, but the words get stuck in my throat and a weak "bye" is all that comes out. The screen goes blank and part of me shuts down to keep Wil tucked into a secret corner.

Zoe: Have you seen Daniel Davison's last article?

A screenshot of *Hollywood Happening* comes up, titled "First Picture of Rocker's Son."

My finger shakes as I scroll to a grainy photo of Rocker and Sylvia's backs with the baby's car seat between them.

I text her as I walk down the hall.

Me: You scared me. I thought this was about Wil.

Zoe: Daniel hasn't caught on to that one yet. How's Wil adjusting to LA life?

Me: He only sees school and Dad's office. He needs to get out. Can you reach out, maybe take him to the movies?

Zoe: Movies? He's dating you, not me.

Me: Just take him somewhere.

Zoe: You do know I'm swamped preparing for my show.

Me: Maybe he can help. He's not just a DJ, he's a sound engineer. He can do the music.

Zoe: Only for you.

A too-familiar voice in the kitchen halts my progress.

". . . Melodie Rockerby is making waves again." Daniel Davison's snide tone steals the glee of my chat with Zoe. His constant water references feel like his own personal vendetta against me. Despite his numerous attempts to get me to talk about Papa's boating accident, I refuse.

I peek around the corner and am confronted with the gossip-monger's giant head on the big-screen TV in the living room. The reflection in the glass reveals Annalyn and Yoli sitting side by side at the breakfast counter watching the YouTube livestream. "But now she's dragged Blatantly Subtle into the depths of her latest hobby of being a singer. That's right, she has convinced the glam-rock band to add her to the roster on their upcoming West Coast tour. Or was it her famous father who did the convincing?"

"Told you so," Annalyn snickers.

"But daddy dearest might not have the pull he used to, because the little nepo baby is not opening for the band, she's stuck in the back, singing harmonies with"—Daniel mocks a gasp and covers his mouth—"the regular singers. Could it be Melodie didn't inherit any of her parents' musical talents? If you have tickets to one of Blatantly Subtle's shows, send me your videos or pics of the concert. I'll feature the best on Sunday's *Hollywood Happenings* Wrap Up here on YouTube. This week I'll be sitting down with—"

Yoli snatches the remote and pauses the video. "He didn't mention us? Weren't we in the press release?"

"We were." Annalyn taps on her phone and flashes her screen at Yoli. "Should've known we don't stand a chance with El or Melodie or whatever she calls herself around. She's totally gonna steal the spotlight. She's not even that good."

"I don't know." Yoli refills her and Annalyn's glasses with orange juice. "I liked that video with the kissing scene at the end, at the Griffith Observatory."

Warmth spreads across my cheeks at what Nick, Sarah, and Wil did for me to create the *Don't Give Me Comfort* video.

"Sure, whoever shot it made her look good." Annalyn's voice is quiet. "However, we both have more experience, more fans, and tons of videos."

"I loved the one of you leading the crowd in a sing-along at the pub."

"That's my parents' place. I've worked there after school and weekends since I was fourteen." Annalyn croons a few bars of an Ed Sheeran song I recognize. Yoli joins in at the chorus, harmonizing with Annalyn's lead vocals. I'm tempted to step into the light, join them with the countermelody, but I stay hidden.

"That's the fifth song of mine to go viral. El just has the one. El Vella has barely any social-media presence. Same with Melodie Rockerby. Just some staged shots in outfits that cost more than my parents make in a year." Annalyn says my name like she's drinking vinegar, not orange juice.

I rest my head against the wall, the smooth surface cool against my hot temple. Of course, they'd checked my social media. As Melodie Rockerby, I avoided anything online except for my private accounts. Maybe Zoe can help me create a public account on more platforms, and I'll start using those instead of my private one.

"Did you see how she stumbled through the lyrics?" A hole burns in my stomach at Annalyn's words.

After the fittings yesterday morning and the chorography lessons after lunch, my body ached, and my brain was fried by the time we got to working on one of the new songs. The unfamiliar lyrics jumped across the page and I missed my cue. If only I'd had a few quiet minutes to concentrate on the words, I could've memorized them. This is one of the reasons why going to a brick-and-mortar school like my cousins was never an option for me. My private tutors gave me the time and tools I needed to make the letters stay in place.

"They weren't that hard," Yoli chimes in.

The pale reflection of Annalyn in the glass flips its hair over its shoulder. "If Carlee expects us to carry her through the performances, she has another thing coming."

Various versions of Mom's warning echo in my mind. Music is a hard, fickle business. I don't have what it takes to withstand the pressures put on a performer. I can't handle the rigors of a life on the road. My feet itch to turn and run, hide in my bedroom.

Instead, I pull back my shoulders. Carlee chose me for a reason, and it has nothing to do with Rocker. I've come too far to give up. This is my chance, and I'll find a way to make it work. I'll download the songs to my tablet and stay up tonight listening to the lyrics, then reformat the pages and memorize them like my reading tutor showed me. I'll prove myself, climb the ladder, and pay my dues. I'll show the girls, Mom, and anyone who doubts me that I'm not here to play make-believe. I'm the real deal.

I step into the light and clear my throat. "Hey girls." Two heads whip in my direction and fake smiles plaster their faces.

"Oh hey, El." Yoli's leg jitters like Wil's does when he's nervous.

Annalyn leans back on her palms, a cat stretching in the sun. "There's yogurt in the fridge."

"Let's take a break." Beau lifts the strap of his guitar over his head. "I need five." He places his instrument in the holder by the piano Carlee's been sitting at most of the afternoon. "Need anything?"

She pulls the clip out of her hair and the pink stripe frames her face. "I'm good."

"I'll get you some tea, just in case. Kamo?"

The drummer sets down her sticks and pops up. "I'll come."

Yoli's gaze trails Beau across the rehearsal space in Carlee's basement. "Hot and thoughtful. How do I get me one of those?"

"Wipe the drool off your face." Josie reaches for her water bottle. "Don't you have a boyfriend?"

"We agreed the long-distance thing is too hard. So it's not cheating if I sample some goods while on tour."

"You're such a flirt." Annalyn elbows Yoli.

Yoli turns to me. "Who's the guy you talk to morning and night?"

I want to tell them Wil is my boyfriend, but Carlee's words ring in my ears. I don't know if I can trust these girls. Someday soon the world will find out Wil is Dad's son, and I don't want to give either of them a story to sell. I can see the headline on Daniel Davison's blog now: "Bandmate Overhears Lovers Conversation—Stepsibling Sideshow." "He's a friend," I say. It's not a lie. Wil is my best friend, right in line with Zoe.

"Oooh." Yoli smirks. "I have lots of friends with benefits. In fact, I'm meeting one again tonight."

Annalyn slaps her arm. "You can't keep sneaking around. You'll get kicked out."

I step away from the gossiping girls, not wanting to talk about boys. It hurts too much.

Carlee catches my eye and I approach the side of the room where she's sitting. She pats the spot on the piano bench next to her and I perch on the edge.

"I listened to your track again." Carlee scrolls through her phone. "The chorus you sent me, I think I know what the issue is."

"What?" Curiosity wins out over my anxiety.

"Clarity. Specificity." Her thumb taps on the words on her screen. "These lyrics are too vague. Anyone could be singing it."

My heart pounds in a feverish tune. "You said it yourself. Love is a universal theme."

"It is, but the interesting part is to see how *you* see it." She tilts her head. "What's the thing that distinguishes this love song from other love songs?"

I draw my eyebrows together, failing to decode her meaning. Carlee nudges my elbow. "You."

"Me?" I twist my hair.

"I need to hear the song and know your perspective. Know what you stand for. What your worldview is." Carlee's hand trembles and she puts down her phone. "Tell me, who are you, El?" Carlee's intense gaze makes me want to move back, but I hold my ground. "I know what your dad's publicist put out there: the perfectly styled image. I see how you're portrayed in the media."

"I—"

She holds up a hand. "I know firsthand how the media contorts something innocent to turn our lives into clickbait. It's part of the business. Something to get used to." Carlee loops her arm though my elbow and whispers, "I want to know the real you. Who is El Vella? Or Melodie Rockerby?"

"El." The word spills from me. "Nothing against my dad. He's great. But I'm more than Bill Rockerby's stepdaughter." My voice is taut and tense. I stand taller.

Carlee pats my hand. "Okay. I get that. Beau's done everything possible to step out from his mother's country star fame. Down to not using her name either." Tanya Martel was huge in the 90's and everyone was surprised when Beau abandoned his Tennessee roots for LA glamour. "But it's more than a name. What do you want?"

This time the lump in my throat is hard to talk around. "To sing?" Why does it come out like a question? I cough and try again. "I'm a singer."

"But what makes you, you?" Across the room Yoli cackles at something and Carlee's eyes drift to the trio of women. "What makes you different from them?"

Just like with the lyrics I studied last night, my thoughts tangle and knot in my mind. The pit in my stomach opens and threatens to swallow me whole. I don't have an answer for Carlee.

Thirteen

Wil

THE FIRST TIME I slept in this room I told El I wanted to marry the bed. After two weeks of a full load of classes at UCLA and interning for Rocker, I'd sleep on the floor in a hallway if it got me some shut-eye. I crashed so hard last night I didn't work on the lyrics for our song, even though El sent me her last changes of the chorus melody. I stare at my beat-up guitar case beside the desk. Rocker insisted I could use any of his at the house or at Rocker Inc. but he might have as well asked me to chop my hand off and leave it at home. Wherever I go, my guitar comes with me.

I pick up my phone. Crap. 9:25 a.m. So much for my workout with Sven and my first class. I scroll through the collection of unread texts as I wipe the sleep out of my eyes. El's message takes priority. Her smiling face pops onto my screen, her signature cup of coffee in hand as she poses in a lounge with airplanes outside the window behind her.

El: On my way to Vegas.

My whole body comes alive. I want to reach out and touch her but it's only a photo. One more week till I visit her in Vegas. I slam my head on the pillow and add the picture to the folder with my photos of her. I scroll through the images. There aren't enough of them. I open Sven's texts.

Superman: Giving up on the gym already? Back at two. Stay put.

Great. I've missed leg day. At least Sven taking Rocker, Sylvia, and Pickle to the pediatrician means I don't have to suffer his indignation in person. I scroll to the next one.

Mateo: Still good for lunch?

Me: Yeah, but I'm not going to make it to class today. Can you come pick me up?

Mateo: Sure.

Me: Don't forget the screen-printing press.

Mateo: Already in the trunk.

El's idea that I help Zoe turned into a phone call where her cousin ranted about her screen-printing press breaking while she needed to create custom designs on three dozen T-shirts. Mateo came through as usual with the agility of a magician pulling a rabbit out of a hat and promised to deliver one. I check Zoe's message.

Zoe: Where is the screen-printing equipment you promised me? I need it now. I'm delivering the shirts this afternoon.

My finger taps on the text from Mateo.

Me: Actually, can you meet me earlier and drive me to Calabasas to drop off the machine?

Seems everyone is glued to their phones. Mateo texts right back.

Mateo: Still no car?

Me: Rub it in, why don't you.

Mateo: Where u at?

My shoulders tense. There's no avoiding this.

Me: Malibu.

Mateo: Pick you up in 30. Drop a pin.

I give him the mansion's address and text Zoe that I'm on my way.

Half an hour later I buzz Mateo through the gates and stand in the driveway as he pulls up in his souped-up Corvette.

"You sly dog." Mateo gives me a slap on the back. "I thought El was the one with the secrets." He surveys the front of Rocker's Malibu home. "This beats the frat house any day."

"I'd rather be living there."

He lowers his Ray Bans and stares at me. "Right. Cause sharing a bathroom with five hungover guys on a Sunday morning is the life."

"I guess." I scratch my forearm. "Anyhow, thanks for offering me a lift."

"I love to drive out here. Lets my girl have a run." He peers up at the second floor, the corner that's El's room. "Are you housesitting?"

"Yeah, about that. I sorta live here now."

"Sorta? This is El's Dad's house, right? You're working for him, right?"

"Sorta."

"Stop with the sortas and tell me what the hell is going on. I don't want to be arrested for trespassing at a celebrity's property."

"You're safe. I'm here legally."

"Spit it out."

"I'm Rocker's son."

"Whaa—"

"No one really knows, so let's keep that on the downlow."

Mateo slaps both hands on his face and rubs it as if it's numb. "Is this a prank show?" He swivels his head. "Where are the cameras?"

"Let's go. We don't have much time. I'll tell you details on the drive." I plug Zoe's address into his GPS. "The sooner we get there, the sooner we can get to lunch." The slice of salmon and broccoli quiche I found in the fridge was enough to tide me over but not enough to make my stomach happy. Apparently Marta goes shopping on Friday mornings.

Mateo revs the engine. "Man, the press will have a field day when they find out about you."

"That's what everyone keeps saying." I don't get it. Maybe that gossip guy will try to spin it for a while but once a high-profile celebrity like Felicity Thomas goes skydiving or whatever, I'll be out of the spotlight.

The drive to Zoe's is fifteen minutes of me filling Mateo in on the deal with Rocker to get the money for Mum and Mateo regaling me with stories of the home cooking he inhaled while at his parent's place for Christmas. I check my phone for messages from El.

El: Did you check the changes to the chorus lyrics?

Our latest song is half-done and getting it perfect might take several more back-and-forths. Our ability to write songs even when we are apart makes me certain El and I are supposed to do this. Together. I need to hold up my end of the bargain and work on the chorus.

El: No rush. My head might not retain any more words at the moment. I just memorized the new order of the songs for the show because they're changing the set again. Removing a heavy-on-choreo song from the latest album and adding a mellow oldie Carlee wrote when Beau and her first started as a duo. I'm grateful for less dancing, and more harmonies, but I've never covered that one. Carlee told me to sit the song out if I can't get the words right.

Bloody hell. Is El in trouble? Can they fire her? I hate the happy buzz in my chest at the prospect of her coming back to me.

Me: Want to hop on a call and run the lines?

El: I'm good. Josie's going to do it on the plane to Vegas with me.

Me: You sure?

El: I promise to call you if I am still struggling.

Me: Call me even if you don't need to run lines.

No response from El.

"Your destination is on the left," the GPS of Mateo's car purrs as we near the entrance to the front of Zoe's parents' place. Last time I went through the back gate as party staff.

Mateo lets out a low whistle as we stop in the middle of the half-circle driveway. "Think I might like this new life of yours."

"You can have it." I climb out of the seat that somehow is molded to my body. Mateo's car is as modified on the inside as it is on the outside. "Where'd you find the money to pay for these things?" is on the tip of my tongue. Do I want to know what goes on in the shady corners of Mateo's life? With my current situation and the potential implications if (when?) it comes to light, no. I do not want to know about Mateo's get-rich-quick schemes.

A man in black slacks and a white short-sleeve shirt opens the door. "Ms. Yilmaz is waiting for you in the music room." He stands to the side as we enter then leads us down the hallway.

I don't think I'll ever forget the music room. The room where El told me the truth about how her papa died. Sitting under the piano, her wet shivering body in my arms as I tried to comfort her after she almost drowned. The realization that there was no way I'd use her to get to Rocker. I couldn't hurt her.

We enter the space dominated by a white grand piano. Soft afternoon light gleams off the hardwood floors like it did that day. I dip my head to see if El is sitting under the piano. Nope. She's not there.

"Finally, you're here." Zoe's voice leads me to an alcove I didn't notice before. It has racks on rollers with clothes in various states of completion hanging off them. A large table is set up in front of another set of windows, with a separate one that houses two different sewing machines and an ironing board next to it.

"Set the press over here," she commands Mateo, who complies too easily. "I promised a dozen T-shirts by 5 p.m. tonight. This model looks different from the one I broke. Show me how to use it."

"Sure, it's fifty dollars an hour. I'll show you anything you want." Mateo runs his thumb over his lip.

"Go on then." Zoe ushers him to continue the setup and turns to me. "What do you think of my design studio?"

"It's different."

"Since my brother moved out, no one plays the piano." Zoe runs a nail along the lid. I had no idea she even had a brother. Zoe narrows her eyes at me. "Unless El's here. And since you stole her away, it wasn't being used." I shove my hands in my pockets, ignoring the dig. "I still keep a lot of my finished pieces in my bedroom, but I ran out of space. The light in here is spectacular." As if to prove the point, Zoe stands and twirls, letting the sun hit the silvery strands in the hem of her dress.

El and Zoe are cousins on their mother's side, but they have very little in common. Zoe's tall, thin, with olive skin, straight brown hair, and hazel eyes. Nothing reminds me of El until she smiles. Although El's smiles are rare and Zoe's are as frequent as the breaths she takes, Zoe draws her lips wide and, just like El, beams with so much sincerity, it's impossible not to feel welcome.

"I like it," Mateo says from behind me and Zoe loses her smile.

"I'm not paying you for chitchat." She indicates the partially constructed press.

"Zoe, this is Mateo. My old roommate."

"I'm this newly minted celebrity kid's best friend." Mateo slicks the sides of his hair.

Zoe's glance bounces between us.

"Don't worry, he knows about Rocker."

"I thought the idea was to keep your new social status quiet," Zoe says.

Mateo steps in front of me and kisses Zoe's hand like he's in one of those black-and-white movies Mum likes to watch. "I'm very trustworthy and good with secrets. I helped Wil and El skip the country last month."

"Mateo is a vault."

Apparently satisfied by our answers, Zoe sizes me up and taps her chin. "You're quite tall." The glint in her eye worries me. She steps back and runs her hand over the outfits hanging behind her. Men's suits and shirts and pants. Alarm rings in my gut. Zoe looks me up and down. "Have you ever considered modeling?"

"No way." I stare at the rack of clothes behind her. El's cousin is out of her bloody mind.

"Why not?" Zoe crosses her arms.

I match her stance while Mateo paws through the collection of hats sitting on the grand piano. "I promised to get you a screen press, run the merch booth, and consult on the music, not be in your show." My attempt to alleviate El's guilt at not being able help Zoe is now backfiring.

"Mateo can run the merch booth, can't he?" She eyes Mateo and winks at him.

"You bet I can." He grins at her. Traitor.

"But I'm not talking about you working my show. I'll hire models for that." She slides her thumb over the screen of her phone that always seems to be in her hand. Her gaze runs up and down my outfit like a doctor analyzing a patient. "You're due for an upgrade."

I glare at Mateo, who's stifling a laugh. No sympathy there. "My clothes are fine."

"Well." Mateo runs his fingers along the brim of an electric-blue Panama hat. "You do dress like a college dropout."

I shoot daggers at him.

"See?" Zoe skips over to Mateo's side and loops her arm with his. "Even your best friend is ashamed to be seen with you."

"I wouldn't go that far." He removes the hat. "But you could step up your game."

Zoe points at my shoes, jeans, and T-shirt. "Look at you. El can't be seen with you like this." She scoffs. "The point is when my cousin quits pretending being a backup singer is good enough for her—"

"Stop." This is El's dream and I have complete confidence in her abilities to know what's best. Blatantly Subtle is just the first step in her career.

"Right." She elongates the word like she's pacifying a two-year-old. "When she's on tour with them there'll be lots of eyes on her. There'll be interviews, club openings, red-carpet events. Being part of Blatantly Subtle even as backup means she'll have an image to maintain. A brand to protect. You need to fit into that. Right now, you do . . . not."

I consider her words, think about my texts with El. She has to fit in, so I guess I must fit into her world.

A devilish smile spreads across Zoe's face like she knows she's won. "Luckily I'm here to help."

"Lucky me."

"So you'll do it?" The smile fades, and her face softens into an expression somewhere between serious and considerate. "For El?"

I crumble. "For El."

Zoe attacks me, wrapping her arms around me and jumping up and down. I stiffen but she doesn't let go. I'm not used to this. It took months to be able to hold El, and it feels wrong to be hugged by her cousin. But Zoe ignores my attempts to untangle myself from her. "Thank you, thank you, thank you. You won't regret it."

"I better not."

"I promise, this'll be good." She finally lets go of me and starts pacing the room. "Remember to quote me when the reporters ask who you're wearing. We should take some photos too, for my lookbook and Insta. How do you feel about a haircut?"

"No." The memory of El running her hands through my hair on the couch in Bremen causes my heart rate to accelerate. "I'll wear your clothes, but you don't mess with the 'do."

One side of Zoe's lips curls up. "I guess the tousled look is in these days. I can make it work." She rifles through the hangers and pulls out a brown shirt with off-centered buttons. "Try this on to start."

"Don't you have something a little more . . . normal?"

She holds the shirt against my chest. "No sense of adventure. I honestly don't know what El sees in you."

FOURTEEN

SVEN EMERGES OUT OF the afternoon sun with an outstretched hand. "Your bag." He says his first words of the day after he spent our workout and the ride to class this morning giving me the silent treatment.

I look around campus, as if I don't know what he means. "Is there a first grader here somewhere? Cause I can carry my backpack to the office just as well as you can."

I face Mateo. "Are we still good for the dry run at Zoe's this weekend?"

"I have the equipment lined up." Mateo winks. "I'll pick you up?"

"No." Sven lays his hand on top of my backpack and takes the handle. "I drive." He moves me forward against my will. "Move it. You can't be late for work."

Mateo looks down unsuccessfully hiding his grin. "See you at Zoe's."

My huff is supposed to show I don't like Sven manhandling me. He doesn't get the message. "Let go of me already."

"Keep up." Sven returns his arms to his sides. Even without dragging me behind him, it's hard to mistake him for a friend. Instead of his usual blue, gray, or black suit, he's wearing jeans and a polo shirt. He looks like a preppy bodybuilder. Not a good combination, nor a good disguise.

"Did they place the order already or do you know what every-one wants?" I stash my water bottle in my backpack and turn in the direction of Blend for our standard coffee pickup for Rocker and whoever is in the studio.

"Not today." Sven does his best impersonation of an air-traf-fic controller to turn me around. "Let's cut through the mar-ket."

No coffee then. I put both arms through my backpack and stifle the nostalgia the stalls of the Farmers' Market bring with every step. The busker playing a saxophone in the spot El and I last played has no audience. I fish out my wallet and drop a twenty. I hope he'll be as excited as El and I would've been. I snap a photo and text it to El.

Me: Recognize the place?

Sven takes my elbow. "This is not a leisure stroll. We're late."

The rest of the walk to the office qualifies as cardio. I'm sweating when Sven lets go of me once we make it through security. I pass by the open breakroom and give my best I'm-your-friend-and-I'm-harmless smile to employees who haven't succumbed to my charms and still give me quizzical looks. At least it isn't because someone recognized me for pretending to deliver coffee from Blend the first time I set foot in this place. Although Rocker introducing me as his intern wasn't supposed to be a big deal, I was the coffee machine gossip for the first week because he's never had anyone shadow him before.

"Good job cataloging the latest batch of demos." Mandy, Rocker's assistant, catches up to my long strides. "Can you send me the notes you took from Monday's A&R meeting? Thanks for covering for me. I drop my kid off late on Monday and never make those on time."

"I'd love to do them every Monday. I learned a lot."

"My savior. I owe you one." She opens the door to Rocker's office and ushers me in.

My palms sweat and I clear my throat to draw his attention. Part corporate with black leather couches and a massive desk, part rock-n-roll with platinum records in a glass case hung over a bar in the corner, Rocker's rockstar-turned-producer office still sets my heart on presto. He's on the phone but signals I should sit on one of the couches.

"Is this what you are wearing?" Rocker asks once he hangs up.

My blue helix T-shirt is in decent shape, barely a year old. Mum gave it to me last Christmas, and although I lost weight last year, with the way Sven and I have been training, I'll fill back out in a couple of months. "Ashamed to be seen with me?"

"Making an impression is part of the job." Rocker closes his laptop. "You're meeting groups you want to potentially sign. If you look like you are less successful than them, they'll look at other offers."

I unclench my teeth. "Not everyone is as shallow as you are. Even in LA people want to make music first and make money second. I know music. My skills don't lie in the clothing department, but I can make them feel like Rocker Inc. is the right place for them. They won't care about the label on my pants."

"The arrogance of youth. I'd love to see how that plays out." A knock on the door interrupts what was sure to be another spiel I don't want to hear. "Come in."

Harper's head with black spiky hair pokes through. "You ready?"

"We have a half hour before we head out," he tells his publicist.

"Plenty of time." She sets her laptop on the cabinet under a large flatscreen and with practiced movements connects the two. "The team and I brainstormed some options on how to break the news of Wil's arrival." Her gaze flashes to me before turning to the slides on the TV littered with headshots, arrows, and the names of a few websites I've searched with El for mentions of her. "We have a *Rolling Stone* article, the safest.

They owe me one and we control the narrative. We get to edit out anything we don't like, but it'll take a few months to get into their editorial lineup. I don't suggest we wait that long. It's too"—her gaze finds me again—"risky."

"Is that aimed at me?" I bristle at her tone.

Harper shifts on her feet. "Of course not. It's just with the new baby and rumors of a feud between him and his stepdaughter, there's more eyes on Mr. Rockerby than usual. That means more cameras and more opportunities for this to get out. We don't want someone like Daniel Davison to break the story."

"You mentioned other options?" Rocker leans forward in his chair.

"Right. Option two is a press conference, invite the usual favorable crowd, let them take photos of the two of you, ask a few questions. Not as glossy as a one-on-one interview and no matter how much we vet the questions, there's always a chance someone will go rogue and ask things we are not ready for or interested in answering." She flips to the last slide. "And the edgiest one is to book a late-night TV appearance. We have friendly territory, vetted questions, but even in a pre-recorded studio interview there are always unknowns. Things may go sideways, especially with live audiences."

Harper taps her laptop and the screen goes blank. "Thoughts?"

Why do we even need this? They are blowing this thing out of proportion. "Can't we just do nothing?"

"No." Rocker rises from his desk chair. "Arrange the *Rolling Stone* interview. Invite the reporter to our place in Malibu. Have Sylvia and Pickle there too. Give them a little tour of the nursery. Sweeten the deal and pull the attention to the happy family side of the announcement and not the—" Rocker stops before he finishes the sentence.

"Got it." Harper gives Rocker a placating smile. "Still not involving El?"

"Keep her as far away from this as possible, like we discussed."

"Okay." She shuts the lid of her laptop. "I'll set it up and get you some dates."

My fate as part of the official Rocker's family has been sealed. I'll be a Rockerby, if not in name then in people's minds. I don't know if the gnawing bitterness in my stomach is the result of the approaching announcement or of the fact that once it's out, the label of Rocker's son will be impossible to shake. I'm not worried about trending for a week or two. When the secret's finally out, El won't have an excuse to keep me out of the spotlight and we can finally be together in public.

Rocker puts on a leather jacket I've never seen him wear at the office. He takes a pair of oversized sunglasses out of a cabinet in the corner, even though it's getting dark outside, and changes from loafers into Doc Martens. "Let's see what we have in store today."

Sven drives us across the city, and we pass a line of people snaking down the sidewalk and around the corner. We get out in a back alley that smells like piss, but once we're through the back door we're in a high-end club I haven't had the chance or money to visit.

If The Devil's Martini is the Burger King of bars, Ultra Green is a Michelin-star restaurant. The roped-off area we are seated in is close enough to the stage, but away from the main floor of posh clubbers, some dressed in less clothes than I've seen people wear on the beach, yet probably cost more than a plane ticket from Bremen to LA.

"Your usual?" The server bends and aims a relaxed smile at Rocker.

"You know it."

"And for you?" She turns my way.

Beer would be nice, but this is work. I've no idea what Rocker's usual is. At the mansion, he has a collection of beer he doesn't shy away from. "Water. No ice."

The server ignores Sven and heads for the bar.

"The second and fourth groups are the ones I've been eyeing," Rocker says. "They've been growing their social-media followings steadily and each had one of their singles go viral."

"Are they the only ones we are here for?"

"This industry has some rules, and we are rarely in a position where we can go for an already signed talent. Other than that, you hear something you like, find out what you can. Check their numbers. Bring the information to me, and we can talk. I'm looking to add a band to our roster."

A host announces the first performer, and a tiny girl with flyaway curls dances onto the stage. Within three bars, the club is hopping to a tune so upbeat my left leg shakes of its own accord. "She's not on your list?"

"She's signed. And we're looking for a band, not a solo gig." Rocker throws an elbow over the back of his chair. "I'll send you a list of the acts next time we're out on a hunt."

Next time? Is he planning to do this a lot with me? And a hunt? Icy spikes jab in my gut. "Is hunting for young girls a regular thing you do to get away from Sylvia?"

"Way to make my business sound gross. First, I never want to get away from Sylvia. Second, this is work." He points to the stage. "Third, pay attention. Death Elbow is up next."

The club bursts in applause when the number is over. Whoever signed her is going to be rich. Per Rocker, most A&R scouts these days ask for a percentage of the future earnings of the performer when they sign contracts. Not that I'll be signing anyone. Rocker will, I'm just along for the ride.

Music that reminds me of rock groups in the eighties fills the space. The electric guitar solo starts off, and when the drums join in, the walls of the club are shaking with squeals.

Rocker shouts into my ear, "Corbin is the lead. Watch him."

I keep my eyes on the stage, where a topless guy in chunky heels kicks his leg up so high, I'm not sure how his pants don't split. The gut-wrenching roar must hurt his throat. Not like I've ever had formal singing lessons, but that type of pressure can't possibly be healthy for the vocal cords. The clubgoers roar back in response. As the mood and lighting shifts, the crowd that during the previous song looked like a swarm of kindergarteners jumping in excitement now appears to be a gang of non-verbal zombies about to tear into each other's throats. The transformation is almost instant. The pulse in the pit of my stomach urges me to join this angry worship.

Rocker's hand lands on my shoulder, and I realize I'm vibrating with the beat. "Powerful, aren't they?" he shouts into my ear again.

Bloody hell. The rush of blood in my chest runs my heart ragged. I'm not even out of my seat, we are not even through half of the song. Bloody hell. "They've got the It factor."

"That they do." Rocker squeezes my arm. "Glad you can feel it too."

Even a dead person could. I can't wait to tell El about this. The rush I felt when El and I were performing, with the audience facing us, singing with us, shouting our names, I'm getting the same swirling in my chest and ache in my heart watching this group give it their all. The energy erupts with the kind of explosive potency that fills arenas. They are destined for much larger stages than this club that is shrinking with every minute of their song.

"You bet," I whisper back to Rocker. The plan forms in my head. I'll look them up online, see what else they've got. When Rocker said "hunt" before, it seemed like an exaggeration of an aging producer. But I get what he means. I've never hunted, but this is so very much like a regatta. The excitement I got from pushing into the final distance as our boat was nose-to-nose with another, as we were not sure who would cross the finish line first. I like that feeling. I grin. This might be the best part of working for Rocker.

I pull my phone out of my pocket and record the remaining part of the song. The live performance is different from a studio recording, but I'm already calculating what we could add. How can we make the backup singer's voice come out more? Maybe we layer some natural noise during the biggest booms to trick the listener into thinking they are in a big space, not just at home or in their car.

Scribbling in the dark in my notebook is a bit harder, but for the first time since recording the song for *Indigo*, ideas of how to produce the song I'm hearing, how to make it better, and what would enhance the sound bombard me.

My brain is on fire. And I love how alive it makes me feel.

FIFTEEN

My hand shakes. I almost scrape mascara across my freshly applied eyeshadow. I've been practicing the smoky eye from the makeup tutorial Zoe sent me and although it's not as good as the perfect model in the video, the results make me look older. More like the rockstar I'm singing backup to.

"Is everyone ready?" Beau pokes his head into the room where Annalyn, Josie, and I are putting on our last touches. "I need you onstage in fifteen."

Josie stands, brushing her tresses over her shoulder. "Yoli isn't here yet."

"Has anyone seen her?" Beau scowls.

"Not since sound check," I say.

"I need to warm up." Annalyn shakes out her hands and heads for the hallway. She claims the acoustics are better in a hallway and she can think there. She launches into the chorus of *Make the Truth Hurt*, the first song in the set. I prefer the bathroom. Sound bouncing off the tiles gives the illusion of extra power in my voice. To each their own.

Beau tilts his head to the door. "Josie, let's talk."

On the table, my phone vibrates. I tap the notification to see texts from Mom. First one is a picture of a younger version of myself smiling. Exactly one year younger, illuminated by the candles of a giant cake, Mom and Dad beaming on either side. The memory from the lavish eighteenth birthday party they threw in Rome last year is bittersweet. I was touring, but it was with Rocker and luxury: fireworks, a private party, and champagne. Happy Birthday and Congrats from every person on the crew. Today none of the people around me have a clue it's my special day, but I like it this way.

Mom: Happy Birthday, baby girl.

Another holiday without Mom. The mascara wand shakes in my hand, and I steady it by placing my elbow on the counter in front of the mirror. My eyes prickle but stay dry. I told myself during Christmas that missing time together was a right of passage on the way to becoming an adult, that I'd get used to it. A month later, my heart still aches every time I think about the fun Mom and I used to have celebrating together. This is my price to pay for chasing my dreams. Cap back on, I give up on the makeup.

Mom: Nineteen. Seems like yesterday you were as tiny as Pickle.

She sends a photo of sleeping Pickle next.

Is that a dig at me not coming to see my baby brother? I had no time. I had to join the rehearsals. Without them I wouldn't have been ready for today. My first performance with Blatantly Subtle, the first of five nights in a row in Vegas. I have dance moves I still can't manage to remember in the right order that haunt me like the Ghost of Christmas Future. Mom and Pickle will have to wait.

Wil's name pops onto the screen. He already called and wished me happy birthday first thing this morning, then twice on the drive to Vegas.

Wil: We made it. In our seats. Top left corner last row.

Me: I'll make sure to look your way.

Not like I'll be able to see him with the bright lights pointed at the stage. I could barely see Carlee at sound check this afternoon.

Wil: Are you really okay with Zoe and Mateo coming as well?

Not like I can tell them to leave now.

Me: Zoe made it clear that even though I'm missing her big party, she is not missing mine.

Wil: She doesn't take no for an answer.

Me: Didn't take you long to figure that out.

Wil: She probably was an emperor in a previous life.

Me: Or a goddess. At least we get our own room.

There have been so many lessons learned on this tour, like earplugs are a necessity when sharing a room with someone because your roommate might snore. Or sleeping with an eye mask while Yoli binges serial killer documentaries.

Wil: It was the flight or the hotel room and I thought you'd enjoy having a room of your own for a night.

Me: I don't mind having a roommate if it's you.

Wil: You sure?

Me: More than sure.

Although he's not asking me directly, I hope he knows I want him to sleep with me tonight. The kind of sleep that includes no rest. No roommates. No Mr. Peters. And no clothes. I've seen Wil's chest without a shirt on and my hands completed a thorough inspection of as many parts of him as I could during our stay in Bremen. Yet those were worse than dangling a delicious butter tart in front of me, allowing me an occasional lick but never a mouthful. I want to see all of Wil.

My cheeks heat at the thought of what I can do with him behind a closed door. I can peel his shirt off and run my hands up his torso. Maybe kiss every inch as I uncover those abs he crushed me against. Or maybe I'll wait until he performs that tug-the-shirt-from-the-back-forward thingy he does that ruffles his hair and makes me want to scream from the tension rising in my core. Or maybe we play strip poker. No. I don't have patience for that.

In my imagination a naked Wil advances, wrapping my legs around his hips, and takes me to a giant bed in a hotel room. The soundtrack in my head matches our ragged breaths and heated kisses, as his lips drag across my collarbone, up my neck, and over my lips that are tired of waiting. Heat spreads from my cheeks down to my chest.

"Is Yoli here yet?" Josie's bellowed question pulls me out of my imaginary embrace.

I smooth my skirt and rearrange myself in my seat to relieve the pressure. "No. It's just me here."

"I can't believe she's pulling this stunt." Josie reapplies her lipstick. "C'mon. We need to get onstage."

"But what about Yoli?"

"El, the show waits for no one. We'll go on without her."

My legs don't want to move. "But we practiced with her."

Josie holds the door open. "We adapt. That's what showbiz is about."

I follow her, my brain frantically working on the puzzle of how to move on the stage without Yoli between Annalyn and me. The dress rehearsal yesterday was brutal. I didn't tell Wil how bad it was because I don't want him to worry. Him being part of the crowd I'll be singing to is not like having him next to me onstage.

Performing. Onstage. Without Wil.

The butterflies in my stomach dodge the stabs of fear. I twist the bracelet Wil gave me to distract myself.

Josie, Annalyn, and I stand behind the stage as the audience screams and whistles, demanding the show to begin. No amount of dress rehearsals prepares me for the nausea in my stomach.

"Here's the plan." Josie puts her hands on my and Annalyn's shoulders. "Remember, enter stage left, wait for the music, and once the performance is over, exit stage left. No rushing." Josie draws a curve on her face. "Smile at the crowd. And have fun."

Fun. That's what this is supposed to be about. Singing with Wil, either at The Devil's Martini or at the Farmers' Market, those experiences were some of the best times of my life. I was riding high. Right now, I feel like I might vomit.

We line up and I take Yoli's spot. Josie's at the front, me last. A deep voice announces, "Las Vegas, give a warm welcome for Blatantly Subtle." The applause deafens me.

I step onto the pitch-black stage and fumble my way into the corner where our microphone stands wait in the darkness. My boot snags on a cord and I bump into Annalyn. She swats me away like I'm a fly threatening to land on her salad.

The pounding back beat of *Making the Truth Hurt* blasts from the speakers twice my size on my left. The sensory overload makes me dizzy. I grit my teeth to stave off the rising bile, then catch Josie staring at me, huge grin, and huge eyes. Right, smile. I'm enjoying myself. Convince the audience this is fun.

Darkness shatters under the blaze of the stage lights. I squint into the glare as if looking at the noon sun. Carlee steps forward, hands on hips, and sings the first line. My throat wants to sing with her, but I clench my teeth and wait. Hand wrapped around the cold microphone, I join Josie and Annalyn, delivering our harmony as we trail Carlee's progress across the stage. Beau joins Carlee, guitar runs battling her voice. She ends the last word on a perfect pitch, spreads her hands wide and claps, inviting the audience to join her. The three of us in the back shout in unison, as practiced, "Are you ready, Vegas?" Josie and Annalyn raise their arms, pumping up and down to encourage the crowd. I remember to join.

The choreography starts. Microphones in hand, we stand behind Carlee and Beau, weaving in and out in our figure eight, hip checking each other, high fiving, and locking arms. What worked well with four of us is a mess with just three, one of us without a partner to play off. The awkward dance disorients me. I can't tell which direction to look and when I finally find the marker, I'm facing the wrong way, my back to the audience.

Instinct must kick in because I'm already singing my line. I remember Dad's words a year ago: "Keep going. That's what the audience needs. A good show." I turn my head only, addressing the audience over my shoulder as I raise the microphone above my head and I belt out the powerful C-note. As I hold the word "go" Carlee revs her vocals and goes even higher. Beau falls on his knees in front of her, his fingers ripping a frenzied squeal from his guitar. The audience goes crazy, clapping and cheering.

I suck in air, attempting to catch my breath, and fully turn to face the fans. I peer up to my left, wishing I could see Wil, but I don't know which of the thousands of shapes I can barely see is him. Carlee roars into *Fire*, the world shrinking to her spotlight, and I'm plunged into darkness. My fingers find Wil's bracelet and worry the rough strips. I can almost hear him whisper in my ear: *You're past that.*

I *am* past that. I sang on stage. I didn't freeze. My debut as backup singer for Blatantly Subtle wasn't a flop. I didn't trip and fall. There won't be headlines blasting my failure online tonight. Daniel Davison will have to pick on someone else.

Kamo's rolling drum launches us into the next song and I raise my head, ready to make this a success.

Sixteen

Zoe spins on the concrete pavement outside the arena and points to my toe. "Stop that tapping."

"Stop your pacing," I snap back.

"Now, now, boys and girls. Let's play nice." Zoe and I both glare at Mateo. He holds up his hands. "She'll be here soon."

Blatantly Subtle put on an entertaining show and watching El on stage was surreal. The images on the giant screens showed what we couldn't see from afar. The fans' screams still ring in my ears. Performing live, the group still sounded like they didn't need an autotune. Even though we cheered, it felt wrong. The harmonies with the backup singers were on point, but El shouldn't have been in the dark for most of the concert. She deserves the spotlight.

Zoe throws her arms in the air. "At last."

I spin in the direction of her gaze, and my heart double-times at the happiness coating El's face as she runs toward us. My legs shake, but my feet are on the move, and we crash into each other, my world whole again. She wraps her arms around my neck. "You made it."

I squeeze her against me and my concerns fly away. I'm lost in her. The sight of her. The scent of her. The feel of her. My fingers slid over the bare skin her dress exposes. She shivers in my arms.

"Okay, you two. Get a room." Zoe's demand pulls us apart and thoughts of the hotel room I checked into earlier cause my body to harden uncomfortably.

"Your makeup was on point and I like this outfit on you." Zoe side-hugs her cousin. "Even if it is basic black. But I thought there were four backup singers? I saw only three."

El clasps her hand over her mouth and shakes her head.

"What?" Zoe pulls her hand away. "Spill."

"The fourth girl, Yoli." Her eyes swivel between Zoe and me. "She missed the first half of the show. She said she was on a hot streak at the blackjack table and couldn't walk away. Beau fired her on the spot."

"No way." Zoe slaps her shoulder.

"Yup."

Zoe pulls out her phone. "I wonder if Daniel Davison knows yet?"

El nestles into me, her pinkie tucking into the beltloop of the pants Zoe insisted I wear tonight. "So, what did you think?" Her smile wobbles and I can't believe she still has doubts. She was amazing.

"Carlee can sing, but I like our version of *Love Is Not a Sin* better." It's Carlee's song but El gives it more heart. "Maybe I'm biased." I swoop El up and spin her. "Who am I kidding, I'm totally biased."

Her body shakes with laughter, the sound music to my ears.

Mateo elbows into the circle and brandishes a plastic card with a red bow in the air. "Your birthday present." He offers it to El like a knight offering a sword. "Specially made."

El's nail traces the thick black letters with her stage name beside the photo of her. She bounces up and down. "A fake ID?"

I kiss her temple. "There's nothing fake about El Vella."

She taps my shoulder. "El Vella isn't twenty-one."

"El Vella can be anything she wants to be." I trace a small circle on her hip.

Mateo offers the second card to Zoe. "Made one for you too."

She snaps it up and inspects the photo. "Not my best pic but it'll do."

"Let's go prove it." Mateo winks at El. "Got us on a VIP list at Rev23."

"What?" Zoe's voice climbs two octaves. "Lassie Poverly was photographed there just last week. It's one of the hottest clubs on the strip."

Mateo checks his watch, light from the streetlamp reflecting on its onyx face. "We gotta go before the shift change."

I open the door to the Corvette and pull up the passenger seat, gesturing for El to get in. "Your chariot awaits." Settled in the backseat, my hand rests on her thigh. It's like I need to touch her to believe she's really here. My phone pings. I read *Melodie Rockerby Stayed Out of the Spotlight in Vegas.*

El glances on my screen. "Daniel Davison doesn't miss a chance to use my name for clickbait."

"I don't actually read his stuff." I swipe the notification away. "Just never deleted the alert I set up for your name."

"I haven't deleted the one for yours either. I just hope mine never gets any results." She looks at the pile of empty chip bags and candy wrappers we demolished on the seven-hour drive here. "Do you have anything to eat?"

"No, but I have some water left." I hand her our dinged water bottle.

El checks our W&E signature on the bottom. "You're still using it?"

"Almost lost it at school a couple of times, but the water always tastes better."

Mateo takes a right and El slides across the leather seat, crashing into me. She doesn't move away, her head resting on my shoulder. Up front, Zoe insists it's her turn to choose the tunes.

"They bickered most of the way from LA," I whisper in El's ear. "Next time I'm flying."

Her hand lands on my chest as she twists in the seat. "Worth it though?"

I pull back to study her face. She can't possibility doubt I wanted to come. But the crease between her eyes, too dark in the backseat of the car to see the vibrant blue I adore, indicates she might. I trace the edge of her jaw. "Every second to be with you."

The lines of her face transform to joy then blur as her lips find mine. Her palm moves north, her cool fingers teasing under the collar of my shirt. Zoe and Mateo fade, and I'm consumed by El, covering her body with mine. Our kiss is slow as we taste each other, trying to make up for weeks of not being able to touch, to kiss.

I could spend the rest of the night in this back seat.

We break apart but my lips can't leave her, peppering kisses on her neck. El nibbles my earlobe. "I missed you."

My turn to shiver, from her teasing caress or her words, I'm not sure. I'm positive it's not from the chill in the air as my body feels like it's on fire. I want to respond, say something, but my throat is clogged. I breathe in El, searching for my bearings. As if she understands, she rests her forehead against mine. "At least we have tonight."

"Think you two can keep your hands off each other long enough to get in the club?" Mateo shouts into the backseat.

I break away from El to discover the car is parked outside a building lit by strobing blue lights, a neon sign flashing the club's name over the glass entrance. The interior lights of the Corvette are on, and Zoe is standing outside the car.

The last thing I want to do is leave our cocoon, but El is already getting out. I slide across the leather and follow, clasping El's hand as soon as I'm able.

Instead of taking us to the entrance, Mateo veers to the left around the side of the building and down an alley. At a gray steel door with a black sign labeled STAFF, he knocks three times. I'm about to ask who he knows when the door swings open and a large man dressed in head-to-toe black embraces Mateo. They speak in Spanish too quickly for me to catch anything, but when Mateo points to me I recognize "amigos."

The guy flashes a mouth full of pearly whites and waves us in. We climb a set of stairs, music pounding against the concrete walls, and I can barely make out El in the darkness.

"Are you sure about this?" Zoe's voice echoes at the top of the stairs.

Mateo turns around and walks backward. "Trust me." He pats his friend on the back. "You'll love this, princess."

I laugh. That's what I used to call El, back when I assumed she had everything.

At the end of a gloomy hall, our guide opens another door and we're ushered into a room with low lighting from the pot lights in the ceiling and three red couches arranged in a circle. Platters of food sit on a table in the middle. One wall is floor-to-ceiling glass and overlooks a massive dance floor full of swaying dancers. On a dais, a DJ is spinning a beat that pulses against the glass, but it is muted here.

Mateo clasps the hand of the guy who let us in, and they bump shoulders. "I owe you one."

"I'll be in LA soon. You can hook me up."

"Deal."

"Mateo and his deals," El whispers in my ear.

Zoe spreads her arms out and twirls. "VIP indeed." She picks up a bottle from an ice bucket between the couches and reads the label. "Champagne anyone?"

El steps away from me to help her cousin pop the cork and every cell in my body screams to follow her, like she's magnetic north. I help the girls fill four glasses with the bubbly liquid and pass one to Mateo.

"Happy Birthday." Zoe raises her glass. "To El and Mateo."

The chilled drink does nothing to quell my thirst. Alcohol is not what I crave.

El plucks a shrimp off a plate. "I was too nervous to eat before." I hand her a napkin and move her closer to the food. Does she look thinner? Is she not eating enough? The 2D version of El I've had to live off is a pale comparison to the in-living-color girl I can now embrace. My fingers play with the ends of El's hair as she munches.

"The knob from the LA Institute of Fashion declined the invite to my show." Zoe shrugs, like this means nothing, but she's been nattering about it for weeks. "His loss. When my show is the talk of the town, he'll suffer major FOMO."

"I can't believe I'm going to miss it." El picks at the shrimp in her hand.

Zoe pouts at her cousin. "I'll livestream it for my YouTube channel. But you'll have to make it up to me for missing my big debut."

"Wil, come check this out." Mateo calls me over to the glass partition. He clicks a button and the wall moves. Pounding music blasts into the room. We step onto the balcony like royalty and scan the writhing bodies below. "Good crowd tonight."

Zoe and El join us, El carrying her half-empty plate of shrimp. Zoe hangs over the railing waving to a crowd that probably doesn't even notice her. She tugs on El's sleeve. "I want to dance."

"Let's dance here." I'd rather have El all to myself.

"No way." Zoe pulls on El's arm, dragging her away. "We want to dance down there."

El glances back. "Dance with me?"

Like I'd ever say no to her.

The music is so loud, the floor vibrates. El's palm is sweaty in mine, but I refuse to let go as Zoe leads us into the crowd. A techno beat drops to a dull thrum and the people around us throw their hands in the air and yell, "Up." The sound spikes and the dancers jump. El places her hands on my shoulders and bounces, the lights from the ceiling shimmering across her face.

Again, the music mutes. This time El joins the clubbers, her hands in the air, and screams, "Up." In response the speakers blast and I jump with El, her jubilance infecting me. The DJ knows what he's doing and revs the crowd with a few more rounds. El, Zoe, Mateo, and I are high on the music. I love watching El, free and happy.

The beat morphs, a slow track overlayed on the dance song. Zoe sways to the bass. A group of girls on our right catch Mateo's eye and he peels off to join their circle. El slows her motions, the smile on her face making the base of my neck tingle. Her fingers grip my shirt and tug me to her, closing the gap. Our chests crash together, then our lips.

El's hands are everywhere. In my hair. On my arms. At my waist. She pulls up the hem of my shirt and her nails brush against my skin. My breath halts and I feel her smile against my lips. I should tell her to stop. This isn't the place. But I can't.

A wall of people surrounds us. Except for the strobe lights, it's dark and we're pressed so tightly together no one can see what El's hands are doing. Which right now are dipping into the waistband of my jeans.

Hell.

This woman will be the death of me.

What a sweet death it will be.

I've waited weeks to hold her like this and paid for a room in the hope of spending this night with El. Even if holding her is all I do. That would be enough. She drags her teeth over my lip and I gasp into her mouth. My abs contract. It seems my princess has other thoughts. Ones I'm completely on board with.

Following her lead, I run my finger under the strap of her dress, tracing the line of the material to where it ends at the top of her chest. My hand doesn't want to move, like this is a line I'm not sure I want to cross. El breaks our kiss, meets my gaze, and takes control of my hand, dragging my finger under the material.

We cross the line together.

Between her soft skin and the excitement in her eyes, my resistance evaporates. Never in my life have I wanted a girl like this. Want isn't the right word. I need El. I need her in my life. In every way I can have her. Here in this club, we're anonymous, and I can be the man in her life. Her boyfriend.

No cameras, no distance.

Just us.

She bites her lip, the plump flesh taunting me, and I need a taste too. It's not the frenzied kiss from before, but a leisurely stroll where my tongue is on promenade across her lips, teeth, inside her cheek, getting to the best part last—her tongue. She takes over and turns my savoring into a claiming ritual.

Her tongue glides along mine, possessing me. I want to be possessed, pronounced hers and only hers. Because I am. The backbeat of the music can't keep time with my heartbeat, accelerating with every invasive stroke of her mouth. My body unites in rhythm with the burst of adrenaline pushing through El's skin into mine. Her fingers dig into my scalp like she can't get close enough.

"Tell me we have our own room," she says.

I barely hear her above the pounding music, but our hearts and minds are one. "Yes."

"Good." She sucks on a spot on my neck. "Let's go. Now."

No need to ask twice. "You tell Zoe, I'll let Mateo know we're leaving." I reluctantly release my grip on her hips and tear myself away. I'll have all night with her.

Mateo is sandwiched between two women. I interrupt. He kisses them both on the cheek and moves to the edge of the crowd with me. "El and I are heading to the hotel. Call you in the morning."

A grin breaks across his face. "Enjoy."

Mateo returns to the girls and I scan the dance floor, already missing El. My fingers feel cold without her hand to hold. I take another lap around the club. No sign of her.

No El.

Since getting in the car with Zoe this morning, she's pissed me off ten ways to Sunday. Right now, I want to murder her. I check my phone. It's been ten minutes already. Where are Zoe and El? The only place I haven't looked is the restroom.

The music changes pace and a stream of girls filter through the hallway leading to the restrooms. Zoe appears in the hall, her mouth a thin line. I look over her shoulder, but there's no El. A hole forms in my chest.

"Tell Mateo to start the car." She pushes on my shoulder to turn me toward the dance floor.

"Wait." I ground my feet. "I'm looking for El."

"Look no further. She's currently in the restroom, throwing up."

SEVENTEEN

El

THE MARBLE FLOOR OF the hotel bathroom is hard and cold under my knees. I'm hugging the toilet bowl with both hands, avoiding the full-length mirror to my left. What designer decided that having a mirror this large next to the throne, as Dad calls it, is good for anyone? My sides hurt from the last round of vomiting and I'm pretty sure my body can't possibly contain any more of the delicious on the way down, disgusting on the way up shrimp. But is my stomach empty enough to actually leave?

I tear off a piece of toilet paper and run it under my eyes. The white comes back with makeup. "I must look terrible." My throat hurts. "And Wil saw me like this."

"You never look terrible." Zoe's sitting beside me, her back against the glass shower enclosure. The gold dress she rocked at the club is wrinkled and might have a spec of my vomit on the cuff. "You remind me of a baby raccoon we rehoused when a whole brood of them made a home in the palm trees in our backyard."

My stomach seizes, and I prove that even more can come out.

"They probably smelled like garbage, like I do." I throw the paper into the bowl, slouch against the wall, and flush. "Just go. You don't have to suffer through this. This is supposed to be your Vegas adventure."

Zoe pushes a damp strand of hair off my cheek. "What kind of friend or family would I be if I leave you here? I don't need your death on my hands. Your mom would kill me."

I ignore Zoe's mention of Mom, but can't ignore the ripple in my heart, like it wants Mom here too. "I'm not planning on dying. I have a concert tomorrow. Besides, this isn't my first food poisoning."

"You wolfed down those shrimp appetizers like you've never had seafood before."

My stomach spasms. "Don't."

"Don't what?" Her eyebrows draw together.

"Don't say any words that have food in them."

"You will feel better tomorrow. I sent the guys to get supplies: ginger ale and saltines."

"No." The spasm rolls through me. I hover over the clear water, but only a burp comes out. "Please. I beg you. Stop mentioning food."

Zoe checks her eyeshadow in the gigantic mirror. "You'll thank me tomorrow morning."

"Maybe. Right now, it feels like I'll never be human again." My bones hurt. My head is a giant bell that echoes every sound. My nose is burning. Even my fingernails hurt.

"Are you ready for a shower?" Zoe knocks on the glass behind her. It's a D-sharp. So sharp it slices through my brain, enters the cavern inside, and ricochets against my skull.

"Ready?" I clutch my temples. I'd love some painkillers but the thought of putting anything into my stomach is more unbearable than the pain. Hot water beating on my shoulders, removing the slime and grime, is not the worst idea. "As ready as one could be."

"Come on, then," Zoe says.

I use her forearm as leverage to get up. The high heels from my stage outfit scrape against the tile floor. Why am I still wearing them? Did I think I'd be dancing more tonight?

My chest aches, but this time it's about the bad timing, not the bad shrimp. I've missed Wil, his arms around me, his lips on mine. Tonight, I couldn't get close enough to him. Only the fact that we were on a dance floor stopped me from undressing him. At least he doesn't have to see me like this.

Zoe helps remove my outfit. Last night I couldn't fall asleep, imagining Wil doing this. The clothes lie on the floor like the discarded shell of a snake. I'm trembling as I get into the shower, and Zoe sits me on the metal built-in bench.

"You okay in there?" Zoe shouts over the water. Her worried face is not that of a fashion mogul in the making, but of my cousin, my partner-in-crime, my family.

"Fine. Thank you for being here." The heat of the shower soothes my trembling sides. Tears join the water on my cheeks. The crippling loneliness of the last month hits me. I've never been away from the people who love and know me for so long. My body's been on high alert, overtightened, and I can't stay that way any longer. I sob in exhaustion, grateful I'm not alone. "You're a real friend," I say through the layers of liquid.

Zoe puts her forehead on the glass. "You didn't drink enough to get sappy on me, but if you're okay, I heard the door slam. I'll go and see what Wil and Mateo are up to."

"Thank you." I rub my face and eyes. "You're the best cousin ever."

"I'll remind you of that next time Bailey invites you to New York for her art show featuring portraits of you and you decide you like her more."

"I always like you more." Maybe it's because she's so close, living in LA, or maybe it's because she's so different. We complement each other. "Just don't tell her about it. I'll deny it."

"Your sense of humor is coming back, so I feel safe to leave you for a bit."

I stay in the shower for what feels like an hour. Too tired to blow-dry my hair, I tug on the clothes Zoe left for me on the sink counter. The nightgown and underwear are more suited for a lingerie shoot, perfect for seducing my boyfriend. But no matter how hot and ready I was to get Wil naked and into my bed, I'm not sure I even want to see him in my current state.

The bedroom in the suite Wil rented for us for tonight is not intended for sleeping. The mirror motif continues on the tiered ceiling over the bed. Still, I'm so tired I crawl under the covers and curl into a ball. Through the door I hear a sea of muffled voices, Zoe and what I hope is Wil and Mateo.

"You can't go in there." Zoe's words are clearer now from the other side of the door.

There's a sound like scraping. "Try and stop me," Wil says.

"Nice try. You're not getting into bed with her. I saw you at the club. She's in no condition to do anything you planned."

The door handle jiggles, and I consider getting out of bed to stop the argument, but the sheets are remarkably soft, and this mattress is like a cushion.

"Piss off. I only want to take care of her."

"Take care." Zoe's sarcasm bleeds through the door. "I thought you were different."

"Hey, you two. Stop it." I can't lift my head, but I shout in what I hope is the direction of the door. "Your arguing isn't helping." My voice cracks on the last word. My mouth is so dry.

Silence greets my plea. Just when I think I've drifted off, the door creaks. Light spills across my pillow as someone enters. A calloused hand lands on my forehead.

Wil.

"How're you feeling?"

"Better now you're here." I thought I didn't want him to see me, but his cool fingers take the edge off the pounding in my head.

"Can I join you?"

I wince. "My breath smells."

"I don't care about your breath." The bed dips and he climbs in with me. My body molds to his, differently than it did in the club. Wil's not only scorching fire, he's my comfort.

The tears from earlier return, stinging. "I'm sorry I ruined our night."

"Hey." He kisses my temple. "You didn't ruin anything. I wanted nothing more than to spend time with you." His arm tightens around me, pulling me closer. "Now I have you all to myself. Just how I like it."

The rise and fall of his chest is like a lullaby. This may not have been how I wanted to get Wil into bed, but this is . . . nice. Except for the food poisoning bit.

"I'll get you a drink." Wil strokes my back. "The lady at the pharmacy said you'll need electrolytes so we got this purple stuff she recommended."

My fingers bunch the cool cotton of his shirt to hold him in place. "No. Don't leave."

His torso relaxes and I squeeze closer. "Not going anywhere."

Except he is. Back to LA in the morning. Without me. What do we have left? A few hours? I have no idea how long I spent in the bathroom.

The minutes with Wil are disappearing, like a timer on a bomb that will explode our world and fling us far away from each other again. I burrow into his neck, soaking up as much of my boyfriend as possible. For a flickering moment I consider giving up, going home with Wil. And Zoe. And Mateo. Just be a girl in love with her boyfriend.

But the temptation gives way to my need to prove to myself and my doubters that I deserve to sing.

"You sure you don't want to go back to the club?"

"There's no place I'd rather be than here." Wil's voice is far away, like he's gone already. I try to fight against the drowsiness but it's easier to sink into Wil. There are words said after that but they chase me down the rabbit hole of sleep. I lose them to the dream I have of Wil and I on a boat in Malta, the sun shining as Papa smiles at us from the driver's seat.

Eighteen

The intensity with which Rocker, Death Elbow, and I are shouting over each other could lead an outsider to wonder if we're arguing about which team should win the World Cup. Since showing interest in the group, Rocker insisted I shadow him every time he interacts with them. Hands-on learning, he called it. Apparently, that involves mediating which plugin to use for the song they are working on.

"I don't think the reverb works here. It's like I'm sitting on a motorcycle while singing. Who wants to listen to that? I need a natural growl," Corbin says.

Rocker focuses on the lead singer. "Don't you have enough? If every song has the exact same sound, you'll lose the audience."

"But they are fans of our sound." Corbin tosses his long hair out of his face. "They want more of what we've given them."

"Yes and no." Lead singer pitted against lead singer is like watching my own private battle of the bands. "They want your flavor of music, but if you give them the same exact thing over and over, they'll be bored. Think Imagine Dragons. They rose to fame with *Radioactive* and *Demons* on *Night Visions*. What was their next big hit?"

"*I Bet My Life*." Corbin hums the first lines.

"Right." Rocker joins him. "See. Different vibe. You need variation. Subtlety, not hitting them over the head with the same damn hammer. Let's switch to a war mace. It's sexier."

Corbin grins. "Never heard of a mace referred to that way. But I get it. Let's try."

We've been messing with the song for two hours. When it was Nick, El, and me working on the *Indigo* track, three heads were better than one. With the six of us pulling the song in different directions, I'm close to giving up. Corbin records the passage with the new plugin. I merge the previous version and the new one on the soundboard in Rocker's home studio, ignoring the five pairs of eyes watching. I can't see them but I swear I feel their hands twitch, trying to take my place at the switches. I hit play.

The part we're working on ends and the room erupts into a frenzy of shouts worthy of a busy market with buyers and sellers haggling over prices. The ruckus grows, and my eyes will roll into the back of my skull if this does not end.

I rise and lift my hands in a timeout gesture. "Shut up every-one," I shout.

Maybe they are stunned, maybe they are actually listening to me, but they all stop talking. The expressions on their faces range from incredulity to anger. Rocker's face is the only smug one. Did I just blow it? Screaming at the group we're trying to persuade to sign with us might get me kicked out of Rocker Inc.

"How about a different approach?" I say. Their gazes are skeptical at best. "Let's record an acoustic version."

A collective groan is my answer.

"Listen. Listen." I walk between them and pull down one of the guitars. "You're a rock band, I get it. You want to keep the growl but shake it up, show range and draw people's atten-tion. I don't think adding more noise to your already aggressive performance is the answer. But if you go quieter, the roar, the intensity, that can stay."

Corbin cracks his knuckles. "Quiet intensity? Isn't that an oxymoron?"

"It's intriguing." Rocker picks up the black Gibson Hum-mingbird I've been too afraid to approach since I googled its price.

Corbin spreads his feet wide and crosses his arms. "How the heck do you silently roar?"

I strum the guitar. "Start with the second verse."

He talks through the lines and falls into the growl that's his signature. I let his voice be the star and only resume playing when there is a moment of breathing space. "See?"

"It's weirdly awesome."

I can take weirdly awesome.

His eyes narrow. "The whole song can't be like that."

I raise my hands. "Not proposing that. This is your lure and intrigue. Why do they sound different? The first chorus will accelerate. The second chorus will get louder, and we hit them with the full sound there. The buildup is important. Just like foreplay."

The group chuckles, and I choose not to look at Rocker in case he's wondering what I am or am not doing with El.

The latest version of the song we recorded with Death Elbow streams from the speakers. Rocker works the grill while Sylvia entertains Pickle on the outdoor couch. You'd think this is a normal middle-class family if you ignored the mansions lining Malibu beach.

"You made them sound so much better." Rocker takes a swig of beer and flips the lid of the grill built into the side of the covered patio. "That was inspired thinking."

"Working with them was such a high," I say.

"Which part?" Rocker rubs the back of his neck and drains the rest of his beer. "Did you like helping them with the sound on this one song, is that why you are studying sound engineering?"

I shrug noncommittally. I'm not interested in discussing my future plans with Rocker. I'm here for a couple months, then I'll be glad to never see him again.

Rocker restarts the song. I hear the spots I want to amplify, but we're close to the final version. He points at the speaker. "How about working with various artists on an array of songs? Is that appealing to you? Or would you prefer sticking with one artist, like Death Elbow, and impact their career trajectory? They don't officially have a manager yet. Would that role appeal to you?"

Curiosity piques. I've never considered that career path. I raise my gaze to him.

His lips twitch. He must've registered my interest. "As a manager you work with the group on all fronts: schedule their events, promotion, might oversee their finances, guide them in their career."

"Sounds complicated."

"But interesting?"

I shrug again but can't hide that I'm intrigued. Working on *Indigo* last year and the month I spent at Rocker Inc. showed me the music business is more complex than I had expected.

"You could do either job at Rocker Inc. Part-time, of course, so you can still go to school while getting real-life experience." His eyes sparkle with hope.

I recognize that look. He had the same one in Bremen when he negotiated me coming here. I let him win once, but I have other plans. I can explore careers in Germany just as well. "Won't be in LA long enough."

Pickle gurgles as if he's disappointed with my answer. Or am I the one who's disappointed at the idea of leaving him?

Sylvia cradles the baby in her hands as he squints and shakes his head and arms in jerky moves that seem to go along with the music. I'm sure it's an impossible feat for a barely one-month-old, but they are too coordinated to be random.

"The boy has rhythm." Rocker crouches next to them. If a paparazzi snapped a photo of Rocker's backyard right now it would be called, "A Perfect Family." I'd be cropped out, but the three of them would be ripe for the modern family magazine cover.

Some families have it all. Others fight to survive. Why can't there be a happy medium?

Rocker picks him up. Every time he gets his face close then moves away, Pickle makes one of his adorable grimaces.

Sylvia stands and stretches, like a bear waking up from a long winter's sleep. "I'll go tell Marta the meat is almost ready. We'll set the table. Bring in the food as soon as it's done."

"Yes, Mommy," Rocker answers in a childish voice as he continues the game with Pickle. "We'll be right there, Mommy."

Would he have played the same way with me when I was a baby, or would my only contact have been child support checks in the mail? Not that the money would've been a bad thing.

The timer on the meat thermometer beeps. Instead of returning Pickle to the basket thing Sylvia was rocking him in,

Rocker offers the baby to me. "Hang on to him, I need to get the tri-tip off."

Baby powder replaces the scent of fresh-cut grass in the backyard and Pickle squirms in my arms. One of his tiny hands clutches the collar of my T-shirt and pulls it down. If he's looking for milk, he's not going to find it here. He gurgles at me. No need to react. He doesn't need to get used to me. I won't be a permanent fixture in his life.

Pickle stares at me as if daring me to not love him, his head bobbing toward me. The organ in my chest reacts, proving Rocker right—no one with a heart can resists Pickle's antics. His eyes have settled into a blue that reminds me of El's, and not our father's.

Rocker closes the lid again and sits beside us on the bench. "Five more minutes." His mouth breaks into the smile he reserves for family. Between work and home, I see the difference now. This one is aimed at both of us. "So glad you're here. Your brother needs you."

Not a sentiment I agree with. He has more adults hovering around him than a single child requires. I smooth Pickle's black tuft of hair. Rocker rests his forearms on his knees. "Your mom sent me pictures of you as a baby after I sent her some of Pickle, and the way your hair only existed on the top of your head in a weird mohawk just like his is uncanny."

"We are related." I don't want to sound mean, but I'm not here to reminisce about the days he missed.

"Your mom seems to be doing better."

"For now." The retesting the clinic did after the first month of treatment is not a fair indication of a final result, but there is no regression. There's even slight forward progress in her numbers. "We'll know more next month."

"Are you still planning to see your mom next weekend?" Rocker adjusts Pickle's onesie and pats the baby's back. Pickle turns and reaches for his nose.

I extend my half brother to Rocker, but his hands are busy playing peekaboo. "I need to book my tickets. She's too weak to travel."

Rocker's face appears from behind his fingers. "You can take the jet."

"Coach is fine. I'd rather you spend the money you'd waste on fuel and a pilot and donate it to someone like Mum. Someone who actually needs the money. Where it can make a difference."

His hands drop. "You forget, I didn't always have money. I give back through my Music and Munchkins charitable organization. Plus, ten percent of my income goes to support other charities."

"Ten percent," I say. Pickle seems to get frustrated at the cessation of the game and wags his arms furiously. "What a sacrifice."

"What percentage would be enough?" The mirth has left his eyes. "Twenty? Fifty? Ninety-nine? When would you not look at me like I'm the villain?"

"It's your money. I'm not here to tell you how to spend it."

"But you are doing exactly that."

I bounce Pickle, who I swear growls in frustration. "I'm just pointing out that you could do more. Mum wouldn't have had to suffer for years if she had the money for the treatment when she first was eligible. There's medicine out there that can help. But the people who need it don't have the money to get into the trials."

Rocker studies me for a long while. "Let's change that."

"Right. Like it's that easy."

"No. These things take a lot of work. But we can find a charity that supports RA patients who require experimental treatments or whose treatments are not covered by their insurance. Or we can start a charity in honor of your mom." His eyebrows shoot up like when I played the guitar for Death Elbow. "I was late in helping her. I can be on time to help others. We can work on a plan together."

Together? Do I want to work with Rocker on something other than the temporary A&R duties? No. But I'd do a lot less pleasant tasks if they'd help people in Mum's situation. "Are you serious?" A simple nod from Rocker. Pickle moves his head too, as if to say C'mon Wil, do it. "Are there deals or strings attached? Will I be required to pose with you in front of cameras?"

"I can't guarantee there won't be any pictures. People see celebrities and tend to donate, but you never have to do anything you don't want to." He raises his hands and Pickle looks at him, probably assuming the game is about to restart. "No strings. Purely voluntary. However, I take these things seriously. I give my money and my time. You would follow suit, be part of the organization. Maybe not the day-to-day operations, but you'll be on the board, making decisions with me. Your sweat and my dollars. Does this sound like a fair distribution of responsibilities?"

"Fine," I say. Pickle gurgles like he needs to burp, or like he'd like to be on the board as well. Maybe one day.

The timer beeps again.

"Head inside." Rocker directs me and Pickle to the house. "Tell Sylvia the good news."

NINETEEN

EL

IN AN ATTEMPT TO escape the messy room I'm sharing with Josie and Annalyn, I search the second floor for the hotel gym. A familiar line from *Give Us a Chance* halts my progress. A Blatantly Subtle jam session? Beau and Kamo riff off each other during sound checks and I've witnessed them read each other's minds like Dad and his bandmates do. Like Wil and I do. But I didn't take part. It was their thing. There's always an invisible wall around their circle that I don't dare break.

The unmistakable sound of Beau's guitar continues. I tighten the knot of Wil's T-shirt over my stomach and cautiously open the door leaking guitar licks and drumbeats. With no perfor-mances or rehearsals planned, today is a rare night off before a packed three days of publicity appearances and shows.

As I step across the threshold two sets of eyes lock on me. The room is most likely used for meetings or conferences. Kamo sits at her smaller drum set while Beau holds a guitar on his lap, singing to two empty metal chairs. I'm still on the outside of their group looking in, but when Beau signals for me to come over to the empty spot in front of him, I step through the forcefield of their gazes. Maybe I'm in, but I am not part of them.

"You can take Carlee's part." Beau's words are not a question.

"Sure." I twist Wil's bracelet between numb fingers.

"Take it from the top." He starts the familiar chords of *Give Us a Chance*, the song I busked to so many times.

The first verse spills from me without thought. I'm not at my best, but I'm singing. Wil would be proud of me. The second line comes out with more conviction. My ears note Beau joining in, the melody building, but my head is showing me the well-guarded footage of Wil in Bremen, with his guitar, his eyes full of encouragement, and I sing to him like I always do when we busk. I tell him my struggles, how the world is against us, how we will get through it because even apart, we are together.

I'm lost in the melody that captured me the first time I heard this song, and I slide from the original version into the one my heart hears. A crescendo. A slowing down. A harder push on the emotional line about not giving up, where the original was softer and more lyrical.

Beau matches my speed, his guitar echoing my elongated B-flat. Like in the game of follow the leader my cousins and I used to play as kids, he builds on the little wobble I add to the harmonized note. Kamo plucks out a beat. We're climbing and diving in our own pattern. Beau brings in the swoops that take the song into a swell of emotion.

Without Carlee in the room, I'm the one they are following. We're no longer playing the original. They are with me, and our version is even better than the arrangement I came up with for Wil and me. I let myself go and my voice shakes the walls of this temporary stadium.

I'm in heaven.

I belt, and I whisper, and I don't care anymore. That's one of the gifts music gives me. The ability to forget my inhibition and chase what feels true. Be myself. Not the girl who lost her father. Not the rock star's daughter. Not the patsy the paparazzi paint me as. Just me.

Today the direction this song is taking is the truest I've felt since I've joined the tour. Such a relief to be me and unapologetically do what I want. What I'm good at. What I'm supposed to do. The music moves through me, the energy flowing from my lungs to every cell in my body. I push my shoulders back and get up, swaying to the song. My blood heats and my lungs expand. I'm powerful and happy.

I love myself at this moment.

The slow clapping starts when the last note still rings through the room. I turn to the door. Carlee's gaze is glued to my face. Chills run down my spine. The intensity in her eyes scares me. Did I just mess this whole thing up? It's one of her favorite songs, and I know my version was the reason she picked me, but this is beyond that version. This is me with her group. This is me impersonating Carlee Waters while she's away. Cold, heavy blocks pile on my chest.

Carlee strides into the middle of the circle and lifts her hand in a high five. That's a good thing, right? I hit her raised palm, but my heart isn't in it. I can't read the room, or her. The way her lips are pressed into a thin line, I think she's upset. Is it a sarcastic high five or is she genuinely happy with where I took her song?

"This is what you get up to when I'm resting?" The sound of her voice is extra loud. "Maybe we try again, and I lead this time?" She gets an enthusiastic thumbs-up from Kamo.

Carlee moves the other chair next to her rightful spot beside Beau. Kamo taps away lightly on the base drum, her tempo matching the beating in my chest.

"Three, two, one." Carlee gives Beau the look they exchange at the beginning of every show.

The opening notes float from his guitar, even though he never takes his gaze off her. Kamo kicks in the throughline and I shrink into the background.

I wait in silence for the portion where harmonies are required. Wil is much better with that side of our duo. I sing the lead—he finds ways to complement me. I came to rely on his expertise. Here I listen for Carlee and Beau and follow their lead. My voice is part of the sound, but my heart is not in it. I'm back outside the circle, my moment in the spotlight powerful but brief.

I miss it already.

"Think we're done for today." Carlee claps again but these are fast, happy claps. "Don't know about you all, but I could use a drink," she says. Kamo hoots and Beau puts away his guitar. "The hotel bar makes a mean cosmopolitan." Carlee looks at me. "We'll find something non-alcoholic for you."

Singled out again, my cheeks flame.

The bar is not full. At 11:30 p.m. most of the hotel guests must be tucked in for the night. Carlee's bodyguards are part of the group, and by the way hotel guests try to come over and talk to Carlee and Beau, I understand why. I've been there. Well, Rocker and Mom have been there, and I've been there with them. Dinners at restaurants where our bodyguards are part of the deal—asking people to be respectful, let us eat in peace.

Beau nudges my arm. "They can probably make a Shirley Temple."

Way to make me feel like a child. I might not be allowed to drink alcohol legally in the US, but I handled my beer in Germany quite well, thank you. No one was mad at me for getting tipsy there. Nineteen is not thirteen. I'm an adult and can vote. This whole not drinking until twenty-one makes no sense to me.

"Water is fine," I say.

Beau sets his elbow on the bar next to me and whispers in my ear. "You're doing great. Relax."

I unclench my jaw. Beau is not my enemy. I catch Carlee and Kamo laughing over their martini glasses full of vodka and cranberry juice at the table to our right. Maybe if I get a red drink too, I won't feel so out of place. "Do they have watermelon juice?"

"Watermelon? That's an interesting choice." He winks and slides a coaster my way. "Hang in here, I'll ask."

The part of the bar the band and crew are in is roped off, but every now and again a flash catches my eye as people who recognize Beau and Carlee snap pictures from behind their drink menus. Others blatantly stand and aim their phone lenses at us, probably filming everything. Not subtle at all. I pull my phone out and see a missed call and text from Wil.

Wil: Did I tell you you're awesome?

Me: No. What's that about?

Wil: The chorus you came up with? It's genius. You always surprise me how you start with our little idea and take it in a bigger and better direction.

Me: Carlee helped.

Wil: Thank her from me.

I glance at Carlee and Kamo, hesitate, then text her a thank you. She can't be mad at me for that.

Carlee glances at the screen and turns the phone upside-down on the table. She picks up her drink and clinks it with Kamo's.

Wil and I cheered like that in Bremen with his rowing mates. Everything was so much better with Wil around.

Me: I miss drinking beer with you.

An ounce of dread evaporates at his instant reply.

Wil: Is that the only thing you miss about me? Winky emoji

Me: Are you fishing for compliments?

Wil: Always. You know how insecure I am. Grinning emoji.

More like the least insecure person I know. It's as if he expects the entire world to automatically fall at his feet. I have no such expectation.

Me: I miss your words. Especially when you whisper them into my ear.

After I hit send, the phrase I was trying to make sound romantic looks dull and uninspired. I twist Wil's bracelet and throw my face to the ceiling. What must he think of my lame attempts to express myself?

Wil: I miss your breath tickling my neck, and the heat of your eyes when we kiss and you don't close them because I imagine you are capturing every moment of us together. I miss your little sighs when our kisses end, because I too feel the loss of your lips. There are never enough kisses. I miss the way you feel under my fingertips, and how your voice reaches into my soul every time you say my name. Like a little present. I miss you so much.

The heat behind my eyes might be tears, but also the longing to hear these words from his mouth. I don't mind spending several minutes untangling the letters on the screen, reading and re-reading them until they are a sound in my head I can play on repeat.

I want to tell him that my feelings for him are more than miss. They are more than like. They are more than a craving for a physical touch. My feelings for him are untamable, and unruly, and they make me want to drop the tour and my responsibilities to Blatantly Subtle, hop on a plane, and be with Wil in the comfort of his arms, with his hands and lips and hugs that feel like home.

Me: Same.

"They didn't have watermelon, but I got you cranberry, and I asked them to put it in a martini glass so it at least looks like you're drinking with everyone." Beau sets the wide glass with its long stem in front of me on the coaster bearing the hotel's name. I sip and pucker. That'd be my reaction to a martini as well, so maybe it's okay.

Beau raises his similar glass, the red liquid sloshing to the edge of the rim. "To the next chapter."

We clink our glasses. I take another sip of the mocktail.

Beau throws a longing glance at Carlee. This isn't the first time I've caught him doing this. Were Beau and Carlee an item when they first started, like Wil and me? I don't remember Daniel Davison gossiping about a relationship between them. But then the world doesn't know about us either.

"Let's join them," Beau says as he slips off the bar stool and heads to where Carlee and Kamo sit.

I set my feet on the ground and step to follow, but my shoes tangle and the world goes sideways. The glass with the juice tilts and I yelp. Beau turns in time to set his hand on my elbow to steady me, but I faceplant on his chest. We tumble to the ground, red liquid all over us.

The clicks of cameras drown out my "Sorry."

TWENTY

SVEN REALLY LIKES LEG days. I'm willing to bet that in his world the expression on his face counts as a smile. El says he's a man of few words, but he's also a man of few facial muscle movements. Scowls, now for those he has a million variations.

"What are you grinning about?" Sven adds another ten pounds and resumes the thigh crunches.

"Seeing Mum. My flight leaves in"—I check my phone—"less than four hours." The first phase of the trial is over and Rocker insisted I take his jet and visit her this weekend. With El playing in San Fran for four nights, she won't miss me.

"Is your mom feeling better?"

The fragile happiness over Mum's current health improvement makes it easier to breathe. "Opa says she's spry as a spring chicken. His words, not mine, but in our calls I can tell she has more energy." My phone dings. "We might even go to Oberneulanders, this restaurant Mum loves."

I glance at the screen and five words slash my giddiness.

Rocker's Daughter Drunk and Disorderly

Before I can click the notification, two more pop up.

Melodie Rockerby Can't Keep Hands Off Bandmate

Like Father, Like Daughter, Melodie Rockerby Tears Up Hotel Bar

"What the heck?"

More notifications flood in, the pings bouncing off the walls of the gym. Sven abandons his machine and glares at his phone. "Shit." I'd fear for the device's life if I wasn't so busy opening mine to read the story. I click the top article. Bloody Daniel Davison again.

A picture of El sprawled across a man's torso pops up. Her eyes are wide, her mouth slightly open, her red hair splayed across her face like she's trying to turn away from the photographer. Into Beau's chest. His hand on her back. Acid hits the back of my throat.

I bypass the "click for more photos" button, dreading the slander Davison's written.

"I called it. Back in the US for barely a month and Melodie Rockerby goes overboard again. Only to land in Langdon Beau's arms. Not sure how a girl her age got served at a bar (I'm looking at you SF) but she didn't waste any time getting tipsy and snuggling with Blatantly Subtle's most eligible bachelor.

We know the rockstar's daughter has daddy issues, but this is going too far. Is Beau a cry for Rocker's attention? Or is Melodie another temporary distraction for the lead guitarist's wandering eye?"

The phone in my hand creaks. "Are you seeing this?"

Sven grunts. Cold eyes meet mine. "It's not true."

"I know." Of course it's not true. El wouldn't cheat on me. At least I don't think she would. No, I know she wouldn't. "This Davison guy twists everything. He's got some vendetta against El."

"Paparazzi slime."

"I gotta call her."

She answers on the second ring and the stress in her voice grates my nerves. "It's not true."

"I know. Are you okay?"

"I mean I did spill the drink on Beau. I tripped on my shoelaces. It was only cranberry juice." Her words fly.

"El?" The cavern in my chest fills with worry, doubt, and every other horrible emotion possible.

"I wasn't even drinking." Her voice cracks. "Most of the band was there including Carlee, but they make it look like we were on a date or something. It's not like that."

"El. It's okay."

"It's not." Her words end in a sob and the sound breaks my heart. I should be there, not here in Malibu, protected behind the gates of Rocker's mansion. El needs me and I'm useless.

My fingers form a fist, wanting to knock Daniel Davison's front teeth out. He shouldn't be able to do this to her. I pace the floor, counting the floorboards like they can provide a solution. "What can I do?"

"Why me? Why does he do this to me?"

"He's an asshole. Ignore him."

"Easy for you to say. They aren't after you yet." Her sharp intake of breath rings in my ear. "I didn't mean that, Wil."

"I know. It's okay." Why can't I think of anything better to say?

"I never want this to happen to you. This is why we can't go public. He'll twist our relationship; focus on the fact we're stepsiblings," El hisses.

My knuckles crack from the pressure of flexing my fingers. I've held my tongue on this subject because it upsets her, but we can't keep our relationship under wraps forever. "Who cares?"

"I do," El shouts. "I'll be the evil witch who seduced Rocker's long-lost son."

"It's not like that." The buzz in my ears isn't from the notifications. "We can fix this." There's silence on the other end of the call. "El?"

"I hate this." Her voice is barely above a whisper. "I want this to end."

My heart stops. Does she mean us? She can't mean us, can she? My throat is clogged, and I can't get a sound out, can't beg her not to do this.

"Subtle's publicist is working on a statement." Another sob rattles through the phone. "Beau's on a call with them now, but it won't stop Daniel's attacks. One minute they say Dad's the one getting me this gig, the next they gossip Dad and I are fighting and I supposedly can't stand him."

Finally, I find my voice. "I know." I can't believe I'm about to say this. "He's a good guy." Her words the night before we left Bremen.

"Oh, Josie's here. I gotta go." The line goes dead before I can tell her again everything will be okay. Which is probably a good thing because I have no idea how to make it okay.

"She's upset," says Sven.

"No shit."

Sven holds up his hands.

"I need to fix this," I say.

Silence hangs in the air between us. He crosses his arms and stares at me.

"What?" I jut my chin at Sven.

"You know who can help."

I rub a thumb across my brow. "Got any celebs that can break up or go to rehab and get El off the front page of Daniel Davison's website?"

"Nope."

"Then who?"

"Think about it." He cocks his head toward the window. My gaze follows his direction to Rocker's mansion.

"No. I'm not asking him."

"He's involved, whether you like it or not: 'Is this bad behavior in response to the feud between Melodie and her legendary father?'" Sven reads from his phone. "Rocker making a statement might help. Take the heat off."

"No."

Sven puts his hands on his hips. "Guess you're not the man I thought you were."

Now I want to smash in Sven's front teeth. "Fine."

My nails dig into the palms of my hands as I stomp across the yard and throw the door open. Voices in the kitchen greet me.

"No. I want a solution now." Rocker's tone could freeze a roasted marshmallow. "Give me a plan," he says into his phone and stabs the screen to hang up.

"I knew this would happen." Sylvia's blonde hair hides her face, her hands massaging her temples. "Can't we sue him for slander?"

Our eyes lock across the expanse of marble between us and she presses her lips together.

Rocker follows her gaze, and I don't have time to retreat. "Wil. There's—"

"I saw the article about El."

"You mean Melodie?" The bitterness in Sylvia's voice grates my already frayed nerves. I want to sneer, tell her Melodie is the child she tried to lock in an ivory tower, El is the woman with the guts to break out and make her dreams come true.

Rocker steps over to his wife and puts a glass of slushy moss-colored mush in front of her. "Drink this." He's so attentive, I hate it. Eyes far too similar to mine look my way. "And the photos?"

The plastic speaker sitting on the countertop squeaks to life as Pickle wails like he has to have his say on this situation. Sylvia winces, and Rocker puts a hand on her shoulder. "I'll go."

Sylvia turns on her stool. "No, I'll go. He's hungry." She pushes away from the island.

"Don't forget your smoothie." Rocker slides the glass with green liquid to her.

"As if today wasn't bad enough." She sighs but takes the drink as she leaves the kitchen.

I approach Rocker. "Why do they make these things up about El?"

He nurses his coffee. "This is part of being in the spotlight. The paparazzi make a living following us, snapping photos that can be spun into stories. It's what Harper warned us about. Why she wants to get ahead of the news."

The urge to correct him, tell him there's no us here, itches in my throat. I tap my fingers on the black marble. Damn it, I have to ask. "Can you help El?"

"Oh?" He lifts an eyebrow.

He's going to make me say it. "Get Harper involved? Put out a press release or something denying the allegations. I'm really worried about her." Rocker throws his head back and a roaring laugh belts out. Flames fan up my neck and I grip the countertop. "This isn't funny."

The laughter dies and his shoulders slump. "Welcome to my world."

"Sorry?"

"Two months ago, you stole El away in the middle of the night, and I had no idea where she was, never mind if she was hurt." My stomach rolls at his words. "Take what you're feeling now and multiply it by a thousand, and you'll have an idea how her mother and I felt."

"It's not the same." I trace a vein in the marble.

"I beg to differ." Out of the corner of my eye I see him straighten in his seat. "How about we agree that we both care about her well-being?"

"Are you going to help or not?"

"Of course I am." His hand lands on my arm. I stare at the long tanned fingers digging into my slightly paler skin. This may be the first time he's ever touched me aside from that one time in the club. In the car he keeps his long legs angled away from me, in the elevator he stands on the opposite side, at lunch he shuffles his chair away to give me room.

His hand is warm. Like really warm. His skin is dry, and I might be imagining it, but I think I recognize the callouses on his fingertips from playing the guitar. They're like mine.

"I'd do anything for my family," says Rocker. "I called Harper as soon as I saw the article. Her team are working on a strategy as we speak."

I shake my head, a stone stuck in my throat. Why is he having this effect on me? My eyes sting. I jerk my arm away and refill my water bottle.

His phone buzzes. "Harper." He taps the phone. "Whatcha got?"

"The first draft of a release." Her voice echoes in the kitchen. Did he put it on speakerphone so I can hear? "But we want to go further. Dispel the rumors of you and Melodie in a feud. Take control of the messaging and spin it into a positive. Would you consider visiting her?"

"If you think it'll help."

"I've been in contact with Blatantly Subtle's team. The top options are you attending the concert tonight, you hanging out with the band at the press conference before the show, or . . . Carlee is visiting a children's hospital this afternoon. You and Melodie could join."

"Hold up." He hits mute and turns to me. "I'll need my plane." He rubs the back of his neck and one side of his mouth hooks in an apologetic frown.

The jet he talked me into taking to visit Mum this weekend. The gifts I had for her, the reservations to take her and Opa for brunch. The planned dinners now that she has some strength back to cook. I was promised the birthday blueberry muffins to celebrate my half-birthday because Mom missed my twentieth.

I rub away the guilty lump over my heart. El or Mum? Alternate plans churn in my brain. I could fly coach but that would mean maybe twenty-four hours with Mum and Opa, if I'm lucky. With midterms coming up every class counts.

My hand reaches for my phone as I press my lips to hold in the damns I want to throw around at this bloody situation. "I'll call Mum, tell her I'm not coming." Mum will understand.

"I'm sorry. We'll find another time to fly you home." He unmutes his phone. "We can be there by lunch."

We?

"Sylvia by your side is a good idea," says Harper. "The family unit together."

"No. My wife needs to stay here with our son. Wil will join me." Rocker raises an eyebrow as if asking for my consent.

I nod. I get to see El.

"Are you sure that's a good idea?" Harper's voice cracks.

"I don't care if it is. He's coming. If you must spin the story, say Wil works for Rocker Inc. There's nothing unusual about an employee accompanying me on the trip."

Rocker hangs up and smiles at me. "Won't make up for me messing up your plan to see Hanna, but I thought you'd like to see El."

Him being considerate pinches my heart. He did ruin my trip, but I would've given up a lot more than seeing Mum for a long weekend if that means helping El.

An hour later, my fingers shake so badly I can barely buckle my seatbelt on the plane. Rocker insists on sitting beside me with Sven across from us. The jet engines hum. We're all on our phones. Sven switches between arranging a car in San Francisco and coordinating security with venues. Rocker is on his third phone call, negotiating the photo op with Harper and Blatantly Subtle.

El's ringtone blares from my phone on the table between us. Rocker and Sven watch as I hit answer.

"You're coming here with him?" She sounds breathless.

I slide to the edge of my seat like that sliver of distance gives me any privacy. "We're in the air."

El sighs. "He's sitting beside you, isn't he?"

"Yup."

"Of course." I hate the resignation in El's voice.

"We have a plan."

"No need to worry about me."

I want to scream that I'll always worry about her, but Rocker doesn't need to witness me acting all smitten. Well, more smitten.

"But I guess I don't get a choice." She sighs. "Again."

TWENTY-ONE

THIS TIME I KNOW where the cameras are. They snap photos of Rocker and me as we walk down the hall of the children's hospital. Everything's been planned. Staged. Set up.

Not by me.

No one asked me.

The mask of polite delight I've perfected over years of standing by Rocker and Mom's sides slips into place. Slight tilt of my head, hint of smile, appear casual. Never let them see the truth.

"Rocker! Rocker! Over here." He turns and the clicks of the cameras cover the phone ringing at the nurse's station. "Are you playing a set with Blatantly Subtle tonight?" The reporter in a wool beanie shoves his phone in our direction.

"A Rocker/Blatantly Subtle collab?" Carlee beams at him like he is a rock legend come to life. Which I guess he is to her. "Are you up for it?"

Rocker drapes his arm over my shoulder and pulls me close. I do my best not to cringe at the side hug. His cologne reminds me of the Malibu mansion, sitting on the couch bingeing movies as a child and him trying to give me a hug. Then, I freaked out; now I just grind my teeth. Unlike Mom, Rocker usually respects my no-hug zone. But today it's about the show, not the reality. The publicity stunt trumps my personal space boundaries. "And miss the chance to watch my incredibly talented daughter perform? No way."

The reporters mock-sigh in disappointment and Carlee joins in. At least I hope she's not actually disappointed.

Another reporter asks Carlee about tonight's lineup and Rocker whispers in my ear, "You look a little pale. Are you okay?"

Am I okay? Is that a joke? I've been working my ass off singing backup for weeks: no sun, no days off, dealing with Annalyn's death stares and the confusing choreography. The one night I let down my guard and try to fit into Blatantly Subtle's inner circle I literally mess it up. The red of the cranberry juice sloshing onto Beau's white shirt, me stumbling over my feet and slamming into him, both ending up on the bar floor, broken glass around us, cameras and phones from every angle.

The energy I've spent keeping up appearances today drains my already low batteries. The sour flavor in my mouth is a permanent thing as I taste the disappointment: my own, Blatantly Subtle's, Rocker's. The pinching sensation between my ribs hasn't left since last night's fiasco.

Rocker leans in, so close only I can hear him. "Wil's hiding in the basement. Hang back while Sven gets us to the first room and he'll take you to him."

My heart beats in my throat. "Thank you," I say. This time my grin is genuine.

Rocker gives me a last squeeze and turns to the reporters, leading them down the hallway toward one of the patients he's here to visit. Sven's already escorting Carlee, who asks my former bodyguard something. Feet shuffle and cameras swivel to follow Rocker, leaving me like a discarded ice cream wrapper. I melt into the beige wall of the emptying corridor and wait for Sven to reappear.

"El." I hear his voice and swivel, my shoes squeaking on the linoleum floor as I speedwalk toward the hulking blond standing by the elevator.

"Sven." I crash into a wall of muscle. We don't hug but I relish every second of contact and take comfort from pressing my face into his chest. Sven sidesteps and blocks me from the outside world.

"In." My ex-bodyguard points to the elevator doors he's holding open.

I let go of my security blanket and follow his orders. "I've missed you."

Metal doors drag close and we're alone in the metal box. "So Wil says." Sven stabs at a button.

If I didn't know better, I'd think Sven was mad at me. "I wasn't drinking last night. Those photos are a lie."

His glacial gaze cuts to mine, and I almost jump away at the intensity. "Don't you think I know that?"

"I . . . Thanks." My hand finds the familiar coarse white strand of my hair. Why is this so odd? Sven and I were thick as thieves before I left for Germany. Zoe might be my bestest friend, but until I met Wil, Sven was the closest person around me. My partner-in-crime. Sven is family. I raise my gaze to the ticking muscle in his jaw. When was the last time I actually spoke to Sven? It's been months. Wil's been our translator these past weeks. "Sorry I haven't called."

Sven's gaze drops to the floor and my stomach falls. Damn. He can't be that upset, can he? I chew on the side of my lip. "Really, I meant to. But the band keeps odd hours and I never want to interrupt you in case you're doing, you know, important bodyguard stuff."

The elevator shudders and the doors clank a low D-note as we continue our descent. "You are never an interruption." The toe of one of Sven's big black boots kicks the floor. "I'll always answer your call." His head tilts my way. "Always."

The dissonance between us evaporates and my shoulders slack. "My personal Superman."

There it is. A rare Sven grin.

"Same here, you know. If you ever need anything," I say.

Sven grunts in reply.

I poke him in the ribs. "So . . . what's new?"

"Not much." His mouth splits into a full-on smile. Something's going on.

"Spill." I poke him again.

He holds up his hands in surrender. "Okay, okay. My business loan got approved and I signed a lease on an office space."

A laugh trudges through the labyrinth of anxiety and bursts out of my chapped lips. "The place on Century Park?"

He nods.

I bounce on my heels. "You're doing it. You're opening your own agency."

"I take possession at the end of the month." His eyes smile now too with symmetrical creases around the corners that should be documented somewhere as a once-in-a century occurrence.

"Does Rocker know?" I ask.

"He knew I was ready to start my own business." Sven's smile falls. "I officially gave him my two weeks' notice yesterday."

"Don't worry. He'll be happy for you." I squeeze Sven's forearm. "Wil?"

"I was going tell him today, but . . ." He points to the ceiling. "I'll tell him tomorrow. Maybe don't mention it."

I hate keeping anything from Wil, but this is Sven's news to deliver. "I'm so proud of you. Mom and Rocker both know you are destined for big things."

"You are too," says Sven. I roll my eyes. My parents are more likely to have faith in Sven's bright future than mine.

The elevator doors ding another D and we jerk to a stop, saving me from my bitter remark. I don't need to spoil Sven's joy with my misery. I follow his trail as we weave through corridors. The happy tingles in my chest for Sven's big step, the gnawing dread in my gut over the press dragging my name through the mud, and the flares of desire at the thought of seeing Wil, they all combine to wreak havoc in my body. Sven opens a door, ushers me through, and I'm engulfed in my favorite scent.

Wil.

His arms seal me in a cocoon and I sink into his familiar chest, soaking up the comfort of him. Since meeting Wil, my stance on hugging has evolved. With Wil, hugs are addictive. Even tight ones like this. Ones that make it hard to breathe.

His mouth presses against the top of my head and the turbulence I've been carrying inside since last night settles. I missed this. I didn't realize until right now how much I miss this. Vegas feels like months ago. How was I ever going to last until the end of this leg of the tour to see him again?

His fingers are in my hair, and the amber eyes I love have traces of concern that make my chest ache. They study me, landing on my mouth. I rise on my tiptoes desperate for a kiss.

"You're here." The glee lacing his voice increases my forward momentum.

"No time for talk—" Our lips crash together, the reason he's here forgotten. Wil's lips linger softly on mine, and I drink in the seconds. The temptation to press into him wins and his eager mouth comes alive. Heat spreads from my face down my neck and ignites the fire that burns other emotions. My ears fill with the music of our contact. This time it's strings: violins, cellos, ukuleles, and guitars. Every string vibrates to our unique tune—the sound of Wil and El.

I dig my fingers into his neck; his sink into my hip. Each of us is trying to get the most we can from the little time we have. My lungs scream for air, but I ignore the pain—the pleasure of Wil's embrace the only lifeforce I need. My back hits the wall of whatever room we're in, and I'm grateful because the lines of Wil meet my curves. His groan reverberates in his chest and mine.

He breaks the kiss, and I object. Too soon. I need more. I stretch toward his lips again but they're just out of reach as he cups my jaw. "I love the paparazzi right now," Wil mumbles. I try for his lips again, because I don't want to talk about this, but he evades my attempt. "Maybe if we told them about us, it would kill the rumors about you and Beau."

The music screeches to a halt. Images of the press hunting Wil down, finding out he's Rocker's son, hounding him, mocking him, all because of me, kaleidoscope through my brain and give me an instant migraine. I step out of Wil's arms and gulp the cool, slightly damp air of the basement. We're in some kind of storage room, with metal shelving laden with boxes and bottles. "That's not a good idea."

"I know you're . . . concerned. But it'll clear the air." He stands before me, his finger hooked under my chin, asking me to look at him. "If you have a boyfriend, the press will move on."

My blood heats for a different reason. "You don't get it. They will never stop." I slam my palm against the wall. "Nothing will ever be enough."

I hear the hiss of the air-conditioning in the chilly silence. A vein beats in Wil's temple. "What's that supposed to mean?" he snaps. How did we go from kissing to fighting? Wil narrows his eyes. "Do you plan to keep us a secret forever?"

I shake my head.

"How long then?"

"As long as I can protect you" is what I want to say. Like he protected my secret those months as we busked in the Farmers' Market because the anonymity was what I needed. Except Wil doesn't understand that this is what he needs. What's good for him.

"A few more weeks. After the tour's done, I'll come home, you finish your semester and complete your deal with Rocker. Then. We'll decide on a time then." If Blatantly Subtle renews my contract. If I haven't screwed things up with Carlee. If I can find a way to protect Wil from the slanderous barbs the press will poke at him when they find out he's my boyfriend. Or us when they find out he's my stepbrother.

"Please, Wil." I tug on the sleeve of his shirt. The material is soft and patterned, not something Wil used to wear before Zoe took over his closet. "Give us a little more time before they ruin everything."

"There's nothing the paparazzi can do to us." He inches closer, his eyes liquid honey. "You're the melody to my words. We belong together." His knuckles caress my cheek. "I'll always worry about you." I open my mouth to protest, tell him I can take care of myself, but he presses a featherlight kiss against my lips. "Like a boyfriend gets to." He hums and pulls me closer.

My heart sputters, and I want to stay here all day.

TWENTY-TWO

Wil

I PUSH THE WEIGHT with my legs and lock it. "Final rep."

Sven scowls. "You're still struggling with form. But no more wobbling. Maybe it's possible to make your legs not look like twigs after all."

"Zoe threatened me with bodily harm if I gain more muscle. She's set on using me as her human hanger." Parading about in Zoe's outfits during her fashion show was not what I had in mind when El asked me to help. Music I can do. Modeling? Not happening.

"Well, it's your body." Sven holds out his hand to help me up. "If you want to gain more muscle, you know where to find me. My office building has a great gym. It's a fifteen-minute walk from campus."

I stretch. "I'm dedicated, but getting to campus by 5 a.m. is not an option."

"We can do lunch hours, weekends." Sven's insistence fills my heart. I don't want our sessions to end either.

"I think you like having a workout buddy," I say. Sven snorts and I grab a towel from the stack. "Good thing for you that DNA test came back positive."

Sven's brow wrinkles. "Sorry?"

"The DNA test you made me take outside Rocker Inc. that day." The soft material of the towel twists in my fingers. "The one you used to convince Rocker I was his son."

"No."

"It didn't come back positive?"

"No. Rocker never saw the test." Sven crosses his arms and lifts his chin. "Ran it myself. To see if I could trust you. Why do you think I let you leave with El?"

But . . . Rocker didn't know before he came to Bremen? That night, the insistence on me coming to live with him, get to know me—why would he do that without solid proof I was his son? It wasn't a thought-out plan based on a biological responsibility, just a whim? Something he decided in the moment? He believed my mum—believed *me*—not because he had to. He chose to.

I had it wrong. Do I have *him* wrong? All these weeks we've lived and worked together in LA, his attempts at getting close to me, were steady and clear. Maybe there's less sense of obligation in his feelings for me and more genuine want. The rusted door of possibilities of having a father who loves me cracks open. Maybe this is more than a quid pro quo. Maybe . . .

I catch Sven's gaze and ask, "Rocker didn't know about the test at all?"

He shakes his head. "It was for my eyes only. Too bad the test didn't indicate what a pain in the ass you are."

The complaint doesn't jab as hard now. I sort of get what El sees in him. And in Rocker. She's always loyal to the right people, good people, people worthy of being her friends. I throw the towel over my shoulder. She asked me to give Rocker a chance and I didn't pay attention. *I'm paying attention now, El.*

"I won't miss your sense of humor," I say.

Sven scowls and I try not to laugh. El's voice sings from my phone, and I hit answer.

Her face pops up. The dark circles under her eyes are more prominent and the spark in them is harder to see every day. "I have your surprise." I tip sideways and Sven pops into the frame.

"Sven?" Her smile eases the ache in my chest. "You're still there?"

"My last day is today." Sven angles the phone to get his big head into the frame. "Couldn't leave without saying bye."

"Not bye, see you later. You're not going to the other side of the world. I can walk to your office from Rocker Inc. The moment the tour is over, I'm flying to LA to see your new place, a bag of butter tarts in hand." Sven squirms, like me finding out he's addicted to sweets is a state secret. "I bought doughnuts yesterday to share with the band," says El. "Annalyn stared at me like I offered her drugs. Carbs is on the banned list, and the food we end up eating is so healthy but also so bland I sometimes feel I've lost the taste for food as well as music."

"That bad?" I thought she felt smaller in my arms at the hospital, now I'm certain. "Can't you cook?"

"The last time I saw a proper kitchen was at Carlee's house in Atlanta and her live-in chef got upset when I unwrapped his knives." She rubs her eyebrow. "Even if there were one, most of the time I don't have the energy to cook. Between travel and performances, everyone is exhausted. Sugar and coffee seem to the only two things keeping me going. I've had dreams about butter tarts."

"Butter tarts are always welcome at Anders Investigations." Sven smiles at the screen. "And we can trade. You bring butter tarts and I splurge on your caramel cappuccino from Blend."

"It's a deal." El scratches her temple. "You'll be safe, right? Won't do anything I wouldn't do?"

Sven cocks his head. "Like pay off a thug to get someone out of jail?"

El chuckles even though her eyes don't get brighter. I want to hug Sven for kidding with El like this, for bringing light into her intense days. I'm glad he was around to watch out for her before I was.

"If you have to help a friend, you'll always have my permission," says Sven.

As we walk to the kitchen to refill our waters, Sven takes over my phone and the conversation, updating El on the office furniture he picked up from Asher Menken's latest movie set. The man has three sentences to say to me all morning and now I can't shut these two up.

I run my finger around the bottom rim of our bottle, where the W&E El wrote is fading. Maybe I shouldn't use it so much, keep it for special occasions. I stash the treasured item on the topmost shelf and grab a generic one. Fill it up and refill Sven's as well. I never wanted him to be my bodyguard, but Sven leaving is like losing the only ally I have in the mansion. Apart from Pickle. But Pickle is more like my personal kryptonite.

Sven hangs up on El. "Gotta go say goodbye to the boss."

"You're the boss now." I grin at him. "Sven." I push off the counter. "Don't be a stranger." I use El's words because they ring true. "You know we're friends. Ditto to what El said. If you need something I can help you with—just ask."

In a house full of people, the one person I want is not here. I crave El. My fingers need something of El's to touch, something I can keep with me, something that smells like her. I wander to the opposite side of the house, far from the ocean. The silence in El's bedroom wraps around me like a cold mist. Photographs of my girlfriend with her papa, Rocker and Sylvia, Zoe, and people whose faces I don't recognize dot the wall in front of me, minus the empty hook of the one we smashed the night she kissed me for the first time.

Heat prickles across my skin. The end of the tour can't come soon enough. Quality time together trumps the incessant texting and calling we're surviving on now.

The Starlight trophy with "Best Song" etched into the plaque on the base reminds me El can win anything she puts her mind to. Another few weeks and this forced separation will be over. Writing songs, sitting in the same room, regaining the ability to touch her, feel her skin and the beating of her heart under my ear as I lay my head on her chest.

"What are you doing in here?" I jump at Sylvia's question.

I pick up the trophy. "Looking for this."

Sylvia plucks the statue out of my hand and inspects it. "Where did she get this?"

I want to scream at the woman. How can she not support the genes she herself passed on? The videos I watched of Sylvia Vella in her youth, at La Fenice Opera House in Italy with Matthew Vella, showed a powerhouse who captivated audiences. Just like her daughter.

I've never doubted my mother's love for me. It's always been there like the air I breathe. She's only ever wanted what's best and put my needs before hers more times than I've ever understood. One of the debts I can never repay. "She won it. For the song we wrote together, and she performed. It's in our friend's movie, *Indigo*."

"Never heard of it."

"Yeah, figures." I bite back my resentment. Will she be like this with Pickle if he decides he wants to sing?

Her face crumbles and I regret the harshness of my words.

"I had my reasons you know. I only wanted to protect her," she says.

"After what happened to El and your husband, I'm not surprised."

Her stare makes the hair on the back of my neck rise. "What do you know about . . ." Her voice is barely above a whisper.

"The accident? El told me everything."

She sinks onto the edge of the bed. "Everything?"

"Yeah. After the incident at Zoe's birthday. With the pool. She—" My chest hurts at the thought of what El went through on Lake Como when she was ten, and on the day of the party. "She was upset."

Sylvia lifts her head. "I remember. We met that day." She holds my stare. "I suspected you were Rocker's son the moment I saw you."

She actually called me by his name, but I'm not about to bring that up.

"My daughter has always had to pay the price for my fame. For our fame." I'm not sure if Sylvia is talking to me or to herself. "After Matthew's death it got much worse. The press was ravenous for the details. Hounding a ten-year-old for the story she couldn't even tell me. We couldn't step outside without questions being flung at us." Sylvia shudders.

Her overprotection might be misguided, but I see how much she loves El. I get the feeling.

Sylvia's fingers turn white where she's gripping the base of El's trophy. "I want to shield her from everything. The accident. The nightmares." She hugs the piece of gilded plastic to her chest, but it's not her daughter, and Sylvia telling me her side of the story is not going to solve the disagreement she and El have. Sylvia's eyes plead with me, as if there's a chance I'd be on her side. "I did what I could. I kept her close. Under my protection. Overnight I had to be mother and father. Make life decisions by myself. I was Melodie's only parent, her only caretaker."

Her gaze glides over my shoulders. "Like Hanna was for you, I guess."

Mum is nothing like Sylvia.

Yet that's a lie. If Mum would've told me about Rocker earlier, what would that have changed in my life? If Sylvia gave El room to grow into an adult and spread her wings, we wouldn't have met at The Devil's Martini. The thought clings to my chest like plastic wrap, constricting my breathing. "I wish Mum would've told me about Rocker earlier. Even if that hurt more."

Sylvia shakes her head. "Mothers only want to look out for their children, safeguard them from anything that hurts." She brushes moisture from her eye. "If I could, I would've switched places with Melodie, been the one on that boat when it crashed. Your mother was protecting you too. That's why she never told you about Bill."

The plastic wrap around my body suffocates me. Mum and I haven't had a chance to discuss why she hid the truth from me. Though that isn't exactly true. She did try to explain, but the raging fire in my chest refused to accept Mum's attempts.

Sylvia offers the trophy to me. "We don't blame Hanna." A rocket goes off in my head. Rocker and Sylvia talk about my mum? My fingers curl into a fist. "She did the best she could for you given the facts. But Wil . . . It's not Bill's fault either."

She stands and moves toward me, but when I back up to keep my distance, she hesitates. "He's hurt too. My husband has wanted a family, to be a father, since the day I met him. Before that. Those charities and Music and Munchkins children"—she points to the photos on the wall behind me—"they represent what he wanted most in life. A family. We tried for years to conceive with no luck. I felt like a failure because I couldn't give my husband the one thing he never asked of me, but desperately wanted—a child."

"But you did. He loves Pickle."

The corners of her mouth tip up. "He does. He's an amazing father to our child." Her lips flatten. "But he wants to be a father to both his sons." Her words ring in my ears. Not news, but it's the first time she called me her husband's son to my face. I remember the look in Rocker's eyes in Mum's living room when he first learned about me. He didn't have proof I was his son but chose a relationship with me anyhow. Because he wanted a family. Even with Pickle about to be born, he accepted me as his son without question.

Sylvia places her hand on the base of her throat. "I'm not asking you to play catch in the backyard, but you're leaving in a little over a month, and he's scared you'll walk away and he'll never see you again. Maybe open your heart to the possibility of letting him be part of your life." Her fingers flutter like she wants to reach out. "Give him the chance he was robbed of by fate. Can you do that, Wil?"

My brain screams no. Rocker doesn't get to send his wife after me to argue for him. He abandoned Mum. It's his fault she's sick. If she didn't work day-and-night to raise me, her health wouldn't have suffered. He's not a good guy. Yet those phrases I repeated every day since Opa told me the truth don't hold the same weight anymore.

El's voice rings in my head. *Give him a chance.*

Sylvia sighs. "Just think about it, Wil." She sweeps her hand around the room. "He does what he can for those he loves. And he loves you. Unconditionally. If you ever decide you want to come back to LA, you have a home here. With us. No matter what."

The image of Sylvia walking out of El's room blurs and the ball of fire in my chest burns the plastic that was suffocating me. I choke on the toxic fumes of letting go of my anger at Rocker. It's stupid but I pick up El's pillow and bury my face in it, wishing it was her. The material is cool, but there's the faintest whiff of the scent of my girlfriend and I inhale it like fresh air after running out of a house on fire.

Twenty-Three

THE STAGE IS NEW, but the act is the same. The movements I perform behind Carlee follow a similar pattern. The notes I hit are identical to the ones I've been singing week after week, day after day. I might not know what it's like to operate an assembly line, but the life of a backup singer is far from the glory and excitement I imagined. Carlee, Kamo, and Beau get to mix it up for each city, altering the lyrics to fit with the locals, making improvised references to the places, the chitchat between songs, while I stand mute out of the spotlight.

The shows are high velocity, high volume. Costume changes, guitar licks, attitude every minute, all designed to drive the audience to cheer, chant, demand more. For the public we paint on our bright and cheerful faces, but behind the scenes the long nights and short days are taking a toll.

Carlee doesn't meet us for sound checks anymore. Annalyn, Josie, or I stand in for her. Instead she takes a nap during the pre-concert hours every day. I wish I could force my body to take a catnap. I just scroll through gossip sites, manically searching for mentions of my name. The buzz over the photo of Beau and me is replaced by images of Dad's smiling face at the hospital, me almost out of frame. Articles applaud his generous nature, including a dig now and again about how he arranged my chance with Blatantly Subtle.

My fingers itch to call Daniel Davison and arrange an interview, set the record straight. But I know it would be pointless. He'd find a way to twist the truth. The tabloids only hear what they want to hear. What they can sell.

I harmonize with the chorus on the second to last song in the set before intermission and breathe while the crowd whistles, shouts, and shows they are ready for the next song. *Light It Up* has been everyone's favorite for a reason. The lyrics punctuate the yearning in the melody, and anyone can sing it, in the shower, at a karaoke, while driving your car. Unlike our national anthem, this is the kind of a song that stays in your head as an earworm, and you don't sound like a rooster attempting to perform it.

Carlee takes her position by the stationary mic in the middle of the stage and moves her head side to side. Her hands shake on the metal rod, not really in rhythm, but she seems to be vibing with the songs today more than usual. As Kamo adds her drums to the mix I join Carlee centerstage and hum to get the crowd ready for her voice to start the first line. We get to the beat where she should join but she doesn't. I flash back to Wil and me on the stage of The Devil's Martini for the first time, me forgetting the words, and him restarting the verse.

The first rule is to make it look like this is part of the plan. The audience doesn't know what arrangement we use. Blunders happen. Beau and the band are pros and they do just what Wil did for me. They circle around to the beginning, and I break my choreo like I did in the first performances where I messed up my right and left and no one watching knew better. I look at Carlee and realize she's not shaking, she's trembling. Her gaze catches mine in a plea I don't understand.

When the moment to start her line comes again, I make the leap and pull a Wil. I sing the verse and the relief on Carlee's face in unmistakable, although my concern for her only grows. Something is wrong. She sways, like I did when I had too many beers with Wil in Bremen. Carlee is way too professional to get drunk before the show. That can't be the reason. I don't know what's happening, but I can't help her by pressing my forehead to hers.

Instead I wrap my arm around her waist. She slumps against me. My grip tightens as I take on her weight, and we move side to side as if this is part of the act. Her smile comes in and out. I try to make it a game, so those who watch us think she's encouraging me, not struggling.

Josie appears on Carlee's other side. She slides her arm around Carlee, and we form a harness to hold our lead in place. The show must go on, so we move and sing and pretend. The many days I sang this song with Wil free my brain to think ahead and plan an exit strategy. Even together Josie and I won't be able to walk Carlee offstage. Annalyn rushes next to me, her fingers scrape against my skin like a scared cat's as I move her into the position I was and pass the melody to her. She gets the strategy and takes over.

The attention is on Josie, Carlee, and Annalyn now. I find my way to Beau, turn my mic off, and whisper in his ear, smiling the entire time, as if we are discussing something fun. "She needs help getting off stage."

To Beau's credit, he keeps playing and only I detect the tightening of his jaw. His fingers fly over the strings of the guitar, wrapping up the bridge, and in a fluid motion, like this was meant to be, he lifts his guitar up and gives it to me. I know some of the song but I'm an average guitar player at best. Yet, I accept the weight of the instrument and think of Wil's arms around me, teaching me the chords of this song in his living room in Bremen. I strum what I know, hoping the rest of the band will fill in the sound.

Beau struts across the stage, amping up the audience as he progresses to where Carlee stands in the spotlight. He puts his hands over Josie's and Annalyn's shoulders and sings the final part of the song with them. They riff on the last note and the audience is back to screams and whistles. Beau kisses Carlee on the cheek, bends, and throws her over his shoulder. He twirls to the audience, smacks Carlee on the butt, winks, and strolls off stage.

The lights cut out and I don't know where to put Beau's guitar down in the dark, so I slink offstage with it still slung over my shoulder. I catch a glimpse of Kamo's black-and-gray camouflage bomber jacket ducking into the greenroom and dive after her.

"What the hell?" Kamo's hands are waving in the air. "We didn't practice that. You can't just go off half-cocked and—"

Beau's glare stops Kamo mid-sentence. His hand is clutching Carlee's as she slumps against the cushions of the maroon leather couch we laughed on before the show this evening. Kamo falls to her knees, squeezing Carlee's arm.

"Is she alright?" Annalyn whispers and clutches Josie's torso.

I run for the dressing table where Carlee's phone sits. "I'll call 911," I offer, hoping someone has already done it.

"Don't," Beau shouts like I'm about to take a photo. I drop the phone and stare, my feet wanting to flee. I shouldn't be here. Something's not right and it's not my place to witness this. Beau squares his shoulders, passes Carlee's limp hand to Kamo, and stands. "We don't need an ambulance. I called Dr. Kim."

"Is she sick?" Josie bites the side of her thumbnail. "Was it something she ate?"

Beau's fists clench at his side, the move so familiar. Wil does this when he's frustrated. "No. We didn't want to tell you like this."

We? Beau's in on it, whatever the "it" is?

"Is she going to be alright?" My voice cracks.

"Shut the door," Beau barks, his usually soft tone forgotten.

Annalyn complies. We stare at Beau. "Remember you signed NDAs. None of this leaks to the press or the public or you'll hear from our lawyers."

Beau glances at Carlee, who's clearly having trouble concentrating. Her nod unseals his lips. "Carlee's been diagnosed with MS. She's having a relapse."

"What?" Josie and Annalyn gasp.

My hand hits the solid metal of Carlee's dressing table, knocking over a tube of lipstick. Multiple sclerosis. Mom performed in a benefit concert for the MS Society of America the year we moved to LA. Visions of people with canes and wheelchairs overlay Carlee's sitting figure. I shake my head in disbelief. Even though I know the disease often strikes mostly women in their midtwenties, she's too young to be sick.

"Again?" Kamo brushes a strand of pink hair off Carlee's face. "I told you we needed a shorter, easier tour."

Carlee doesn't move.

"What can we do?" I address Carlee even though I'm not sure she can reply.

"I'll be fine." Her voice is weak, and I want to believe her but my gut churns at the ramifications of Carlee unable to perform. To stand even.

A knock on the door sends Kamo and Beau into silent conversation.

"Who is it?" Kamo asks.

A low voice responds, "Dr. Kim."

Beau crosses the room and cracks open the door.

The tall stooping man with graying hair and a large bag in his hand enters the room that already feels too crowded. He surveys our faces and frowns. "Can I please have everyone out?" His firm quiet voice belies his frail appearance.

"Are we canceling the rest of the show?" Josie asks the question that has been burning in my mind.

"No," says Carlee.

"Yes," say Dr. Kim and Beau.

The doctor pushes up his sleeves. "Even after I start you on the intravenous Solu-Medrol, it'll be three to five days before you can perform. Although I'd advise you to take a longer break."

"Just follow plan C." Carlee falls back on the couch.

My brain scrambles, trying to remember what plan C is. Kamo and Beau shake their heads.

"You promised me." Carlee ignores the doctor who's taking her pulse. "Go out there. Play. Have the girls sing. I'll be fine."

Beau ushers us out, closing the door. He jerks his head to the left. "My room."

The hallway vibrates with the chants of the crowd as we silently follow. His door clicks shut, Kamo standing in front of it, arms crossed like a sentinel, as Beau digs into the back of his guitar case. I shift his guitar on my hip and take one of the papers he distributes amongst Annalyn, Josie, and me.

Carlee was not kidding. At the top of the page in bold letters is "Plan C." But the numbers and indentations and paragraphs on the paper do their regular dance, refusing to reveal their secrets. "We made a plan if she couldn't perform. Josie you sing *Fire* and *Stupefy Me* using the center microphone. Annalyn you take over the piano with *Making the Truth Hurt* and *Never Forgive Again*. El, you and I handle the duets, and the final song."

My rendition of *Give Us a Chance* must have not offended Carlee so much if she designated me as the lead vocalist on it in case of emergency.

"Stick to the plan. Let me handle the crowd, take the heat. Ignore any booing." Beau takes a bottle of water out of the mini fridge, unscrews the lid, and gulps it down in one smooth motion. He wipes his mouth with the back of his hand. "No matter what Carlee thinks, Dr. Kim is right. She will take a break." He walks to me and takes his guitar back. "Everyone just got three free days. Use them well."

TWENTY-FOUR

MY COUSIN FLOATS TOWARD me in the ocean of people, tents, flashes, and fashion like a fish designed solely for these waters. "You made the flight." She takes both of my arms and twirls me. "And mustard looks perfect on you. Did you change here or at the airport? I told Mom to not let you step foot into the event until you put on something decent."

"As in something from your collection?" I ask.

"That's what the invite says. Attendees must wear something styled by me. Did you see the merch shop Mateo set up at the entrance? Now everyone can buy a Zoe Yilmaz original. And the proceeds will go to supporting Wil's new RA charity. Mateo is a genius."

How much of a cut is Mateo getting from his brilliant idea? Zoe looks so happy, I don't want to spoil anything. My ear still hurts from her scream of joy at the news the tour is on hiatus and I could make her fashion show. "Where's Wil?"

"He's around here somewhere." Zoe spreads her arms. "So, what do you think?"

Aunt Patti's backyard is a sea of striped tents where a menagerie of artists entertain the guests Zoe invited to her Fashion Event. No boring runways. Zoe, being true to herself, has cameras streaming the event, backdrops for photos ops, and tags for social media. The more you tag her, the more chances you get to win an exclusive fitting and a day of Zoe dressing you.

Zoe is her own boss, a leader, not a follower. I won't be surprised if she sets a new trend in runway design. Her support of up-and-coming and established creators over the years paid off when they pitched in for this event. The sound that's pumping around us, both distinct and part of the ambiance, proves Wil was a better choice to set the music programming. He took the melodies I came up with and amplified them with a new arrangement.

Zoe stretches on her tiptoes. Her hand beats against my arm. "El, you need to see this." She points to the edge of the pool. I follow her gaze to a stoic Sven, one of Zoe's "Get lucky?" T-shirts stretched to capacity across his chest.

My hand goes to my mouth as we both giggle. "Did you invite him?"

"No. Or I would have made something extra, extra, extra large for him to wear." Zoe jumps in place. "This means Felicity Thomas is here!"

We both scan the party for the famous movie star, a.k.a. Sven's one and only client. Asher Menken worked with her on *Two Trains to Paris,* his latest movie, and suggested she hire my ex-bodyguard. Not sure what for, but apparently it requires him to be at fashion shows.

"Maybe she's in the restroom?" I offer when we come up empty.

"Yeah." Zoe's face deflates. She resumes scanning the crowd and her eyes narrow. "Oh no he didn't." She storms past me. I turn to find her undoing a button on Wil's shirt. "Stop changing the style. It's supposed to be worn open."

"I look like I should be on the cover of a romance novel. No one seriously wears a shirt with three open buttons." Wil rolls his shoulders but the grin on his face that Zoe misses because she's adjusting his belt belies his grumblings. He's teasing my cousin. Well, these two have certainly become friendly in my absence.

"Tell Sven to go easy on you. Gain any more muscle in the next week and I won't have time to alter the pattern for the tux I've designed for your RA Connect Foundation Gala." She jerks Wil's pants down lower on his hips and a pang of what I do not want to call jealousy jolts through me. For months, the closest I could get to Wil was holding his hand, and now my cousin is adjusting things left, right, and center.

"There," Zoe tuts. "Now you are perfect." Wil could wear ripped overalls and I would still find him attractive. But I admit, with the way the shirt molds against his chest and the slacks hug his muscular legs, both in my favorite shades of blue, I'm not complaining.

"Hell yes I am." Wil's gaze flashes my way and heat floods my cheeks. I take a sip from my glass in an attempt to cool down.

Zoe slaps him on the shoulder. "Don't be so cocky."

Sparkling water almost comes out of my nose. Wil the Cocky German was the name that littered my phone with texts when we first met. But now I know what's underneath the attitude Wil shows to the world. Soon I hope to finally find out what's under that shirt beyond the glimpse I had the day after the Starlight Gala.

Wil must be reading my mind because he ignores Zoe and shortens the gap between us. "Fancy meeting you here." His soft lips twitch. "I shouldn't be happy because . . . you know . . . but I still am happy you're here."

"Me too." I take a step closer. Not close enough. Too aware of cameras everywhere. Why couldn't Zoe have her show in a warehouse with dark corners I could . . . well, corner Wil in? "It's only a few days. I have to be back by Monday night." Did he look this good in Vegas? I forgive Zoe for adjusting his shirt. It gives me more skin to admire.

"Mum says hi by the way. Her last day of treatment was yesterday. She told me to give you a hug and a kiss from her." Wil erases the distance, and our chests touch while his lips brush my temple. The caress, so innocent and brief to any outsider who's paying attention, is the kindling I did not need for the brushfire under my skin. My fingers curl around the stem of my glass. "She misses you too," he says, and I hear *I missed you so damn much.*

"Tell her I miss her as well. And her stollen." My eyes tell him *I missed you more. So much more.*

"Mrs. Yilmaz delivered you here safely."

Zoe inserts herself between us. "Don't ever call Mom that in front of her, she'll go and schedule another relaxation and rejuvenation retreat. Last time a friend of mine called her Mrs., she spent a week grilling me on how old they thought she was and why I don't pretend she was a teen mom."

I push my cousin aside. "Yes, I'm safe, thanks for asking." I fake-glare at Zoe. "Aunt Patti kept trying to persuade me to visit Mom, Pickle, and Rocker, because they are family, and family sticks together. Apparently, no argument is big enough to ever not be part of the gang." I stuff down the part of me that wants to visit my old room that's only a few miles away, meet Pickle, talk to Mom. But not yet. I need to prove myself first so I can show her that I was right, that I know my path. Music is my life whether they approve or not. "Patti asked me if I'm coming to Norway in summer."

"That's my mom." Zoe rolls her eyes.

"I didn't want to crush her hopes, but *mine* are to be on tour in Australia in summer with Blatantly Subtle." I smile at Wil, and the mouth I've been dreaming of curves in the smile that made me wish for hot kiss-worthy fun the day I met him. That El had no idea how kiss-worthy Wil's lips are. How addictive. How much space the thoughts of them would take up in my head. I don't make my way to Wil because if I do get close enough, I might tear her beautiful outfit off him. Or burn it as I internally combust.

"But your deal with Subtle doesn't stop El Vella from singing, right?" Zoe adjusts the three-quarter sleeve of my dress by folding the cuffs up around my elbows.

"As long as I'm not paid."

"Perfect."

My fingers tingle at the gleam in Zoe's eyes. I know that look. It usually leads to trouble. "Why?"

"Well, you know what would make my event the talk of the town?" Zoe takes my hand. "My cousin Melodie Rockerby, or, as her true fans know her, El Vella, performing her viral hit *Don't Give Me Comfort*." I try to pull my hand from her grip, but she holds on like I'm her lifeline. "Pretty please."

I glance at Wil, and he lifts his hands. "I had nothing to do with this."

"Of course not. I don't need my cousin's boyfriend's permission to ask her for help." Zoe puts her hands on her hip. "Do I?"

"No, but—"

"Perfect. You'll do it." It's a statement, not a question.

I take another sip of water, searching for an excuse. "I don't have my music."

"Luckily we have the man who produced your hit here." Zoe puts her arm around Wil. "Surely, he has the track on his phone. I mean, it's not like he listens to it obsessively or anything."

"You do?" I bite my lip and tip toward him.

"Stop it you two." She lowers her voice. "You can't stand here in the open," she ducks her head, "and make googly eyes at each other."

"We're not—" Wil and I squeak at the same time.

Zoe clears her throat. "Anyhow. Your boyfriend who you are not mentally undressing can set Mateo up with your tracks—"

"Tracks?" Wil and I are in sync today.

"Well, yes. The crowd will want an encore. Sing *Our Lines*. It'll put everyone in a good mood." Zoe holds up her hands. "Of course it's up to you."

"Oh, of course." I glance at Wil.

He shrugs. "It *is* up to you."

"Fine. I'll sing."

My cousin makes a sound like a balloon losing air. "Yay. And Wil can join you on stage. Your old guitar happens to be in the pool house." My jaw drops at my cousin's audacity. She was born ten months before me, and she's been ten steps ahead of me all my life.

"You planned this."

Zoe clasps her hands to her chest. "Not possible. I didn't know you were coming." She winks. "But I stocked the pool house with El-approved goodies in case you made it back to LA to visit me." I open my mouth to protest and she shakes her head. "You can thank me later. Meanwhile, Wil"—she shoulders him—"mingle. Show off my designs."

"How much longer do I have to wear this?" Wil's eyes meet mine and the heat in them is hotter than the afternoon sun. My stomach flips and I try to ease the ever-present pressure that builds whenever I think about him.

Zoe checks her phone. "Fifteen more minutes and then meet me in my bedroom."

"Bedroom?" The word erupts from my mouth.

"For his last outfit change." Zoe juts out her hip. "Get your mind out of the gutter."

Wil takes a step in my direction but Zoe grabs him by the shoulders. "Nope. Not happening." She spins him around. "You two have the whole weekend for that. But not until I'm finished with you. Go strut your stuff."

The glowing amber in Wil's gaze blazes. I love my cousin and want her first fashion show to be a success, but I can't wait for this event to be over.

Zoe pushes him toward a crowd of older woman in matching white outfits who gobble him up like he's the first tray of appetizers at a charity event. Her face blocks my view.

"Listen." She glances at the group of women, one of whom strokes the fabric of Wil's shirt. At least I hope she's just testing out the material. "I get what you see in him." I dig my nails into my palms to distract from the returning sharp pain I refuse to call jealousy. "I admit, he's grown on me. Not as much of a jerk as I thought when he stole you away from me without a word."

"I—"

Zoe holds up her palms. "I forgive you. And him." She loops her arm over my shoulders and aims us toward another tent. "You have my permission to like him almost as much as you adore me. Just remember, when I call, you always answer."

"You got it."

"He talks about you all the time." Zoe drags out the "all." "El this and El that. Like I don't know anything about you. Do you know he tried to get butter tarts delivered to you in San Francisco after the Beau thing?"

"He did?" My eyes water. The tenderness swells like Puccini's *O mio babbino caro* Mom sings when she's happy.

Zoe lays her head on my shoulder. "I think your boyfriend might be a romantic." This time my jolt has nothing to do with jealousy. "I've been looking everywhere for someone like him, and you found him."

"I wasn't looking." My heart heard his heart and the two conspired against us, because I was not ready to feel this strongly about anything but my music. But is anyone ever ready?

Twenty-Five

THE LATE AFTERNOON SUN retains some of its heat, but the evening breeze has picked up and the fashion show has morphed into the afterparty. Wil and I stand backstage, like we did so many nights at The Devil's Martini, waiting for our turn to sing. Unlike then, Wil's fingers are wrapped around mine and I feel the current of electricity flowing between us, not just sense it. This is where we work. Every time we walk onto a stage, it's magic.

"Is it odd that I'm excited?" His knuckles nudge my chin.

I meet his gaze. "Then I'm odd too."

His lips twitch. "Can't be, you do this every night. It's been a while for me."

I reach up on my tiptoes and trace the bridge of his nose. "I don't do this with you. And that's my favorite part."

His grin breaks free and my heart accelerates like a speeding car. Wil bends closer. "Maybe we should find some Farmers' Markets to busk at in every city. Make it our thing."

"Now there's an idea." My hand glides over his shoulder, along the collar of his shirt to the buttons I long to undo.

"Ahem." Zoe taps the toe of her transparent high-heeled shoe. "I'm right here."

Wil's cheeks turn pink. Is my boyfriend blushing? The image fills me with a giddy glee like I'm on the teacups at Disneyland. Mateo interrupts the playlist. Zoe straightens her shoulders and steps on stage.

She does her classic double-air-kiss move. "Everyone looks fabulous, if I may say so myself." Her hand flies to her chest in mock humility. "I have one more surprise for you. Put your hands together for El Vella."

Cheers. There're actual cheers. I can't blame the wind for the goosebumps that fly across my skin. I let go of Wil's hand, wave to the crowd, and take the microphone from Zoe as the opening chords of *Don't Give Me Comfort* boom out of the speakers. "Hello, Calabasas."

The guests roar.

I launch into the song Wil helped me create. My melodies and his insight unlocking emotions I couldn't put into words. He joins me onstage, the chords that once lived only in my heart played by the man who now owns the organ.

And it happens.

The spell begins to weave.

Wil and El become WE again.

I'm home.

The lyrics pour out and at last I'm one with the music. My music. After weeks of performing on other people's terms, their music, their chorography, the stage is mine to do with what I like. With whom I like. Too soon I run out of lyrics and I close my eyes, holding the final note as long as I can.

Applause rolls toward me like thunder, bathing me in adoration. I've only ever wanted to have my melodies out there in the world. To be heard. But this, the reflection of what my music means to people, how it affects them, is a high I cannot deny. I scan the audience and soak it in.

"Sing *Our Lines*," someone shouts.

I follow the sound and spot a tall man waving at me like I'm his long-lost friend. I smile and shoot a glance at Mateo. The passionate notes pulse across the stage and my toe taps of its own accord. I clap my hands over my head and the crowd joins in. I'm high on their adoration.

The music flows around me, through me, and out over the audience. Socialites and movie stars sing our words, fill me with their love, but I focus mine on Wil, singing to him. It's Wil I see.

Only Wil.

His gaze trails across my face to my lips, his stare heavy with awe, or lust? Even from this distance the connection is electric like the first time we sang together, his forehead to mine. That move sparked the love inside me that took on a life of its own. Cementing into something tangible, real, unbreakable, capable of withstanding miles apart and separate lives.

There's not much I'm sure of in my life. Except Wil.

His fingers stop strumming, the backbeat fades, and my lungs can't suck in enough air. I'm out of breath but not from singing. I'm breathless at the sight of Wil. I thank the fans, shove the microphone in Zoe's hand, and leave my cousin high on promises and praise. I scramble down the stairs.

Right behind me Wil breathes into my ear. "You're amazing."

Trusting only my fingers to touch his, I take Wil by the hand. Anything more and I'll devour him. Together, we move away from the maddening crowd of models and guests.

"Where are we going?" asks Wil.

I tug him around tent poles and dash between open spaces, hiding our escape. Beyond the furthest tent, the pool house beckons. We sprint across the grass and burst through the front. The music of the party fades as I close the door by pushing Wil against it. He opens his mouth to let out words I know I'll love but right now I want to kiss him more.

My lips do the talking for me, crashing into his. Instead of satisfying my need to touch him, the kiss turns my internal temperature to roasting. A thousand thoughts cram into my mind, competing for space, and the thrumming in my ears drowns the muffled music from the party. Why is Wil still wearing his shirt?

Wil's fingers sink into my hair and he's pushing my head back, removing his delicious lips from my greedy ones. Disappointment drives through me at the speed of the train I took from Milan to Rome the last time I was in Italy. My body tenses. Did I misread this? Does he not want me?

"Hey." His forehead presses against mine. Bursts of hot air fan against my cheek. I need his mouth back on mine. "This isn't a race." He runs his hands up and down my arms. "Give me a minute."

I pry my fingers from his rust-colored shirt Zoe stitched his initials into the collar and cuffs of and force my heart to stay in my chest. He's right. This isn't the ten-minute make-out session in a dank and dark basement, or an hour of grinding against him at a club. We have all night. All weekend. "Right. Sorry."

"No apologies. I want this too." He lets out a frustrated growl. "You have no idea how much I want this."

A guffaw leaves my mouth. "Half as much as me."

"Not even close." He slides away from the door, and cool air coats my skin at the loss of this touch. His fingers entwine with mine.

One tug and I'm in his arms again. They lift me and I wrap my thighs around his waist. "Is this a competition? You know I'm good at winning those."

"I've got skills you haven't been exposed to." He sits my butt on the counter.

Zoe needs a thank you note for insisting I wear a dress and not pants. I press myself into him and pull him closer with my legs. "Not for lack of trying."

The hum that initiates in his chest and ignites mine only makes me repeat my motion. More. I need more. My fingers leave his skin in search of buttons. Must. Get. Shirt. Off. His palms on my back help us crash into each other like we're cymbals. We hit together and can't separate. His body move with mine, and we're using our lips as leverage.

"I'm not sure I can try any harder." There's a shake in his voice and his hand as I try to recapture his mouth. "Can we . . ."

His words are the trigger I needed. We must stop trying. We can actually act on our feelings. I get my feet back to the ground and take Wil where I want us to be. Where I'm ready to be with him.

Without turning on a light, I guide him through the darkening gloom of the pool house and into the single bedroom. My cousin decided I needed my own space while I was in LA. Oh, how I love her even more right now.

I pause before the king-size bed, my hands shaking. The desire to share myself with Wil is an impulse but also a longed-for dream that sets my chest aflutter and releases a flock of butterflies in my stomach.

Warm lips press against the curve of my neck, and my shoulders relax while wings flap under my ribcage. His hand settles on my hip, the move I adore, and I fuse with him, my back molding to his front. I shiver, not from hesitation, but from anticipation. The concept isn't new, but I feel new. Like before was playacting because I didn't know what truly wanting to be with someone felt like.

The craving to turn consumes me, yet I resist. As much as I want him, Wil's set on savoring every touch, and I want to give this to him.

"Every day I wake up imagining doing this." A gentle kiss below my ear fans the flames. "And this." His nail traces the neckline of my dress, like he did at the club.

"I tried to write down the memories of your touch, but they're ghosts on the page, nothing compared to the real you." He glides his hands along my hip. "I wish more words existed so I could reconstruct the way you feel."

My heartrate double-times as his finger reaches the spot between my thighs that's been thirsting for more. My moan surprises me. Maybe we should stop here, because his touch is the best thing I've ever experienced.

"Do you feel it too?" The timbre of Wil's voice has dropped half an octave. It echoes in my ear like a siren, and I'm putty in his hands.

"Wil." I want to tell him how amazing this is, but he gets there first.

"You're so amazing."

"So are . . ." my mind goes blank as his thumb finds my neck, ". . . you."

Greedy to let him roam over every inch of me, I arch and fumble for the zipper of my dress. The material catches, but nothing is stopping me, and I yank harder. In one motion the fabric falls away. His lips and hands cover me better than any cloth. I'm lost again, never wanting to be found. Electricity zips through me.

"Worth the wait." I'm not sure if his words are a question or a statement.

Wil whips the shirt over his head and I don't have time to look at my prize, adore the abs I've been dying to ogle again. I feel him against me.

I find his lips as we tumble on to the bed. At last, my dreams of his hands on my body are coming true. My hands make their own map of his body. Every ridge. Every dip. Rough peaks, taught muscles, and sun-kissed skin.

We're wrapped in each other. Our hearts and our bodies. His heart pounds against my chest as he hovers over me. My heart syncs to his as it's done since we first sang together. It's not just violins or cellos I hear now, it's the whole orchestra. Every instrument perfectly in tune.

If only I had the words, I'd write him a love song, an album of love songs. Instead, I attempt to show him, erasing any distance between us. It's not enough. Will never be enough. But I give him everything I have, like he didn't already have it.

"El," he rasps. The fireworks in his eyes are brighter than the finale on the Fourth of July.

We collapse as one. Not letting me go, he lies on his side and cradles me into him. "Is this reality?" Wil whispers into my neck.

"Our reality." I pull his arms tighter around me.

Our fingers intertwine and I melt into Wil. I thought music was the only thing that made me feel this way. The euphoria of chords and melodies mixing into something familiar and right, yet new and breathtaking. Music might be my first love, but Wil is my first everything else.

Twenty-Six

Wil

EVERY LOVE SONG I'VE ever heard pales compared to the light in my heart. My brain itches to write the words swirling in my head. All the words. Each inadequate. An attempt to capture the sensations. But I don't move, basking in being close to El like this. Her fingers pressing into my shoulder. Her soft skin against mine. Her flame-tinged hair tickling the back of my hand.

Her.

Words can wait. I want more of this. I'm never leaving this bed.

Why can't every morning be like this?

El's chin brushes against the pillow and my heart leaps, partly hoping she'll wake so we can talk or repeat some of last night, partly praying she won't and I can lie here and watch her. She sighs, the crease between her eyebrows smoothing away.

Her eyelashes have traces of mascara and her lips are parted, the lightest pink without the gloss she tends to wear. Nothing like in the movies where girls have a team of makeup artists. We aren't in a movie. She's 3D, alive and warm under my touch. Her every breath, the imperfection of her makeup on the pillow, the sheets that are somehow diagonal over her and the one foot she leaves uncovered even though she tugs the blanket up to her chin.

I drink in her form over and over again, finding new details with every pass. The line of her neck that peeks from one corner of the cover, the tiny curve to her lip as if whatever she's dreaming about brings her joy. Is it me? Because I've been dreaming about her for so many nights, I lost count.

The chase has always been the most fun for me. The rush of adrenaline to gauge if she's interested, the anticipation of her body under my skin. With El my seduction scenario went out the window. We got into this room and I didn't crave the rush. I only craved her. A small part of me wondered, worried—what if I lose the thing that took residence in my head when I fell for her? What if sleeping with her changes things? What if the moments of passion dilute the strength of my feelings?

El's nothing like any other girl I've wanted before, because want doesn't even describe the potent potion of tenderness, lust, care, longing, and whatever else that new feeling is that coats my lungs, throat, brain, and heart. I should've been afraid that every time I touch her, kiss her, sleep with her will distill my feelings, turn them into something so strong and powerful that one drop of it would knock me to my knees.

I know the name for that feeling. My mind serves the four letters to me when I trace the slightly upturned bridge of El's nose with my gaze. My pulse telegraphs it to me when I dip closer and breathe in her scent. Four letters. One person. The life I've never imagined for myself here in this room. A movement away.

El and I. WE. Together. For real. Forever?

Forever.

Not a sentiment I've ever considered, but now that it takes over my body, mind, and soul, I can't fathom not needing it. Why did I fight love for so long? What can be better than this? Nothing. No one will persuade me otherwise.

"I loved singing with you yesterday. I might be jealous of Blatantly Subtle," I whisper to my sleeping beauty.

The phone on the floor blasts "Come talk to me, come talk to me, come talk to me" in Zoe's commanding voice. El's eyes fly open and confusion is clear on her face. The moment her gaze falls on me, it calms. My heartrate skyrockets. I did that.

"Wil."

I press my lips to hers and stay there, touching her again, because I can, because she wants me to. She rests her head against mine. "What time is it?"

"Does it matter?"

"Nope." Her nails scrape along my forearm.

Zoe's voice starts blasting from the floor again.

"Zoe," El groans.

"Ignore her. She can brag about the party tomorrow. We have a whole day together. Just you and me. Not sharing you with anyone."

El snuggles closer and hooks her leg over my thigh. "That is the sexiest thing I've heard this morning."

"The day is young. I'm full of sexy things." I brush the tips of her hair off the shoulder I nibbled on last night. "With you as inspiration, I won't run out of them in the next decade, century, millennia."

Her fingers skim my jawline. "That's a lot of words."

"You know I'm a man of words."

"You are *my* man of words." She presses a kiss against my sternum, and the organ beneath it lights up.

I nuzzle her neck, my tongue enjoying the erratic beat of her pulse. "That is the sexiest thing I've heard this morning."

"Man of words?"

"Your man." And I'm lost in her again. The soft sigh my touch elicits, the slide of her skin against mine.

Zoe's voice blasts through the air for the third time. El inches away, and my body protests. "She's not going to stop. I'll just tell her we're in seclusion for the day and turn it to do not disturb."

"She owes me." My hand can't resist reaching for her arm to pull her back. "For yesterday and for disturbing the best morning of my life."

El smiles. "Best morning?"

"First best morning of my life. I'm counting on having quite a large roster of these with you."

"Hold that thought." She wrenches away and fishes her phone out from the pile of clothes on the floor. Device in hand, she returns to my embrace, and I sling my arm across her waist. On top of the sheet. Because if I dive below, Zoe or not, I won't be able to stop myself.

"What's so urgent you had to wake me up at—" El pulls the phone from her ear and looks at the screen, "9 a.m. Okay, that's not that early but—"

Her muscles tense. My own go on high alert, preparing to step in front of whatever is causing her concern. "What did you do?" she says in a voice laced with dread, anger, and irritation that has no place in the day we are supposed to have. I pull her closer like my body can stop this. "Zoe. You didn't."

My pulse is pounding. I wish I could hear the other side of the conversation. "Speakerphone?" I whisper.

She rolls her eyes at whatever Zoe is saying and hits the speaker button. ". . . about time you talked to her. And meet your baby brother."

Pickle is worth meeting. Everyone in the world should meet Pickle. I might be biased, but that kid has superpowers and wrapping adults around his tiny fingers is one of them. Also, making me laugh.

El squirms. "I specifically asked to stay in your pool house to avoid my family. If I wanted to visit them, I would've."

"Bullshit." Zoe's authoritative tone cracks against the head-board. "You want to see them, you're just too chicken. I'm ripping the Band-Aid off. They'll be here for brunch in ten minutes. You can thank me later."

"Ten minutes?" I whisper.

"Good morning to you too, Wil," Zoe says. "I stashed a change of clothes in the closet for you. Wear the gray pants with the black shirt."

I glance at El, who doesn't look thrilled. "Seems you've thought of everything."

"Don't I always?" Zoe sighs. "Listen El, the choice is yours. Hide out in the pool house with your boy or put your big-girl pants on and face the music. This isn't a press conference, there won't be paparazzi questioning you. This is your family." A door slams somewhere on Zoe's side and a woman's voice tells "Bob" to turn on the oven to two hundred. "Family comes first."

I hate Zoe for putting El in this position, but I admire her balls for trying. I've seen firsthand how much Sylvia misses her daughter. I'll never agree with her tactics for overprotecting El, keeping her from pursuing music, but I understand the desire to safeguard El.

"See you in two," says Zoe. I stare at El. The languid joy of the morning has vacated the premises, and El's fear fills the space. I wanted to protect her, and now it's like I've cornered her.

"We can sneak out the back, go to the movies?" I dig around for my phone. "I'll see how long it'll take to get a ride share."

It's impossible to get around LA without a car. I need to start saving for one.

El's hand lands on my wrist. "Wait." Usually I adore her look of determination, but right now it's laced with something that makes my stomach turn. "Let's just get it over with."

We do the opposite of last night, quickly buttoning shirts and zipping dresses. El runs a comb through her hair. "What were you saying about Blatantly Subtle earlier?"

"Just that they only get you for another week." In the mirror, El sticks her tongue out at me. "Then you're all mine. I can't wait to take my girlfriend on a real date."

The comb clatters on the bathroom counter. "You, me, and Daniel Davison. Won't that be fun."

I nibble my own lip, repressing, 'It'll just be us.' The press won't care enough to tag along. "Zoe will find you a hat." I try to lighten the mood. "Worked for us before."

El covers her face with her hands. "That was before I knew you were Rocker's son."

"What are you saying?" I jam my feet into the shoes Zoe picked out. "We can't hide in this pool house forever."

"Can't we?"

"No." I bite the inside of my cheek. The familiar frustration over El not wanting to be seen with me returns. "You'll be at Death Elbow's first performance on the fifteenth, right? That's in three weeks. What difference does a few weeks make?"

Silence sits like an invisible wall between us. "I can't think right now. My mother is probably in Zoe's driveway. I haven't spoken to her in months."

In the doorway, she presses her lips together, and the need to take away the concern etched on her forehead propels me forward. I bracket her face and brush my lips against hers. "We'll eat, say hi, and then the rest of the weekend is ours. To do what we want."

The electricity I woke up to this morning has fizzled, replaced by the buzz of apprehension.

My fingers find hers. "Pickle's worth it. Trust me."

The jagged shard in my throat eases as she squeezes my hand. "I trust you."

Twenty-Seven

El

Walking by the pool toward the main house is usually the worst part of staying with Zoe. Today the worst part is ahead. My perfect day in Wil's arms just turned into a horror movie of what I assume will be stilted conversation with my parents to the soundtrack of a crying baby. I just might prefer a dip in the pool than entering the room of doom.

I open the French doors into the living room and my heart sinks lower than I anticipated. Heads turn my way, the conversation stills, and the smiles fall off Mom and Rocker's faces. I won't fake happiness. Me being here is enough of a concession. I stand in the door and find Zoe's figure behind her parents making wild eye movements to encourage me to come in.

"How did you sleep?" Aunt Patti is the first to verbally acknowledge my presence.

There was even less sleeping than usual last night. I ignore the heat rising up my neck and step away from Wil. "I appreciate you letting me stay," I tell her. "We were up late working on a new song." The melodies that filled our moments together might be on my first solo album. Wil's words, my tunes.

"Oh, to be young and capable of functioning on sleepless nights." My aunt offers me a glass of orange juice. "Talk to me when you are my age. Eight hours is the bare minimum. You know I slept for twelve hours straight one day, and I thought that was an impossibility—"

"I didn't know you were joining us." Mom props the baby on her hip and rises. "You look good."

She doesn't look good. The glow of pregnancy is gone. Although she's wearing makeup and her hair is twisted in an artful bun that's supposed to look messy but is probably something she spent a while on, the darkness under and redness in her eyes is hard to hide. There is sadness in them too. She's supposed to be happy and excited about motherhood. Her perfect baby. Not store an ocean of sadness in those blue eyes.

"Zoe invited me." Yes, let's blame this insurrection on my cousin.

"You're always invited. You know that." Rocker stands next to Mom and tugs her and the baby into his chest. Protecting. Always protecting. At least I don't need to be under his wing anymore. "Here and in our house. You can come home any-time."

Home. I don't think I have one. The endless string of hotel rooms aren't. Zoe's pool house isn't one either. My old room at the Malibu mansion isn't, not anymore. I'm homeless, but freedom is worth that price.

"No, thank you." I straighten. How long do I need to stay before I can leave?

Mom whispers something to Rocker and he lets her go. She comes within reach but doesn't attempt a hug. She knows bet-ter.

The baby, like a shield between us, gurgles and squirms in her arms. I stare at her, not knowing what to do. Mom makes a cooing sound and offers him to me. "Pickle would like to say hi."

Giant blue eyes lock on mine, his tiny hand reaches out and grabs my hair, tugging on it with a strength I did not expect from someone this small.

"Ouch," I cry and tug my hair back out of his grasp.

A wail shatters the room. I'm underestimating this baby every step of the way, because he fills the spacious living room with a scream that bounces off the vaulted ceiling and makes Beau's guitar solo sound like a whisper.

"Take him," says Mom. I expect her to give him to Rocker but instead she offers the cavern of his crying mouth to me.

My hands refuse to move. "Why?"

"He wants you to hold him."

"Could've fooled me." Does anyone care what I want any-more?

"He's just a baby." How does Rocker's voice remain calm over the endless howls of his son? At least the baby stays on pitch and I don't have the urge to shove my fingers into my ears. Rocker approaches and blocks the rest of the room from my view. "Can't you hold your brother?"

My brother. Unlike Wil, this baby is both Rocker's son and my half brother, a blood relative. I should feel something toward the child, but my only desire is to turn and run out of the room, away from the expectations and noises.

"I can take him." Wil's voice sounds nearby. He removes the now red-faced infant from my mother's hands. "Hey there, buddy. What's the fuss about?" He talks to the baby as if this type of a conversation is something they do a lot. Like the mewling lump actually understand Wil's words.

Pickle's shrill slows, his body shaking, but he grabs the finger Wil offers and brings it to his mouth. The sound I started sub-sides with a hiccup. "Am I delicious? Or are you delicious?" Wil mimics biting the baby's cheek, and the mouth that could've competed with an ambulance siren emits a giggle. Wil strolls away, absorbed in his brother, who stares at Wil like he's his favorite thing in the world.

I know the feeling.

Rocker shadows Wil and sets a hand on his back in the same protective way he did with Mom and the baby before. Staking his claim. "Let's go for a walk, let the girls talk," Rocker says to Wil but in a loud enough voice that I know it's directed at me.

Wil throws a glance my way over his shoulder but still allows himself to be guided by his father through the French doors and away from me.

A hand on my arm brings my attention back to the room. Everyone but Mom has disappeared.

"Melodie. How are you? Really?" She puts her other hand on me and rubs up to my shoulders and down to my elbows in what I assume should be a soothing gesture meant to open a line of communication I shut off when I left for Germany with Wil. A line of communication I'm not sure we can restore.

"Fine. Just fine." I shrug off her hands and stride to the couch. "Doing what I want to do the way I want to do it."

"Sorry the tour is on pause. I hope Carlee's flu isn't going to affect her vocal cords. Have you suggested gurgling with salt and baking soda to her?" Mom clasps her now empty hands.

"She has a doctor for that."

Her face becomes the mask I've seen a thousand times in press conferences and award shows.

"Are you enjoying yourself?"

Enjoying myself is not exactly what's happening. But didn't she say music is hard work? And I am working hard. That is definitely what every day of the tour feels like. Work. Work. Work. "It's a start."

She bites her lip. I pick a croissant off the table by the fireplace and nibble on the buttery goodness. My stomach says I'm starving but my brain doesn't believe it.

"You know what Bill said is the truth, right? You don't have to stay here." Mom edges closer to me. "You're more than welcome at home. Your room is always there for you." Another inch in my direction. "Marta misses you. I miss you."

The dark spot I refuse to acknowledge whenever I think of my mother covers my heart. I miss her too. Even though I don't like that I miss her, I want my mom, and on many lonely nights I want to be in my room staring up at the stars on my ceiling, feeling like I belong.

But I don't belong.

Not anymore.

I'm not the version of Melodie Rockerby Mom and Rocker want me to be. I'm El Vella. When I saw my name on the fake ID Mateo gave me as a birthday present, it no longer felt like a stage name. El Vella is who I am, not just the disguise I used to sing my songs. "I've been thinking about changing my name to El. El Vella."

Mom jerks to a stop. "Is this about wanting to be closer to your father, or trying to get away from Bill?"

"It's about me." Why doesn't she get this? "Finding my voice." I tap my chest. "You moved from Norway to Italy to go to opera school at eighteen." I wash my hands over my face. "I'm nineteen. I don't feel the same way I did at twelve. Rocker adopting me then was sweet, and it felt right at that time, but I'm not a Rockerby."

"If that's what you want." She doesn't look like she agrees with the words.

"I won't ever forget everything he's done for me, but I'm a Vella." I square my shoulders. "I know it now, and I want others to know too."

"I can try to call you El like Wil. But isn't it a bit drastic, actually changing your name on paper?"

I abandon the croissant. "Maybe I need drastic."

"You always avoided drama." The veneer of calm cracks, and the light of my true mother peeks through. "I don't understand you. We've given you everything. You have the world at your feet, and you abandon it to chase after fame? When did fame bring anything but heartache?"

"I'm not chasing fame."

"What then? What have we not given you?"

"Freedom."

She throws her hands in the air. "You had more freedom than most people. How about those who can't waste their days with the hobby of the week and do their nine-to-five jobs or work two jobs to earn enough to take care of their families? People survive. I didn't think I raised a child who wouldn't appreciate the privileges we've provided."

"I appreciate the privileges. But I don't want them." My fingers form hard balls of tension. "Maybe money and status are something you were after when you started singing, but music is what I'm after. The ability to create what I want, to follow my passion, to do what I'm supposed to do in this life. And it's not working at Rocker's company or attending parties and photoshoots with you and Zoe. I know I have music in me. It's my job to bring it into the world and share with people. The freedom to do that is worth more than all the money in the world to me."

"Is it worth more than your family?"

The sentence slices my skin. "If you want to give me the world, why do you make me choose?"

"How can I show you what the music world looks like from my side, with my years of experience and heaps of failure?" Mom's cries are nothing like the baby's. They're soft, and guttural, and they bury me. The last time she cried like this, her previous round of IVF was unsuccessful, and I was encouraging her to try again. There was hope in those tears, unlike these. "I don't know what to do anymore. How to protect you. How to prove to you this is idealistic and will only lead to pain and hardships that I want you to avoid." Her pitch-perfect voice turns nasally. "I'm proud of how hard you're working. Your songs showcase your talent. Even though I don't understand why you chose to be a backup singer, I won't stand in your way. But music is a fickle business. Can you blame me for not wanting it to hurt you?"

"No, but you need to let me make my own mistakes." I wrap my arms around myself. "I'm not a baby. Worry about the child out there that needs your care and protection." I point to the door Wil and Rocker exited through.

"You will always be my baby."

My heart crumbles. Once we were as close as best friends. "I'm an adult. Maybe you can try treating me as one."

Mom rests her head on my shoulder and before I notice, my arm is around her and I pat her on her back, as if she is *my* baby. "Support me instead of trying to control me."

"So you'll come home after the tour? We'll be back to how it was?"

"No, Mom. I love you but I'm part of Blatantly Subtle now." Carlee needs me, but I can't tell Mom that. "When I'm in LA, I'll find my own place to live."

She sobs into my shirt and the wet spot grows on my shoulder. "Okay . . . El. Let's try it your way," she mumbles into the cloth.

"Thank you." I exhale. The tension that was stretching my lungs from the moment Zoe announced this forced reunion disappears, and I drape over my mother as we hug each other.

One battle won. Being an adult is not that hard.

Twenty-Eight

THE BRUNCH TABLE COULD seat twelve, and with just eight of us, El is nowhere near me. Unless my arms grow to ten feet, I can't even touch her under the table. Rocker's elbow keeps bumping mine though. Sandwiched between him and Zoe's father, the conversation has been hopping from the latest deal on the development in Singapore Mr. Yilmaz's company got the tender for to the plans of visiting Norway and Ohio to show off Pickle to the grandparents and extended family.

"Pickle will be the star of the show," Rocker says.

"Like his father. Only fitting, right, Wil?" Mr. Yilmaz bares his veneers that are so white they leave no illusion of natural teeth. I don't laugh at the joke. "Do you sing? Play an instrument? My son is great at the piano. You two could probably jam.

Unfortunately, he's all the way in New Orleans getting an MBA at Tulane. Are you in school? What are your goals in life? Are you going to be a star as well?"

"I think El's doing a good job taking care of that." I cut into the eggs covered in some white sauce that tastes delicious. "I'm more a behind-the-scenes guy."

"He's been instrumental in bringing fresh talent to Rocker Inc. We just signed a band, Death Elbow. We think they'll be the next Måneskin. I offered to promote Wil from intern to a part-time A&R rep." Rocker's eyes brim with pride when he looks at me. Now and every day. "He was the one who produced Melodie's first video."

"The one with all the views?" Mr. Yilmaz perks up, like I'm suddenly much more interesting now I'm known for a post with almost two million views. "You and Melodie are friends then?"

The eggs get caught in my throat and I take a sip of coffee. We are so much more, and if it were up to me, I'd be shouting about it from the rooftops, showing her off on dates at the best restaurants, and resting my hand on the small of her back on red carpets.

When I see us living together, it's not under Rocker's roof, but in an apartment of my own. El Vella and Wil Peters, not Melodie and Wilhelm Rockerby. That is not us. A simmer of irritation burns my stomach. Having the option to admit to her uncle that I'm her boyfriend would be a good first step. But I guess being part of a relationship means I'm not the only one who can make this decision.

"Something like that." I ball the cloth napkin and set it next to my egg-covered plate. "I'll be right back."

El throws me a glance from her human sandwich between Sylvia and Mrs. Yilmaz, who each have one hand on her forearms, as if to keep her permanently attached to the table, unable to go back to her life on tour.

The room where Pickle is sleeping is at the end of the hallway. His car seat sits on the ground by the bed. He's the only one who doesn't have any preconceived notions about what I am. He loves being around me, using me as his chew and drool toy, and smiles at me like I'm the sun and moon. Not because I'm supposed to be someone, just because he likes my company.

"Here you are." Rocker bursts into the room.

I've been out of his sight for two minutes and he's acting like this is some kind of an emergency. I press my finger to my lips and point to his sleeping son. Rocker's eyes widen and he urges me out of the room.

"We have a problem." Rocker drags me into a room with a billiards table and a small bar. He runs his fingers through his hair and the wild expression on his face scrambles the eggs in my stomach. Is something wrong with Mum? I reach for my phone, but he places one hand on mine, pinches the bridge of his nose with the other, and closes his eyes. "We're out of time."

"What are we talking about?"

"Sven called. One of his contacts in the press alerted him about a photographer trying to sell pictures and videos of you, Pickle, and me."

My stomach settles and I shrug off Rocker's hand. "That man at the club on Thursday took our photo."

"As my new intern. We've hidden the fact that you live in the mansion. Harper managed to squelch the few rumors the press asked for comments on. I thought you'd be safe, but they have been all over Pickle. Everyone is trying to get photos of the baby. We've already set up an exclusive interview with Rolling Stone magazine, and they'll donate part of the sales to your RA Connect Foundation."

My RA foundation. The sound of that is still so foreign. "How does that relate to them figuring out I'm your son?"

"The paparazzo was after Pickle's photos. The photo Sven sent is of us on the lawn." He cringes. "Changing Pickle's diaper."

Gross. Why would anyone take a picture of us dealing with baby poop?

"And there's a video of us singing to him."

Or film two men dealing with baby poop?

"It still doesn't mean anything," I say. "You introduced me to your son. I'm a nice guy."

The wrinkles etched into Rocker's brow ease as he laughs. "That you are." Then they reappear. "But I tell you to pick up your brother and head back in. My words are clear. No doubt

I'm referencing Pickle." He washes his face with his hands. "Damn. Now they'll put it together."

Damn indeed. I run my fingers through my hair. "Bloody hell. What do we do? Do I go back to Germany? Will this follow me there?"

"Don't bother trying to solve this on your own, Bill Rocker-by." Sylvia joins our little circle, trailed by . . . everyone. My gaze falls on El. Is it the lighting in this room or is El's face paler? "This is a family matter."

Rocker slips an arm around his wife and kisses her temple. "Sven said he can hold this off until Monday but only because on a weekend it won't get as much press, even if TMZ reports it. When it gets out the press will have a field day. Cute Pickle and Wil."

I grab the side of the table and force myself to look at the triangle of balls in the middle and not El, who's been studying me as if I'm about to die. Fame is not anything I ever wanted, but Zoe and Mateo have been warning me this was bound to happen. It's not that serious. Can't be that bad. Rocker's been dealing with it for most of his life. "What are our options?"

"I spoke with Harper." Sylvia adjusts her blouse. "She insists we get ahead of the story. Call a press conference. Have Wil and Bill talk to select members of the press, answer questions we plant. Her theory is if this comes out before the pictures or video, the public will assume the video is a follow-up, not gossip. This way we control the narrative."

Mr. Yilmaz reclines against the wall. "Getting the right journalists will take time."

I pick up a red ball and roll it in my palm. "Can't you just buy the video. Pay them off?" His money has to be good for something.

"Sven offered. Like he did with Melodie's footage, and when someone filmed me and Sylvia getting into the car with Pickle at the hospital." Rocker checks his phone. "But there was nothing to see beyond a covered car seat and two tired people wearing sunglasses. This video is gossipmongering. The delay is a huge favor, and even that costs."

"You want the press to show up quick?" Zoe takes a cue stick off the wall and rubs something on top of it like she does this for a living. "Invite Daniel Davison. If he's there, everyone will clamor to attend."

El pushes off the wall. "He's the last person we want there."

"No." Zoe turns to El. "He's the exact person. If you take his questions head-on, there won't be any room for misinterpretation. Everyone knows he can't be bought."

Rocker and Sylvia exchange glances while El's gaze drops to the floor. I know she despises Daniel. So do I for what he's put her through. But what Zoe is suggesting makes sense. If we get everything out in the open, they'll have no reason to hunt for more. My solar plexus burns at the possibility of telling the truth, of no more secrets, of telling the world about El and me.

I could go to her concerts, not as Rocker's assistant, but as her boyfriend. Meet the band, be the one El spills drinks on in the bar. I don't want to betray El, but my soul starts to sing with the concept of the freedom in telling the truth.

"The press conference needs us to be a united front." Rocker's gaze flicks from his wife to El and lands on me. "We do it as a family." I hold his gaze, resisting the urge to find El's, get her permission to do this. Then it hits me. I don't have a choice. This is happening whether I want it to or not. Whether she wants it to or not. She's being pulled into my orbit and has to face the press because of me.

Rocker opens his mouth as if to say something, but El's voice cuts in. "Family."

My gaze rushes to her, but she's not looking at me. My insides squirm at her raised chin and the hard lines of her mouth. I've seen this determined expression before and I know, whatever she has set her mind on, I'll have a hard time changing.

"Wil?" Rocker steps between us. "It's up to you."

He makes it seem like if I say no, he'll accept it, find another way. There's no falseness here, only sincerity. Rocker is not a bad guy. Whatever Mum saw in him when they met, I see it now. Maybe our lives would've been different then, but they will surely be different now. I check my phone. 10 p.m. in Bremen. "I need to call Mum first."

His face melts into that odd look he gets whenever I mention Mum. "Of course. Tell Hanna . . ." He clears his throat. "Give her Harper's number. We should set up a call and brief her on how to deal with the press. They'll figure out ways to contact her for her side of the story. She doesn't need to pick up. And if anyone bothers her, we can set up a security detail." Rocker taps his phone. "She can always call me directly as well."

Great. Another thing we'll need Rocker for.

"I'll tell Harper to set the press conference up for Monday." Sylvia trails out of the room, followed by Mr. and Mrs. Yilmaz.

Rocker says, "I'll text Sven back." He follows his wife.

Zoe bounces on her heels. "And I'll go choose your outfits."

El and I both groan at the same time.

"What?" She does what I call the confidence pose, putting her hand on her outstretched hip. "Wil here has to look good for his big debut." Her other hand fans across her face. "His big debutante ball. He'll be a real man now."

"I'll just wear my Energie Berlin T-shirt." Make my rowing team proud.

"No." El stands beside her cousin. "You don't want to give the press ammunition to dig into your past. Wear what Zoe recommends." El offers her cousin a fleeting smile. "She knows what she's doing."

"Damn skippy I do." Zoe brushes a few strands of El's hair behind her ear. "And I have the perfect electric-blue jacket for you. Part punk rock, part dutiful daughter."

My girlfriend's shoulders sag, like she's resigned to her fate. "Let's go try it on while Wil calls his mom."

My throat constricts as El walks away from me. I want her to stay, let me hold her for a bit before calling Mum. But as I work up the courage to ask, the billiards room empties. I collect the balls and arrange them back into the neat triangle. I eye the undercounter mini fridge with beer and the shelf with alcohol I'm not even familiar with. The dread in the center of my torso is not as much for what to tell Mum, but what others will say about her. I wanted to call her with an update on when I'm coming to see her, not that the paparazzi are about to descend.

"Wil?" Mum's voice, groggy and quiet, feeds the worry in my chest. She doesn't need this stress. I should hang up and tell Rocker to stop this.

"Did I wake you?" I slide into German.

Rustling on her end of the line is answer enough. "I must've fallen asleep on the couch."

My fingers grip the phone. "Are the symptoms back? Are you more tired than you should be?"

"Not at all. I went out with the girls for brunch. They treated me to Oberneulanders." I can hear Mum's smile through her words.

"Is Opa there?"

"Sure, yeah, he's in the kitchen." She shouts, "Dad, Wil's on the phone. Come over, I'll put him on speakerphone."

"What is it?" Opa's voice is now close.

I breathe in, looking for the best way to break the news. "They know."

"Who's they and know what?" asks Opa.

"The press. There's a video of Rocker, Pickle, and me where Rocker refers to Pickle as my brother. Rocker's trying to hold the story until we can do an impromptu interview and get ahead of the news. He's going to announce to the world that I'm his son."

The phone hangs in silence and I can almost see Mum's and Opa's faces. The worry.

"Are you okay with this?" Mum's concern is exactly what I expected.

"I'll be fine." It's not like much will change in my life. Being his son makes no difference to me. "But there will be questions. About you. Harper, Rocker's, publicist is working on a list of questions for the reporters to ask." I grip the phone tighter. "There's no way not to mention you."

"I knew this day was coming." Mum sighs. "I hoped you'd have a bit more time to adjust to your new life, but . . ."

"Mum. I'm not worried about me. They'll call you too. Rocker wants you to be prepared. I'll text you Harper's number and you can—"

"We'll be fine."

"You don't know that."

"I'm feeling much better. My health is good, I promise. The rest is not important. Stop worrying about me."

"When is the interview?" Opa asks.

"Monday morning sometime."

"Good." Mum doesn't sound concerned. Maybe this is good for her too. Everything will be out in the open. "Go tell the world who you are."

TWENTY-NINE

NOTHING UNDER EL'S ROCKSTAR outfit is a secret anymore. Images of El's body under mine, next to me, over me, multiply. Even after Zoe messed up our plans and the paparazzi spoiled the rest of Saturday, I couldn't let go of El. I don't want her to leave me. I got lost in her this weekend. And there is a part of me that has permanently become a part of her. "Are you sure you can't stay tonight and fly in the morning?"

"Sure." El evades my fingers and crosses the conference room off the main lobby at Rocker Inc. "They emailed us about a 9 a.m. meeting. There's no way I can make it if I don't fly tonight."

"I'm sure Rocker's pilot can fly out before dawn."

Her shoulders tense as I come up behind her. "Wil. You promised."

I nuzzle her ear with my lips. "Promised what?" My blood sizzles in my veins and floods me with the desire that only increased with every touch of El over the weekend.

El places her palm above my heart. I dip to fuse my lips with hers, but she holds me in place.

"We aren't telling anyone outside the family about us."

I circle the empty room with my chin. "I don't see anyone."

"The press is behind that door. Harper is due to come in any moment."

One more kiss.

"Harper won't tell anyone." I inch my lips to hers with every word.

The door behind me swings open and El jumps away from me, scurrying to the opposite side of the room.

"This has the changes we discussed last night." Harper, dressed in a black pantsuit, rushes in, Rocker on her heels holding Sylvia's hand. On the other side of the door, a crowd of reporters are gathering, lured in by the tease of a major announcement.

"Wil, El. Perfect. We've got everyone." Harper taps away on her tablet and a word document pops up on the large TV screen. True to his word, Rocker has made sure we have been part of crafting our own message every step of the way.

"I changed the second line in the third paragraph to mix-up." Harper sounds like a schoolteacher I had once. Her suggestions are more like orders. "Appears more like there was a misunderstanding than Rocker being an absent father."

Rocker searches my face, as if me agreeing to this absolves him of some crime he didn't commit. He was an absent father, but not because he made that choice. I understand that now. I reread the sentence. "How about miscommunication?"

Harper changes it on the screen. "Works for me."

"Good. Email this to me." Rocker pulls out his phone.

Gone is the casual man I live with behind his guarded gates. He's in his full rockstar glam getup today, black boots, jeans, jacket, Rocker Inc. T-shirt. Sylvia is the polar opposite, blonde hair swept up in an immaculate design that took hours this morning for her stylist to create, her makeup making her look ten years younger. Diamonds sparkle at her neck and a deep maroon dress gives her a 1950s housewife look. The strongest similarity between El and her mother are their eyes.

El's electric irises jump out at me any day but radiate in the blue jacket Zoe selected. She looks every bit the rockstar's daughter. I was prepared to hate the ridiculous outfit Zoe had in mind for me, but she surprised me with blue jeans, a plain white button-down shirt, and a gray blazer with a thin blue stripe. Maybe we can't say we're a couple out loud, but Zoe made sure we are the only two who match. Any photos taken today will hint to anyone who pays attention that we're together.

"Let's undo one more button." Zoe reaches for my collar.

"Not on the runway here." I bat her away. She insisted she come for moral support for El and me, but I suspect she's here to ensure we don't wrinkle her precious fabrics before the cameras can snap pictures.

"Don't bitch at me. I'm on your side." Zoe brushes the top of my shoulder. "I told El she's missing an opportunity here to come clean about you two dating as well. Get it over with. They'll find out eventually."

I huff.

El crosses the room and stays just out of reach. I freaking hate it.

"Everything will be fine," she says like a prayer.

I hope whoever is in charge of this new twist in my life is listening to El's favorite phrase in the face of adversity. If she'd let me, I would comfort her, take her hand, kiss her until she forgets to be nervous, make the rest of the world recede until the only thing that truly matters is the two of us. But I remain glued to my spot, ordering my body to behave.

El's fingers play with the bracelet I gave her. "Rocker'll field most of the questions. He's a pro at this."

"It's . . . so fake." My fingers drum against the polished wood of the table. The undercurrent of the conversation that we would like to have swirls around me.

"You don't have to be fake." El's hand twitches at her side but she doesn't move. "Be Wil. Everyone I know loves Wil."

My heart goes boom. Did El just say she loves me? I can barely hear over the thunder in my chest. The room shrinks to only El's sparkling eyes, and I move my lips in a silent attempt to form words. I need to say something.

"It's time." Rocker's hand is on my shoulder. I glare at him.

"Wil, you first." Harper stands with her hand on the doorknob. "Then Rocker and Sylvia. Melodie last." I want to correct her, insist Harper call her El, but today she's Rocker's stepdaughter, not the girl I—not my girlfriend.

In the lobby, four microphones are set up on a long table in front of four empty chairs. There's a small murmur as we walk in front of maybe a dozen people. Not sure what I was expecting, but it was more than this. Years of watching press conferences at film festivals created this image in my mind of a packed room, cameras on. This group is more like a bunch of commuters waiting for a train that's been delayed. A cloud of boredom hangs in the air.

My chair squeals as I drag it out from under the table and all eyes train on me. My mouth turns into the Sahara Desert. This is nothing like being on stage. The audience is not quite hostile, but neither are they here for a good time. I can't wow them with music or a joke.

"Thank you for joining us." Rocker's voice is as calm as when he orders a coffee at Blend. Years of practice, I guess. He recites the first few sentences of the statement we crafted. The heavy beat thrumming in my ears muffles his words and I concentrate on trying to figure out if the design on the patterned scarf a woman in the front row wears is penguins or dogs.

She speaks up and the sounds of the room rush back in. "Why are you only finding this out now?"

"His mother tried to contact me on many occasions, but there"—Rocker's knuckles are white where they press on the table—"was a miscommunication. My manager thought it was a prank." The reporter opens her mouth to speak but Rocker barrels on. "Turns out she didn't need me." His hand clamps down on my shoulder. "She raised an amazing young man."

Twelve sets of eyes turn to me, and my insides liquefy. I've been on stages in rooms packed with ten times more people than this watching me perform and never flinched. But here, with the weight of expectation etched into each stare, words fail me for the second time in an hour. The urge to run, to flee, makes my toes tap. A drop of perspiration trickles down the back of my neck.

Rocker's fingers dig into my shoulder, and we lock eyes. His gaze calm and confident against my surely scared one. I must be imagining it, but I hear, "We got this," and my pulse slows.

"My mum is amazing." My voice squeaks and camera flashes temporarily blind me. I toss off Rocker's grip, clear my throat, and aim for the mic. "Raised me on her own. I never imagined I was Rocker's son. I'm much better looking." I give them an eyebrow raise and a wink. There's a round of chuckles from the reporters, and one of the knots in my stomach unties. El's right, I can do this. These people are just like any audience in the club. A joke here and there, and I'll have them eating out of the palm of my hand.

"Why find your dad after all these years?" a man with a full beard shouts over the din.

I'm not telling them about Mum's illness, confess we're poor and desperately needed the money. Again, I think of El protecting the story of her papa. Is this what it'll be like from now on?

"We discovered the connection when he became friends with my daughter." Rocker's voice draws the paparazzi's attention back to him. "I visited the family in Germany when Melodie stayed with his mom."

I blink. He didn't lie. Well, after Sven's assurances he never told Rocker about the DNA test, what Rocker is saying is true. Even though he's glossing over my relationship with El. I prepare for more questions about her, more needling for the facts, but the reporters move on, satisfied with the answer.

"Melodie, what's it like gaining two brothers in one fell swoop?"

The water El was sipping must go down the wrong pipe as she bursts into a coughing fit.

I lean into the microphone. "I'm not her brother."

Scarf lady snaps her head in my direction. "You have the same father."

"But he . . . Rocker adopted El. We're not related."

"Who's El?"

"I—" El's voice is soft and drowned out by her mother.

"That's her stage name. El Vella. Melodie chose it to honor my late husband, her papa." Sylvia pats El's arm. "Her music is quite outstanding. It's why Blatantly Subtle handpicked her to join their band."

I've never heard Sylvia praise El's music. Did Harper write these words for Sylvia or is that genuine admiration? I hope the latter. For El's sake. She deserves her mother's support.

"Melodie." Another reporter's up. "Are you dating Langdon Beau?"

"No." El and I both speak at the same time. Rocker's knee taps against mine. I bite the inside of my cheek.

"Beau has been a mentor during this tour." Even bent forward, I can't see El's face, but her voice is stronger. "He's a friend."

"Rocker, what do you think of your daughter dating a fellow guitarist?"

I stare at the opposite wall. We've never really discussed the fact El and I are dating. Not sure I want to find out this way. Rocker clears his throat.

"All I care about is her happiness." Rocker's knee taps mine again.

In approval? Or in permission. Not like I need it. Yet my lungs expand as if the most important part of this press conference is over. Without the world knowing about El and me, treating her as my girlfriend around family will have to be enough. For now.

"Will you play a concert with Blatantly Subtle?" Daniel Davison directs his question at Rocker.

"Maybe someday. I have nothing but the utmost respect for them."

The bearded reporter throws a question at me. "Can you play guitar, like your dad?"

I try not to wince at him calling Rocker my dad. Harper insisted I appear happy to be reunited or the press will sense a story. Show something negative and they hound us. Present positivity and they'll lose interest. This is our chance to set the stage. I plaster on my best smile. "I play. Maybe better than him."

"Is that true?" The reporter turns back to Rocker.

Dad grins and shakes his head at me, happiness streaming from his face. Not the fake one. He's not that good of an actor. "Wil and I have a lot to learn about each other. Maybe someday he'll even join me on tour."

Yeah, right. I match his smile. His praise warms my heart, but the only person I plan to tour with is El. Camera flashes explode in a frenzy of blinding bursts. I can imagine the headlines: "Father and Son Stare Down." The questions segue to Rocker's career until Harper walks out and ends the press conference.

We file out of the room and this time I go last, my chest lighter, my steps unburdened, my head clear. I pull my shoulders back and raise my chin. It's out now. The world officially knows I'm Rocker's son. I'm glad it's over. Now my life can return to normal.

THIRTY

THE TV SCREEN MOUNTED on the wall in Carlee's penthouse suite is on mute, but Daniel Davison is pointing to an online article with the headline, "Rocker Got Two Sons for New Year's." Not the worst one I've read since the press conference yesterday. The photo of Wil and Rocker staring each other down, identical cocky smiles and amber eyes, is worth a million words. Any rumors that Wil is not really his son vanished once that image hit social media.

Like father like son.

"Exciting weekend, huh?" Beau flops onto the couch beside me, his heavy boots clanging on the glass coffee table.

I sip my coffee, heat rising to my cheeks at being caught staring at the photos.

"From only child to middle child in a month. That sucks," says Beau in his supportive-big-brother way that is nothing like the show he puts on for the paparazzi. If the reporters witnessed this, the speculation about the two of us would dissolve faster than the sugar in my coffee.

"It's not that bad." Thinking of Wil as family feels both right and wrong. I need a distraction. "Why are we meeting so early?" The 9 a.m. summons surprised me.

The light in his eyes dim. Panic spreads in my gut. "Is Carlee worse?"

"No. Not worse." His voice is flat, not the playful guitarist who makes the girls squeal, but the man who has something on his mind. A knock at the door sends Beau to his feet. "Refill your coffee. You'll need it."

Josie and Annalyn burst into the room, Kamo sauntering after. Beau kisses Kamo on the cheek. Josie gives me a shrug as she settles in beside me, while Annalyn, looking slightly bored, perches on a stool at the bar behind the couch. I don't get her. Doesn't she get emotional about anything?

The door to Carlee's bedroom cracks open. She looks a thousand times better than the last time I saw her, slumped on the couch in her greenroom. Her hair is pulled into a loose bun and her usual black clothing is replaced by light-blue jeans and a plain white T. She walks to the center of the room, blocking the weather report on the TV.

Cartoon suns surround Carlee's head. "I'll get straight to the point. This will be my last tour with Blatantly Subtle."

I have no coherent thoughts. I expected some changes to the tour schedule while she recovers, but this doesn't make sense. She can't leave Blatantly Subtle. What would the group even be like without her? She is the soul of Subtle. Josie's and Annalyn's blank shocked stares assure me I'm not the only one feeling this way.

Beau moves to Carlee's side and takes her hand. Her gaze at him is soft and I almost feel like an intruder. Kamo brackets Carlee on her other side and takes a wide stance.

I lick my dry lips. "Is this because of your MS?"

Carlee's chin dips.

"Is the group breaking up?" Josie's voice trembles.

"That's the last thing I want." Carlee lifts her face. "Beau and I started Subtle together and I'm committed to keeping our vision alive. I might be," her eyes search the ceiling, "retiring, but the band will go on."

Retiring. The word doesn't make sense. She's only twenty-seven. Goosebumps spread from my chest to my fingers that dig into my thigh.

"If you're leaving and the band isn't breaking up, then what's going on?" Annalyn addresses Beau, like Carlee doesn't matter anymore.

"Since the original diagnosis, there was always a plan. It's just happening a bit faster than expected." Carlee frees her fingers from Beau's. "We're going to need a new lead singer."

Her sentence breaks the numbness. Who can possibly replace her? A few options pop into my mind but are quickly dismissed.

This is madness. The pressure in my head pushes on my temples from the inside out, refusing to contain the idea. There is no Blatantly Subtle without Carlee.

"Do you have someone in mind already?" Josie squirms beside me.

"Not Kat Adams?" Annalyn's upper lip climbs in disgust.

Carlee chews on her cuticle. Her glossy eyes land on each of us. How painful this must be for her to even talk about quitting music, about someone else taking her place. I can't imagine my life without music. My heart tears for Carlee.

Kamo steps forward. She smiles as if she's happy about this whole situation. "We handpicked you as potential contenders. The idea has always been to assess you on the road, in a live setting, see how the crowd reacts to you and you to them." She shrugs. "Now we speed the process up and decide. Pick one singer to lead the new Subtle."

Blood races through my veins faster than the notes in *Flight of the Bumblebee* by Rimski-Korsakov.

The lead singer position. No more backup. No more following. Me upfront, the face of the band. Making decisions as an equal, not an afterthought. A permanent job with a paycheck. A big one. The cup shakes in my hand and the pounding in my ears drowns Josie's words.

This would mean instant acceptance into the higher tier of the music community. Me sitting at a table at the Grammys not as Dad's plus one, but as a real musician. Mom would have to embrace my choice of music as a career. The press would have to acknowledge I have talent of my own. Adrenaline makes it difficult to not leap for joy. Subtle picking me would be proof to everyone I'm not just a child of famous parents, but a singer. A songwriter. A musician in my own right.

"Don't you want this?" Kamo flaps a paper in my face.

I stare into her face. Want this? I've never wanted anything more. I yank the paper from her. "What do I need to do?"

Kamo's teeth flash. "I knew you'd be in."

She nods at the paper. "Read the terms. Sign and return it to me before the final performance on Saturday."

"Who's singing tonight?" Josie asks with a concerned tilt to her head.

"If Dr. Kim had his way, not me." Carlee's sitting in a chair, her legs curled under her. "But I can't let the fans down."

Beau crosses his arms. "Your health is more important."

Her hand settles on his forearm. "They paid to see me and I'm not disappointing them." His jaw settles into stone. Carlee addresses us. "I do have to ask you something I was hoping we could delay until after the tour." The three of us hinge forward like she's about to reveal the secret to life. "Part of being in Blatantly Subtle is the creative writing process. I'm not dying. Not yet, but the next album needs fresh songs that represent the new Blatantly Subtle."

"We cowrite songs?" asks Josie.

"Maybe, eventually." Beau abandons his post at Carlee's side and stares out the window. "First we need to see what you can do on your own."

My pulse quickens. Write a song for Subtle? One I might someday perform on stage?

Josie squirms in her seat. "Like write a full song?"

"Yes." Kamo braces against the TV stand, her green jacket matching the lawn of the commercial onscreen. "And perform it for us. Friday morning."

"This Friday?" Josie's head swivels between the two band members. "That's in like three days."

Annalyn rubs her hands together. "Do we have any parameters?"

Beau speaks to his reflection. "Something you can see yourself lead Subtle with. Show us what you've got."

I keep silent, because this is how I know I've got the job. Carlee helped with the chorus. She knows out of all of us, I have the most experience with songwriting. Annalyn does covers. I've not seen Josie do anything but backup singing. I fight the smile that is creeping its way onto my lips. I catch Carlee's eyes, and I swear a tiny spark runs between us. She knows I can do this. She wants me to show everyone else as well. They might not be fans of me fumbling the choreography, but I can write a song they won't be able to say no to.

My body is bursting from wanting to tell Wil. They believe in me. Carlee picked me not just as a backup but as a lead.

Potential lead, but that's exactly what makes my heart perform somersaults in my chest. Potential. She sees potential in me. Not because of who my father is or what my name has to offer, but me. El Vella. The real me. I'm not just stubborn or delusional when I imagine myself center stage, because Carlee and Blatantly Subtle imagined me in that spot when they considered hiring me.

I run out of the hotel lobby doors into the chilly midmorning air of Vancouver. I can't go back to the room I'm sharing with Annalyn. I aim for the park across the street. I need to think. To scream. To fly.

Wil was right. I am more than a backup singer.

The NDA pinches at my conscience. I have to tell someone. Talk to someone. If I call Wil now I won't be able to resist telling him. Zoe will sniff out the news and pry me open like a jar of Mormor's lingonberry jam. I bring up my contacts and scroll for the only person who won't badger me, but give me the advice I need without asking questions.

Four rings later I almost hang up, but then I hear a click and rustling noises. "El?"

"Is it a good time to talk?"

"Are you okay?" Sven's whispered delivery is hard to hear.

"Yes and no. I need help."

"Where are you? I'll come get you." There's a squeak like an old hinge opening.

"No, no. Not that kind of help." I stare at the water gushing from the mouth of the stone fish at the center of the fountain.

"I have news but I'm not supposed to share. I really want to, but I don't want to mess up this opportunity because it's big. It's really big, Sven. It's huge." The burbling river of my sentence leaves me breathless. "I signed an NDA though."

The hinge or whatever squeaks again. "This is about the band?"

"Yes." I stand up. "Thing is, if I don't tell Wil it's like I'm hiding this huge thing from him that will affect me and my life and thus him and his life." I sit down again. "So I can't not tell him. Right?"

"Right." I hear a woman's voice calling Sven's name.

"Are you . . ." Does Sven have a woman in his place? Is he still dating the girl from The Devil's Martini? I can't even remember her name. "Do you have company?"

He growls. "Not wanted company."

"What does that mean?" There's another shout of his name, this time closer. "Are you in trouble?" Every horror movie I've ever watched plays in my head. I've no idea what I'd do if he were in danger. Call the police? Call Rocker? My shoulders stiffen.

Sven's voice drops. "Yes and no."

"I'm calling the police."

"No!" His half-yelp, half-whisper freezes me. "You can't laugh."

The tension in my muscles eases. He can't be in real danger if his worst nightmare is my laugh. "I promise, I won't laugh. Where are you?"

"In my closet." He sighs. "I'm hiding from my assistant."

I sink onto a wooden bench and clasp my hand over my mouth to stifle the laugh.

"You promised," he grumbles.

"I'm trying," I say unconvincingly. "Why are you hiding from your assistant?"

"It's possible I hired a matchmaker instead of a temp agency. I woke up this morning with her standing over my bed, offering me coffee. I didn't have any clothes on and I've no idea how she got the key to the upstairs apartment."

My fingers press against my lips again, trying to suppress the hyena-like laugh that's eager to break free.

"It's not funny."

"No." I try to be serious. "It's not." I clear my throat. "Where is she now?"

"In my bathroom." The squeaking sound eeks again. "I think she's brushing her teeth with my toothbrush."

I shudder. "Sven, just fire her."

I swear, he whimpers. It dawns on me. Of course Sven can't fire her. My Superman's kryptonite is anything that causes a woman pain, be it a papercut, kicking her out of his apartment, or delivering bad news. I've seen him eat cold pasta to not hurt a server's feelings.

"You can't stay in the closet. Just tell her to leave."

"I'm trying."

I can't stand hearing him like this. "Hold up. I have an idea."

I text Zoe.

Me: Can you do me a favor?

Zoe immediately responds.

Zoe: Need me to kick Wil's butt? This fame thing is going to his head. Though every photo I'm tagged in as his designer does increase my following.

It's been one day. How famous can Wil be already? My breath hitches as my fingers fly over the screen.

Me: No.

Me: Can you get to Sven's new office ASAP?

Zoe: Picking up coffee at Blend. Be there in less than ten.

Me: Thanks. There's a woman in his apartment. His assistant-turned-stalker. He needs someone to fire her.

Zoe: Dancing Lady emoji

Zoe: A hundred new followers and I get to save Superman. My morning is looking up.

Zoe: Tell Sven to hold on.

"Sven?"

"Still alive."

I cringe at the dejection in his voice. "Zoe's on her way to save the day."

The woman's voice calling for Sven sounds farther and farther from whatever closet he's in. Sven's problem solved, I need him to solve mine. I pick at the green paint on the park bench. "So what should I do? Do I tell him?"

"Tell who?"

"Wil. About the thing."

"Do you trust him?"

My answer is unequivocal. "Yes. One hundred percent."

"Then tell him."

The churn in my stomach halts. "How do you do it?"

"What?"

"Help me while barely saying anything?"

There's more rustling and I imagine Sven sitting below a row of suit jackets. "Because you already knew the answer."

A stupid, happy tear leaks from my eye. "Thank you."

I hang up with Sven. It's okay if I talk to Wil. I bask in the excitement and certainty and dial my boyfriend's number.

THIRTY-ONE

"THAT'S INCREDIBLE." I KNEW El wouldn't be a backup singer for long. My girlfriend is going to be the lead of Blatantly Subtle.

"But you can't say a word to anyone." El's face on the screen of my phone is shiny and happy. My heart pinches. "Promise. I could lose this chance just by telling you."

"El, you can trust me. I got you."

"Do you mean that?"

"Always."

"Do you think you could come out here and help me with the song? I know you have classes but your midterms are over and I thought you might have more free time. I know we can write something that will blow Blatantly Subtle away." For the first time in this conversation, El's smile falters.

"I'll go ask Rocker for the jet now."

She perks up. "Really?"

"I'll call you right back."

"Wil." El places her fingers over her mouth. "I could be Blatantly Subtle's lead singer."

"It's a done deal."

I would cross an ocean to see El for a couple of hours, never mind a night. Giving up sleep to make up a few days of missed classes? Worth the hassle. I just need to be back for the Thursday rehearsal for the RA Connect Foundation Gala and getting Death Elbow ready to perform at the afterparty.

I pull out my duffle and start throwing in clothes. A knock on my door interrupts my packing.

"Can we come in?" Rocker's voice from behind the door is perfect timing. Saves me tracking him down in this massive mansion.

"I'm glad you're here. I need—"

"Wil?" Mum's voice makes me spin. She enters my room with Rocker looming behind her.

"Mum?" The gears in my brain screech to a halt. She runs to me, and I press her to my chest, her blond hair is all I can see but this is my mum. In LA. In my room.

"Mum!"

Her hug tightens, and I can't breathe. She's gotten so much stronger.

"Mum." I close my eyes and let myself absorb the moment.

"I told you he didn't suspect anything." Rocker enters the room, his smile so wide he shouldn't be able to fit through the doorframe. He's vibrating with energy. "You're surprised?"

"Very," I say as I let air back into my lungs.

Mum detaches herself from me and takes my face into her hands. "Have you grown? You look bigger than you were on Christmas. Less skinny. I like this look on you."

"You're one to talk." I've seen her on our videocalls weekly if not more, but even after a transatlantic journey she is beaming. "You must be tired."

"First-class travel is closer to spending time at a resort than traveling. I had my own little cabin, and they brought me so much food, and I caught up on movies I meant to watch but didn't have time for. I even got a massage in the first-class lounge in New York."

"Is Opa here too?" I search the hallway behind Rocker.

"His passport expired. You know how he hasn't left the country since Oma died. No reason to travel. 'Waste of money.' But if you stay here, I'll make sure he renews it."

Me staying here is not the deal Rocker and I made. I'm leaving once the winter quarter is over, but Mum doesn't know about our agreement. My happy and healthy Mum is worth much worse deals. I still can't believe she's here. I grip her arm tighter to convince myself. "Why didn't you tell me you were coming?"

"It was so last-minute." She glances at Rocker.

"I figured it'd be best to get Hanna out of the house for a bit, avoid the reporters until we have a proper plan." I meet Rocker's eye, gratitude flowing through my veins. He really does look after his family. "Marta's setting the table for dinner and Sylvia is dying to meet Hanna. She should be back from her walk with Pickle any minute." His silly grin widens. "I have so many plans for your stay."

"Plans?" says Mum.

"We'll sightsee. Asher Menken, he's our neighbor, got us tickets to the premiere of his latest movie tomorrow, so we'll do the whole red-carpet experience. Treat you like a movie star. Then there's a spa day on Thursday for you and Sylvia, and . . ." Rocker stops as he watches Mum's face elongate with every item he lists. "Or not. We can just chill in the backyard by the pool as well. If that's what you want. Or we can—"

"Bill." She lays a hand on his forearm. "Just being here is lovely. I appreciate the planning, but maybe Wil and I can have a moment? He can show me my room, right?"

"Yeah. It's the silver one. He knows. I'll be down the hall. Join me when you are ready. No rush." Rocker backs out the door and the reason I wanted to talk to him clangs in my mind. El.

I glance at Mum, who sits on the corner of my bed and looks out at the choppy ocean. "I've seen your room on video, but it's so much bigger in person. Everything seems double the size."

I'll settle Mum in and then ask Rocker for the jet. Mum will be fine with Rocker taking care of her. "My sentiment exactly when I first got here. I don't notice the difference anymore." I plop next to her. "How long can you stay? Are you missing any treatments?"

She pats my hand. "The doctor cleared me for the flight, and I have everything I need with me. You're stuck with me for five days."

"Five days." If I leave tomorrow instead of tonight and come back Thursday morning, I'll only miss one day of Mum's visit.

Mum lays her head on my shoulder. "Not enough, I know, but I have to get back for my tests. Plus, I can't leave Opa alone for too long. If the reporters find us, we don't want him talking to them, do we?"

I laugh. "That would be bad." My stomach rolls. I can't leave now. I can't just vanish the first day she's here. If I tell her, she'll probably insist I go, but what do I tell El?

"Are you not happy I'm here? Should I have stayed home?"

"What? No. I love that you are here. I get to show you everything. The campus, Rocker Inc."

"Do I get to meet Sven and Mateo?" Mum's lips tip up. "And the infamous Zoe?"

I fake groan. "I'm sure I can arrange that."

"Can we grab coffee from Blend?"

"That is the easiest. I can take you there tomorrow morning." I wince. That's if I'm not in Vancouver with El.

"And the beach? I heard about these hot air balloon rides with a view of the coastline." I haven't seen Mum this excited since . . . ever?

My nerves are buzzing, and I can't sit still any longer. I pull her up with me. "We can do anything you want. You tell me and I'll arrange it."

"Bill said he had plans . . ."

"You're the star of the show for five days." I loop her arm around mine. "I want you to be my arm candy during the RA Connect Foundation event, but the rest of the time, anything you wish for that we can accomplish with money and connections is yours."

Mom tilts her chin up. "Is it true Asher Menken is your neighbor?"

"On the left side." Mum loved the video I sent her last September when I met him at the Starlight Gala. My heart does a cartwheel. I can't wait for Mum to meet him in person. "Some architect lives on the other side."

I walk Mum into the hall. "All of my friends already think you're a model or a movie star," she says. "If I tell them where you live, they'll be certain you're LA royalty."

"I'm not. Rocker is. And this is just temporary."

She pushes hair away from my eyes. "It doesn't have to be."

"Are you kidding? The legal drinking age here is twenty-one. I'm not waiting six more months to drink a beer." I open the door to her room. "You get settled and I'll be back in a few to help you find the kitchen." I kiss Mum on the cheek. "I can't believe you're here."

I slip back into my room and call El. It goes straight to voicemail. "Call me when you get this. Rocker flew Mum over. She's here in LA. Maybe I can fly out tomorrow instead?" Even as I say these words, I know how unlikely it is. The wish to split myself in half and be in both places at once cleaves my heart into two. El vs. Mum. Mum vs. El. I let Mum down when I canceled my visit to Germany and chose to fly to San Francisco to help El. This time I'll let El down. My chest is heavy. "Call me."

Mum's oohs and ahs intensify with every step in Rocker's house. Her bed with a canopy she was certain only existed in the movies. A bath that can fit her tall frame. The balcony with a lounger and the view of the ocean. I see the place through her eyes. That was me on Labor Day visiting El here and finally getting what her level of wealth meant. I no longer register the intricate detailing of the wrought iron banisters, the Italian marble floors, the thousands of dollars each piece of furniture must cost. Getting used to money was so easy. Effortless.

We pass the piano and harpsichord on the way to the kitchen. I hug Mum into my side, my arm over her shoulder when we enter the room. Sylvia and Rocker are kneeling on a blanket as Pickle reaches for them, then switches his attention to where I am, stretches, and rolls over. "You did it. Bill, did you see him roll?" Sylvia repositions Pickle onto his stomach. "Can you do it again?"

"Our guest is here." Rocker rises.

Sylvia's head snaps our way. The genuine smile that makes her look so much like El wavers. She scrambles to her feet and smooths the silk blouse she's wearing. "Hanna, you're . . . I've heard so much." Her lips stretch back into a smile, but her eyes are uncertain.

"Did Wil give you the tour yet?" Rocker puts his arm on Sylvia's shoulder.

Mum answers in English. "My room, and the stairs, the music room. The views of the ocean are breathtaking. It sounds so serene, better than any white noise."

"That's what I said when El and I moved in here. The views." Sylvia plays with the huge diamond on her finger.

"Lovely views." Mum's unease is palpable.

No one moves. The tension grows as the awkward moment balloons. Should we sit on the couch? The stools at the kitchen counter?

"Ba-ba-ba." Pickle breaks the silence then blows raspberries, a sign he's upset at no longer being the center of attention.

I rescue my half brother and introduce him to Mum. "This is Pickle."

He lurches in my arms, tiny hands grasping for Mum's hair. "Aren't you adorable."

Sylvia leaves the shelter of Rocker's embrace and pats Pickle on the back. The baby's forehead crinkles, and he changes direction to pull on his mother's hair. With Sylvia and Mum side by side, the similarities between them click. Blonde. Blue eyes. Mum's taller while Sylvia is average height. They might not be mistaken for sisters, but Rocker has a type.

"The roast is resting, and the Yorkshires should be ready in five." Marta enters the kitchen with a tray of mini quiches.

"I'm—" She notices our silent group. "Is this your mother?" she asks me, setting the tray down. "Wil passed me the stollen recipe and that's been the best fruit cake I've ever made. Took me a bit to change the measurements but it was worth it."

Mum says, "My mother said it is a secret family recipe, but Wil's . . ." She stops and throws a glance at Sylvia.

"Wil's part of the family." Sylvia steps forward. "And so are you."

Sylvia wraps her arms around Mum who reciprocates. The sight of polished worldly Sylvia and my mother in her cheap jeans and T-shirt is odd. My two worlds coming together. Maybe this is indeed possible. Maybe I don't have to pick one over the other.

What if I can have both?

THIRTY-TWO

I'VE NEVER THOUGHT ABOUT writing songs as a task. Calling myself a songwriter and actually writing songs on demand is a leap I thought I was ready to take. It worked for *Indigo*, but then I had the story, the premise, the point to make with the song. I had Wil to be my sounding board, my interpreter, my inspiration.

But Wil's not here. I can't blame him for staying in LA to be with his mother. Yet I can't deny I want him here. The physical and emotional comforts Wil provides are my safety net. Without them, without him, I'm more alone than when I sat in my room in Malibu. Vancouver is only three hours away. Rocker would lend him the jet. Wil could've flown here for a night and been back to spend the rest of the week with Hanna. The ache in my head spreads. My heart wallows in self-pity. I rub my chest and struggle to take a full breath. Nothing is the same without Wil. Especially songwriting.

Sitting in a rented studio full of any instrument I might want, with the programs and plugins at my disposal, I stare at the walls and count the nails in the paneling. One nail on top and one on the bottom. But the two next to it have three.

The file I'm working in isn't blank. It's also not the first. Or fifth. In the twenty-four hours since Carlee asked Josie, Annalyn, and me to write an original song that represents the vibes of Subtle that could be on their next album, I've had a hundred ideas.

None good.

None inspiring.

Music swirls and sparks, but I'm like a car that has a tiny tank of gas and can't get to the final destination. Instead of finding a gas station to refuel, I get into a new inadequate car. On and on. Time passes. The hours in this studio are miles on the road, but I'm also driving in a circle.

Erratically.

I put my face into my palm and massage my eyelids. Inspiration is usually everywhere, and when a snippet of something real comes to me, the euphoria is unmatched. A blessing and a curse.

Even if I'm not actively writing, my brain is turning over the melodies, arrangements, instrumentation. Songs swirl and morph and occupy every waking moment. I run to the beat of the song. I hear it in the background as I talk to my friends. At night it keeps me awake. If I manage to sleep, it haunts my dreams.

But despite the deadline, the music escapes me. The urgency to write what's in my brain is absent. Maybe it's the studio. I move to the patio. Nope. I walk down Water Street back to the hotel and lie on my stomach on the bed. Not working. I sit at the foot of the bed and stare at the pristine white ceiling.

Nothing.

I sprawl on the floor of the hotel room Wil rented for me for the rest of the week even though he couldn't come.

I listen to the playlist of my favorite songs on repeat. Emotions flit over me, but nothing seeps in. I tear the buds out of my ears and toss them on the coffee table. The tiny things clatter ineffectively, just like the scraps of lyrics that one good song do not make. I growl, hit the floor with my fist, my foot, shake my head, and roll on the stupid fluffy throw rug.

Annalyn's voice from the hallway halts my thrashing. I still, listening to the harmony and the words. I don't recognize the song. I scramble to my knees and push my ear to the door.

Scrappy, and bright, even though I'm not right
For everyone.
For myself I'm the only one.
For myself I'm the height.

I press my eye to the peephole. Annalyn stops pacing the hallway, mutters, types something into her phone, and resumes.

> Scrappy, and bright, even though I'm not right
> For everyone.
> For myself I'm the only one.
> For myself I'm the titan,
> The muse,
> I don't use . . .

She's too far away for me to hear the rest. With just her voice, the words and melody give only a glimpse into what she's working on, but I'm one thousand percent sure that's the song. THE song. She's not done either, but she seems further along than my million bits and pieces with exactly zero words to accompany them.

My lower lip trembles. I was certain I had this advantage over Annalyn.

I can't fail. I've come too far. I reach for my phone and call Wil, even though I promised myself I'd let him focus on Hanna this week, no matter how much I want him to hop on the plane and cowrite this thing with me. Wrap his arms around me. Give me the words I can't seem to find on my own. Just be here.

"How's day two of the visit going?" I try to sound interested.

Wil's face is relaxed against the headboard of his room. "Mum thought the Japanese toilet she has in her bathroom is the best thing she's ever used. I thought she'd love the pool or maybe the beach. No, she mentioned the toilet so many times Rocker is set on having one installed at our house in Bremen. Can you imagine?" Wil's laughing, and the brightness that surrounds him is a testament to how close Hanna and he are.

"What did she think of the three ovens Marta has in the kitchen? I emailed her about them, and she thought I was kidding." I play along, not sure I should be breaking his mood with my inability to come up with something decent.

"They baked blueberry muffins this morning to celebrate the birthday Mum missed and are conspiring to make a secret dinner with a proper stollen. Marta has a friend for life in Mum."

Saliva pools in my mouth at the through of Marta's cooking. "And Mom. How's she getting along with Hanna?"

"Best buds they are not, but it's less awkward every day." The smile returns. "Pickle is the big diplomat. I used to ask Mum why she didn't have more kids, and she always said I was enough. Seeing her with Pickle, I think that maybe if she found the right person . . . not that I'm going to micromanage my mother's life."

"Maybe she can join our call tomorrow morning—"

"About that. The only time we could fit in the sunrise hot air balloon ride was tomorrow."

I fight the wave of bile burning at the base of my throat. "What time will you be back?"

"It takes like four hours." The pit in my stomach grows wider. Wil must see the disappointment on my face. "That was the only thing Mum asked for."

"How about the afternoon?" Probably too late, but he might offer some last-minute advice on whatever I come up with.

"I go straight to Asher's *Two Trains to Paris* movie premiere. Rocker promised Mum the whole red-carpet experience. Zoe is fitting a special dress for her, and they hired a glam squad with hair and makeup. You know the drill."

I throw my shoulders back and put on my best I'm-loving-this press conference face. "Yeah, I get it. Don't worry. Go. Spend time with your mom."

Wil's face fills more of the screen. "Are you sure?"

"Absolutely." Not, but I know how much I miss my mom, and she doesn't live half a world away. I rub my temples. "I was going to ask you tomorrow but . . ."

"What's wrong?" When Wil's worried about his mother, two little crinkles form between his eyes. Like now.

"I'm still stuck." Even I hate the whine in my voice.

"The song?"

"I wish there were a song." I clasp my hands in my lap. "I haven't settled on one yet." Let alone completed one.

"Hold on." Wil's little black book appears at the corner of the screen. "How about the chorus you sent me this morning."

Ah, my 6 a.m. epiphany. It held so much promise. In the shower, I heard a rhythm in the pulsing water and the beginning of a melody. Words about water flowing, water shifting, sparked and then flew away. I ran to write them down, but what came out was like a child's drawing compared to the Rembrandt in the bathroom. "It went nowhere. I can't have a chorus without the rest of the song."

"I'll talk to Mum, maybe Marta can take my place tomorrow." He's scribbling in his black notebook and I long to see the words. "You should've stopped me talking about Mum, we could be working on it now."

"I love listening to you talk about Hanna."

He shakes his head. "If I'd come to visit like I promised we'd be done by now." The mouth I love to kiss forms a thin line. "Still, we can accomplish a lot tomorrow morning as well."

"Wil." I try to grab his attention. "Maybe this is for the best. This is not about WE anymore. I'm supposed to do this on my own. Are you going to be in Blatantly Subtle with me? I can't rely on you to write my songs. I just need to settle on an idea."

His eyes darken, like I've said something wrong. "But I can still help, can't I?"

I replay my words and realize what I said. I shake my head. "Of course. I always want your help. Enjoy the balloon ride. Say hi to Hanna for me and make sure Zoe sends me the photos of you and Hanna dressed up."

The crinkle doesn't disappear. "I just wish you could be here with us. That'd make this week perfect."

Being with Wil would be perfect even if hot air balloons or sunrises weren't involved, but I'm not sorry I'm missing the red-carpet frenzy. We hang up and I scroll through the voice file from the morning. The upbeat rhythm reminds me of the happy feels of our song, *Orange.* Not something you can dance to but not a ballad. The arrangement I did on *Love Is Not a Sin* was a hit. I can do something along those lines but amplify it, make it more rock or more full-on dance mode.

If I am lacking joy in my life, maybe this is the way to create it. I think of Wil's excitement over spending time with his mother, of his face blooming when he played with the baby, with his friends in Bremen, his jokes with Mateo.

I glance at the bracelet on my wrist. Stealing Wil's joy might be the inspiration I need.

Rushing across the lobby of the recording studio on Water Street I spent hours at yesterday, I almost bump into Carlee and Josie hugging. My gaze falls to the floor. "Oh sorry."

The women break apart, Josie wiping her eyes. "It's okay, El." She offers me a sad smile. "I was—"

Kamo and Beau enter through the main door. My heart rate slows. I'm not late. But even if I were, practicing the new words of the chorus would've been worth it. I pull my hair out of my ponytail and fluff it in a last-minute attempt at not looking like I didn't have time for a shower. Or makeup. Or running a brush through my hair. Worth it when they hear my song. Wil's song. The song I wrote for Wil.

Beau claps his hands. "Ladies. Are we ready to get this show started?"

"I am." Annalyn steps from the corner, giving me a fright.

"Wait." Carlee puts an arm around Josie. "Josie wants to say something."

Josie takes a deep breath and squares her shoulders. "I love Subtle and singing is my passion. I'm honored to even be considered for lead singer." She glances at Carlee. "But I know myself. The spotlight is not where I belong. I'm bowing out."

The pulsing in my temples drives the sounds of the foyer away. This is huge. I glance at Annalyn, who is failing to suppress her grin.

Beau wraps Josie in his arms. "You'll still stay with us, right?"

Josie rolls her lips between her teeth, her eyebrows in an upside-down V. She blows a long breath out. "If you'll have me."

"Can't imagine Blatantly Subtle without you." Kamo rubs Josie's back.

Josie turns to Annalyn and me. "You're both so talented. Good luck."

"They are." Carlee walks between us. "Time to see what kind of songwriters we have on our hands." She disappears into the hallway. Showtime.

The sound engineering side of the studio that was too big and empty without Wil yesterday barely fits the six of us. Beau has a coin in his hand. "Heads or tails?" He looks at Annalyn.

"Heads," she says.

Beau tosses the coin above our heads, catches it, and slaps the shiny silver onto his palm. "Your lucky day, Annalyn. You pick the order. Would you like to go first or last?"

The streetwear jumpsuit that skims her body is the exact opposite of my lucky outfit of green palazzo pants and beige top. Her cat-eye liner could pierce someone standing too close. My face hasn't been washed today. Her lips are glossy and outlined. I'm rummaging in my pocket for ChapStick. She's edgy vibes. I'm comfort. Without Zoe and an expensive hair-and-makeup squad, I'm a pale young girl to her polished diva. We couldn't be more different if we tried.

"First. Always." She gives Carlee a broad and triumphant smile as if she's already won.

She hasn't and she won't. Today is about songwriting. This is my time to shine. Even though Wil hasn't heard the words I came up with or the final melody, this song is gold. I know it in my bones. In my soul. My smile is full of confidence. "Break a leg."

Annalyn walks into the recording booth and sits at the keys of the piano. She hums then switches into a-a-as that span three octaves. Annalyn's runs compete with the melody she's playing, interrupting each other. The first line of her song is sure. I was expecting the quiet effect to continue, for her to use an ethereal voice or to whisper-sing, but instead she sounds like a babbling river. Words chase music running from the piano. Her competition seems not to be with me, but with herself, as she talk-sings a story.

Her story.

The images of her childhood struggle to fit in, her family's expectations, how she immersed herself into being an artist. I hear it. I feel it. The composition might as well be about me. I recognize myself as a child searching to belong, finding refuge in music, looking for a way out of parental disapproval.

The words are personal to her, yet universal. The big band sound is unnecessary. She shines solo. She leads Carlee, Beau, Kamo, Josie, and me through her tale and captures us. Captures me. Damn. Tears burn my eyes, and I sniffle. At least I'm not wearing any makeup. I blink away whatever I can as the keys beneath her fingers fall silent. Carlee, Beau, and Mille stand, clapping their hands raw in applause. I do too, because she deserves a standing ovation.

She's good. That's why she is here. But that doesn't mean she's going to win.

Annalyn strolls into the booth and stops next to me. "Good luck." The unsaid "you'll need it" lingers.

"You were great." I extend an olive branch.

"I know." Annalyn bites her lip as if she wants to say something but knows she shouldn't.

I stretch my hand her way. "May the best singer win."

She watches me for several beats and shakes her head, then brings her mouth close to my ear and whispers, "This isn't about being the best. It's about being the one they want. That's me."

Why do I even try with her? "We'll see." I drop my hand as she takes the chair I perched on the edge of for her entire performance.

My knees shake when I take my position on a tall stool in front of a microphone, my guitar over my chest like a shield. I'm channeling Wil today, and piano was part of the reason the song didn't want to come together. This is not about me or for me. The guitar is part of Wil. Today I'm conquering my fears and trusting I can do Wil justice. I strum the first chord and it vibrates in my chest, jostling the insecurity Annalyn re-introduced. I crumple the doubt and shove it away. Joy. I'm singing about the light Wil pours into me. I will be the sun to Annalyn's darkness. Happiness has to be more powerful than despair. I launch into the song, as if I'm in Rocker's Maserati, revving at the start, pushing my vocals, stretching to go high and low.

Full volume.

Full speed ahead.

I channel my inspiration.

Wil.

"When I cry,

I cry

with my fingers on the piano,

the guitar strings,

the five lines

that reveal

what hides

inside my head.

When I laugh,

I laugh

with your fingers on my skin,

my cupid bow,

the pages of your notebook.

The guitar takes center stage to guide the listener. I need them to hear Wil's ability to leave a mark wherever he goes. The sunshine of his smile when he's joking with his friends, with me, is in the chorus. The heat of his stare, the electricity of his touch, the happiness of his soul. Every facet of my boyfriend pours into the words I struggled to write.

I give the performance everything I feel. I forget about being lead singer. I unzip my heart and expose the corners I haven't shown anyone before. Even Wil.

They clap. Like with my first performance at The Devil's Martini, I fail at gauging if they're clapping as hard as they did for Annalyn. Everyone is on their feet, which is what I want, but there's no one thing that clearly screams I won. There's nothing that tells me I'm not it either.

Unlike The Devil's Martini, I don't have Wil by my side as I wait. I'm alone, and I need to get ready for my solo performance tomorrow at Blatantly Subtle's concert.

THIRTY-THREE

THE LAST TIME I was in a stretch limo, every seat was taken and Asher Menken's now-girlfriend was attempting to climb out the sunroof. Tonight there's plenty of space with just Zoe and me in the backseat as we head to Asher's latest movie premiere. The red-carpet experience Mum was both excited and scared of. She floored me when she walked out in her dark pink dress. Mum looked both younger and the most glamorous than I've ever seen her. Zoe styled her perfectly, but Mum's smile was her best accessory.

Hopefully I'll see loads of those. With the official launch of the RA Connect Foundation tomorrow, we'll make sure many more people in Mum's situation get the help they need and have a chance for smiles, not winces of pain.

"So nice of Rocker to invite Hanna to ride with Aunt Sylvia and him," says Zoe.

"Harper insisted the three of them show up together tonight, to squash any rumor that there's something going on between Rocker and Mum," I huff.

"Twenty years too late."

"You always have the right comeback. You could've been a comedian."

"Have you seen the outfits they wear? I'd break out in hives."

I recline against the headrest and wish for the fourth time this evening that it were El and not Zoe in the car with me, but my girl is making her dreams come true. I can wait one more day to hug and congratulate her.

"What is it with you and buttons?" Zoe tugs on my collar, opening the gap between the material further. "It's like you're a prude or something. Show some skin. Work it."

I brush away her hand. "Stop fussing."

"You're such a newbie. You're not exiting this car as Wil Peters. As far as the world cares, Rocker's son is walking the red carpet."

A week after the press conference and I'm learning to spot the paparazzi. The worn baseball caps. The bulky jackets that hide their long-range lenses even though it's eighty degrees out. Campus is pretty safe, security is swift at removing them, but walking to the Farmers' Market to get lunch isn't worth it anymore. Mateo's frat brothers aren't asking many more questions than before, and most of them are about how possible it is for me to get my hands on games that don't release for a while, and if Rocker really wears his leather jacket to bed.

But in a few minutes, I'm walking straight into the fray.

Zoe runs her hand down my chest to flatten her latest design, a three-piece suit that is surprisingly comfortable. Not that I'll admit that to her.

"I want each and every one of those reporters to capture you wearing my designs," she says. "The coverage will be off the charts for your red-carpet debut."

I stare at the crowd eating up the passengers that exit the car in front of us. "Is that all you care about? The world seeing your designs?"

No response. I turn and Zoe's arms are crossed like I've suggested we attend this movie premiere naked. "C'mon, you are not sulking."

"Everyone underestimates my ability. My parents don't care, too busy jet-setting around the world to even notice if I'm home or not. Too concerned about my brother and his . . . issues." The only thing I know about the guy is he goes to school in another state, can play the piano, and didn't show up to her fashion show. I open my mouth to ask but Zoe pokes me in the chest. "I work damn hard. I can't feel my index fingers from the million times I've poked them with a needle sewing these outfits. But it's worth it. This is what I am meant to do. I feel it in my bones and you and everyone else who doesn't care can kiss my ass." She sinks back into her seat, the glossy lipstick she reapplied moments ago reflecting off the glass of the car window.

In the last two months I've seen snobby Zoe, pushy Zoe, grifter Zoe, bickering Zoe, and hyper Zoe. Right here, right now, I see the real Zoe.

"I'm sorry," I say.

She snickers.

Zoe's like the sister I never had. A swell of protectiveness hits me for the girl who has to post her life on social media just to get her family's attention.

"Really. I am." I bump her elbow with mine. "I don't underestimate you. If you say you'll succeed at this, you will. You and El are alike in that way." Her shoulders drop. "I'm not used to being fussed over. This model/spotlight thing is not for me."

Her head snaps in my direction. "Wil, you're dating my cousin, one of the most sought-after women by the press. Even if you weren't Rocker's son, you'd be in the spotlight."

I cringe at her words. They're almost identical to what El keeps using as the reason to keep our relationship out of the press. But not for long. Soon she'll finish her tour with Blatantly Subtle and we will be able to go on a real date. No more hiding in basements and pool houses. I'm taking her to the movies, to concerts, to the restaurant Rocker took Mum and me to yesterday, to Disney Land if that's where El wants to go.

"That's why I 'fuss' as you call it. I want you two to have a fighting chance." Zoe twists a butterfly ring on her finger.

My turn to snicker. "The press won't influence my relationship with El."

"Says the man who's had the luxury of not having his every move scrutinized." The car inches forward and she picks up the tiny box she calls a purse. "I hope you're right."

"I am. Nothing can come between El and me." Zoe doesn't understand. El's it. Our weekend together in the guest house blew away any pretense of us being casual. My first girlfriend will be my last.

"My cousin is so freaking lucky," Zoe mumbles.

"Do me a favor?" Her black-rimmed eyes find mine. "Can you help make sure Mum and Sylvia aren't left alone together at the RA Connect Foundation Gala tomorrow?" Zoe and Mum bonded at the spa yesterday, after I suggested to Rocker maybe sending Sylvia and Mum to a half-day retreat, just the two of them, might be a little too much for the women in his life. Zoe offered to act as buffer. In typical Zoe fashion she refused to give up her phone at the entrance and did a deal with the spa to promote their services. Mum was live on Zoe's channel and felt like a movie star.

Zoe chuckles. "Count on me."

The strange thing is, I do. I have no idea how it happened, but I think Zoe and I might be friends. I might even miss her when I go back to Bremen.

The car door swings open and a flood of noise rushes in. I step onto the red carpet and someone calls my name, followed by another and another, a chorus of Wils. Zoe takes my hand and exits the car like a queen. Now the throng is chanting her name.

One side of the walkway is crammed with reporters holding microphones, men and women wrangling cameras that emit flashes like strobe lights at a dance club. The other side of the walkway is a wall covered with the logos of the premiere's sponsors.

Zoe pushes me against the wall. "Put your hand in your pocket." I do as she says. She retreats and a thousand bulbs go off.

Faceless voices shout. "Over here, over here, Wil. Look this way." And "Wil, who are you wearing?"

My mind goes blank. Zoe prepped me for this moment for days and the only thing my brain comes up with is El's cousin. El's cousin.

Zoe's at my side, her arm on my shoulder. The rhinestones of her dress scratch the thin material of my shirt where she's pressed against me in her side pose. "Why my designs of course. Wil only wears Zoe Yilmaz originals."

Her ploy works as the reporters refocus on her. My brain takes a minute to catch up while my eyes try to adjust to the bright lights. Just when I think it's safe to look up, a million more flashes blind me. Zoe nudges me to move but I stumble.

She grabs my hand and pulls me toward the entrance. Voices shout at us.

"Zoe. Are you and Rocker's son dating?"

"Wil, is she your girlfriend?"

No. My girlfriend is a thousand miles away.

Thirty-Four

"El," Annalyn calls from the couch in front of the TV in the greenroom. "Look who has a girlfriend. Didn't take him long."

The image onscreen is the video of the celebrity-studded red carpet for Asher Menken's *Two Trains to Paris* movie premiere. The photographers shout at Wil, smiling and confident in a stunning charcoal suit, Zoe's arm draped over his shoulder, the diamond butterfly ring I gave her for her birthday catching the light of the flashes. Pressed against Wil's left side, every curve of her body is highlighted like they were made to complement each other. "Isn't she your cousin? Did you know they were dating?"

"They're not," I say almost too fast.

Annalyn pulls on the hem of her skirt. "Your new brother is objectively hot. I'd tap him if I had a chance. They make perfect sense. Your cousin is gorgeous."

"They are not dating." Heat spikes up the back of my neck. "Trust me."

"Maybe they're keeping it a secret." She gulps some water. "Daniel Davison will find out. Bet he'll interview them for his *Hollywood Happenings Wrap Up Show*."

She pauses on my boyfriend, who fits in with the diamonds-and-couture crowd, his smile as dazzling as Zoe's ring. I've never doubted my cousin's talent when it comes to fashion, but her creations for Wil are inspired. How does she make basic black look so . . . not basic? Or is it just because the material is draped over Wil's increasingly wide shoulders? I trust Wil. I trust Zoe. "You can't always believe what these celebrity gossip shows say."

"Could've fooled me." Annalyn walks over to the giant screen and points at Zoe's arm. "Her hand looks mighty cozy on his chest."

Typical paparazzi. The group photos Zoe sent me before they left the house showed the whole gang dressed up and goofing off as they were loading into their limos. My favorite was of Wil and Hanna alone, her fuchsia-pink dress a perfect contrast to Wil's darker ensemble, framing Wil like a flower. She deserves some time to feel like she's royalty. I'm so glad the trial is working and she's feeling better.

Annalyn unpauses the video. The screen morphs to a story about Asher Menken and his new flame, Siobhan Casey, whose purple hair is longer than her barely-there dress. I'm saved by Josie bustling into the living room, Kamo following. Josie takes the chair to my left, giving me a "no clue what this is about" look.

"Ladies." Kamo claps her hands to get our attention. "After today's show Dr. Kim wants Carlee to take more breaks."

Annalyn's back straightens. "She still wants to finish the tour?"

"With two nights left, she's not budging on that one. It's her swan song. We have to give her that." Kamo flicks her box braids over her shoulder. "So each of you will be taking over more songs, like last week."

I ready myself for what else she has to deliver. "Also, Saturday night, before the encore, Carlee will announce her retirement." Kamo meets my eye. "And her replacement."

"But that's too soon," Annalyn whispers.

"With some rumors about the canceled dates, our publicist wants to get ahead of the press before the news leaks." Kamo grins. "One of you will join Carlee in the interview with Rolling Stone about the new lead singer."

Beau pokes his head in the room. "Kamo, Josie. Carlee needs you." His eyes meet mine. "Let's have a great show tonight."

My nerves pop and fizz. This is what I want. More time in the spotlight. "Imagine my name in *Rolling Stone*," I mumble to myself as I stand up, intent on finding a quiet place to call Wil.

"I don't need to." Annalyn flicks her hair. "You've been featured in it twice already."

"That doesn't count. Those were interviews with Rocker. I want to be known as a singer and songwriter, earn my own money with music."

"Money is money. You have plenty. Do you know what this could do for my life?" Annalyn tilts her head to the side, a move I know so well after sharing a hotel room with her for months. "You're second-generation wealth and grew up with a silver spoon in your mouth. You have everything. You don't need this like I do."

"Who says?"

"I do." Her empty water bottle slams onto the coffee table. "You have everything. You're not the daughter of immigrants who left their homeland so their children could have a chance. You didn't go to school during the day then work at a pub evenings and weekends. You didn't scrimp and save every cent to pay for the piano and vocal lessons your parents couldn't afford."

My spinal cord tightens. "I didn't have it easy either."

"Are people depending on you?" Annalyn's mouth twists and she crosses the room. "There's a generation of my family relying on my success, and I'm hellbent to give it to them. I worked for this for ten years. I deserve to be here."

"And I don't?"

"Stop lying to yourself." Her hand grips the doorknob. "This is a vanity project you'll abandon when your daddy buys you a recording studio of your own. For me this is life-changing."

I squeeze the plastic bottle in my hands, wishing it were the soothing metal of our water bottle. Wil's and mine. "For me too."

"You're selfish. You already have everything: money, fame, opportunity." She yanks open the door, walks through, and slams it. The doorframe rattles in her wake.

Selfish? Have everything? Her accusations trigger memories of Mom's words, of Rocker's. Do I have everything? Am I really not appreciating my life? What does Annalyn know about me? I glance at the TV, where a reporter is interviewing Asher. That's what Annalyn knows. The stories the media weave from innuendo and snippets taken out of context. Annalyn doesn't know me. But she will. The world will when I become the lead singer of Blatantly Subtle. I'll control the stories they tell.

By the end of the second set on Friday, I not only have a plan to win Subtle's attention during my solo, I know how to show them I'm their new lead. I won't only sound the part, I'll also look like Carlee. With Josie singing backup harmonies for Annalyn's solo, I have enough time to transform my outfit. My fake eyelashes are heavy. Without reminding myself to keep opening my eyes, I'd stumble over my feet. The black high-heel platformed boots Carlee loves to wear that go to mid-thigh and almost touch the tight pleather shorts are not aiding in my attempt to stay balanced, but the discomfort will be worth it when Carlee picks me. I tug on sequined gloves the costume designer has spares of in case Carlee misplaces one or throws them to the begging crowd.

I'm ready.

In the shadows backstage, my skin itches with goosebumps as Annalyn hits the G of *Making the Truth Hurt.* Unlike me, she's in her plain short skirt and T-shirt outfit, relying only on the power of her voice to beat the higher pitches Carlee usually goes for. From where I'm standing, I can see Beau nodding in approval behind Annalyn on stage and Carlee scribbling something in a chair next to me.

Yeah, I get it. Annalyn's good. A hard act to follow. She no doubt has the lung capacity to pull off the love song, and the fans can't seem to take their eyes off her long legs. She may have manipulated the crowd, but at the cost of spending most of her time standing at center stage glued to the microphone stand.

The melody fades, and she gets a standing ovation. My stomach cramps worse than after the bad Vegas shrimp.

Annalyn glides off the stage with her slow measured strides, like the applause is the invisible train of her outfit, and takes a seat by Carlee.

"That was fantastic." Carlee shouts above the hoots and hollers from the audience.

"Thank you." Annalyn drapes an arm over the back of her chair with the confidence of a CEO whose company's stock just doubled. "That song made me believe love is possible."

Who's the suck-up now?

The backstage crew scurries to remove the standing mic. The lights dim, bathing the room in almost sheer darkness. Channeling Carlee, I find my way to the keyboard. I studied this song. Besides watching her perform it night after night, I found every live version on YouTube. I studied every angle, every breath she takes, every smile at the crowd. Each detail, every mannerism is fresh in my head.

Fire became an instant hit in the clubs. The techno tune kicks off with repeated bass amplified by the heels of a flamenco dancer they hired for the sound. I lay my fingers on the keys and play the catchy melody like Carlee would do it. In the dark.

Mouth close to the microphone, I sing the first line of the chorus, giving it a dragging quality in this ultra-slow version Carlee chose for this tour. Josie's vocals in the background merge with the melody. My head down, my stance muted, I imagine myself the spitting image of the lead singer. The second line of the chorus ends and my fingers halt.

I wait.

One.

Two.

Three.

The stage floods with lights and I snag the microphone as I yelp the start of the second verse with every ounce of confidence

I have. I strut to the edge, the flare from my bedazzled gloves make me the cold flame to match the lyrics. Carlee assured me I don't have to do the next bit, that staying on stage is an easy adjustment for the light crew, but I'm going to show them I can tackle any challenge they throw my way. Careful not to stumble in my heels, I mimic her swagger and bounce out onto the catwalk and into the crowd of screaming bodies, hands clawing at my feet.

I wink at Kamo and Beau on the stage, smiling and singing like I don't have a care in the world. Like my heart is not racing. My pitch is perfect and the music in my earpiece pushes me along, the words flying off my tongue. I strut the Carlee strut and every element aligns. The high is heady. I make it back onto the main stage in front of Beau. Now for the riskiest part of my plan.

I sink down to my knees in time with the backbeat and wink in his direction. The corner of Beau's mouth slides up and I know this is working. I wag my finger in a come-hither gesture, asking him to join me.

There's no hesitation, just like with Carlee.

He joins me center stage. Hand on the outside of his leg, I glide up his body, over his waist, my fingers clutching the lapel of his jacket. I share my mic with him and together we launch into the chorus. The next round I swing the mic between us in time with the rhythm.

The music crescendos, signaling the end of the song. I take control of the microphone and Beau steps back. At the perfect spot the backtrack cuts off. The lights cut out, and I sing the last line. Just like Carlee.

Acapella.

I think the room falls silent, but I can't tell over the pounding in my ears. It takes every ounce of strength in my body not to move, not to surge with the adrenaline, not to kick off the next song, sing a whole set. Keep chasing the high.

My pulse slackens and the applause seeps in. The lights rise and I return to earth, my high slipping away. A pair of arms crash around me. Beau is hugging me. I remind myself not to tense. Beau is hugging me. This must be a good sign. Kamo joins him, and I'm the soft gooey middle of a huge doughnut.

"You rocked that" and "I could've sworn you were Carlee" and "That finale" come at me at once.

Backstage Annalyn offers me a half-hug. "Damn. With your lack of dance training, I didn't think you could pull off the catwalk." I plop down beside her not even trying to hide my grin. I killed it. That's right, I'm El Vella. The daughter of Matthew and Sylvia Vella slayed Carlee Waters's performance.

Carlee rises for her closing song. I wait for her to tell me how much she loved my rendition. "You are talented, El." The crowd roars as she retakes the stage, waving at her fans.

My fate is in their hands. Out of mine. That was the deal from the start. I clomp to the backstage hallway. My heart and my stomach collide. Cold sweat covers my skin beneath my polyester and pleather outfit. I remind myself to breathe and keep my eyes ahead.

Hallways blur and I'm glad I'm trailing Annalyn or I wouldn't have been able to find the way back to the greenroom. On the TV in the corner of the room Carlee takes the microphone and turns the stage into a gloomy haunted place without the tricks of lights. She's the beacon these people are here for and she mesmerizes them, lulls them into waves of a human ocean that wooshes right and left in sync with her tilting body.

She is the master of this game.

She is the act that is hard to follow, but I accept the challenge.

Thirty minutes after the stage goes dark on the TV, Kamo bursts into the room, followed by Beau, Carlee on his arm, and Josie. I shove my phone in the waistband of my skirt.

"Annalyn." Beau gives her a smile. "El." He gives me one as well. Both full and significant. Both offer zero indication of who he prefers.

Beau focuses on Annalyn. "You've been amazing to work with. Your voice soars without any effects. No matter what you wear you're a star. Your edginess and excellent dancing abilities put you in the lead from day one." That sounds like a but is coming. A but that is in my favor. I squeeze my fist and ready myself. "But."

My chest expands. I won. It's me.

"El, you are a true singer and songwriter. We loved your sound yesterday. That song was love in verse and melody. The epitome of falling for someone." Beau locks eyes with me. "Tonight, I almost forgot Carlee wasn't on that stage with me.

You nailed the fearlessness, the vocals, the ability to get the audience revved up—"

"Unfortunately," Carlee interrupts. "There can be only one lead singer of Blatantly Subtle." She steps forward. "Welcome to your new family, Annalyn."

Annalyn.

Not Melodie Rockerby.

Not El Vella.

Not me.

What do I do now?

Kamo hugs Annalyn. Another thing I can't do. Josie has tears in her eyes. Beau whispers in Carlee's ear. My heart slams against my ribs.

Carlee steps toward me. "El—"

I don't hear the rest. Because I'm running.

Out of the room.

Through a maze of hallways.

I rip the gloves off and wish I could rip the boots off as well.

Of course they didn't pick me. The press had it right from the start. I was the publicity stunt. The rock star's daughter who made headlines to get Blatantly Subtle into the spotlight. Possibilities tumble in my head like laundry in a washing machine. Maybe Beau tripped me that night in the bar, the reporters a plant. Maybe Carlee only invited me as a favor to Rocker to boost my confidence. Maybe Rocker paid Subtle to hire me.

I scramble into the first bathroom I see and hang over the counter. I claw at the fake eyelashes, peeling off the black feathers. As my costume comes off, so does my composure. The girl in the mirror is not me. I don't think I like her anymore. I don't think I like Carlee anymore either. They just wanted to use me for my name.

What do I do now?

The dark hole of nothingness yawns in the background, ready to take over. I turn on the faucet and wash off the heavy makeup I stupidly worked on, trying to be what they wanted me to be. Everyone else probably knew this was a pity gig. They were probably laughing at stupid little trusting me.

"Here you are." Carlee's voice jerks me away from the mirror. Her makeup isn't smudged by tears. Her stage outfit is not wrinkled or torn. "You're a fast runner, especially in those heels."

I shut off the water and compose my face into something resembling an acceptable façade. "I've run most of my life."

"I didn't know that." Carlee tugs at the paper towel holder and offers me two sheets. I snatch at them. "You're excellent at many things, El. The way you used the crowd today, and got Beau into the song, followed every tiny moment of my routine." She stops herself. "What was my routine. I'm not the lead anymore."

"Neither am I." I spit the words at her. Is she going to confess and tell me Rocker paid her to make me part of this?

"It was the right choice. For Blatantly Subtle. Annalyn is a good fit." I hear Carlee's message, loud and clear. Talent is not what decides these things. Mom tried to warn me that the music business is fickle. Carlee's throat moves with a deep swallow. "You're not band material."

The words slice through my broken armor. I dab my damp burning eyes. The lights inside me shut off. I'm scrambling in the darkness to see what I'm supposed to feel because I no longer feel anything. I'm cold, and dark, and empty.

"...live. So much more potent than YouTube. And the writing screams of talent." I can't listen to Carlee praising Annalyn. I get it, I'm a failure. Carlee takes my hands in hers and I see the gesture, but I feel nothing. Carlee's mouth moves but I hear nothing. I'm deaf to her criticism. We are frozen in time. There is no way back, and the future is a black hole I can't possibly face.

"Did you hear me, El?" Her fingers squeeze mine.

I didn't, but I can pretend.

She meets my gaze. "I understand if you don't want to perform with me for my last night tomorrow."

I jut out my chin. "Despite what you think, I'm not a quitter."

I'm just not good enough.

Alone in the bathroom again, I search for the rage I must feel for Carlee, but I find none. I find nothing inside. The shell of El Vella wipes down the counter and blows her nose. One more day. One more show. I can do it. I sit on the toilet bowl, peel off the boots, and shove them into the trash can. I don't feel okay, but I know how to fake it.

There's one person I can be real with. I need to hear his voice. I struggle to see the call button on my phone through my tears. Wil will know what to do.

Thirty-Five

"You look so handsome." Mum straightens the lapel of my silver-gray jacket. "I think Zoe has outdone herself."

I fiddle with the cufflinks Zoe had custom-made for the event for Rocker and me. Silver squares engraved with the new RA Connect Foundation logo. She even had a set made for Pickle. Sylvia, Mum, and El got pendants on a silver chain. "She outdoes herself every chance she gets."

"I like her. She's fun." Mum smiles back at me. Her cheeks are rosy, even through whatever Sylvia's makeup artist applied to make Mum's skin look as if she's eighteen and not thirty-eight. Gone are the purple bags under her eyes that I stared at every morning across the breakfast table. My fear of losing her that's been weighing on me most of my life is gone too.

My worries that Rocker's show-off-LA tour would exhaust her, or worse cause a relapse, never came to fruition. From the morning hot air balloon ride to the red-carpet premiere last night, she jumped in with both feet.

Sylvia also had her stylist pick a dress for Mum. The full-length bronze gown is a far cry from the navy-blue pantsuit she wore to my high school graduation. Diamonds, another loan from Sylvia, twinkle at Mum's neck and wrist. Someday I'll make sure she has permanent versions of the jewelry. And more.

"Wanna dance?" I ask Mum.

Death Elbow kicks off the second, more fun portion of the night in twenty minutes when the party transforms from ball to rock concert. I can't wait to watch them perform the song we crafted in Rocker's home studio live in front of an audience for the first time. This might be my only chance to dance with Mum.

Rocker and Sylvia grin as we join them on the dance floor while an instrumental version of the latest Blatantly Subtle hit plays from the speakers. My phone buzzes with a two-thumbs-up text from Mateo, confirming the stage is set. I'll miss him too when I go home. My stomach twists at the thought.

I take Mum's hand in mine. "What's your favorite part of the trip?"

"Aside from spending time with you?" Her eyes twinkle. "Meeting Asher Menken." He sat beside her at the premiere and half of Mum's phone memory is photos of them together.

I laugh. "Of course."

She tilts her head. "What's your favorite part of living here?"

The chuckle catches in my throat and I concentrate on my steps. "Not sure."

She pats my shoulder. "Hard to choose?"

"What? No." I shake my head vehemently.

"It's okay to like it here."

I glance at the stage, unable to meet Mum's penetrating gaze. "I don't. Can't wait to get back home."

"Luv." Her fingers stroke the top of my hand. "I see how happy you are here."

"Hard not to be happy when you have Marta making anything you ask for and a chauffeur driving you everywhere."

"Sure." She tilts her head. "I guess that stuff is nice. But it's not about that." Her eyes wander across the dance floor where couples sway to the music. Zoe is chatting with a tall blond. Mr. and Mrs. Yilmaz, or Patti and Bob as they insist on me calling them, spin and laugh. The crowd parts and I get a clear view of Rocker and Sylvia. "You have a life here now."

"Do not."

"Wil." She gives me the look she adopted to call me out when I faked a stomachache to skip school. "Are you telling me you don't like your classes?"

"They're fine. But I can get just as good an education in Bremen or Berlin." I might miss access to the sound studio on the third floor of the Herb Alpert building where El and I recorded the first song we wrote together.

"But you won't get a chance to do A&R at a record label. Discover new bands like Death Elbow." She points to where the band's poster promises a sound explosion.

Rocker's daily habit of reminding me about his offer to permanently work for him could be a drinking game. "I can still go to clubs at home, still find talent. With my experience at Rocker Inc., maybe I can land a job at a music studio somewhere." Preferably one with sound boards like Rocker's. My favorite is the one in Studio B. There's something about the acoustics in that room.

"What about your friends? Zoe and Mateo? Won't you miss them?"

My phone buzzes in my pocket, as if Mateo can hear our conversation and wants to contribute. I ignore the interruption. "As much as I miss Leon and Jan."

"And El?" asks Mum.

Now that's a low blow. "El and I can live anywhere."

"But her family is here."

I clench my teeth. "And mine is in Germany."

"Not all of it." Mum glances over my shoulder.

I shake my head. "I'm not staying here for him."

Mum squeezes my shoulder. "I'm not asking you to stay in LA for your father. Or in Bremen for me and Opa. I'm asking you to stay where you want to stay. For you." The softness in her voice causes my throat to burn. She tilts her head. "You've given up too much—"

"I haven't given—"

"Yes, you have." The fake nails they applied at the spa dig into my arm. "I'm grateful to have such a wonderful son. What you've done for me is . . ." Her voice trembles and the burning in my throat intensifies. "Was too much but greatly appreciated." She squeezes my bicep. "I want my wonderful, joyous son to be happy. Not for anyone else. For himself."

I've spent half my life worried about Mum, planning for her, trying to make things better. For her. There wasn't much time or space for me to think past the urgent need for money or new meds or windows that needed replacing. My only free time was the summers in England I spent with my cousins, and that was only to give Mum a break. Another string of buzzes from the pocket inside my suit jacket. What does Mateo need now? I search for him in the crowd, but he's nowhere.

"Luv." Mum's finger traces my chin. "What is it *you* want?"

I meet Mum's eyes. Clear blue eyes, free of tears or red streaks from stress. "I could stay and finish school."

Her smile cracks the rusty chain around my heart and the links fall away. "I think that's a good option."

I suck in the concept and hold onto it. The longer it sits there, swirling in my chest, the more it seems viable. The music ends and the dancers part, clapping their appreciation. El's ringtone sings and I fish my phone out of my pocket. "Hello."

It's too loud in the ballroom to make out what El is saying. I jam my finger in my free ear, but it's no good. "El, hold up. Let me find a quiet spot."

I escort Mum back to the table and duck out the side door. The hallway leading to the restrooms is empty. "Sorry. Didn't know the old crowd could be so rowdy."

"Wil." The wobble in El's voice punctures the balloon of happiness in my chest. "I screwed up." She sniffles and my heart squeezes. I mentally calculate how long it would take to fly to Vancouver to get to her. Even with Dad's jet it'll be hours. "They didn't choose me."

I shake my head as if I can unhear those words. "How? I mean why?"

"Carlee hates me. She said I'm," El hiccups, "not band material."

"There must be some mistake. You're the best singer they have."

"Mom and Rocker were right. I'm a failure," she whispers.

"Stop that. You are not." The silence on the other end rips at me. "Carlee made a mistake. She blew it. But this is not the end. This is just the beginning. I believe in you. We'll figure this out together." El's sob bursts like a dropped mic. "Come home."

THIRTY-SIX

I STEP AROUND A woman and her now-sleeping baby that wailed the entire three-hour flight from Vancouver to LA. My sneakers feel like they are weighted with my dashed hopes, and I drag my feet along the worn gray carpet of the corridor leading to the terminal. Shame at the silent tears I shed in the back of the plane prickles along my spine.

They didn't choose me. I wasn't good enough.

This was not part of the plan. Return to LA, tail between my legs, a loser. I should be spending the night celebrating with Blatantly Subtle. I should be preparing for a career in music. Instead, around me there is silence. It's like music abandoned me in Vancouver. After singing backup in the final show, I couldn't stand being onstage anymore. How could the vision of being a lead singer wrap around my heart so quickly? Maybe that was always my dream. If backup singing would've never satisfied me, why does it hurt now that I don't even have that?

The bright lights of LAX hurt my eyes and I squint, searching the arrivals area for . . .

Wil.

I'm in his embrace. The warmth drives out the cold of the recycled air from the plane. Strong arms cocoon me and hold me together. His lips press at my temple. "I'm so sorry," he whispers.

My throat won't work, and the burning behind my eyes attempts to restart the tears. I grip the soft cotton of his hoodie and inhale the scent of him. Wil is here. Wil will make it better.

We stand there for a minute or an hour, I don't know. Or care. My face tucked into his neck, his hand runs light strokes across my back as he presses soft kisses into my hair. Passengers part around us. The world shrinks to him and me. I focus on the pulse of his heartbeat pounding where my ear is squished against his neck. I use that constant drum to knit together a thin layer of protection against my emotions, gaining just enough strength to push back the tears.

"Let's go home." His voice is low.

The temporary wall almost buckles. "Okay."

Only when I peel myself off Wil do I remember we're at the airport. I search for signs of someone recognizing me. The fear creeping up my spine. If the paparazzi get pictures of Wil hugging me, it'll be the incident with Beau all over again. No, worse. Headlines of the stepsiblings hooking up will dominate the internet. I can't let that happen.

There's nothing.

No one.

The arrival area is void of people, never mind cameras and paparazzi angling for a shot.

Wil reaches for my hand, but I step back. "I need my bag."

My yellow suitcase is the lonely item on the conveyor belt, and Wil snags it before I can. We walk out the sliding doors and climb into the back seat of a waiting SUV. There's a dull thud when the driver closes the door and we're plunged into murky dimness punctuated only by passing streetlights.

"Are you sure you don't want to come back to Rocker's place with me?" Wil's voice cuts through the silence.

The damned ache behind my eyes pulses. "No. Zoe said I could crash at the pool house."

"Whatever you want."

I find his hand in the dark. "Can you stay with me tonight?"

"For a while. A reporter is coming by in the morning for the interview with *Rolling Stone*. They'll be expecting me for breakfast."

His unsaid words are if I came back to Mom and Rocker's house with him, we could be together. But I can't. Can't walk back into that house draped in failure. Can't face explaining to them that I tried and screwed up. Again.

In her driveway, Zoe offers her condolences with a hug, and this time I let her hold on as long as she wants. She pushes back the hood of my sweater. "They'll regret it. When you're a famous singer, they'll beg you to sing with them."

I don't even shrug. What's the point? What I haven't told her, or Wil, is that the music has stopped singing to me. On the plane all I heard was white noise. In the car, the usual rhythm of the tires against asphalt meant nothing. It's like I'm in a locked isolation booth where inspiration can't enter.

"The pool house is ready for you," Zoe whispers in my ear. "I stocked it with the essentials. Popcorn, chocolate, and licorice."

"Thanks." My head rests on my cousin's shoulder as we stroll across the backyard.

At the door, Zoe gives me one more squeeze. "We'll talk tomorrow." She runs a hand down Wil's arm and skips across the grass to the main house.

Inside everything looks the same as it did the last time I slept, or rather didn't sleep, here. Wil takes my bag into the bedroom, and I follow him. He startles when he turns and I'm right there. "Hey."

I lift up on my toes and press my lips to his. We're in our bubble, and I want to dissolve in him. His hands mold around my arms and he gently separates us, pulling back to meet my gaze. "Maybe we should—"

"No maybe."

Wil's fingers play a melody I can't decipher across my upper arm. Even with the lack of light I see the heat flare in his eyes.

"I'm not sure—" He drops his hand and rocks on his heels.

The dull ache in my chest that disappears when Wil's near peeks back into the tiny space between us. I scooch closer to him, pressing my cooling skin against his warm torso. He's always warm.

"I am." I dive for his lips again. I'm always sure about Wil. With him I have the grand prize. With him I am a winner.

In the bedroom, we take our time because there's nothing to rush back to. I have nowhere to go. I wait for the music to return, for the orchestra of WE to start the opening chords. We make sounds: our moans, the rustling of the sheets, his name on my lips. But there's no symphony.

The black licorice I snagged in the kitchen as I got us water tastes artificial on my tongue. Snacking at midnight isn't my thing, but it's the first time my stomach doesn't revolt. When did I eat last? I snuggle next to Wil in bed and offer him a bite of the sweet stick. He shakes his head. "Mum loves this stuff, but I don't get the fascination."

"It's a Norwegian thing." I throw my leg over his. "I'm sorry Hanna left before I had a chance to see her."

"Mum too, but she had to fly to Bremen for her tests. Rocker persuaded her to take the jet. She thought first-class was a luxury. I'm sure she'll be raving about her trip home for a month."

The happiness in Wil's voice bumps up against the bitterness I'm holding back. Happiness I can't convert to my own.

"I'm sorry too." We've emailed a few times, mostly updates on her health, a few recipes from when I stayed in Bremen. Maybe that's the solution. Maybe I should go back to Bremen with Wil. Back to where it went wrong.

"I can't wait to introduce you to the band." Wil wriggles underneath me. "You'll love them."

Death Elbow. Wil has a band. I press my hand to my quivering stomach.

He nibbles at my ear. "Everyone's excited about their first concert under the Rocker Inc. label."

I want to be happy for him, I do, but I can't pull together my fake face. I can't lie, especially not to him. I press my lips against his shoulder.

"Can you believe it's sold out?"

"Yes," I say. Because this isn't a lie. Wil being a success is inevitable. People like him. People love him. People want to be near him.

"Will you put on the dress you didn't get to wear for the Starlight Foundation gala?" He brushes tangled strands away from my neck.

Eyes closed, I focus on his touch. My stomach flutters. If I can stay in this moment, with Wil's caress jolting my sadness away, everything will be fine. I arch my neck, giving him more access.

"I can't wait to see you in it." The trail of kisses along my skin stokes the embers in my belly. "Finally get to go to one of these things with you by my side."

I picture walking down the red carpet in the beautiful dress Zoe designed last September, supporting Wil, like he's always supported me. My boyfriend by my side, smiling, happy. A tiny firework of excitement explodes in my chest at the image.

"It'll be our first official date." His hand grazes my chin and flashes go off in my brain.

In the movie in my head, cameras flash.

Reporters shout questions at me.

How does it feel to be a loser?

Are you here to support your brother?

Why are you holding your brother's hand?

Ice prickles along my spine. I'm not even there yet and my feet move to flee. Escape the questions. Escape the prying eyes.

"Everyone will be there. Except Pickle of course." Wil's chest rumbles with his laugh.

Everything'll come out. Daniel Davison cackling at our relationship, mocking Wil. I clutch Wil's arm like I can keep him here, in our bubble, until I can find a way to stop it.

"What's wrong?"

"The . . ." The ache in my chest rises, stifling. It's too much.

Wil's hand leaves my body. "What?" The tenderness in his voice is replaced with something I haven't heard in months. Maybe frustration.

"Please, Wil. I can't." The razors in my throat make it hard to talk. A sniffle escapes. I can't ruin this night for him. All my boyfriend wants is to take me out for date. He has no idea of the pandora's box he'll open. "I can't face Mom." Not a lie, but also not the whole truth. The floodgates open, and it's not gentle tears that escape, but ugly, ferocious sobs. I can't stop them. They coat my tongue, and I can't breathe.

Wil's arms wrap around me. "Don't cry." The steel ribbon tightens. "Please, just don't cry."

I try to stuff the hurt and disappointment back into the box in my chest I carried from Vancouver to LA, but it's no use. The lid is gone, and I exhale the sad, pitiful cries of a loser who has much more to lose.

THIRTY-SEVEN

MOM DOES A SLOW loop around my room and peers into the suitcase and two boxes I've been packing to take to Zoe's pool house. "Are you sure you don't want to come back and live with us?"

"I'm sure." After a week of living out of the suitcase in Zoe's house, I've made up my mind. No use giving Mom hope.

Mom lifts her head. "How come you let Zoe help while ostracizing the rest of us?"

Her question pricks in a familiar way. Mom and I used to have this shorthand. Somewhere along the way that changed. Maybe when she started dating Rocker seriously, when our world expanded beyond just the two of us?

My hand clutches at the wool of the sweater Zoe knitted for my sixteenth birthday. Why doesn't Mom get that I'm not a little girl anymore, that my leaving is normal. I'm trying to figure out what to do with my life and if I'm sure of one thing, it's that coming back to my parents' house is a step back, not forward. I clench my teeth but fail at controlling the swirls battering my ribcage. "Because she doesn't ask anything of me."

"If you move back here, you don't have to work for Bill. And we'll reinstate your allowance."

What's the use? If my mom were listening, she'd help me pack, not try to keep me tethered. Isn't my failed music career and the fact that she's already proven me wrong with Blatantly Subtle enough? I cram the sweater into the suitcase and yank the zipper.

Mom takes a framed candid picture of Rocker, her, and me laughing off the top of the pile I haven't packed yet. "We love you. Come back to your family."

Wil's more part of this family now than I've been over the last year. And Pickle takes up most of her time. "You have plenty of people here already."

"You'll be closer to Wil. Bill told me about you two. No sneaking around?" Mom watches me like an auctioneer at Christie's, waiting to catch a yes that just might tumble out of my lips. "Wil can help you settle back into your life."

Her assumption that I'll be settling stirs the unease in my chest, but my guilt over not telling her about Wil and me brings the acid up from my stomach. "I was going to tell you."

"Melod—El. I know you." She used to, but I no longer think she does. Mom rummages through the pile of photos I intend to take with me and extracts a photo of Papa and her staring at each other like they are the only two people in the world. "I know what a man in love looks like. I've been lucky to have two look at me that way."

"Do you love Rocker like you did Papa?" The question spills out and I look away, expecting her to be upset.

Mom's low hum is pensive, but not angry. She returns Papa's photo to my bed. "Bill's amazing. I've no idea what I did in this life to deserve such a kind, compassionate, good-looking partner." She laughs at the last bit. "We're so different yet have so much in common. He treats me like a treasure, even when I don't deserve it. He's my best friend, and I love him. It's possible to love more than one person. I have plenty of love to give and now that Pickle is here, I'm certain love is not a finite resource. More comes when you need it." The corduroy of her pants rustles as she sits on the side of my bed next to the canary-yellow suitcase full of parts of my childhood I don't want to leave behind. "But with Matthew, with your father . . ." She touches my hand and stills my anxious packing. "Your father swept me off my feet, and I'm not sure they ever touched the ground again when he was around."

I'm intimately familiar with the feeling, because that's the effect Wil has on me—the weightless feeling of possibilities to counteract the constant drowning I can't seem to outswim. I don't deserve his strength. I'll just drag him down. Wil needs someone who'll shine with him, who's not afraid. That could've been me, but it's not anymore. I drop the dress I was folding, sit next to Mom on the comforter that no longer feels like mine, and stare at the ceiling full of stars that no longer bring comfort.

What would've happened if Rocker hadn't found me in that hotel room in England? With my music video produced by Mr. Astor, I wouldn't have needed to sing at The Devil's Martini. Never met Wil. Spared him from cleaning up my messes. The thought that I need to let Wil live his life without my baggage pins me to my spot.

"You don't remember, but I used to be fun." Mom probably interprets my collapse as her winning me over. Her fingers reach my way then halt. "Your papa loved my extravagance. Your grandparents not so much. They thought I corrupted him, made him focus on the wrong things." Mom smiles the smile I only see when she talks about Papa. One I haven't seen in years. "But he took risks alongside me and came on the grand adventures I'd dream up for us. We always had fun."

She plays with the gold band on her finger. "Our greatest adventure was having you. Matthew was over the moon. Our world of two became three: our perfect little family." She cradles my hand in hers. I slide it out and grasp for my hair, the only thing that isn't changing in my life.

"At first, the press was kind. Photos at events, snapshots of us walking through the park with you in the stroller, and pre-arranged interviews and photoshoots. We were proud to show the world our perfect baby girl. Until . . ." She gulps, smile gone, face frozen in a stony mask of bad memories. "Until the accident. You probably don't remember but they snuck into the church during the funeral we closed to the public and took photos of me trying to calm you down."

I do. I remember the camera flashes and Mom dragging me through the back door of the church. Mom trying to wrap me in her arms and her embrace hurting my heart. I remember wanting to run back to stay with the closed casket that held Papa, even if I couldn't hug him anymore. Without his hugs, I didn't want anyone else's.

Mom reaches up, takes the strand of hair out of my hand, and tucks it behind my ear. "I was still playing nice. I asked for privacy and only got more paparazzi trailing us. There were photos taken through the slats in the fence, images of us boarding planes. Eating. They followed us into a bathroom in Vienna. You were a child. I had enough. I wasn't asking anymore. I did what I had to. Keeping you safe was the only thing that kept me going." Her finger traces my cheek. "Did I make your childhood hell by protecting you too much?"

The painful, muddled images of the months after Papa's death click one after the other in the slideshow of my memory, but they are not the only ones. I see plenty of colorful ones, of hearing the sounds of the world as we traveled, Mom and me, always together, always close, frequently laughing. "No, Mom. I had a childhood many would envy." I sink into Mom's fingers that are caressing my cheek. "I wasn't ready to face the reporters either."

"I've mulled it in my head so many times. What if I'd used a different strategy and told them the story of the accident, gave them the facts from the beginning? Would they have left you alone? Would the fascination have faded? Did I make it worse?"

What if I followed the instructions Blatantly Subtle gave me for my performance? What if Wil was anyone but Rocker's son? What if I were strong enough to face the world with him? My what-ifs are as numerous as hers. "You can't change the past."

"I hate that for most of your life, you had to hide. I want you to be able to go anywhere. With anyone." Mom lifts my chin. "You are my brave girl."

"I'm not brave."

"You are the bravest of us all. You fight for what you want. Even though I'd much rather you choose an easier route, I understand. I was like you. I wanted the world, and I can't deny the world to you. You have so much ahead of you. You're going to do amazing things. If a career in music is what you want—go get it." Love shines through her eyes. "Wil told me how you sang at a club. That you won an award for your song in that movie. How he helped you put your video into the world that caught the eye of Blatantly Subtle, your busking, and your covers. They selected you out of hundreds if not thousands of people. Thought you had potential to lead that group."

The reminder stings. "But they didn't choose me."

Mom laughs. A sound I haven't heard in months. "So what?"

"Well, that was kinda the point."

"Baby girl, I keep telling you: the music business is fickle. I lost a spot at the Norwegian Academy of Music and ended up in Italy. And you know what happened there?"

"You met Papa."

"Exactly. Life rarely takes the straight road. If I weren't trying to hide you, I wouldn't have insisted on a private tour of the Griffith Observatory while visiting Aunt Patti the same day Bill had a private tour at the same place at the same time."

I chuckle. "You almost ripped him a new one insisting he change his to another day. I don't think anyone had talked to him that way in years."

"And you insisted we could do the tour together."

"The docent was so relieved when you stopped glaring at each other."

"You were so happy watching the stars—"

"And Rocker was happy watching you," I say. We laugh, remembering. "You two made me believe in love at first sight."

Mom's laughter faulters. "Love at first fight is more like it."

Pickle's demanding wail crackles through the baby monitor Mom brought with her, snapping us into the present. We glance at the shadowy baby on the screen trying to escape the wearable blanket contraption Mom's testing to prevent him from waking himself.

"Go. He needs you." I stand.

"Thanks." As the reminiscing stops, the circles under her eyes return. "Go downstairs. Marta must have dinner ready. You're staying for dinner and movie night, right?"

We pause at the part of the hallway that will take us in different directions. "I wasn't planning on it. I'm just waiting for Wil and Sven to get back from their workout."

"You can invite Sven to stay too."

"Maybe I'll stay for dinner. No movie night." I slip away before she tries a different tactic to convince me. It's hard enough to keep up the smiles when it's just Wil and Zoe. I slink through the house that used to be my home, feeling empty inside.

Marta's cutting the homemade margarita pizzas she made in the brand-new pizza oven installed on the patio, just because Wil mentioned he loves California Pizza Kitchen to Rocker last week. I scowl at her.

"Would you like to sneak a taste?" Marta places a slice with still-bubbling mozzarella on a plate for me.

"I'm not hungry." I reach into the water cabinet for one of the Rockerby-house generic water bottles and freeze. The row of glass and black metal cylinders is disturbed by a partially peeling dented water bottle. Wil's bottle. The bottle I gave him on our last night together in Bremen. The one he promised to keep close. Never leave his sight. Our bottle. We have so many memories attached to that thing. What is it doing here and not with him?

"I'm back," Wil shouts into the living room. His T-shirt is drenched and his hair points in every possible direction. He needs a trim.

Rocker pokes his head out of the media room and shoots past me to bearhug Wil, patting him on the back like he's dislodging something from Wil's throat.

"You might need to do the same with this little guy, he refuses to burp." Mom enters with Pickle propped against her shoulder.

"I can do it," Rocker and Wil say as they outstretch their hands toward Mom and the baby.

"I haven't seen him today." Wil mock-elbows Rocker as if he's fighting his way to his brother.

Rocker fakes battling him then grins and lifts his hands in defeat. "Fine he's yours. But it's my turn tonight to sing him to sleep."

My boyfriend wiggles his hands at the baby and makes weird noises like he's communicating as a cat. He takes a cloth with a giraffe design from Mom and drapes it over his shoulder. "There's my favorite brother." Pickle gurgles and lolls his head in Wil's direction.

Rocker and Mom bookend Wil as he taps the baby's back like he's a maestro orchestrating a soft staccato.

"Let's eat," Marta calls us into the dining room and the four of them shuffle off without me.

I shut the door of the water bottle cabinet with enough force to make it shake. The vibrations match the angry ones in my gut.

At the noise, Wil glances back at me from the entrance to the dining room. "You coming?"

"Go. I'll be right there." I lean against the counter and shove my darkness out of their sight. I push my fingers into my eye sockets, scraping for the energy to last through this meal, and locate the appropriate smile in the catalog I've mastered for cameras. As I join the happy family, I suck in a breath. And in the one place I used to feel safe, I pretend.

Thirty-Eight

Marta's pizza is better than Mum's, even though I'll never admit that. El cuts her slice with a knife and fork. Pickle babbles in his contraption. The conversation around the dinner table flows. The pleasant post-workout ache lingers in my muscles. Too bad Sven couldn't stay. He needs to hire more people or he'll run himself ragged. I take a swig of the good German beer Rocker has cases of. A chuckle makes it past my lips. I can get used to this. I *am* used to this.

When I landed in LA in December, I had three goals: complete a quarter at UCLA, work for Rocker, and earn money for Mum's treatment while waiting for the end of El's tour with Blatantly Subtle. I was anxious to get my old life back. Here in this dining room, with El on one side and Rocker on the other, I want time to slow down.

In the adjoining room, a TV the size of a football field blasts a baby tune I find myself humming in class daily. Across the table from Dad and next to the baby corral, Sylvia watches Pickle's every move as he bats in rhythm to the tune, a spotted whale that hangs from the arch above him getting the worst of the hits. She looks prepared to dive in and save Pickle, as if the toy can fall and suffocate the kid if she takes her eyes off him.

"Did you start without me?" Zoe's voice comes from the archway to the front alcove. She emerges, laden with a rolling suitcase and three bulky garment bags in her arms.

I jump up and grab the heavy bags, laying them across the fancy tufted bench. "We just started. Full warning, Pickle is in a mood."

Zoe dramatically crouches across the room, her fingers wiggling at the baby. "Is someone cranky tonight? Does he need his big brother to sing to him?"

Pickle stops his attack on the whale, his legs kicking as Zoe approaches. She tickles his tummy and we watch Pickle TV for two minutes.

"What a day." Zoe plops into a chair beside El. "Sven's phone was ringing off the hook. I can't play his assistant for much longer. Took me an extra hour to swing by the house and pick up outfits for everyone. Wil, I think the navy blue or the burgundy might look best. Both will match the dress I made for El." She nudges her cousin, and I grin at my girlfriend. Death

Elbow's big premiere is next week and I'll finally get my chance to see her in the dress.

I swallow a bite of pizza. "Sven says thanks, by the way."

"What for?" Rocker wipes his fingers on a napkin.

Zoe pours a glass of watermelon juice. "Your ex-bodyguard needed a little help firing his latest assistant/stalker."

"Stalker?" Sylvia interrupts her Pickle vigil to stare at Zoe with real concern on her face. I grin at El and she smiles back.

"She was harmless. Simply had a big ole Sven crush." Zoe cuts into food. "Thanks, El, for hooking me up. I haven't fired anyone since that handyman I hired to build the gazebo in the backyard."

El huffs. "He showed up without a hammer."

Zoe sighs. "This was more fun. Best part is, now Sven owes me one." She jabs the pizza with her fork. "Not the hardest thing I had to do this week. Tracking El for a fitting has been much harder. And we live in the same house."

"I live in the pool house."

"Po-ta—to, po-tah-to." The fork swings in the air. "I'm here. You're here. The dress is here. I have my kit with me. The second dinner is over we're going to your room and finishing this dress." She pokes El in the ribs. "You've lost too much weight on tour."

"I agree. El, you're too thin," Sylvia says.

El's fork clatters against her plate. "I'm fine."

"She's perfect." I'll always have El's back. And she is perfect.

Rocker clears his throat. "Is everything confirmed for the show? Triple-checked? We can't mess up Death Elbow's first performance under the Rocker Inc. label."

"You can count on Wil. He even made a spreadsheet," says Zoe.

I glare at my plate. I showed that to her in confidence. Turns out there's a lot more to planning a live concert with a band than just DJ'ing at a club.

Zoe wipes the napkin on her red lips without leaving a smudge of lipstick. "And I'm meeting with the Death Elbow guys tomorrow for a final fitting. I'll make sure their outfits are at the venue the day before the show."

"Mateo will help with the merch booth." I meet Rocker's discerning eye.

Zoe takes a sip of her drink. "I've hired him to design my new logo in exchange for a Zoe original. Bill, you have your stylist working on your clothes for the event?"

"All taken care of."

"Aunt Syl? Am I designing something for you?"

Sylvia clutches her napkin. "Your mom invited Pickle and me to the new resort and spa up the coast."

"You deserve the R&R. Wil can get you tickets to any upcoming Death Elbow concert." Dad speaks of my future with Rocker Inc. as if it's set in stone. "Or other up-and-coming artists he's been keeping tabs on. Wil has an eye for talent."

The pizza sticks in my throat. Over coffee this morning, like clockwork, Rocker repeated his offer of me working for Rocker

Inc. I said my usual no, even though for the first time, it didn't feel right. After Mum said the idea of staying longer and finishing school wasn't bad, I've been considering the option. With El not touring, this could work. I have two weeks to decide if I stay, or if I ask El to return to Germany with me. I try to catch El's eye.

She peers at her plate, not meeting my gaze. "I'm finished." El stands, her half-eaten pizza left on the table. I reach for her hand, but she steps away. "Are you ready, Zoe?"

I want to ask her to talk to me but my mouth is full of pizza. Zoe points to her full plate. "Give me five. I'll meet you up there."

"Pickle," Sylvia yelps. We turn to catch his little fist gripping the whale, as if he's trying to pull himself up.

Rocker shoots out of his chair. "Isn't it a bit early for him to be gripping things?" Both parents beam at the child like he is the next Mozart or Lebron James.

I puff out my chest. "Takes after his big brother. Mum says I was running round the house at nine months." Both Sylvia and Rocker stare at me. "It's true. She has a video."

Dad's eyes light up. "Can she send it to me?"

Heat rises to my cheeks. "I can ask. It might not be backed up." I push away my empty plate and glance at Zoe. "Time to check on El?"

She stuffs the last piece of crust in her mouth. I tickle Pickle on the way past and head toward the hall. I pause at the end of the hallway and wait for Zoe. "Before we go in, we need to talk."

"You're wearing a suit. I don't care how much you hate them, you are representing Rocker Inc. not—"

"No." I stop her tirade. I've learned when it comes to fashion, it's easier to just give in to Zoe. The tightness in my throat has nothing to do with her. I swallow. "Rocker wants me to work for Rocker Inc. I was planning on going home, but now that El's not with Subtle, I was thinking I could stay for the spring quarter at UCLA, finish the year, if she wants to stay in LA."

A crinkle forms on Zoe's forehead. "I'm confused. Why are you asking me? Isn't that something you should be talking to El about?"

I slouch against the wall. "I've tried. Since she's been back, she avoids any conversation of the future." I draw circles on the wall. "It's like she doesn't want to move forward with me. I'm trying to be patient."

"I don't know what to tell you." She pats me on the shoulder. "Grow a pair and talk to your girlfriend. Tell her how you feel. El would want to know."

I exhale. "You're right."

She runs her hands through my hair. "Can you please do something about this before next week?"

"Zoe?" I turn to find El staring at us.

"Hey." Zoe strides toward her. "Convince your boyfriend to get a haircut. Messy suits his brand. Shaggy is just lazy."

"What do you think El?" I rub the top of my head. "Is Zoe right?"

My girlfriend wraps her arms around her body. "She usually is."

Thirty-Nine

WIL'S BRIGHT FACE IS hard to wake up to. Harder to smile back to. I should be happy for him. I am happy for him. LA becomes him, like Zoe's clothes. Like working at Rocker Inc. Do I become him anymore?

He takes my hand and kisses the knuckles, giving me a look. The look. The one I can't say no to. One that might just be the only thing that lets me forget that empty space where music used to be. If my melodies are not coming back, how bad could it be to fill the echoing caverns with the liquid fire of Wil's touch. "Don't look at me that way."

"You're the one who's doing the looking." I lay my hand on his forearm and walk my fingers up to his bicep that's straining the sleeve of a slim-fit T-shirt. I sneak a finger under the fabric and move up to his shoulder.

His eyes morph from hard amber to liquid honey. "El. We have plans."

"Running is not plans," I say. "I know better ways we can get sweaty without leaving these walls."

Wil places his palm on my fingers that are now touching his clavicle. "It was supposed to be a surprise."

"A good surprise?" I rise and repeat the same maneuver up his arm on his other side.

He halts me before I get to the sleeve. "I can't believe I'm saying no to this but, we must go."

"Why?" I target his lips.

"Because you haven't been running since you've been back." He twists so my back is to his front.

I look up and back to catch his gaze roaming my neck. "I know you want to accept my offer."

"Always. But trust me. You'll love this surprise." He kisses my temple and walks us to the door.

Wil borrowed Zoe's car for the day. The drive to Runyon Canyon on this sunny day shouldn't bring on the resentment I've been hiding from him since he signed Death Elbow. Hiding from myself, because I'm his girlfriend. His smile wakes the ache in my heart that doesn't belong there. Why am I so bad at this?

"The next step is to get them on tour. We'll start with one around the US, see how that works. I've been talking to Rocker about getting them on a talk show, and our publicists are working on finding a spot. The single got a million views in the first ten days. No video, just the song and the lyrics on screen. Imagine what we'll get with a video. Thanks to yours I have ideas, and I am considering asking Nick and Mateo, gather the old crew maybe. But Rocker thinks we should get someone more established. He actually mentioned Leonard Astor. The irony." Wil stops and throws me a side glance. "Did you ever tell Rocker you were planning to film with him?"

"No." The word erupts from me as if Wil was asking if I've been swimming recently.

"D'you want to try again? If we talk to Leonard about Death Elbow, we can see if we can do something for you. Your dream collaboration, no?"

I shrug. "I thought so. What the *Indigo* team put together turned out to be the dream one. The dream I didn't know I needed." He's the dream I don't want to wake up from. My heart pinches and tears mist my vision of Wil glowing on this sunny Friday morning, eyes on the road, fitting the energy of the city.

"We did well, but you can't compare that to Leonard. Rocker said he's like a sure bet if you want people to talk about your video," he says. I know. That's why I chose the famous director. "Your followers have been growing. The covers you've been making are getting views."

"Hardly."

"If you put another original song out, that might be the push you need to recapture attention. Start talking to the recording companies again." He reaches for my hand. I pretend I don't see it and cross my arms. "We can finish your love song we started in Bremen. A new song can change your life again."

"That's our song, not my song." I hit my head against the headrest.

"Does it make a difference?"

"It does to me," I snap. "You've already proven you can win at everything you try. I wasted every opportunity I had." I dig my nails into my skin. "You don't get it. I'm a failure."

"You're not a failure." Wil's tone is kind. Too kind.

Easy for him to say. He's the golden boy. Straight A's at school. Managing Death Elbow. Pickle adores him. The press fawns over him. Even Rocker loves him more than me now. I grind my molars and glare at my knees.

Wil turns into the parking lot. "What about the song you wrote for Blatantly Subtle? I still haven't heard it. And they never took the song, right?"

"That should tell you everything you need to know about how good it is." I cringe at the sound of my voice, but the hope in Wil's delusion of where my career is going pierces the already thin wall of my belief in myself. "I'm a one-hit wonder. There are no more songs. The music is gone. I told you."

Wil parks the car and puts his fingers on my downturned chin. "Your music is not gone." He steers me to meet his eyes. "You will never run out of music."

"How do *you* know?" I release my anger.

"El." His gaze borrows into my soul. His stupidly handsome face sends tendrils of heat into my core. "I know." That look again. He's killing me with that look of his. "I know because I know you." His thumb caresses my cheek. "You *are* music."

I scoff. "Only in your eyes." The rage and desire burn from the inside. Being so close to him used to be my dream. Now it's my nightmare. I move my face out of his hand and settle my gaze on the car parked next to us. "I'm empty."

Palms on my face, he gently turns me to the left. "Hey," he whispers. "Emptiness is music too."

The liquid fire is back, flowing down the walls of my soul, heating me with the emotions I can no longer generate on my own. Stealing his joy for my song was one thing. Stealing his fire to keep my ambitions going feels wrong. Is wrong. "Not *my* emptiness."

"El."

Hearing his pleading voice only hurts more.

"We can stay in LA," Wil says. "I'll accept Rocker's offer and we'll have enough money to rent an apartment. You'll work on your music. I'll go to school. We will figure the rest out. Together."

I stare blankly at him. His vision of our future is as good as a fairy tale. Because that's all it is. In my view of that story there are paparazzi in the shrubs next to our door. "Siblings Shacking Up" slander in every corner of the internet, and me the burden again. Off Mom's shoulders and onto Wil's. His bright future forgotten as he carries my baggage for me.

A knock on the glass startles us apart. "You're late."

That voice. I recognize that voice. I whip to my window. "Sven?"

Out of the car in a second, I hit the wall of Sven's chest. His arms offer not a hug, but protection I forgot the sensation of.

"I told you I have a surprise for you." Wil's lips bend in a smile. "Worth getting out of the house for?"

"More than." I step out of Sven's non-hug.

Sven's non-hug slides into a non-smile. Lips straight, but his eyes don't lie. He's glad to see me. "Let's run. I told Zoe I'd be back by noon."

We get to the trail entrance and switch to a light jog to warm up. If I were only looking to my right where Sven's running next to me, it would be like no time passed. Like we're on our usual run. Like I haven't run away from that Melodie. I move my head, and to my left, Wil is keeping pace with us. My life has changed. I changed. El Vella might not have the music on her side, but I make my own decisions and I pay for them. My legs pump as I run ahead of the men. I push and let my lungs do their job. Being in charge is less fun than I imagined. I accelerate. Being in charge is damn hard. My feet hit the dusty path. My throat burns but I go faster, pushing through the discomfort.

The trail curves. Goes up. Goes down. I follow the familiar landscape and I don't stop. The pounding in my chest rises to my ears, my mouth dry, I find my stride and feel lighter than I have in days. This I can do. I push harder and my lungs scream, the pounding of my soles on the path quieting everything else. I run like I can outrun my mistakes.

The end of the trail comes faster than I thought and there's nowhere left to run. I bend down, sweat dripping from my brow, ribs expanding with every breath, as I prop my palms on my knees.

"What are you running away from?" Sven's tree-trunk legs appear next to me, his breath ragged.

"No idea." My heart slows and the familiar heaviness claws at me, dragging me down into the mire.

He drops to one knee and reties his laces. "You can talk to me you know."

I nod, the block in my throat preventing any response. When most people meet Sven for the first time, they're intimidated by his stern looks, cold stares, and massive muscles: great aspects for keeping people away. But what they miss is that underneath that bulk beats the heart of a gentle giant.

What would I even tell him? That I'm jealous of my boyfriend's success? Even Sven couldn't forgive me for that. I'm heinous.

He places a palm on my shoulder. "I mean it. Tell me any-thing. No judgment."

My chest caves in and I open my mouth, trying to force the words out. It's like the night I first stood onstage at The Devil's Martini. Birds carol in the nearby trees, the wind rustles the leaves as percussion, and I can't push the black goo out of my lungs.

"It's okay," Sven whispers. "I'm here when you're ready."

"It's—" Over Sven's shoulder I spot Wil making the last turn and the words die on my tongue. I can't do this to him. Wil collapses by my feet and hangs his head between his knees.

"Is this"—his chest is heaving—"what you call running?" He stares at me from under drips of sweat.

"Just a jog. Barely exercise," I tease.

"I can't go to work like this. I'm heading home to change." Wil manages to scrape himself off the ground. "Are you coming with? Death Elbow has the last cut of *Brass Balls*. We can talk to Rocker about Leonard Astor for you."

"No." Apparently my tongue has no problem snapping at Wil. Why am I like this? "I have a better idea." I angle my shoulders to Sven. "I want to see Sven's new office."

Sven studies me. "I have a client at one. But sure."

"I'll see you tonight." I peck Wil's cheek.

Neither Sven nor I speak on the ride to downtown. We pass by the Farmers' Market Wil and I busked in last summer and the bubbling bile returns. Now that Wil is out as Rocker's son, we'll never get those days of anonymity back. Singing for the joy of it, just the two of us. If we go public, it'll never be the two of us again.

The parking lot we pull into at the back of the two-story building has three empty spots and Sven swings into the first. I point to the black "Mr. Anders" printed on the plate fixed to one of the red bricks on the wall. "The boss has his own parking spot?"

Sven climbs out of the car. "Your powers of deduction are unparalleled."

"Ha ha." I stick my tongue out at him and follow him through a white wooden door. "If I never sing again, maybe you can hire me. I can be the Watson to your Sherlock."

"Can Watson answer the phones, schedule appointments, and pick up my dry cleaning?"

"Depends." We climb two steps. "If the pay is right, I'm sure LA is full of Watsons who'd love to have a flexible gig that lets them go to auditions."

"Not hiring another wannabe actor." Sven's jaw ticks. "The last one didn't know H comes after G."

"And the temp agency wasn't much help." I hide my snicker, thinking of Zoe having to come to his rescue. I suck in air and force myself to take this seriously. "Can Trevor help you?"

"My brother in an office? He'd steal the pens and sell them on the black market."

Wherever Trevor goes, trouble follows. "He might surprise you."

"The last thing I need is a surprise." Sven holds open another door, ushering me into a mostly empty room.

From behind an L-shaped desk, Zoe scoots out. "Did you bring coffee?"

Sven makes a face like a dog that had an accident. "Forgot. I'll make a pot."

"El, please explain to your friend here the importance of a proper coffee maker." She backs up into a row of cupboards in the corner that could be a small kitchenette and points to a tiny one-cup coffee maker that looks like it belongs in a cheap hotel room.

"Disgusting. El, lets go to Blend and grab some *decent* java." A phone rings and Zoe holds up one finger as she dives for the desk. "Ander's Investigations . . . yes." She smiles at Sven. "Let me tell you about our services."

Sven whispers, "Don't tell her I said this, but she's a lifesaver."

"Secret's safe with me." I meant it as a joke, but he nods like he knows it's the truth. Because it is.

"My office is back there." Sven points to an opening behind the desk where Zoe chats on the phone. I try to figure out the color on the wall behind him. A shade between beige and light green, maybe. "And my apartment is up there." He opens another door revealing a staircase. "It's only a studio but I get by."

I forget sometimes that Sven had a life before he became my bodyguard. One where he never really had a permanent home. I don't know the whole story of his childhood, but I know after his years in the military, he came straight to us. This might be his first real home.

"No commute," I say. "Nice."

He looks at his watch. "I gotta change. Talk soon?"

"Sure." I make myself smile and ignore the yearning to follow him as he charges up the steps.

"How was the run? Were you surprised?" Zoe makes me jump as she hip-checks me. "Wil was giddy as a kid in a candy store when he came up with the idea."

"You talked about me?"

"Of course. He's worried about you. We all are." She steers me to one of the empty seats in front of the desk. "I told him you just need to get back to singing. That's why I suggested you make another video. Speaking of, did you know Carlee is moving to LA? Her assistant contacted Sven about setting up a security system at her new office."

I tune Zoe's voice out. The fumes from the dumpster-fire of betrayal cloud my visons. Wil and Zoe have been conspiring behind my back. Together. Are they trying to get rid of me? Do they want me to go back to England to make this video not to deal with my mood?

The phone rings again. A repeat of three boring notes. Music is mocking me even here.

"Hold that thought." Zoe reaches over and hits a button on the keypad. "Ander's Investigations." She twirls her hair. "I had you on the schedule for Monday at three, but if you need to move it, I can squeeze you in on Tuesday at 8 a.m."

"He really needs to find someone full-time." Zoe hangs the receiver up. "I've been helping out here and there but this isn't me. I have a photoshoot in an hour and he has this client coming in. It doesn't look good if there's no one here to greet them. Image is everything." She tilts her head. "Of course you know that better than anyone."

"I could stay." The words fly out of my mouth.

"Really?" She looks me up and down. "You'll have to change. Luckily I have a few outfits stored in the closet." She flicks invisible dust off her shoulder as I give her a look. "What, you know my motto. Always be prepared for a fashion emergency."

Twenty minutes later, my look has transformed from sweaty runner to semi-professional assistant, my jogging outfit exchanged for a black pencil skirt, white cami, and a pale green jacket that might match the office walls. Zoe pulls my hair back into a clip and gives me a mini makeover.

She settles her hand on her hip. "Oddly, this look suits you."

For the rest of the day, I play the role of assistant. I answer the phones, make coffee for the two clients that come in, and water the ficus. Best of all, I don't think about music once.

FORTY

I SLIP INTO THE pool house and a brick sinks in my stomach. El sits on the couch, popcorn bowl in hand.

"Why aren't you dressed yet?" I ask. "Zoe's almost ready."

She startles and kernels fly through the air. They land on the blanket and my T-shirt she's been wearing for three days as she's been helping me study for next week's finals. "Didn't you get my text?"

"No." I bend down to help pick up the loose popcorn. Butter coats my fingers. Not wanting to stain the new outfit Zoe made for Death Elbow's big debut, I grab a tissue and wipe off the residue. "I was driving."

"Driving?"

"Yeah." The plan was to surprise her. Not like I'd put a bow on it or anything, but I thought the sight of Dad's gift might, I don't know, make her smile. "I got a car."

"You bought a car?"

"No. Rocker bought the car as my bonus for signing Death Elbow. I had no idea. But I can sell it and use the money to rent our apartment."

El whips off the blanket and the brick in my gut lifts. Finally, she's moving. We need to leave in twenty minutes to walk the red carpet for the band's photo op. Maybe Zoe can do El's makeup in the car on the way.

Except El doesn't head for the bedroom, veering to the fridge instead and pulling out a can of soda.

"So let me get this straight." She cocks a hip against the granite countertop. "I lived with Rocker for six years and I had to be chauffeured everywhere like a child. You live with him for what, three months," her free hand flaps in the air between us, and I don't correct her that it hasn't been a full three months yet, "and he gives you a car of your own."

"I earned it." I move into her orbit, attempting to calm her down. "Every A&R member gets a bonus when a new group signs on the dotted line."

Pinched brows, pupils down to pinpricks, lips pressed so tightly together they're almost white. The last time El glared at me like this, she thought I'd slept with another girl after the Starlight Gala. "Oh." El widens her eyes. "You *earned* the car."

"Not like that." I'm not sure what she means, but I'm pretty sure I'm supposed to apologize. "It's my reward for doing a good job." My phone vibrates. A picture of the merch table from Mateo. I give him a thumbs-up emoji.

"What the hell?" El slams the soda on the counter, shoulders past me, snatches her tablet off the corner of the couch, and storms into the bedroom. Well, at least I got her in the right room. I check my watch. Fifteen minutes now.

I follow but the bedroom door shakes against the frame as she shoves it shut forcefully. "Think of what this means. No more bumming rides off Zoe. I can drive us anywhere you want to go."

Silence.

I roll my shoulders. "You can't really be that upset about this?"

My phone pings again.

Rocker: I'm at the club. Are you close?

Bloody hell. I text back.

Me: I'm picking up El.

The door flies open and she pushes on my chest. "Why? Because you're a big success?"

Where is this coming from? "No."

"Oh, I see. I'm the loser here so I'm just supposed to fit right back into Melodie Rockerby's life. Where everyone drives her around like the baby she is."

"That's not what I said." I jam my hand in my pocket. "Can't you just be happy for me?"

El blinks. A slow exaggerated movement that hides the electric-blue eyes I love. Her teeth gnaw at her bottom lip. "Get out." Her voice is so quiet I barely register the command.

"Sorry?"

Her hands hit my chest and I stumble backward. "I said, get out."

"This isn't you." I try to grasp her arms, but she slaps my hands away.

"Get out. Get out! GET OUT!"

"El, you're being ridiculous. Death Elbow are waiting. We have plans."

"You have plans. The band needs you." Another push against my chest. "I don't want to go to that club. I don't want my picture taken. I don't want to be seen with you."

This time it's her words that slam into me.

"We can't be late." Zoe's nose is in her phone as usual as she enters the room. "I can't trust those musicians to wear—" She double-blinks when she notices El. "Why aren't you dressed?"

El's arms cross and she glares at me. "Take Zoe. I'm sure she's happy to hang on your arm again."

"Zoe? What—" My phone rings. Death Elbow's lead guitarist is calling now. "I need to take this." I yank open the door and step into the cool night. "Hey."

"Are there any extra VIP passes?" Corbin asks.

I scratch my neck. "I think so. Ask Mateo, he has the list."

"Good, good. You'll be here soon, right?"

I look back at the pool house. "Almost there. Just picking up my girlfriend."

Zoe throws open the door. "Stay here then." She storms across the walkway and tugs on my arm.

"Wait. What about El?"

"Forget her."

"Hell no."

Zoe's nails dig into my wrist. "Wil, I love my cousin, but you can't mess up your life because she's being her usual stubborn self." She points to my new Lexus. "Get your butt in the car."

I do as she says, and we take off for the club. Zoe tucks the backstage pass the owners gave us into the strap of her dress. "Hard to make this thing look fashionable."

I tug on my shirt. "You made the collar too tight again."

"Don't blame my designs for your grumpy mood." Zoe glares out the passenger side, the headlights of oncoming traffic illuminating the green stones in her earrings. "El is so selfish sometimes."

My phone rattles on the console. I glance at the screen. A message from the club owner. I'll deal with him when I get there. I reach for my water bottle and knock it flying. Water sprays around the inside of my new car.

"Hell, Wil. This is silk." Zoe pats her dress. Her gaze meets mine and the frown wipes off her face. "What happened?"

"I don't know," I shout.

"Hey." Her hand lands on my bicep. "I'm on your side."

"There's something wrong, Zoe. Like seriously wrong. This is not the El I know, the El I—"

"I agree." Zoe sounds almost as pissed as me. "After the concert, when we get home, we'll do an intervention."

That's the last thing El needs. Another person forcing her to do what she doesn't want. I can't do that to her. "No." I squeeze the steering wheel. "Maybe we should go away, back to Bremen."

"This is not the time to make rash decisions," Zoe mutters under her breath.

I hit the brakes. "I need to talk to El."

"Wait." Zoe's hand is clutching her seatbelt. "What about Death Elbow?"

"I don't care. I . . ." I pound on the driver's door of my new car, my cufflinks scratching the leather.

"Okay. Okay. Let's go home." Zoe pulls out her phone. "I'll text Mateo, tell him to get the band onstage. We'll deal with Rocker once you're not driving."

Rocker. Damn. I'm letting him down. Why do I always have to choose? It's El or Mum. Or El or Dad. I spin the car around, putting the ocean on the opposite side. The tires squeal as I merge back into traffic on Highway 1.

I barely hear Zoe through the pounding in my head. "Everything is going to be fine."

El's words are coming out of the wrong mouth. I want them to come from her. I want to go back to the way it was. Just the two of us. The car in front of me brakes and I smack the horn. "Get out of my way."

"Wil. Take a breath."

"This isn't fair. I didn't do anything wrong." I swerve around a motorcycle. "I followed her rules. I waited. I was going to stay here." The road is getting blurry. "All I want is for her to be happy. Why isn't she happy?" Happy with me.

I turn to Zoe, desperately hoping El's cousin has answers. A bright light washes the color from her face. "Wil! The bike!"

My head spins but the road is not in the right place, the motorcyclist cutting across the asphalt. I jerk the wheel to the left and push on the gas to bypass him, but the car surges and launches us into the tree-lined divider.

Forty-One

El

I pop the tab on the can and the fizzy water explodes, drenching me and Wil's T-shirt in a pale pink fountain of watermelon-scented wetness. The anger boiling in my head breaks the thin tissue between my rational self and the twister of emotions I've been hiding. I slap the puddle on the counter, splashing the liquid around, dripping from surfaces like the tears I can no longer shed because hot jealousy evaporated it from my eyes.

Annalyn has Subtle. Zoe has her fashion. Rocker and Mom have Pickle. Sven has his new business. Even Wil has Death Elbow. What do I have? A minuscule number of followers who beg me to cover songs that are not mine. No job. No money. I'm not even a burned-out has-been mooching off other people, living in my cousin's guesthouse because she pities me enough to play host. I'm a never-been.

The cloth of Wil's T-shirt burns like ice against my skin. He was supposed to be the answer, the one who liked me for me, but I shouldn't have been this trusting. Wil doesn't want us to stay private. That's not enough. I'm never enough. I drag his shirt off and throw it on the counter. The stains spread like a new-age Rorschach test. I see my doubts eating through me, the not-enoughness sending its tentacles into the spaces I thought were safe, stealing everything from me.

My music.

My family.

My boyfriend.

Because I'm the problem. The shiny-but-fake Melodie Rockerby had it all. The raw and real El Vella is the pauper. No fresh content. Just interpretations of what others have.

At least I'm good at that one thing. I rifle through my closet struggling to find something that is not Zoe's creation, a piece of clothing that does not have memories of Wil. Plain white T-shirt and jeans on, I grab my guitar, set my phone on the tripod, and immerse myself in other people's words and melodies, rolling my feelings in the expressive wrappers of their creations.

Wil doesn't get it. People who say that there's no such thing as creative block just haven't been there. Get your butt in the chair and come up with stuff. I wish it were that easy: an on button, a lever I can flip and force the creative juices to flow.

My fingers and my voice do the heavy lifting, mopping the soggy mess of my emotions. Other people's chords and lines bring my pulse down, even out my breaths, and the empty room around me is no longer witnessing me drowning in myself. I turn off the last recording and recline with the phone in my hand. My voice on replay is never like what's in my head, but what I have is good. If they want me out there, this is the version I choose to present. No more gloss and glamour. I post the first video of what I see when I look inside myself.

Recording content for social media is when I'm in the zone in my head, but the editing, the posting, the interacting with the comments are the tasks that creep into the space I left to try to find whatever I lost inside. The posting turns into a mindless scroll of witty confessions that sell books, cute family dances that are perfectly in sync, makeup tutorials, lives from people's rooms, their workplaces.

I want Wil to be here, with me, in our little bubble. Or I want to climb into bed, hide under layers of blankets, and pretend I'm in my old room with the stars on the ceiling. Or better, with Papa on a picnic blanket listening to him telling me about Orion's belt: safe and happy, before everything started. Before he left me alone, and I became this scared insecure version of myself.

I rip the towel off the hanger in the bathroom and mop up the pink liquid in the kitchen, wipe the walls, the counter, and the floor, erasing the evidence of what most days look like inside my chest. I return the room to the condition it was in before I told Wil to get out. It's empty here without him.

My phone rings in the bedroom. I rush back. Not Wil. Aunt Patti. Are Mom and her coming back early from their trip up the coast? I hit ignore and walk away to throw the now-pink towel and Wil's T-shirt into the laundry hamper. My phone rings again. And again. What can be so important? I flop on the bed and answer, "Yes?" I don't want my annoyance to show but it's hard to hide. Annoyance and frustration seem to be my core today.

"Oh, thank goodness. You're okay. Where are you?" Mom's voice is on the other side.

I pause. Why wouldn't I be okay? My chest tightens at how strained her voice sounds. "At the pool house."

Mom lets out a long breath. "Baby girl, there's been an accident."

Cold dread drowns my limbs, and the phone is a lead weight in my hand. "Is it Pickle? Aunt Patti?"

A baby cries in the background as if Pickle's yelling, "It's not me."

"No." Mom's voice fades. "It's Zoe, and Wil."

He left me alone. I let him go. "Wil?" I clutch my middle. My fingers dig into my ribs as I struggle to breathe. Icy fear encases my heart. My knees shake.

"We're on our way to the hospital." Mom's voice grows louder as the cries next to her get more pronounced. "It's all over the news."

Why does it feel like I'm in the middle of the conversation?

"What happened?" I slide to the floor, set her to speakerphone, and google Zoe Yilmaz and Wil Peters. Images of a crash from various angles. Ambulances. A fire truck. Glass everywhere. What's left of a car with the front left side smashed. My lungs refuse to do their job and my vision blurs.

Is that Wil's new car?

I push the words past the anvil in my throat. "Are they hurt?"

"We don't know, baby girl." My fingers go numb and the phone drops onto the comforter.

Wil's hurt. I know it. He left me and I know he's hurt. The tears I couldn't cry earlier rush forth.

Not again.

Please, not again.

"Bob's getting on the next plane in Türkiye and won't get there till tomorrow. We just left the resort but are still three hours away." Mom's voice of steel cuts through my silent sobs, commanding my attention. "Bill's on the way to the hospital but he can't be in two places at once. Patti doesn't want Zoe to be alone. Can you go?"

I stuff my feet into sneakers, find my purse, and order a rideshare. "I'll call you as soon as I know more."

FORTY-TWO

THE BRIGHT LIGHTS OF the ER feel like the spotlights from my stage performances, concentrated and trained on me. Eyes are everywhere, the seats more full than Rocker's sold-out concerts. Why are so many people here this late? I tug my cap lower. Not like anyone expects me here, but I'm not the only one who's seen the news. Didn't seem like the paparazzi figured out which hospital they brought Wil and Zoe to, but that won't last. I know the drill. I give it an hour before they set up camp under the roof of the porch outside the main entrance.

"I'm looking for two patients that were brought in by ambulance," I say.

The nurse at the reception lifts her head. "What's the name of the—" Her bored, tired face changes into a smile as she glances over my shoulder.

Rocker steps beside me. Not hiding. Fully himself. A worried and pale version of himself, but everyone in the lobby knows who he is.

"Mr. Rockerby, how may—"

"My son. Where is he?"

"He came in a few minutes ago. I'll take you to him." She presses a pass against a black square on the wall and the wide hospital doors open. I try to walk through. "Please," she holds her arm in front, blocking the entry way. "Wait here until someone helps you."

Rocker puts a hand on my shoulder. "She's with me."

The nurse peers at my face beneath the bill of the cap. Recognition blooms in her eyes. She guides us to a tiny room full of medical instruments. "Wait here. Someone will come get you shortly."

Rocker paces from corner to corner, four steps in each direction. I sit on a chair and clutch my bag and hat to my stomach. "I'll go see Wil. You check on Zoe, then we switch." His voice trembles. "We'll take turns till Patti gets here or till they are released."

"How bad is it?"

Rocker freezes. "I don't know. When they called they told me Wil was unconscious at the scene. The police suspect he was drunk and veered into oncoming traffic."

Wil and a DUI? No way. He drinks an occasional beer, but he doesn't get wasted. Or is this the new Wil I know so little about? He's been to so many events and parties, and there's alcohol there. No one would card him.

"They'll test his blood to be sure." Rocker pounds a flat palm against the wall. "I threatened to sue if a word of this gets out to the press."

Finally, two people appear. One of the nurses leads me down a hallway, while a doctor escorts Rocker to the opposite side where they have Wil. "Is Zoe okay?" I ask.

"She's awake. I can't share medical information with anyone other than family." I want to protest that Zoe is my family.

The nurse drops me off at a glass enclosure with curtains hiding what's inside. My stomach churns as I tap the makeshift door.

"Come in."

I move the curtain aside. Zoe's propped up on a hospital bed, a gown wrapped around her shoulders, a tube attached to her wrist, a pulse monitor on her finger that punctuates the room with the sound of her heartbeat. Her makeup's smeared, hair in disarray, a huge bandage on her forehead. She seems okay. The air I've been holding in my lungs since entering the hospital releases. "You look good enough to livestream even from a hospital bed."

Zoe goes to cross her arms but winces in pain. "This isn't funny."

I scoot forward. "I know. I was so worried when I saw the report."

"You were worried?" Zoe glares at me. "*I* was scared."

The sudden impact of the collision. Flying through the air. Being submerged long enough I thought I would drown, only for the life jacket to push me to the surface. The disorientation. It all rushes in, and the popcorn from earlier threatens to make a return. "Accidents are scary."

"Hell, El. I'm not talking about our accident." Zoe closes her eyes as if she's going through her version of the scenes that just ran through my mind. She sighs. "That. That was . . ." Zoe runs a hand over her face. "I don't know." She looks at me. "I'm talking about Wil."

"You were scared of Wil?" So he was drunk. Drunk enough to scare Zoe?

She rolls her eyes. "For Wil. I was scared for Wil."

"I don't understand."

Her hard gaze meets mine. "You know the accident was your fault, right?"

"My fault?" Papa didn't want to go out on the lake that day but I begged him. The beeping of the machine accuses me as well. YOU did this. YOU did this. "I wasn't even there."

"Exactly," Zoe snarls. "Tonight was important to him. He simply wanted to share it with you. Hundreds of people were waiting for him, his new group, Rocker, and you know what he does? He turns the car around to go back to *you*. He picks you even after you picked yourself and refused to go. You only care about what you need. What about what Wil needs?"

"You sound jealous." I clench my jaw and allow indignation to fill my eyes.

Her mouth falls open. "You did not just say that to me."

"You spend so much time with him. Dressing him up. Changing him."

"For you." She spits the words at me. "Because he's important to *you*." She shakes her head. "If I'd had any idea you'd be this selfish, I never would have pushed you to make that music video."

"Selfish? Me?" I gasp. My jaw slackens.

"Yes you. Ever since you've been back you've been moping around my parents' place while Wil worries and frets over your feelings. Did you know he gave up a chance to be at Death Elbow's first photo shoot to watch old movies with you for an afternoon? To make you feel better?"

"He didn't tell me that."

"Because you didn't ask. You never ask about what he's doing."

"Because it hurts." I point to the side of the hospital where Wil's at. "He doesn't even want this life, yet these good things are happening for him, and my dreams are crushed."

"So Wil's not allowed to be happy if you are not?"

"That's not what I mean." I draw my eyebrows together and shake my head.

"Sounds that way from where I'm sitting." Zoe lifts her hand and winces again. "You know what?" She runs her fingers through her hair and puts the flyaway strands behind her ears. She takes a second to adjust herself to as straight a sitting position as one can in a hospital bed. "You need to leave." Her cold voice sends chills down my sternum. The meaning of her words sinks in and goosebumps spread along my spine. She manages to cross her arms on her chest. "Come talk to me when you realize that not everything resolves around you." Zoe raises her chin, and I crumble under the weight of her stare.

"Zoe?"

She turns her head to the side and pretends she's inspecting the picture of an otter decorating the wall.

"Zoe."

The curtain behind me moves.

"El. Wil wants to see you." Rocker steps into the room.

I give Zoe's sullen figure one more glance, hoping to meet her eye, but the same nurse who brought me here ushers me out. Zoe's words scream at me in my head. Where's her bitterness coming from? She can't really think of me this way.

Wil's room is identical to Zoe's but what I see is not. Tubes, machines, bandages, bruises. My knees threaten to buckle. The injuries I see paint a different picture from what Zoe's condition appeared to be. What about the ones I don't see? Wil's flat on the bed, and the beeping that was but an accompaniment in Zoe's room is the major tune in his. His breaths are labored. Eyes closed. I can't wake him up if he's asleep. He needs rest, not my tears that burn behind my eyes.

Wil's eyelids flutter. His gaze travels to my face, and one corner of his mouth moves up, not in the cocky grin I'm used to, but a deflated version of it.

This is your fault. Zoe's words slice through the brave face I'm attempting to master. My heart in my throat, I tiptoe to the chair next to him.

"El." His hoarse whisper pokes holes in my resolve to stay calm.

"Are you okay?" I sniffle the tears away.

He stretches his hand with the heart monitor clamp on it to the edge of the bed, as close to me as he can. "I am now that you're here."

"I'm serious." I clasp my hands on my knees, afraid to touch him. To hurt him even more. "Look at the tubes." There's a clear mask next to him, a line leading to a bag with some liquid. Cables going from another machine through the collar of his robe and under it. "You were in a car accident." I state the obvious, trying to make sense of it. Because of me? I can't meet Wil's eyes. I inch my fingers to the sandpapery sheets and set my pinkie over his, the only touch I'm certain won't cause him further pain. "How bad is it?"

"I'm fine." Wil moves his hand over mine and a sharp intake of his breath combined with accelerated beeps on the monitor tell me what he refuses to say.

He is *not* fine. There're scrapes on his face and a strip of what looks like a rash on the slope where his neck becomes his shoulder, a patch of raw skin on his jaw. His other hand is bound in bandages. And his eyes. His beautiful amber eyes that glow when he kisses me are streaked with red. Each detail tells me the violence of what he went through. My chest deflates with every new trace of the crash that's not covered by the gown.

My nostrils prickle with tears, my cheeks burn with shame and anger, the top of my chest heavy and aching. "What happened?"

"I don't remember much." Wil tries to smile to mask his pain. "The paramedics said the airbags saved me but," he circles his eyes over his body, "this is the payoff." His index finger grazes the top of my hand. "I'll be fine. The doctors said so. A couple days in the hospital, and I'll be back home." I clutch my hand to my mouth to prevent the sob that's about to escape. His eyes soft and exhausted, he keeps looking at me as if I hold the answers, while I only have questions. Questions I don't even know how to ask. He squeezes my hand in a weak attempt to reassure me. "How's Zoe?"

Zoe. The sob wins. It rattles my chest and heaves into the room. Tears follow. I shake my head, internally screaming at myself to stop it, to get it together. To not be selfish. Wil doesn't need this. He needs calm. He needs rest. The sobs ignore my pleas and grow in volume and frequency.

"Is she alive?" Wil's expression alert, he attempts to lift his head. The machine beside him beeps faster.

I lay my hand on his shoulder to keep him in place and he winces. "Sorry." I jerk my hand back. "Yes. She's fine. Better than you are."

This is all your fault.

I slide my hand from under his and gesture at his prostrate body that I should be swaying with at Death Elbow's concert, not watching struggle on a hospital bed. "Did I cause this?"

Wil closes his eyes and presses his pale lips together. His pulse, audible thanks to the machines, picks up. The dashes of it sound like morbid confetti falling through the air.

I sway forward, ready to catch his denial. My heart speeds up to echo his. Why isn't he talking? "Did I?"

"No." He moves his head minutely side to side, eyes still closed. "You didn't cause the accident." His voice is low and hard to hear over the accelerating beeps. "I did." He lifts his eyelids as if they weigh a ton, and his gaze finds mine. "I was distracted."

"Because of me." The words leak out of me.

He shifts in the bed and one of the wires goes taut. "I shouldn't have left with Zoe."

"You should have. You just should have stayed with her. You picked the wrong cousin." I look around at the machines keeping him alive. "I'm bad for you."

"Don't ever say that." Wil's fingers reach for me again, but I can't touch him. Every time I touch him, I hurt him. "I want you by my side every step of the way."

"On the red carpet you mean." I stand up.

Wil runs his hand through his hair and winces as he touches the stiches on his cheek. "Stop. Stop putting words in my mouth. Stop blaming me for wanting to take my girlfriend out on a date, not just make out in a dark room and worry who might find out. I don't want to be your dirty little secret."

"But the press." My lip quivers. "They'll make things worse."

"Worse than what? What we have now is a shell of a life."

He does regret being with me. Or if he doesn't, he will soon.

Wil takes a shallow breath. "Aren't you tired of secrets? You've been hiding for half your life. I tried to do it for two months, and it nearly ruined me. I just want to tell people about us. They know about Dad—"

"Dad? Since when do you call Rocker Dad?"

"You're the one who told me to give him a chance." The muscles in his neck strain. "And you were right. He is a good guy. Isn't that what you wanted? Me choosing to have him in my life?"

"Not if it means you choosing him over me."

"Why do I always have to choose?" The machine monitoring Wil's heart beeps a long angry alarm that pierces my eardrums.

"You don't." I take a step back. "I'll choose for you."

"El." Wil tries to sit up. Another alarm joins in. I have no idea where it's coming from. I look at the door. Shouldn't someone be coming to do something about it? Wil ignores the noise and clutches at my hand, coughing while trying to speak.

"No." I wrench my wrist out of his weak grasp. The bracelet he gave me for Christmas slides off.

The nurse rips the curtain open, brushes past me, and forces Wil to lie down. She sets the mask over his face and touches something on the wall above him. "You need to leave," she tells me.

Wil's eyes don't stray from mine. My legs refuse to comply with her command to move, to leave the room.

"Now." A male nurse rushes in and stares at me.

A doctor strides between us. "Why is she still here?"

Someone takes me by the shoulders and moves my body through the blur of hallways until I'm back in the burning brightness of the lobby. I made him worse. I'm the common denominator. I make everything worse. They're better off without me.

I stumble through the sliding doors. The cool night air touches my skin. A group of paparazzi give me a tepid glance, but a shivering girl in a plain T, jeans, and baseball cap is of no interest. I speed away before they make any connections and run along the pavement until my legs can't hold me anymore, ending up slumped on a bench.

What am I supposed to do?

Where do I go?

I can't go back to Zoe's pool house.

I can't go to the mansion.

The anger, guilt, and desperation spin into a ball in my chest. Nausea rolls through me as tears fight for a way out. My brain freezes, unable to process the avalanche of emotions. I shove at them and focus on the task at hand: getting myself away from this damned hospital.

I pull out my phone and dial the only number I can trust to answer.

"El?" The concern in Sven's voice guts me.

"Sven." Why is this so hard? Thinking. Breathing. Talking. I cough, hoping the scary clump will come up and free me.

"I . . ." Fear pushes on my sternum. Am I being selfish dragging him into this?

"I need . . ." I can't say it. But I must.

"Help."

"Stay put."

FORTY-THREE

My wrist aches.

The pain reminds me of her.

The day I met El, the reason I got to be in her life was because she hurt her hand and needed me to play guitar. The day I got to hold her hand for the first time at the showing of our movie *Indigo*. The day I couldn't take her hand and stop her from leaving me in the emergency room.

Where the heck is she? And why isn't she answering my calls, my texts?

My phone pings and my muscles tighten in hope. I flip it face-up. A text from Mateo. I'm grateful my friend saved the day the night of my accident and got Death Elbow on stage. I sink back into the hospital bed. My heart sinks. He's not her.

There's nothing from her.

I scroll to the last text I sent El.

Me: Let's talk. Give me half an hour and we can solve this. I know it.

"What time is it?" Rocker's head peaks out from under a blanket.

"Almost eight." The private room is as nice as the fancy hotel we stayed at in Vegas. Beside the obligatory bed, there's a set of small couches and a large TV. Everything is muted shades of brown and blue, down to the plush blanket covering the bottom of the hospital bed. "You should go home. Pickle will be missing you."

Dad hasn't left my side since he arrived at the ER. No matter how strict the hospital policy on staying past visitation time was, he found a way around it. Did he promise to build another hospital wing? I don't know, but he slept in a chair the first night, when the nurses brought him a pillow and blanket. Since then, assistants bring in food and coffee, and he takes meetings in the hall on his phone while I sleep.

He sits up and yawns so widely I can count his teeth. "Not leaving, Wil. Get used to it."

I have. He's become part of my world: seeing him every day, working with him, discovering we both like pilsner and hate spending time away from Pickle. If I stay here, what else will I learn? When I leave, what will I miss? "Isn't Death Elbow's interview today?"

"It sure is." Rocker pulls a lever at the bottom of his bed and the flat surface folds back into a couch. "Harper can handle them."

"One of us needs to be there." A blaze of pain flashes across my torso as I forget to regulate my breathing to the shallow ins and outs the doctor recommended as my rib heals. My injuries were mostly superficial. Except for my rib. The doctor said I was lucky, but weeks of rest are in my future.

Warm fingers settle on my forearm. "Don't worry, Wil. We've got this."

The wrong we.

Or maybe a different we.

I meet Dad's gaze. "Thanks. But I'd feel better if one of us were there. It's their first TV performance. We promised we'd be with them every step of the way."

His lips press into a fine line. "You're not just trying to get rid of me?"

"I mean . . ." My mouth curves. "Seriously though, I'll just be sleeping. Or studying." Exams are coming up and the extra study time while I'm sequestered in this hospital room has been the only silver lining.

"Okay. If you promise to stay in this room."

I hold up my injured hand. "Where would I go?"

"On that topic. Any decisions on staying for the spring quarter?"

The deal was a round of the clinical trial Mum needed in exchange for me staying with him for one semester at UCLA.

Now the bargain is complete. "Can we make another deal? I'll stay for another term if you pay for another round of Mum's treatment."

He perches on the edge of my bed. "I'll pay for any treatment your mother needs. Or wants. If she wants a new dress, I'll pay for that too. Replace that boiler in her basement, or get her a new house for that matter." Rocker fingers hover over my forehead, as if he's about to push my hair back, but his hand recoils. Cool air brushes against my skin without his touch. "And if you want to go home, I'll drive you to the airport myself. No strings attached."

There are always strings. What does he want from me this time?

"I just want you to be happy." He licks his lips. "I'd be thrilled if what you want is to stay, here, in LA. With me. With Pickle. Be part of our family." There's a plea of hope in his eyes. "If you miss your mom, I have the jet at your disposal. You can visit her whenever you want or we'll fly her here again. Your grandfather too."

"Good luck getting Opa on a plane."

"Your mother might convince him." Rocker moves on the bed. "So, do you want to stay?"

My lungs sting as oxygen stalls in them. He's serious. He honestly wants me to be in his life. I let the concept float in the air between us. Out in the hall, the wheels of a trolley squeak by my door, footsteps following. Rocker watches me intently and I exhale the last shreds of resistance. The back of my throat itches. I honestly want to be in his life.

"Okay," I whisper.

The rockstar grin that has graced a thousand interview photos blasts across Rocker's face. "Excellent." He leans forward like he wants to hug me, but stops, jumping from the bed instead. He rubs his hands on his jeans and paces the room. "Excellent. I'll get the team working on your visa and an application for a green card." He pauses and turns to me. "You do want to stay for a while, right?"

"Yes, Dad." My hand flies to my ribs as they twinge with the pain of my chuckle. "Until you get sick of me."

His cheeks turn red, and he drums his fingers against his leg. "Yeah." He turns to the window. "Okay." He rotates to the door. "That's good."

"How's my celebrity patient today?" Nurse Ken strides into the room with two tiny cups on a tray.

"Good," Dad and I answer at the same time.

"What I like to hear." He pushes the buttons on the remote and the back of the hospital bed lifts. "Word on the street is you might go home tomorrow. Meantime, let's get these in you." He hands me the tiny cup with the pills and another with water. I swallow the meds as Ken records my vitals in the computer. "Everything looks good. I'll be back after breakfast." His scrubs swish as he leaves my father and me alone.

My father and me. My father, who I no longer want to avoid. My father, who is not the enemy I imagined him to be. My father, who it turns out is a good guy. Just like El promised.

"Have you heard from El?" I resent myself for asking, but maybe she contacted him or Sylvia, just not me.

Rocker's face falls and I get my answer. "She hasn't reached out to any of us."

I clutch at the thin hospital blanket. "Sven hasn't said anything?" The thick eyebrow identical to mine rises on my father's face. "Right. Sven wouldn't say anything." Sven was my second call after I got the message El wasn't talking to me. He confirmed he's heard from her but nothing more. At her request.

Rocker places a hand on my shoulder. "She's safe."

Safe and with Sven is not as good as safe and with me, but better than her staying at a seedy hotel because she refuses to use any of Rocker's credit cards. "I want to go to Sven's office today."

"Not happening. You are under doctor's order to rest. No bending. No sharp movements. No twisting. No risking your cracked rib turning into a broken rib and perforating vital organs."

"I'm not that fragile."

He settles into the chair that by now must be molded to his butt, he's spent so many hours in it. The hospital could auction it off as Rocker memorabilia and pay for a new MRI machine. "Let's not test the theory."

"She can't ignore me forever." I don't even know if she's read my texts with my pleas to talk. I close my eyes as if denying reality will be enough to not face it.

"Give her some time." Rocker huffs. "If you push her, she might run. As you well know."

I block out the accusation. "I get it. I'm sorry okay. We shouldn't have left like that."

"No. You shouldn't have." Rocker's voice is low, like he's talking to a frightened child. "But if she was going to run, I'm glad she ran with you. She came back. She'll be back again. Running is the thing she does."

"You don't understand. This is more than running." I cradle the broken bracelet she left when she ran out of my room. "She's got this notion that she's bad for me. That she ruins things. I know being fired from Blatantly Subtle was a setback, but was it even the right thing for her? She's so talented. Why can't she see herself through my eyes?"

Rocker's laughter is bitter. "For as long as I've known El, her face and words have been plastered on the pages of magazines and in celebrity gossip shows. They are the mirror she sees her reflection in."

"I get her relationship with the press is nothing like mine. I understand the hesitation over the scrutiny. That they might make a big deal about us being stepsiblings." I scrape my uninjured hand over my face.

"The press will always find something. I'm proof of that."

"But you and Sylvia seem to be doing great. Why doesn't she have faith that we will as well?"

"Sylvia and I met after we were famous. We both chose the limelight. El inherited it. The paparazzi hounded her after Matthew died, but when Sylvia married me, I made it worse." Rocker pushes out of the chair. "If I had my way we'd live in a compound on a private island, but as Sylvia keeps reminding me, she needs her family around. And she's right."

"I get it. I want El to feel safe, but I also want her by my side." My arm gets tangled in the line of the IV and my chest burns again. "How do I get both? I don't see a way out."

"Whoa, whoa." Rocker lands a hand on my shoulder and stops my movements. "Calm down. I don't want a repeat of what almost put you in cardiac arrest in the emergency room. We'll figure out a way to get her back."

I groan at the ceiling but relent to the pressure of Rocker's secure touch and surrender to the hospital bed, the drugs causing my eyelids to droop. I wish my father was right, but I'm not sure El even thinks I'm worth fighting for anymore.

Forty-Four

"Ander's Investigations, how can I help you?" I use my polite assistant voice.

The man on the other end of the line offers to solve my marketing needs. Apart from Sven, his clients and the cold callers are the only people I've spoken to in the last three days. He promised he won't tell Mom, Rocker, Zoe, or Wil where I am, even though I know how angry my parents will be at him once they find out where I'm hiding. The least I can do is answer his phones.

"Stop calling here." I pour my anger out at the minimum-wage worker on the other side of the line and slam down the receiver.

"Where did they find my number?" Sven sets his elbow on the pile of my boxes we picked up from Zoe's pool house that don't fit in the upstairs bedroom I took over. My guitar still lies in the case on top. The thought of touching that thing sets my brain on fire.

"Maybe that temp Zoe fired for flirting with you gave your business cards out at a convention or something?"

His eyebrow arches. "I was wondering if I was missing a box." He scratches his jaw—the telltale sign he's uncomfortable. "Listen, I'm going out of town this weekend. Will you be okay here by yourself?"

"Of course."

"Sure you wouldn't rather go back home or to Zoe's?" I glare at him. He holds his hands up, palms toward me. "Okay, okay. Thought I'd ask."

"If you want me to go—"

"El." He sighs my name. The name I want to go by. Sven switched to it the moment I asked him to. "I don't want you to go, but this is wrong. You can't stay here and answer the phone for me."

"It's not a bad gig. At least you don't have to hide in the closet from me."

"I love having you here, but you can't answer phones for the rest of your life. You can't sleep on my bed forever. I need my room back."

My phone buzzes. Notification of another one of Wil's texts. I flip the screen down. I should just block his number. Would be much easier not to accidentally text whenever I make coffee and the aroma reminds me of him. How do I put a stop to the longing for him that doesn't want to listen to the decision I made? I'm bad for him. I'm not even good for myself.

I jiggle the mouse. What the hell am I going to do? Not talking to him doesn't seem to curb my appetite for his voice and his hands and . . . him. Maybe distance will. I could move away from here. There's nothing holding me in LA anymore. The whole world is my hiding place. I could move to Malta. I can go spend the spring and summer there and untangle the Gordian knot my life has become.

"Fine—I'll go to Malta."

"I love Malta." Carlee's voice sets confusion to my thoughts. Why is she in my head? "But that sounds like you're running away, not running toward what you want." A tall blonde with a pink stripe in her hair walks through the door. "You can't live your life running."

Carlee Waters is in Sven's office.

"What are you doing here?" I say.

Carlee plops her bag on one of the chairs in the waiting area. "Sven was doing a security consult at my new office and we got to talking about you."

"Sven, you promised."

"I didn't tell anyone you asked me not to. Carlee was not on the list." He taps the side of the reception desk.

"He told me you work for him now."

"I need to earn money some way."

"Why didn't *you* call me?" Carlee perches on the corner desk.

Sven steps between us. "I'm heading to Blend. For coffee. Can I get you anything Ms. Waters?"

I give Sven my don't-you-dare-leave-me-alone-with-her look, but he studiously checks his phone.

"That's kind of you. I'll have a green tea with honey." She winks at him as he flies from the room faster than the real Superman.

Carlee returns her gaze to me. "I told you to reach out once the tour was over."

I remember her telling me I don't belong in a band. I do not remember her telling me I should be reaching out. "There's nothing for us to talk about. I'm done with music. My parents know me well and maybe they recognized that I'm not a real musician." I stack the mail on the side of the desk. "Only playing pretend."

Carlee's nose scrunches. "Nonsense. You're extremely talented. I wouldn't have picked you otherwise."

"Helped that Rocker greased your palm."

"El. Your dad had nothing to do with it. I didn't know your real name until it was time to sign the contracts. I'm not going to deny that we used that fact once you were on board, we'd be stupid not to, but Bill Rockerby is not the reason we were considering you."

"Really?"

"I watched the footage of you I found of you online. I talked to Pauline, I even watched the *Indigo* movie you wrote and sang for. I wanted you to be Beau's new singing partner. I wanted you to replace me."

"Wanted. What changed?"

"Are you ready to believe me now?"

I lounge back in my chair and cross my arms. "Depends on your answer."

"It's the same. You're not right for Blatantly Subtle. The way you sounded during the jam session compared to your performance of *Fire* at the concert, when you were trying so hard to be me, that was what convinced me. You can't replace me, because you need to be you."

I pick at my cuticles. "I don't know who I am anymore."

"Based on *Don't Give Me Comfort*, you are a musician I want to work with."

"I'm not doing backup singing. I'm looking for a real job."

Carlee crosses her legs. "I'm opening my own company and I'm hiring."

"You need an assistant to answer your phones?"

"No." Her fingers knit over her knee. "I've got people for that. But I'd like you to write songs for and with my clients."

"Why would you want that?"

"You're not listening, just like you didn't listen the last time. I keep telling you that you have the music inside you, and I want to help you share your gift with the world. Working with you on the chorus during the tour . . ." Carlee hangs her head low. "For the first time in a long time I was inspired, wrote a new song." She lifts her eyes to me. The fire of creativity burns in them. "I forgot how much I needed that feeling, the high of writing the music. Songwriting is where it all started. I had mentors that helped me. I want to pay it forward." She takes a brochure out of her bag. "I started a company here in LA." She gives it to me.

I clutch the paper without looking.

"I can introduce you to other artists. You'll learn how different people write, you'll collaborate, you'll get to know yourself as a songwriter." Her voice paints a picture I refuse to fall for. "Once you do, hopefully you let me produce your next album."

Now I know she's making this up. "That's not how the music industry works."

"It's how *I* want to work." She squares her shoulders. "And I, not the music industry, am making the offer."

"Can't do it." I can't live in the same city as Wil.

"Why?"

"This isn't about you." The phone rings. I let it go to voicemail. "I can't stay in LA."

"What's wrong with LA?"

"My ex-boyfriend is here."

Carlee rolls her eyes. "LA is a large city. I'm sure you can figure out how to avoid him."

I groan and roll a pen between my fingers. "Not when he lives in the same house as my family."

"Rocker's long-lost son?"

"Yep." Now people outside my family know about Wil and me.

"Isn't he your brother?" Carlee squirms on the desk.

"Stepbrother. And that's one of the reasons why we can't be together." My phone buzzes again. "Wil doesn't get it."

"Hold on." Carlee makes a timeout sign. "Did you break up with him or he with you?"

"Why does it matter? None of this matters."

"Is this why you're running away to Malta? From him?"

"I'm not running away. I'm giving Wil the life he deserves."

Carlee places both palms on the desk. "Is that what he wants?"

"No, but he doesn't get it. He's only seen the good side of the press. They adore him now, but wait until he shows up with me on his arm. They'll turn on him and he won't be able to live a normal life anymore. I had to protect him."

"Protect him? Or yourself?"

I dig my fingernails into my palm. "The press already lies about me. I'm not losing anything."

"Have you ever tried telling them the truth?"

"Why? People like Daniel Davison will just twist it. Pick the juicy bits and bury the rest. Their job is to produce more clickbait. They don't care about my story."

"You're wrong." Carlee slides off the desk. "You'll never be able to control what people say about you. Especially if you choose a life in the spotlight. Those lies sting, but you can't hide who you are. What kind of a life is it pretending to be a safe, boring thing because that's draws the least attention?" Carlee rounds the desk and paces to the door and back. "Stop being afraid to show who you really are. You were pretending to be me during your solo on stage, and that did not get you the spot. Maybe that's a sign. Stop doing that. Be braver. Be brave enough to be yourself."

"Even though I'm afraid?"

Carlee takes my hand and shelters it between hers. "Especially because you are afraid."

My fears cover me like an extra layer of skin. Fear of telling the world about my failure to save my father, about my struggles with words, about how music was my world, about Wil.

"What if it's too late?" I whisper.

"You won't know if you don't try."

I stare at my guitar case on top of the pile of boxes. I'm not a quitter. I open and close my hand, imagining touching the strings again.

My fingers take the G7 position.

My throat tickles.

I hum the first word of the song I wrote about Wil.

As the lyrics entwine with the melody, the music crescendos in my mind. I want to play the chords. To sing the words. I still want music in my life.

Music *to be* my life.

I look back at Carlee. "Where do I start?"

"From the beginning." She lets go of my hands. "Tell your story, on your terms, the way you'd like the world to hear it."

"Like an exclusive interview?"

"Or a live one?" Her eyes sparkle. "Much harder for anyone to edit you out."

The thought of a live interview sends shivers over my skin. Maybe I'm not done being afraid, but I could be done letting my fears guide my life.

Forty-Five

THE SQUEAK OF A door brings me out of the murky semi-consciousness back into the hospital room. Real sleep is impossible when the nurses come to measure my temperature and monitor my vitals every hour.

"Wake up, sleepyhead." Zoe's chipper voice grates against my anything-but-happy insides. "You need to get dressed."

I lift my head to fight off the drowsiness. "Hello to you too."

"Chop chop. No time to waste." The suit bag in her hand lands on the foot of my bed.

Did I sleep for twenty-four hours? I check the date on the board the nurses use to keep track of my vitals. Nope, still March 18th. "You're a tad early. They aren't releasing me until tomorrow."

"Whatever." She waves a hand in the air. "I'm breaking you out. You've been cooped up in here for too long. You need real ice cream."

I drop my head to the pillow and glare at the tiles of the ceiling. "Not in the mood."

Her finger pokes my foot. "Get in the mood."

"Zoe."

"Wil."

She's as stubborn as her cousin. "Have you heard from El?"

"Maybe." Zoe crosses her arms. "Get dressed and you'll find out."

What is it with this family and deals? Carefully, I swing my legs over the side of the bed. "Could you turn around? These robes aren't exactly useful."

"Not anything I'm interested in seeing."

She spins and I drag the suit bag over to the bathroom. Inside is a pair of weathered blue jeans and a dark-orange Henley. It reminds me of the afternoon at the Farmers' Market when El told me colors had the power to shape life into what we want. If only it were that easy.

Zoe knocks at the door. "Do you need help with the zipper?"

"I'm not two." It's bloody difficult one-handed but she doesn't need to know that. At the bottom of the bag is a pair of boat shoes. No laces. Smart girl. I fling open the door, ready for my inspection. But Zoe's not there. I peak around the corner. She's perched on the edge of my hospital bed, her face anything but chipper as she stares at her phone. "What's wrong?"

Her eyes flicker at me then back to the screen. "I got an alert about El."

I cross the room in three strides, pain slicing up my spine and into my temple. I snap up my phone.

Daniel Davison Dishes: Melodie Rockerby going live now.

My butt hits the mattress. "What the hell?"

Zoe scooches over to peer at my screen.

The man in question's face fills the screen. "Ladies and gents, do I have a treat for you today. After years of playing cat-and-mouse with me, the one and only," the camera zooms out and the girl who dumped me while I couldn't breathe joins him on the screen, "Melodie Rockerby has finally agreed to an interview."

My heart leaps at the sight of her. My ribs send currents of pain through my chest at my sudden inhale. The tremor in my hand prevents me from locating the volume button.

"Hello." She wags her fingers for the camera and her smile is the fake one she practices in the mirror for photo shoots and run-ins with the press. I hate that she has to hide behind it. The pain below my ribs intensifies. "Thanks for coming on a walk with me."

Daniel looks up. "Where are we?"

El turns to the building behind her. "This is Rocker Inc." She points to the logo above the door. "My stepfather, Bill Rockerby, you might know him as Rocker, owns this studio. He recently signed a group you'll want to interview, Daniel. Death Elbow are about to blow up."

"She mentioned my group," I say. "What is she doing?"

Zoe shrugs. "I have no idea."

The camera wobbles as it follows Daniel and El walking down the street. "I worked at Rocker Inc. for a few months. Managing a record label is a lot tougher than I thought. Of course, I didn't get much into the day-to-day stuff, but I did a lot of coffee runs." They pause outside of Blend. "The barista in here knows my order by heart."

Daniel peers into the window. "Do you want a coffee?"

"I'd rather have a butter tart." She swings her arm at the camera. "A new vendor just opened at the Farmers' Market. It used to be one of my favorite places to spend my lunch hour." I loved our time together there. Best part of my day. El leans into the camera. "Want to know a secret?" She doesn't wait for Daniel to respond. "I performed here as El Vella last summer. You might've heard of my song *Don't Give Me Comfort*."

"Great video." He winks at the camera. "So are you Melodie Rockerby or El Vella?"

El's laughter is light but doesn't make it to her eyes. "Both. I was born Melodie Vella, to Matthew and Sylvia Vella. Their only child." A small smile tugs at her lips. Mine mirrors hers. "When my mother remarried, her second husband Bill Rockerby adopted me at age twelve, and I became Melodie Vella Rockerby." Her smile shrinks. "When I started singing, I took on the name El Vella."

"Why not use Melodie or El Rockerby?" asks Daniel.

"I didn't want people to judge me or treat me differently because of my famous stepfather." She glances at the camera. "The goal was to be recognized for my abilities, not as a Rockerby. I also wanted to honor my papa."

Beside me, Zoe gasps. This may be the first time El has ever said the word papa outside of the few family members she trusts.

"Music is in my blood." El's voice sounds wrong. Is it the tiny speakers of the phone or is she nervous?

Her look burns a hole in my heart even through the screen. I miss staring into her eyes, having them marvel at the effect she has on my body. With her lips on mine we could talk for hours without saying a thing.

"Most know my stepdad's music. But my father, my papa, Matthew Vella, was an amazing singer too. He starred in operas across the world. His bass-baritone singing lullabies was my favorite sound to listen to growing up." She twists the white strands that make her so recognizable and pushes them behind one ear. "He was at the top of his game when he died."

Bloody hell. Despite the California sun streaming through the glass, my skin turns cold. My fingers squeeze the case of my phone like I can stop her from doing this. Just by mentioning his death she's stirring a hornet's nest. The paparazzi will be all over her. The online articles will swirl again.

"Wil. What is she doing? He'll ask—"

"Right." Daniel steps closer like he can smell blood in the water. "And you were how old when he died?"

"Ten." There's a slight wobble in El's voice. She can't do this. I've witnessed how this story hurts her to tell, how she relives it in her dreams, what it costs her to even mention the accident. She's kept it from the world for almost a decade.

"Were you with him when he died?" Daniel licks his lips.

My fist clenches. Don't do this, El. Walk away. Run.

"Yes." She flicks her gaze to the side, composes herself, and faces Daniel. "We were on Lake Como. He loved taking me out on his boat. Called me his co-captain. We'd spend hours on the lake. My parents used to call me their water baby." Her fingers weave in and out of each other. "As we were heading home one afternoon, a speedboat cut in front of us. Papa veered to avoid them and hit a rock. We were both thrown from the boat." She pauses, and I hope it's over.

El's eyes lose focus. "Papa was . . . hurt. He had a large gash on his arm." I touch the cast on my wrist. My heart stutters. What must it have been like seeing my injuries? She clears her throat. "He was having trouble staying afloat." Her fingers clutch at the sleeve of her jacket. "He didn't like to wear his life vest, said he'd been on boats since he was a child and didn't need one."

Zoe's nails dig into my thigh. "Oh, El," she says quietly.

A text alert covers El's face, and I flick it away, not wanting to miss anything. As if me taking my eyes off her would be cause enough for something bad to happen. Again. I should be there with her, holding her hand, but I'm not. Because she doesn't want to be with me.

"What about you?" Daniel Davison taps his chin. "Did you have a life jacket on?"

"He promised Mom I'd always wear one. He always kept his promises. Except for one."

"Which one was that?"

"His last promise." El looks down and takes a deep breath. When she looks up again, I see her determination. Oh, how I love that look of defiance, of I-know-I-can-do-this. "He promised me everything would be fine. Told me to swim for shore, that he'd be right behind me. I started swimming but he stopped talking, so I turned back, and he was gone."

El's voice breaks on the last word. Zoe's head droops onto my shoulder, and she emits a sob. I put my arm around her, holding her because I can't hold El.

Onscreen, a tear trickles down El's cheek. She quickly brushes it away. "They found his body the next day. Mom tried to keep it from me, but the official cause of death was drowning. Water in his lungs."

Even Daniel seems upset, his voice low. "I had no idea. That's truly horrible." He rests a hand on her shoulder and squeezes it, as if that would make a difference. "I'm so sorry for your loss. Thank you for sharing with us today."

El stares directly into the camera. She's looking right at me. "I don't want to hide anything anymore."

My eyes burn. I know the words aren't meant for me, but I wish with all my heart they were.

Offscreen, Daniel asks, "What made you change your mind?"

I pull the phone closer, desperate to know the answer.

"I decided it was time to stop hiding, stop focusing on the past I cannot change. Time to live my life the way I want to and appreciate what I have now. Who I have now."

"And who is that?" His tone switches from tender to gossipy.

"My family." El glances to the stall at the Farmers' Market she's standing beside and grins. Her eyes sparkle as she gazes into the camera. "My boyfriend."

The rapid beat in my ears might be the cause for mishearing the last word. Did she really say boyfriend? The thought scrambles everything inside me. My brain doesn't want to believe what my heart desperately wants to believe. A strange noise fills the room, a mix between a sob and a cry. Zoe's arms are around me, gently holding me, and I don't understand why.

My head hurts. My chest hurts.

I can't breathe.

I can finally breathe.

"That . . ." My voice sounds wrong, thick, like I've been screaming at a concert.

Zoe releases me and pops up. "Yes Wil. That was for you." She crosses her arms and bobs her head. "Now what are you going to do about it?"

Forty-Six

El

Daniel Davison, the man I've avoided for half of my life, smirks. I've been here before, cameras in my face, words stuck in my throat, waiting for the biting remark, the shocking question. Normally my skin would be itching, my feet tapping, eager to run, but not today. I've got him where I want him.

Telling Papa's story shredded my heart, just like it does every time I think about that day, but the sympathy in Daniel's eyes was not fake. Which is what I was counting on. If he doesn't want to look like the worst person in the world, he won't have a chance for snarky comments when I tell him the next part of my tale. If he tries to make fun of me, no celebrity will grant him an interview ever again. I lift my chin and face my fate. I can't say I'm not nervous, that the gongs aren't vibrating in my head. This angst is different. It's not terror, but anticipation.

Maybe it's this place. The Farmers' Market has always been where I was happiest. Lunch hours spent with Wil, playing our music, trying new arrangements, experimenting, falling in love.

Maybe it's the fact that there are no more secrets. I'm free. I see now that hiding Papa's story only increased the appetite for gossip. So why not feed it to them? On my terms.

Maybe it's because I don't want to run anymore. I want to live my life, come what may. Everything out there for the world to see. To judge. To like me or not. I won't waste another moment hiding who I am and how I feel. If the press, the people, hate me, let them. There's nothing to fear from them anymore.

Losing Wil is worse than anything the paparazzi can say or do to me.

"Boyfriend?" Daniel's eyebrows rise. "This is new. Do we know him?"

The air in my lungs burns. Here's the risky part of my plan. Saying his name. I don't even know if he's watching. If he still gets the alerts on his phone. I hope so. To trust this is the right thing. Showing the world I'm with Wil, or was, if this doesn't work out, isn't about Wil. This is about me. About proving to myself the paparazzi don't have power over me anymore. And to do that, I have to expose everything.

Say his name.

"You do. I met Wil Peters nine months ago at a singing competition." My lips curl into what feels like the first smile in weeks at the memory of Wil eyeing me up and down while I stood in that bar in my blond wig.

I walk to the empty spot Sven guarded for me. "We became friends as we sang here each day. He played guitar for me when I injured my hand. Together we busked, and we collaborated on a song for our friends' movie." I wave to the camera. "Hi, Sarah. Hi, Nick." I twirl in the spot I recognize well. Our spot. "Wil helped me find the words for *Don't Give Me Comfort*. He even arranged to film the video for it. Somewhere along the way, we became more than friends."

"To be clear, you're talking about Rocker's long-lost son?" Daniel's mouth might as well be salivating, he's looking at me with so much eagerness.

The words swirl in my head. I look into the camera and imagine talking to Wil like I have so many times, because it's not a crutch to rely on him. Sometimes I need help and that's okay. Wil did more than help me find the words, he taught me I can express my feelings through them too, not just music. "I didn't know he was my stepfather's son at the time. He'd only found out himself that year."

"Isn't that . . . weird? Dating your brother?"

The snakes stir and I shut them in a box. "Not at all. We didn't grow up together. He's not related to me."

"I guess. But—"

"I can tell you what he is. If he were a color, he'd be orange. Pure sunshine and happiness. He's creative and caring. If he were an instrument, he'd be a guitar, capable of playing any song. If he were breakfast, he'd be blueberry muffins, the perfect mixture of tart and sweet, bursting with warmth, fresh out of the oven." I can't seem to stop. The elements of Wil pour out of me. "He writes beautiful words that come from his soul and speak to mine. He's musical, plays guitar like his dad. He's confident. Sometimes a little too confident." My cheeks ache from grinning. "But secretly I love that about him too."

I don't tell the camera about Wil's kisses, the way one look from him can melt me, how I didn't know what romantic love was or how capable I was of loving another person that way until I met him. Some things are just for him, and I'll find a way to show Wil those when the time is right.

I turn to Daniel. "And he's kind. If you are fortunate enough for Wil Peters to care for you, you are one of the luckiest people in the world." I slacken the tense muscles in my abdomen and allow myself to take a full breath. The smells and noises of the market give me the strength to finish what I came here for. "He's all that and much more. And if he's watching this, I've been selfish." My lips tremble. "I hope you can forgive me."

"I gotta say, El, when you break your silence, you really go for it." Daniel moves to stand beside me. "We need to take a short break, but when we come back, El Vella will perform her brand-new song live. Don't go anywhere."

We stand grinning at the camera. "And we're clear." He steps away from me, eyes on his phone. "This is good. Lots of comments. Yes, we're trending." His eyes lift to me. "Get set up. We're back in five."

Sven steps out of the shadow, my guitar case and phone in hand. "You did good."

"Thanks." I snatch the phone and unlock it. "I hope it's enough."

Notifications are blowing up my screen and I quickly scan for the name I want. My chest deflates. Nothing from Wil. No calls. No texts. I double-check that he hasn't DMed me on socials. I force oxygen into my lungs. It's possible he hasn't seen it yet. My finger hovers over his number but the cameraman interrupts. "Can you stand here?" I slip my phone into my back pocket. I'll call after I sing.

Sven crosses his arms and the cameraman slinks back.

I drop to my knees and undo the latches on the guitar case. "What if it's too late?"

Sven coughs. "It's not."

"How can you be so sure. I screwed up—"

"El."

"I know, you think he'll forgive me, but I can't stand that I hurt him."

"El." I rip my eyes off the guitar and glance at Sven. He tilts his head toward the gathering crowd.

I stand and look in the direction Sven indicates. My heart leaps into my throat. Wil is weaving his way through the throng of people. Slowly, as if every movement is causing him pain. Is every motion causing him pain?

Heat blazes through me and I charge at him. "What the hell are you doing?"

He halts and steadies himself on the corner of the stall selling baked goods. "What?"

"Are you trying to return to the emergency room?" I slap at his arm, and he clutches it like I've wounded him. "Did you drive here?"

"I did—"

"What if you got in an accident?" Panic careens through me. Wil flinches. "I—"

"Scratch that. Another car accident." I kick his shoe. "What if something happened to you?"

"Noth—"

"But it could have. You don't know." I pace in front of him. "Should you even be driving?" My pulse is thundering in my ears. "You're supposed to be resting."

"Yes, but—"

"But what? You thought you'd whip over here and scare the hell out of me?"

"Well." Wrinkles stretch over his eyebrows. "Yes and no."

"This isn't funny." My legs wobble, and I search for something to stabilize me.

He inches forward. "No, it's not. And Zoe drove. I was too busy watching you tell the world I'm orange."

"You saw?" I point back to the spot where I need to be singing in less than a minute.

"I did."

Even though I'm outside, there doesn't seem to be enough air. I wrap my arms around my middle and try to expand my lungs. His hand brackets my face, the steady fingers stilling the turmoil in my head. "El. Breathe. I'm right here."

Wil is here.

I soak up the liquid gold looking into my soul.

Wil is here.

He came.

"Are you"—my throat doesn't want to work—"here for me?" Every cell in my body tenses, half agony, half hope.

His lips curl in the way they always do when he's about to say something smart, or funny, or sarcastic, or teasing. Things that would normally make me laugh, but not now. The beats pounding in my ears cover the noises of the crowd around us. I hold onto the hope.

"Yes." The word is so quiet, I'm not sure I hear it. He presses his forehead against mine. "Yes."

I no longer need air. Lightness fills me for the first time in so long. How could I be so naïve to think I could run away from this feeling?

"I'd never stay away from you when I know where you are. I'll always be by your side. You and I are a team. WE are a team."

I crash into him, and he yelps. I jump back. "Sorry." His arms encircle me and pull me back to him. I gingerly ease into my favorite spot, molding to the center of my universe. His chest shudders against mine but this time I don't let go. His face presses into my neck as I cradle my love for him. My heart buzzes and sings because I'm holding my boyfriend and I'm no longer afraid. Because home is where he is, and I don't need to run anywhere. I've already arrived.

Joy fills me and reaches into the corners of my mind and body I thought might stay empty and dark. If Wil were a feeling, he would be joy. I should have said that to Daniel. The melody that I wrote for him knocks at my breastbone, begging to come out and show him what he means to me.

"We're live in five, four . . ."

Wil steps back and I swing my guitar to my chest.

"Two, one."

"And we're back." Daniel's voice grounds me in the center of the Farmers' Market. "Let's hear El Vella's newest single *The Joy of You*." He claps and I strum the first chords.

This time I don't look at the camera, I look at Wil. The words flow easily. They're not enough to describe what my heart, mind, and soul experience. I offer the world my vision of Wil.

When I cry,

I cry with my fingers on the piano,

the guitar strings,

the five lines that reveal

what hides inside my head.

When I laugh,

I laugh with your fingers on my skin,

my cupid bow,

the pages of your notebook.

When I spell joy it comes out as y-o-u.

When I spell love it comes out as w-e.
When I stop and play
what I can't spell
I can finally breathe,
because I can no longer hide from myself."

I sing to him to let him know I'll never deny or hide us again. The world knows now, and they have no choice but to accept our reality. Whatever happens, my love for Wil will overcome any obstacle.

The last note rings in the air. Daniel Davison must've ended the broadcast because he shakes my hand. I can't take my eyes off Wil, the soft smile on his face, the shine in his eyes, the expression that causes zings of joy to course around my body. I step into his arms, gently this time. I want to ask him what he thinks of the song, want to know how he'll improve it.

But first I have to ask my question.

I rest my head against his shoulder, listening the solid sound of his beating heart. "Wil?"

"Mmm." The stubble on his cheek ruffles my hair.

"Will you go out on a date with me?"

The pounding in his chest accelerates. "I thought you'd never ask."

He lowers his brow to mine, and I claim him with my breath, my lips, and my heart. We come together, and for the first time I believe our story will have a happy ending, no matter how it started.

**There's one more book to complete
Wil & El's romance.
Catch the happily ever after in WE Balance
Out Now**

Turn the page for a sneak peak!

ONE

WHAT IS THE PRICE of fame?

I click post on the new cover song my followers were asking for and prop myself against the headboard. Sven's bedroom has become my oasis over the last month and a half. Unable to resist, I scroll through the comment section from the video I posted two days ago. Although my heart glows from the encouraging words of fans, the hateful comments about me dating my step-brother leave a bitter taste in my mouth. My fingers fly to my hair and twirl my signature colorless strand. Even all these weeks since my live interview with Daniel Davison, when I announced to the world that Wil Peters is my boyfriend, the haters leave snide remarks and send disrespectful DMs about us, not about my music.

The sound of the water stops and Wil's humming filters through the bathroom door. I should get ready too. I abandon my phone, screen down, on the bedside table and leave the guitar between it and the wall. Sven's bedroom was small for just me and my stuff, but with the addition of Wil's items that have migrated here, the only open spot is the bed. I put on a pair of jeans and a T-shirt. My hands hover over the heels from Zoe's collection, but I pick simpler sneakers instead.

I twist toward the sound of the bathroom door opening and drink in the sight of my boyfriend. Wil strikes a ridiculously overdone pose that somehow sends my heart into an allegro. His hair is styled. His right arm that's still stiff but finally out of the cast hangs at one side and adds debonair swagger to his brown fitted slacks and beige shirt. My thumb digs into the seams of my jeans and I glide my bottom lip through my teeth.

Wil's eyes shine as he crosses the room. His soft lips connect with mine. My annoyance over the post melts with the care of his touch. My head spins, but Wil pushes me gently onto the covers and his hand on my waist grounds me. He teases my mouth, asking permission for more, and when I open, he drinks me in like I'm the only thing that can quench his thirst.

My fingers slide around his neck, urging him closer. I'm quickly learning that Wil's first kiss of the day is like the sample at the chocolate shop we visited in Bremen—a sweet yet hot taste of things to come. This, here, with Wil, is my safe heaven. Unlike fame, this is worth the price.

"Hi." His low tone rumbles to my core.

A breathy "Hi" escapes my lips. Wil's hand roams from my waist along my ribs. My body tightens like the strings on a guitar. Maybe we should dump the current plan of checking out an apartment and make use of the bed we're already on. I skim my palm over Wil's broad shoulders. His liquid heat seeps into me.

The bang of the front door reminds me where and when we are. My sanity slices through the cloud of lust. Sven has clients in the office downstairs and even though it's the end of the workday for most, security firms don't keep regular hours. I turn my brain back on, sit up, and skate to the edge of the bed, out of the tempting cage of Wil's solidity.

"We need to go."

"To be continued." Wil's gaze drags over my lips and I think he's going to kiss me again. I want him to kiss me again, but he sighs and stands. "Do I look like a guy worthy of going on a date with El Vella?"

"This is not a date," I remind him.

I run my hand over Wil's chest, careful not to restart what I just put a pause on. The luxurious fabric is something that would've been in my closet last year. It screams high-end and expensive, but doesn't scream my boyfriend. This Wil is quite a departure from the guy in well-worn jeans and T-shirts who agreed to play guitar for me at The Devil's Martini. This Wil could be on the cover of GQ. My body simmers in anticipation, but the seam of his shirt bumps my greedy fingers to a stop. "When I asked you out, I meant dinner and a movie, you know, normal boyfriend/girlfriend stuff."

Wil's thumb travels along the curve of my shoulder and my skin tingles. His palm continues down as he presses the back of my knees against the bed. "As long as I'm with you, I don't care what we do. Or where."

My cheeks are scorching, because even though we've had to be careful of his ribs and arm after the accident, we've made excellent use of this double bed. With every last ounce of restraint, I pry myself away from Wil. "I care. I promised you a date and it's happening." I straighten my T-shirt. "Today is about getting me out of Sven's bedroom for good. Once I have my own place we can spend an entire weekend in bed."

"Promise?" Wil runs his nose along my cheekbone and lightly bites the corner of my lip.

I twist out of his caress, take his hand, and drag him down the stairs. "Promise."

On the sidewalk, Wil draws me to him. I jerk away and scan the street for camera lenses.

Wil frowns. "I thought we were over this." The long rays of the oncoming sunset make his amber irises deepen to glimmering gold. "Everyone knows we're together."

"Everyone knowing we are dating doesn't call for public PDA." I separate from Wil, putting cold air between us. "We can kiss plenty more inside my new apartment. When I find one." I take Wil's hand to move him along the sidewalk. We're losing the light. "Let's go do that."

The excitement disappears off Wil's face and a muscle in his jaw ticks.

I swing our hands as we walk and try a diversion. "How was the new professor in your sound design for visual media course?"

"Fine, I guess," Wil scoffs. "Mateo was right to insist I enroll. He says hi by the way."

"Is he ready for tomorrow night?" I turn down the street that leads to The Devil's Martini, where Death Elbow will be playing.

"It's all he's talked about. He and Zoe were arguing over the merch booth. The stickers Mateo created are apparently taking space away from the T-shirts designed by Zoe."

I breathe through the ache in my chest at the mention of my cousin. Just because I haven't talked to her since the accident doesn't mean I'm not thinking about her all the time.

Wil steps closer. "She misses you."

I glance at him. "Then she should call me."

Wil sighs. "Or you could call her?"

I take a sip from our water bottle and offer it to Wil. The W&E I wrote on the bottom when we were hiding in Bremen over Christmas is still there. I point to the signature. "It's fading."

"Shall we get a new one?"

"No." I lightly slap his chest. "Don't even joke. This water bottle is the first gift you gave me. It goes with me everywhere."

We wait for the light to turn. Wil leans in. "Will you wear your blue dress tomorrow?"

"No." The walk sign flashes. "That's a bit formal for a rock concert."

He takes my hand. "Someday I'll see that dress on you."

I rest my face on the soft fabric of his coat and for a second let myself imagine a magical night where he gets to enjoy the blue dress on me at the beginning, and I get to enjoy him removing it at the end.

The further we walk from the office, the worse the street art gets. At first the murals are graphic and colorful, but the side of the corner store is covered in scrawled graffiti that's more like tagging. In the distance a car alarm cuts through the air, whining between an F and an F-sharp that makes my ears want to bleed.

Wil's fingers tighten around mine. "Are you sure this is the right street?"

"Yup." I lift my chin. The satellite image I studied this afternoon didn't show the overflowing garbage bins we're forced to step around. "It's just up here."

"El. I'm not sure this is for you."

"You're so overprotective." I drag Wil by the hand. "We'll be fine."

We turn a corner and a four-story rectangular building recently painted snow-white contrasts starkly against the brown and tan townhouses flanking it.

"This is it." I bound up the three steps to the covered portico, search for the name the landlord provided, and press a button on the entry system.

Wil twists left and right, surveying the area, and his eyes land on a woman pushing a shopping cart down an alley. He opens his mouth, but the buzzing sound of the door opening causes him to pause. He sucks in his bottom lip. "Do they just let anyone in?"

"Jon is expecting us." I push down the flutter of anticipation and hold the door for Wil.

The small lobby is cool and murky in the dwindling evening light. A cream sign with black letters states the elevator is out of order.

Wil spots the stairs. "Good thing today wasn't leg day."

I glance at his chest. Are his ribs up to a four-flight climb? "We'll take it slow."

Wil heads for the first step. "I'm fine. Let's get this over with."

Frustration bubbles beneath my skin, threatening to overflow. I follow Wil as we wind around flights, a single bulb illuminating the steps. The air gets stuffier and thicker with each floor. In contrast to the foyer and the stairwell, the hallway is brightly lit, and my eyes sting like I've stepped onto the LAX tarmac at high noon. Crisp, clean white walls are broken by deep red doors adorned with modern brass numbers and hardware.

I stop in front of number 405 and knock. The door swings open and a short, muscled man in a green leisure suit greets us. "El?" He sticks out a meaty palm. "Any trouble finding the place?" He doesn't wait for an answer. "Sorry about the elevator. It'll be fixed by the end of the month."

Parquet covers the floor of the open concept living room/kitchen area that appears smaller than the pictures I showed Wil. My harpsichord would not fit in here. But maybe it's best that Papa's gift stays in Rocker's climate-controlled mansion. Sweat drips down my back and Wil shrugs out of his coat.

"The air conditioner is currently being replaced." Jon strolls to the breakfast bar. "My partner and I bought the building at the beginning of the year and renovations take time." He nods at Wil, like only men understand the concept of installing electrical components. "Next up is the laundry room and the entry system."

We meander to the bedroom, which has a closet the size of Sven's filing cabinet. Wil pokes his nose into the bathroom, takes a cursory glance, and shakes his head.

"What?" I whisper.

"It's tiny." His breath tickles my ear. "We can't both fit in there."

"That's one strike against this place." I run my hand over his chest.

He softly captures my wrist. "Of many."

"It has potential." Like I might potentially be able to afford the rent. I can trade in my shampoo and conditioner for something from the drug store, and find another way to manage my frizzy hair. Maybe live in braids for the next few months?

The warmth has abandoned Wil's eyes, leaving them a flat yellow. "You can't be serious. This place is a du—"

I clap my hand over his mouth. "Jon will hear you." Wil licks my palm and I release him. "It's the nicest place in my price range."

"I will not have you stay here."

My back stiffens. "You sound an awful lot like Rocker right now."

"El, that's not fair. This place is not . . ." His mouth contorts.

"Not what? Good enough for you?" The words vomit out of me. I'm stunned. At me, and at him.

"Safe." His grip on me tightens. "I'd be constantly worried about you walking up those stairs—"

"The elevator will be working soon."

"And this neighborhood?"

I cross my arms. "I'm never going to find a place as nice as Rocker's. I'm not a millionaire." And won't become one any time soon. "I can't stay with Sven forever."

Wil inches forward. "You don't need a mansion. But you do need a place where you feel comfortable." His finger traces my clenched fist. "Think about it this way. If the paparazzi followed you here, they'd easily get into the building."

"Jon said he's fixing the buzzer," I protest weakly.

"I couldn't live with myself if something happened to you." Wil traces my cheek. "Please, El. Let's keep looking. I'm sure you can find a place that's safe."

I glance at the darkening sky and like the last rays of light, my willpower to resist Wil wanes. "Fine."

His arms cinch around my waist, pulling me close enough for his lips to press on my temple. "Thank you."

"But you have to break it to Sven that he's sleeping on his couch again tonight."

A soft lullaby plays as the soundtrack to my dream. The chords shift slowly up, melting into something softer, and I'm chasing the music, the melody spooling in front of me like Mormor's favorite tablecloth. Even though Sven's bed is as hard as a stone pallet, I'm comfortable and safe.

A squeak of fingers sliding on a guitar string cuts through my haze. I force my eyes open but the tune restarts and I sink back into the depths of dreams unrealized. Until it happens again.

I open my eyes and the sight before me presents a different kind of dream.

Wil.

Wil without a shirt on. His back against the headboard, guitar in hand. I float on a cloud of bliss, looking at my small piece of paradise. How lucky am I that fate brought this man to my city, to The Devil's Martini, almost a year ago?

He's balancing the headstock of a guitar in his left—uninjured—hand, awkwardly plucking notes with his still recovering right. The cast came off only days ago and from my experience breaking my fingers last year, I know it'll take him weeks of physical therapy to play like he used to.

So many great and awful things happened to bring us together. His mom falling for Rocker and getting pregnant. Wil not knowing who his father was until last year. Wil's mom getting sick. My father dying in a boating accident by my side. My mom and me meeting Rocker at the Griffith Observatory. Mr. Peters sending Wil to the US to confront Rocker. Me sneaking into The Devil's Martini for the open mic night. The guitarist I hired winding up drunk. Wil being there, offering to play the guitar, and helping me sing when I froze. Mom giving birth to Pickle. Wil and me coming back to the US from Bremen. Blatantly Subtle not choosing me as their lead singer. Rocker announcing to the world that Wil is his son. Wil's mom getting the treatment she needed. Wil and Zoe's car accident—which I know wasn't my fault but still feels like it was. Singing to millions of people live to show Wil what he means to me.

Memories stream in as Wil's music wakes them one by one. I want to cry and laugh and everything in between. My heart spins the reel of what my life has been by his side.

The El of a year ago gave up on love after Dillon's breakup text. The El of a year ago wanted to be center stage. The El of a year ago would not even imagine sleeping in a tiny shoebox of a room above Sven's office.

Today's El hasn't accomplished anything that El wanted, but today's El, today's me is happy. So happy I don't want to jinx it. No denials. No disguises. The last month and a half of being Wil's girlfriend has been the best of my life.

"I could wake up to this every day." I kiss his shoulder.

His finger slips and the off-key E echoes in my ears like feedback from a mic.

I sit up and reach out. "Let me do that."

"I thought I had an idea, but with the bum arm everything is a struggle, so it's gotten away from me." Wil runs his fingers across the scruff on his chin that tickled my inner thigh last night. "A pre-chorus, or something that leads into the chorus."

Muscle memory kicks in and my fingers find their places on the guitar. I replicate what I heard him plucking but add to the tone with my fully functioning hands.

"How do you do that?" Wil stares at me intently.

"Rocker taught me to play."

"No." He moves his fingers in the air. "Just pick up and play back the same tune I only made up a moment ago. No sheet music. Only hearing it once."

I shrug. "I don't know. I can just feel it."

"Here?" Wil traces the skin over my heart and the organ responds with an accelerated beat. "Or here?" His fingers roam across my clavicle, along my throat and cheek, settling on the edge of my hairline, by my ear. The pitter-patter of my thoughts still at his touch.

"Both?" The guitar shakes in my hands. "In my stomach as well."

"Do you have any idea how amazing you are?"

I lower my gaze. "Half as amazing as you?"

"I'm not even close."

"You—"

Wil stops my protest with a kiss and the argument is over because I'd surrender to this any day of the week. This kiss is laced with early morning tenderness, an echo of last night, a taste of what's to come. I drag him closer.

Between us the guitar wails in protest. Wil releases my lips, his eyes finding mine. "Play it again."

Never breaking eye contact, I strum his melody, repeating the notes that are now not only his, but ours. Low and soft, he whispers words that match my plucking.

Love conquers all, the movies said
but when I'm lonely in my bed
I think of you

I come to the end of the portion I heard him play but I don't stop. The melody unfolds before me and I let my fingers run of their own free will. Wil keeps singing, the pupils in his amber eyes expanding like an infinite starless night. It's just his words, my melody, our souls weaving magic, and there is no feeling like it.

Singing onstage with Blatantly Subtle had the high from the crowd, the excitement of singing with musicians who were true professionals, the thrill of knowing what was next on the set list but also the uncertainty of what would happen and how we'd have to adapt. Yet something was missing. A piece of the puzzle never found its spot.

My fingers flex, my memories fade
and on this day, I can relate
I think of you

But this. This here with Wil surpasses anything I experienced during those weeks. It's him and me onstage at The Devil's Martini, busking at the farmers' market, recording our song in the studio. This makes my heart pound, my head clear yet buzzy, my stomach full of the butterflies that show up when I'm happy, not anxious. I'm floating yet tethered. Wil is my anchor.

Maybe they were right,
maybe they were wrong,
maybe I should just give up, give in and fall for . . . you

We weave the cascades of "you" between our voices, harmonizing in perfect symphony. I grin as joy radiates from me, reflecting the happiness inside.

His smile mirrors mine. We are two halves of a whole. A duet.

Maybe him and me singing together is the answer. Maybe we should—

"Damn, El." Wil cuts off the song, my breath, and my thoughts when his lips find mine.

"IT'S EXACTLY THE SAME." El's gaze roams around the semi-darkness backstage at The Devil's Martini. "Even the scuffs are still on the wall."

"I doubt they've done anything since we were last here." I lead her to the green room we were never invited to use when we sang as the opening act on Saturday nights. The "HEADLINERS ONLY" sign doesn't seem as forbidding as it did almost a year ago. I open the door and walk into a wall of smells and sounds.

Corbin, the lead singer of Death Elbow, shirtless with eyeliner pencil in hand, slants away from the mirror and does a sweep of my girlfriend as if I'm not right next to her. "The infamous Melodie Rockerby. We meet at last." He drops the pencil, opens his arms wide, and advances on El.

I intercept the hug instead, slapping him on the back. "I told you she was coming this time." I wince the moment the words exit my mouth. I'm still a little bitter that she didn't want to come to the last performance of the group, but I didn't mean it that way. I'm just happy she's here. "This is Corbin Laceter." I wrap an arm around El's shoulders and kiss her on her temple. "And this is my girlfriend, El."

"El, huh. My pleasure." Corbin picks El's hand up and kisses it like the gentleman he is not. He doesn't know the names of any of his groupies and prefers it that way. He smiles at El, flirting with his eyes as if I'm not standing right there, then straightens. "I hope you enjoy the show."

Did he just flex his abs? I give Corbin a nudge. Playful but also rough enough for him to get the "get your hands off my girlfriend you wanker" message across.

"Are you going to introduce me too?" Like the golden retriever he is, Lucian bounds to us. "I'm Lucian, the bassist, and you are beautiful. The hair is even more gorgeous in-person, I've seen you in magazines since I was a kid and now I get to meet you. I still can't get over meeting so many people I've only seen on TV." Lucian bounces on his toes. "This is my brother Gideon. Our drummer."

Gideon lifts his hand in greeting and returns to braiding his hair. I'm not sure the new style will last through the set. His jet-black hair usually hangs loose to his waist and whips around as he sweats behind the drum set.

Corbin nudges Lucian aside. "This is Xander. Our guitarist."

"If I'd met your boyfriend before I met Corbin, I would've had him join our band." Xander's grass-green eyes take me in.

"Didn't you two used to play here?" Corbin holds his arms wide.

El smiles at me. "We did."

"I love the covers you've been putting out. You can play one of those. Be our opener? A little impromptu throwback?"

Corbin joins Lucian and Gideon in a circle around us. "Warm the crowd up for us?"

I point to my still recovering arm. "I'm out of commission. Plus I wasn't the star of the show. El was." El still is my star. I tug her closer and nuzzle her hair with my chin.

Lucian inches closer. "Maybe El sings with us then."

"Sorry boys." El taps the spot over my heart. "I only play with this man."

Corbin laughs and returns to his reflection in the mirror.

I catch his eye. "Remember the brand team from Vatton are watching. I've placed their water bottles beside each of your instruments." The head of marketing sent over four boxes of the florescent purple canisters. "Try to remember to take a sip during your performance."

Corbin's lip curls. "Is there vodka in it?"

"Water. We'll drink after."

Corbin points his eye pencil at me. "I'll hold you to that. Play first, party after."

"Sure." I rub my hands together. "Now, let's get ready to rock this place to its foundation. El and I will be your hype team and get the crowd revved for you."

The guys roar as we slip into the hallway.

"They seem like . . ."

"Rock and roll." I tug on a strand of El's hair. "They're just pumped for the performance."

At the end of the hall, Mateo has his hands on his head like he's trying to block out sound. He shuffles back and Zoe strides into his space, her arms in the air. They are far enough away that I can't hear what they are saying, but their disagreement is clear.

"Typical." I roll my eyes and bend down to El. "Those two are arguing again."

The smile slides off El's face as she spots her cousin. "I have to go to wash my hands."

Reluctantly, I let her go. I can't make her talk to her cousin. No matter how much I want to.

Zoe spots me. "Wil. About time. Would you tell this design expert"—she air quotes the word—"that fuchsia is a violation of the dark aesthetic I've created for Death Elbow."

Mateo shakes his head. "She wouldn't listen to me."

I wince. "Zoe, those are Vatton's hot-off-the-press signature metal water bottles. That is apparently going to be the color of the summer. I'm trying to lock down a deal."

Zoe cocks her head. "That's not my shirt you're wearing." She steps forward and tugs my belt loop. "At least it works with my pants. Wil Peters, what's going on?"

"I decided to wear something different."

"Without checking with me first?" Zoe places both her hands on her chest. "I'm hurt." Her hands fall, her left settling on her hip. "Are you going to be selfish like your girlfriend and stop talking to me next?"

"I'm not stopping talking to you. You know I love your designs." I tuck the Moderni Look shirt in. The Finnish clothing company is another potential brand deal. "This is business."

The audience screams loud enough all on their own. For a freshly signed group, Death Elbow is growing their followers faster than Dad and I anticipated. The band is all in: the daily short form videos, the Vlogs, their eagerness to go on any radio show or online interview that we can book them. The guys work hard. Concerts, press, writing session, social media—they have been on a roll. But they party hard too, which is something Dad already talked to them about.

"Thank you, The Devil's Martini. You've been the best audience, and we love you! Keep an eye on our socials for a special announcement that's coming soon." Corbin does his usual sales pitch and they exist the stage.

The boos and calls for an encore circle us. I vibrate with the energy the fans are exuding. The feeling of the crowd loving what the performers are dishing out onstage is a drug. I thought I forgot what that feels like, but even just sitting here surrounded by the vibes brings back the longing to play, to be the crowd's focus. If El ever decides to sing again professionally, I could maybe come onstage once or twice, play for her, for old times' sake, just a gag. Just once or twice.

"Do you feel like it's last July?" El's whisper tickles my ear.

"Because one of us has an injured hand?"

She elbows my side gently. "Because we are at The Devil's Martini and the crowd is going wild."

In the shadow of the wings, I glance across the stage. "Do you miss this?"

"The audience? Yes. Singing in front of my phone is not the same."

"Thank you, Death Elbow, you've definitely been on my playlist for the last two months, and I hope you perform in front of many larger crowds." Pauline, the manager of The Devil's Martini, takes the mic off the stand and sighs. "Thank you all who came today and supported this local business that has been in the community for over fifty years." Pauline walks to the other end of the stage. "Singers such as Carlee Waters, Dasher, and El Vella had their start here during our open mic competitions. These walls have heard classical, jazz, rock, pop, country." The crowd roars in agreement.

She runs her hands reverently over the wall. "I've witnessed the last ten years, and what years have those been. I have autographs from so many singers who became staples on the radio, and some who I call friends." Pauline returns to the center of the stage and sticks the mic back on the stand. "It is with a heavy heart that I must announce The Devil's Martini will be closing its doors."

I flinch as if the news physically hit me. Stunned silence stretches around me. This is where I met El. Where we first sang together. Where I felt the magic of WE. That can't disappear.

My stomach and heart switch places. The place where that be-
gan can't just cease to exist.

Beside me, El has her hand on her heart. The heart I found
in this room, on that stage. The heart I can't imagine living
without. I pull her closer, like the threat of The Devil's Martini
closing might somehow take her away from me.

A low boo rumbles from the back. Others join until they fill
the space. If the boos for the end of Death Elbow's show were
loud, these boos are deafening.

Pauline dips her head. "I feel the same way. We've been
searching for a buyer without success. Apparently no one wants
to take this old establishment over." More boos. Pauline waves
them down and gives a sad smile. "If you know anyone who
wants to buy a bar, call me. I can throw in some coasters for
free."

There's a sad communal chuckle from the crowd, and the
buzz of Death Elbow's performance has evaporated. Around
us, people murmur and shake their heads.

"In the meantime, we have a few more bands performing, so
I hope you all come back and see us before we shut our doors."

El elbows me again, not so gently this time. "Maybe Rocker
could buy this place. He has the money," she whispers.

Rocker Inc. definitely has the money, but it's not what they
do. They deal with artists, not properties. "We can ask him. I'm
not sure this is his brand."

"*You* can ask him." Her face takes on a serious quality. "He
can use the venue as a launching point for the singers and bands

he's promoting. Use it as a performance venue for Rocker Inc. Isn't that a great idea?"

"It's an idea." I caress her shoulder. The disappointment of no more The Devil's Martini must be weighing on her too. "But I can't promise you anything. I'm sure Pauline scoured LA and beyond before they came to the decision to close."

"I guess. Still, I can't imagine LA without The Devil's Martini. It's like Nashville without The Bluebird Cafe." El rubs her eye. "We met here."

I'm transported back to that moment, her skipping across the bar floor, her red hair hidden under that blond wig I hated. My insistence on playing guitar for her, needing to spend more time with her. Did my heart know even then that she was the one? El's lips curl like she's reliving the moment too.

"We need to save The Devil's Martini." El squeezes my arm. "I'd do anything to keep its doors open."

"Don't look at me that way. I might be richer than I've ever been, but I'm not rich enough to buy The Devil's Martini for you."

Her chest rises and falls. "We have to find someone who can."

END OF SNEAK PEEK

WE Balance

OUT NOW

ACKNOWLEDGEMENTS

Writing a book is a bit like putting together a band. While the characters on the page perform for you like the best of bandmates, there are many people behind the scenes who bring the story to life.

Our editors help us fine tune the words and the characters. Thanks Kia, Victoria, and Laura for keeping us on pitch.

Our book cover elements showcase what to expect during the performance, helping readers like you discover Wil and El's story. Thank you to María Peña for bringing Wil & El to life and Books and Moods for creating the beautiful blue cover.

Our fellow writer friends help us stick to the truth. We enlisted our fellow writers who are from Germany to help us get the details such as German electrical engineering and how likely is snow in Bremen in December. Thanks Claudia and Sal for pointing out that cedar is not a thing in Germany. Neither DL nor Gala have ever played in a band or been on tour, so we turned to our fellow slow burn romance writer and a talented singer KG Fletcher. Thanks for giving us insight into what touring life is like.

Our Street and ARC teams are our eagle eyes and our cheerleaders, reading early versions and giving us valuable feedback. They inspire us to keep writing and entertain us with their comments, Discord discussions, pet photos, and merch requests.

When our band needed a name, we asked them for ideas on our Discord channel. The instant Ashley M. suggested Blatantly Subtle, we knew that was the name of Beau and Carlee's pop-rock band.

Our PA CeCe is our tour manager, who makes sure everything runs smoothly. Eliza is our concert promoter who makes sure fans know what's going on. Without them, we'd have to cancel sleep and add hours to the day to survive. Thank you for rolling with the changes and understanding us when we can't find the words.

Our families are the backbone of what we do. They listen to our bursts of creativity and our streams of doubt yet stand by us no matter what. We owe them all the tickets to all the concerts they want to see.

Our fans are our reward. We're so glad you found us.

During a recent discussion, a fellow writer asked how, since writing is such a personal thing, we work and write together in such a seamless way. Much like Wil and El, fate brought us into each other's lives. We may not be Lennon and McCartney but we trust each other enough to share our most outlandish ideas and accept help. Like any successful duet, we bring our individual talents but also let go enough to blend our styles.

Wil and El's show continues in the final part if the trilogy, WE Balance. Like them, we have lots more to offer as we expand the Willa Drew Universe.

SERIES BY WILLA DREW

SECOND CHANCE BILLIONAIRES

The Second Chance Billionaires series follows five lifelong friends—a grumpy CEO, a charming playboy, a retiring hockey pro, a British aristocrat, and a sci-fi author—from college roommates to billionaire boardrooms as they each get one more shot at love.

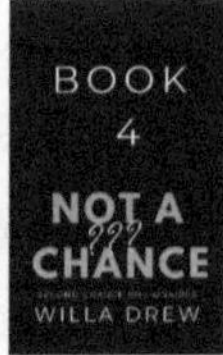

AND US

Watch movies and real life collide with Sarah and Nick in a right person/wrong time, hidden identity, new adult romance. One year, five parts, six major holidays, many twists.

Kisses, Lies, & Us

Passions, Hopes, & Us

Distance, Love, & Us

or binge the complete series with bonus scenes in

Friendzoned By My Crush

FALLING FOR THE ROCKSTAR'S DAUGHTER

An upper young adult, friends-to-lovers, slow burn romance

featuring a reluctant collaboration between two musicians.

WE Blend

WE Breathe

WE Balance

ANDERS INVESTIGATIONS

Meet the men of Anders Investigations, a new contemporary

romance series with a romantic suspense element.

Taming the Grumpy Bodyguard

Loving the Grumpy Bodyguard

FALLING FOR THE MOVIE STAR

If you like an age gap, brother's best friend romance featuring LA's red-carpet glamor, Irish charm, and a reunion written in the stars,

Siobhan and Asher's story is for you.

Two authors. Two countries. One obsession with love stories.

Willa Drew's contemporary slow-burn romances are full of feels, playful banter, and high-stakes emotions. Their globe-trotting characters fight for love as they discover who they are and where they belong.

Willa, a proud Canadian and devoted Leafs hockey fan, and Drew, a Russian-American with a lifelong love of languages, always search for the perfect words to capture heartbreak and connection.

Their books guarantee swoon-worthy kisses and happily ever afters.

Come hang out with them
@willadrewauthor
willadrew.com